MW00452102

the
TALKING
STICK

Other Books by Donna Levin

Extraordinary Means (1987)
California Street (1990)
Get That Novel Started (1992)
Get That Novel Written (1996)
There's More Than One Way Home (2017)
He Could Be Another Bill Gates (2018)

the TALKING STICK

a novel

DONNA LEVIN

ARCADE PUBLISHING • NEW YORK

Arcade Publishing books may be purchased in bulk at special discounts for
sales promotion, corporate gifts, fund-raising, or educational purposes.
Special editions can also be created to specifications. For details, contact the
Special Sales Department, Arcade Publishing, 307 West 36th Street,
11th Floor, New York, NY 10018 or info@skyhorsepublishing.com.

Arcade Publishing® is a registered trademarks of Skyhorse Publishing, Inc.®,
a Delaware corporation.

Visit our website at www.arcadepub.com.

10 9 8 7 6 5 4 3 2 1

Library of Congress Cataloging-in-Publication Data is available on file.

Cover design by David Ter-Avanesyan
Cover photo courtesy of Gettty Images

ISBN: 978-1-64821-031-0
Ebook ISBN: 978-1-64821-032-7

Printed in the United States of America

For David Groff
Poet, editor, friend

Memory, for Freud, is a kind of trickster, a canny yet unreliable narrator, a creator rather than a transcriber of reality.

—Madelon Sprengnether, "Freud as Memoirist:
A Reading of 'Screen Memories' "

People's memories are maybe the fuel they burn to stay alive.

—Haruki Murakami

The truth will set you free, but first it will piss you off.

—Gloria Steinem

CONTENTS

1   The Top of One Mountain Is the Bottom
    of the Next   1
2   Overwhelmed, Overwrought, Overhoused   6
3   Treasure Island Treasure   26
4   Fly Away   45
5   You Never Forget Your First   54
6   Retail Therapy   62
7   The Most Awful Time of the Year   71
8   Swept Away   82
9   Summertime, but the Living Ain't Easy   86
10 All How You See It   98
11 First Meeting Free   102
12 All Downhill from Here   115
13 You'll Be Fine   120
14 In Case You Can't Stand It   126
15 No Place Like Home   132
16 The Placebo Effect   142
17 Harder Than It Looks   150
18 It's Been a Long Time   158
19 Read Him Like a Book   164
20 Moving Day   171
21 No Way to Live   183
22 Plenty of Blame to Go Around   190
23 Seems Like Old Times   195

24	Knock Down Walls, Build Bridges	199
25	Melon Madness	204
26	Gone	214
27	Scraping the Sky	225
28	The Father and the Daughter	232
29	Lemon Meringue Pie	237
30	Rock the Boat	247
31	Four Very Good Years	254
32	Off the Beaten Path	265
33	Only Human	269
34	Round and Round She Goes	276
35	A Large Capacity	284
36	Back to the Boat	290
37	Calling All Creators	296
38	Let's Get Cookin'	302
39	A House Is Not a Home	314
40	Until We Meet Again	323
41	Looking for Love in All the Wrong Places	330
42	Thank You for Your Inquiry	339
43	We Love You, Penelope	343
44	The Truth Hurts	347
45	Search but You Will Not Find	358
46	Return to Treasure Island	362
47	The Final Bridge	368
48	Believe It or Not	370
49	Food for Thought	377
50	Time and Tide	382
51	The Bottom of One Mountain Is the Top of the One Below	389
	Acknowledgments	*397*
	About the Author	*389*

Chapter 1

The Top of One Mountain Is the Bottom of the Next

HUNTER

Hunter Fitzgerald was a tireless hiker of hills and a curious explorer of woodlands, as well as a daily runner. But all that came to a screeching and painful halt on a Sunday in early March, two days after she lost her job.

Hunter and her husband, Peter, had climbed to the top of Mount Tamalpais, a two-hour trek, first uphill, then down a long, rocky, but well-traveled path. If today she needed exercise to battle stress, it helped that this outing was already on her calendar.

There, at the summit, was the West Point Inn, a funky wooden building from the turn of the previous century, a throwback to the era of trains, and now a shrine, well-tended by the acolytes of history and the environment.

At the last minute, Peter had suggested that Hunter's friend Angelica come along.

Hunter wouldn't have minded on an ordinary day. At the moment, though, she was still adjusting to the dramatic role reversal between herself and Angelica. Once upon a time—and "once upon a time" was last week—Hunter was pulling down a comfortable salary, while Angelica was scrounging for rent money. Hunter and Peter had bailed her out more than once, but Angelica could pay them back now, since with the publication of her memoir, *Jesus Warned Me He Was a Jerk*, she would receive the rest of her advance.

The memoir was an account of her disastrous marriage to one Vijay Koka: how it led her to get sober, and then to find Jesus through AA. A major prepublication campaign by the publisher had resulted in the book debuting at #8 on the bestseller list.

Hunter hadn't read it yet.

Now she turned her back on husband and friend, and breathed in deeply. It was sixty degrees—in early March! At her childhood home in Connecticut, the snowplow was likely still at work. But here, the sun was out, and she could see the inlets of San Francisco Bay. In the distance, cupped by trees and hills, and under a thin cover of low-hanging clouds, was the gray-blue of the Pacific. It would be here long after they were all gone.

The thought was meant to give her distance from her own problems.

"I'm so sorry that you lost your job on the same day as my pub date," Angelica commiserated.

Hunter let that pass. She'd climbed the corporate ladder at Energy-4-All Fitness, all the way to Fitness Center Manager. Then on Friday, she and her coworkers had learned that all three locations had closed, with no notice from the powers on high. Nor any explanation.

Now Angelica held her arms out to the early afternoon sun. "How can you not believe in God when you look at this?"

"I watched *Cosmos* on PBS," Hunter said. "Neil deGrasse Tyson explained it all to me."

Hunter's atheism was a reaction to a strict Catholic upbringing. A novena to St. Anthony, asking for help in finding a missing doll (she'd tried that more than once as a child), was little different from sacrificing an ox to Zeus in exchange for a good crop. And men's obsession with virginity crossed all cultures.

"I think Jesus is standing right behind you," Angelica said. "I think He wants us to check into the West Point Inn *right now*."

"The West Point Inn isn't exactly Peter's style," Hunter said. Peter was like her: a lover of the outdoors, of skiing and kayaking, but also a fan of certain comforts. After ziplining, they went to stay at the nearest Ramada. At the West Point Inn, one not only needed to bring one's own sheets and pillowcases, but to share a bathroom with strangers. Peter didn't even like sharing a bathroom with *her*.

"I've stayed here," Angelica said. "Jesus would have stayed here."

I was getting bored at the gym anyway. Hunter had been telling herself that for two days, without making inroads on her attitude. She continued to stare at the clouds over the distant Pacific. A breeze lifted stray hairs off her neck.

There was something not to like about California: Though Hunter herself was never one to read self-help books, as she and her comrades-in-unemployment made their mass exodus from the Energy-4-All Fitness Center on Friday, carrying the bankers boxes that held their pictures and plants, they were all repeating such mantras as, *What you think is failure is an opportunity! Believe it and you will manifest it!*

It was so much hogwash. Enough so that she said to Angelica now, "Have you thought about digging up your yard? Maybe you'll discover golden plates and you can start a whole new religion."

"You'll find another job soon," Angelica said. "You are so talented and smart. And I have news!"

Hunter walked past the picnic tables on the west side of the path, getting closer to the edge. The firs and pines, beyond the reddish-brown slope, were calming. Calming, but not reassuring.

"There's a film option!" Angelica had to raise her voice now. "Mel Scarpetti has bought it for NewFilms. He loves it for Uma Thurman's comeback."

Be happy for Angelica, Hunter thought. *She's paid her dues. The spinning wheel spins and—*

"Th-there's more."

It was Peter this time.

Hunter turned around. Angelica and Peter were holding hands.

And Hunter dropped into a horror movie, the kind where the main character is walking into the house where the bloodsucking, brain-eating monster lives, and you scream *noooo*, but you can't save her. Walk in she will.

Angelica was fifty years old, short, with the kind of frizzy red hair that can't be tamed by anything less viscous than motor oil. She also had an unjust mass of freckles. Hunter wasn't vain, but she wasn't vision-impaired, either. She was tall and alabaster-skinned (she never went outside without a hat and SPF 50 sunscreen), and although, at forty-one, she was too old to be a runway model, she had every other requirement, from the wavy blonde hair to the flat chest and the thighs that didn't touch.

Looks weren't important. Looks fade.

But in what universe did Peter, the same age as she, and who had a jawline that could cut prime rib, prefer a woman whose nose was too small for her face?

"You shouldn't blame yourself," Angelica said.

Hunter heard her from a distance far greater than the ten yards that separated them. On the path behind Angelica, a couple pushed a stroller, and Hunter marveled at the effort they'd exerted to get it up here.

"Alcoholics are very clever at hiding their drinking," Angelica continued, while Peter nodded solemnly. Angelica kept talking: She'd persuaded Peter to accompany her to an AA meeting. Seven meetings in seven days, and now they were in love.

"We didn't mean for it to happen," Angelica added piously.

"They never do," Hunter heard herself say softly. There was a weight in her stomach. *Keep it together. Keep it together.*

"We didn't mean for it happen," Peter echoed, and Hunter thought, *he never did have much imagination.* For earthbound Hunter and disembodied Hunter had merged into one angry and confused woman.

. . . and this angry, confused woman turned away, and this time, instead of gazing across the vista of the Bay, she looked down at the hill that fell away below her. It wasn't all that steep, but it felt like a precipice.

She'd be happy if I jumped, Hunter thought, though she wasn't that close to the edge, at least not in a literal sense.

Besides, it wouldn't cause more than a lifelong disability, and she wouldn't give them that satisfaction.

Chapter 2

Overwhelmed, Overwrought, Overhoused

HUNTER

A hangover must be God's way of warning sinners that Hell is for real.

That was Hunter's second thought upon awakening Monday morning. Her first thought, after a mental bucket of ice water landed on her head, was *oh my God he left me.*

A real bucket of ice water might have been welcome. She was on the couch, where she had fallen asleep. (Passed out was more accurate, but she wasn't ready to confront that.) When she'd returned home the night before she'd gone through both bottles of the Dom Perignon that she and Peter had been saving. She barely remembered consuming them, but she did remember thinking, when she popped the first cork, *Now I don't have to share.*

After all, supposedly champagne was now off-limits to Peter.

The ceiling had grown higher overnight; the whole house yawned around her. She was living alone already; Peter had gone home with Angelica after they came down off the mountain.

Hunter twisted to her left side, sending an invisible stream of pebbles rolling down the inside of her forehead. *They should put warning labels on wine bottles.* She had half of the symptoms that drug companies added to commercials for their newest treatments: nausea, dry mouth, headache, blurred vision. As for decreased sexual desire, that was a preexisting condition. How the hell had this happened? Two nights earlier they'd been planning their next party. When she was going through the guest list, was he already thinking about his escape? In her mind now she could picture a moment in which she'd proposed Angelica as a guest to that party, and one corner of Peter's mouth had turned up.

But now she couldn't be sure it had happened that way.

What was this about Peter being an alcoholic? Ridiculous! Now that she was sober, Angelica saw alcoholism everywhere.

True, at their parties he drank. A lot. But so did some others. So did she. True, of late he'd been drinking at home when there were no parties. She'd shoo him to bed and spend an hour or two scrolling down her Facebook feed. *Like! Love! Care!*

She'd thought then, *all he needs is one good deal to get back on top . . .*

On the drive home from Mount Tamalpais, Angelica did most of the talking. God was love; Angelica loved Peter, but she also loved Hunter, and Peter loved Hunter and Angelica, and God loved them all. Although they were both in the back seat (and still holding hands, Hunter saw, at red lights when it was safe to turn around), Angelica leaned forward to deliver a monologue about how they would have *more* love in their lives, not less! And they could support each other in sobriety!

Hunter had known Angelica before sobriety. Sometimes Angelica would cry over the phone, and say that then-husband Vijay was "narcissistic and withholding," though between sobs she might say that she *deserved* to be treated this way.

Then Hunter would go barhopping with her for an evening. And yeah, she praised herself for being a good person doing a good deed. Over straight bourbon (while Hunter drank frou-frou cock-tails, brandy Alexanders, and strawberry margaritas), Angelica would sometimes laugh uproariously at the perceived foibles of others—including Peter—and just as often become maudlin, reviewing decades of mistakes with both jobs and men.

Even after Angelica stopped drinking, Hunter felt sorry for her. Not long after, she was abandoned by Vijay (though Angelica might say she kicked him out); meanwhile, sobriety had brought her neither love nor money. Yet.

Hunter massaged her temples. It made the headache worse. And when the doorbell rang, it sounded like Quasimodo was back at Notre Dame. Who . . . ? Hunter's Mill Valley neighborhood was not a place where Jehovah's Witnesses canvassed; it was too long a walk between houses to make salvation efficient. Peter. It was Peter, coming back! He'd be on the other side of that door, begging forgiveness, maybe shouting "trick or treat!" No, wait, "April Fools!" She ran to answer it, though each thump of her foot against the floor caused a corresponding thump in her head.

"Well, hello!" It was a woman with short black hair, cut in an asymmetrical bob. She wore a black pantsuit, and carried a bulky tan leather briefcase with more buckles than a straitjacket. "Is this a good time?" The woman didn't wait for an answer. "These are the Sharps. Chad and Bentley. And they aren't looky-loos. They're seriously in the market."

The couple standing behind the pantsuited woman were stunningly blonde and healthy. The man was dressed as a lumberjack, in jeans and a red plaid shirt. The woman was also in jeans and plaid shirt, but hers was a mauve no lumberjack would wear, and hung loosely over a hypothetical waist.

Finally Hunter made enough sense of what the pantsuited woman was saying to ask, "In the market for what?"

"Oh, haha, that's a good one," the pantsuited woman said. She jabbed Hunter with her business card. The letters were wobbly, but Hunter read:

TAYLOR GREEN-COOPERSMITH
SHANGRI-LA REALTY

"My house isn't for sale," Hunter said.

"Oh, but it is!" Taylor Green-Coopersmith tapped on an iPad. "See?" She shoved it close to Hunter's face. The sun reflecting off the screen made the image faint, but Hunter did recognize it as her house.

"It's a mistake."

"No, it's not!" Taylor said brightly. She took the iPad away to do some more tapping, then thrust it even closer than before. "See? Your husband listed it."

"My—my husband?" *He left.* "He doesn't live here anymore."

Taylor cocked her head and made her lips into a flat line. Her expression said, *not my problem, lady.* "You have to let us in."

The full horror dawned slowly. The house had been Peter's mother's. Hunter and Peter had lived there rent-free until she died, when she bequeathed it to them in her will. Left it to *Peter,* that was. It was separate property. Yet Hunter had always thought of it as hers. She'd even christened it Chardonnay Heights, after Peter's second-favorite white wine (Gewürztraminer was too hard to spell).

She'd meant to transfer the title, but what was the rush? Who knew that Peter was going to leave her and sell the house?

The fear started as a stone in the bottom of her stomach. Here she'd been thinking only of herself as abandoned, betrayed, and looked down upon, when her much bigger problem was money. She had savings from her gym salary: savings she'd started after the fixer-upper in Greenbrae cost so much to fix up that Peter lost money on the project. She'd intended the account for both of their use; she just hadn't told him about it because if he spotted the perfect Zegna suit, he would skip "wish list" and go straight to "add to bag." So she had that, but it wasn't enough.

Taylor Green-Coopersmith tapped her Ferragamo-shod foot.

Now on autopilot, Hunter stepped back from the doorway, leaving it open. Hunter was proud of her house, which she cared for to excess, but what if this couple fell in love with it and made an offer? She had nowhere to go.

Taylor stomped in, motioning the Sharps to follow. "This has the open plan that everyone wants!"

Hunter's living room had a view of the Pacific. A billion-dollar view. Once her mother-in-law was out of the way, Hunter had knocked down two walls to create a great room, the better to entertain.

But the Sharps weren't as easily charmed. "The sun will get in my eyes," Bentley Sharp complained.

There were remote-operated shades. Two layers: one mesh, to dim the glare when necessary, and another of heavy material to block out all light. But since Taylor didn't seem to know that, Hunter said, "Yeah, it's a problem. I can't stand to be in this room after about two in the afternoon."

"Let me show you the rest." Taylor motioned them to follow—at least, Hunter hoped that the peremptory gesture included her. She shuffled along behind in her socks from the previous day, feeling too much the supplicant now to tell the realtor and her clients that it was a shoes-off house.

"This is the master bedroom! You've done a beautiful job." Taylor seemed to intend Hunter as the recipient of this compliment, but didn't wait for a response. "The recessed lighting! The clerestory window!"

"Now, it's the opposite problem in this room." Hunter shook her head. "It gets very dark here in the winter months. Also very cold."

"Space heaters!" Taylor traced an invisible lasso above her head.

"Huh," Chad grunted. "Isn't there another bedroom? Maybe we could use that as the master."

Taylor stabbed the iPad with her index finger, then pointed. "This way."

The second bedroom was actually smaller. Peter used it as a home office, though it also served as a pop-up (or plop-*down*) guest room, thanks to the sofa that folded out to a queen-size bed. At their monthly parties, there was usually someone too drunk to call an Uber; after all, you had to be able to remember your home address.

Bentley Sharp crossed her arms over her ironing board chest. "I like the wainscoting," she said grudgingly.

Hunter had carefully chosen the contrasting shades of pale taupe and eggshell. "The molding is hard to keep clean," she said mournfully.

Then her attention shifted to Peter's computer, where the screensaver was rolling: It was a slideshow of pictures from their last trip to Maui. Peter loved taking pictures, and he had no shame about using a selfie stick.

Hunter stared. If he'd left his computer on, that must mean that he and Angelica had decided at the very last moment to give Hunter the news on their hike. What were they thinking, the pair of them, as they climbed? *Haha, won't she be surprised?*

Hunter watched two more pictures go by, then hurried to join the others.

They were in the small room nestled between the two bedrooms. "And this is a natural for a nursery," Taylor was saying. She slyly raised one shoulder to her cheek.

"There's no closet, though," Hunter was quick to point out.

"They'll buy a wardrobe!" Taylor snapped. "You've heard of wardrobes, haven't you?"

Chad Sharp wasn't concerned with closet space. "That's the ugliest thing I've ever seen."

He directed an accusing finger at the Ingraham clock that Hunter and Peter had found at a flea market and restored. At least, it might be an Ingraham clock. It was an old clock, anyway.

Bentley stroked Chad's neck. "Snickerdeepickerdoodle, it's an antique."

"I like modern things," Chad said. He stretched his left arm high; the cuff of his plaid shirt fell back to reveal his Apple Watch. "Who uses clocks anymore anyway?"

How dare he! Never mind that the clock probably wasn't worth that much even if it was real. She'd shown him a picture of her child, and he'd declared it homely.

Even more than entertaining, kayaking, and wine tasting, Hunter and Peter's most passionate shared pursuit was scouting flea markets and garage sales for undervalued treasures. They'd set aside this room for their possibly antique dolls and possibly rare action figures. Hunter was skeptical that they'd ever found anything of great worth, but she liked sorting through what people no longer wanted, or at least were willing to sell.

They called it "the Margaret Keane room," because, hidden behind a bookshelf that displayed the smaller items, was a painting that resembled one of Keane's: a girl with big eyes holding a cat with bigger eyes. Hunter was pretty sure that it was a fake, but Peter thought it might be real, and now that the painter had died, it was potentially much more valuable. ("I knew that was a good buy!" he'd crowed, after reading her obituary.) He was waiting for the first round of fakes to pass through the glutted market, and then he'd try to sell it to a dealer who knew it wasn't real, but who in turn could pass it off as real. And so on.

"Or you could use it as a large dressing room." Taylor held her iPad up, then moved it around to minimize the glare from the window. "You know . . . *until*. Now, let's not forget the other bathroom!"

The details of the second, smaller bathroom, with its seashell guest soaps, embroidered hand towels, and marble fixtures, were lost on Chad. Bentley reassured him, "Honeylicious, we can always remodel."

Hunter said that the toilet was always clogging and that they probably needed a new sewer pipe.

"Now the kitchen!"

As they passed through the great room again, Hunter could have sworn that Taylor was goose-stepping. She let her own knees buckle so that she landed back on the sofa where her troubles—*that day's* troubles, anyway—had begun. She still felt as though an internal organ had been removed. She'd spent over a decade with Peter, most of it in this house.

How could it all go away? If only her head would stop throbbing.

"Look at this granite!" It was Taylor, shouting over the breakfast bar.

Chad: "It's too sterile."

Bentley: "Marble would be classier."

Taylor marched them back. "You, my friend—" she fixed black eyes on Hunter— "are overhoused."

That was the first time Hunter heard that expression, and it reverberated with judgment: She was taking up more space than she deserved. She thought of the scene in *Doctor Zhivago*, where the Bolsheviks force his family into one unheated room.

That couldn't happen here in America. But she was glad to be registered as a Republican.

———

The last thing Hunter heard, when the intruders were on the other side of the front door, was Chad declaring, "The driveway is a total deal-buster."

Hunter listened for the receding thumps of the Sharps' boots, and the lighter clicks of Taylor's heels. Then she hoisted herself up and headed back to Peter's home office.

Now showing on the desktop: a picture of herself and Peter holding pale orange drinks with little umbrellas. A moment later it dissolved and was replaced with a picture of the two of them in swimsuits.

You'd think you could trust a man who shared his computer password with you, she thought as she logged on, although since he used his birthday and his mother's maiden name, she probably could have guessed it on her own.

She needed to see exactly what her financial situation was. The Sharps may have been unimpressed, but Taylor Green-Coopersmith would produce more like them. Realtors were an evil breed: They would convince you to sell a house you loved so you could buy a house you couldn't afford.

Hunter and Peter had two joint credit cards as well as a few department store accounts, and she checked those first. Whew: Everything was as she'd last seen it, on Friday. And their joint checking was intact.

There was a large, ungainly stack of envelopes next to Peter's desktop computer, tilting to the left. She would celebrate by throwing it all away. Hunter paid bills online, but she couldn't quite force herself to stop the hard copy delivery. She lifted the envelopes and flyers one by one, quickly eliminating anything that had URGENT or REPLY REQUESTED stamped in red. Then the offers for insurance: life, health, home. Many giant postcards from realtors (not her favorite cohort at the moment), declaring, "Sold above asking!" and showing pictures of staged rooms photographed with wide wide-angle lenses.

Then another envelope from Bank of America, this one not requesting a reply, but looking all the more sinister from the way Peter's and her names were visible through the plastic window: Peter P. Fitzgerald, with Hunter B. Fitzgerald underneath.

Her hands shook as she tore open the envelope. The horror movie music from the afternoon before, a screechy violin, returned.

Visa bill. A forty-thousand-dollar credit limit. He owed $38,165.23, including the interest and late fee from the last missed payment.

For the next several minutes—or was it an hour?—she was paralyzed, as she stared at the screen saver. More pictures floated by: more cocktails in their hands. Crowded swimming pools. The pre-dawn drive to the top of Haleakala. They'd raided Hunter's 401(k) to take that Maui trip, and others. They were young, and Peter was on the verge of flipping that house in Belvedere for a million-dollar profit! (What had happened to that again? Right . . . the Fed raised interest rates.)

Later, she thought of the sight of the Visa bill as the moment the telescope turned backward, and she saw Peter, and their lives together, through the opposite lens. She still felt as though an internal organ had been removed, but now the organ was malignant, and she was relieved. Her memories were of his boasting, his sulking . . . and his drunkenness.

How did he get her name on that credit card? She needed to talk to a lawyer. She knew lawyers, too; there were at least two who came into the gym after work and flirted with her.

When she forced herself to examine the purchases she saw huge charges at Emporio Armani. Bose—those new headphones were almost $400. Over a thousand dollars at REI. Was that the new kayak in the backyard?

She simply wouldn't pay it. There were no debtors' prisons here in the US of A.

But her name was on the card, and when the collection agency came to call it was her credit score that would plummet. She'd never be able to buy a new car, let alone a house of her own. Maybe she could negotiate a payment plan.

But never mind cars and houses—she had to get a new job, and quickly. Unemployment insurance wouldn't be enough to put gas in her car. But she had enough money in that private (okay, secret—she admitted that to herself now) account to tide her over until she got her first paycheck.

And she wasn't going to wait until tomorrow, either. She took two Advil, and opened an Excel sheet.

There she listed the names of every professional contact she had, along with phone numbers, and notes: who had twins (a weird number of people had twins); whose mother had been ill; who also had family in the Northeast, especially Connecticut. Then she rearranged the order from most to least promising.

By now it was after lunchtime, and a number of people had left for the day. She never did that—well, maybe on a Friday. The general manager (now the *former* general manager) of Energy-4-All, Byron, would give her a glowing recommendation, as would most of the trainers, especially as they knew that she wasn't looking for the same positions as they.

She started with Gwen, sales manager at Forever Fitness.

"I heard about Energy." Gwen clicked her tongue. "There are rumors about Byron." She went on in that excited whisper that people use to spread bad news that doesn't affect them. "Sexual harassment."

"I never had any problems." Hunter was pretty sure that Byron was gay, not that that took sexual harassment off the table.

"I also heard—"

Hunter listened as long as she thought necessary to keep the contact active. Gwen didn't know of anything offhand, but she'd get back to Hunter.

Danielle, recently retired as an assistant operations manager, said she knew of a general manager opening . . .

General manager!

. . . at a spa in Idaho . . .

Idaho? Hunter might be a Republican, but she was a California Republican.

The next person she got ahold of didn't have a job for her, and didn't know of any, but had plenty of ideas: make sure your certifications are up to date. Give classes in your house. Start your own gym! You can get a small business loan—

Hunter had observed this in the past: the less concrete help people have to offer, the more advice they have to give.

There were several promising leads, though: an operations manager opening at RJ's Gym; 101 Fitness might need a new marketing person.

More contacts said they'd ask around for her.

By now the sun was about to set, and the great exodus had begun. Hunter sharpened pencils until their points broke off, and considered whether to call Madison Bloom. She should wait until tomorrow. Madison, as GM of Galaxy Fitness, was her highest-level contact, and she wanted to catch her when they were both at their best. By tomorrow the last traces of her headache would be gone.

But no, she couldn't wait. She only took time for another Advil.

Madison was there. Madison took her call. The rosy glow of sunset, though not visible from Peter's office window, set Hunter's hopes alight.

Madison said she'd love to have Hunter on her team. Hunter was a hard worker, a professional, an aggressive marketer. She particularly admired Hunter's classes, how she targeted different "demos" (demographics). "The narrower the focus, the greater the appeal. What seventy-year-old wants to work out with teens?"

Hunter's internal glow got warmer and brighter as they talked. Yes, Madison knew about Energy-4-All closing. But maybe it was meant to be! Her own fitness manager, Sasha, was about to go on maternity leave . . . was it next month? Six weeks at most. Madison hinted that she might encourage Sasha to leave sooner. What with her swollen ankles and sciatica, she'd be better off at home and on bed rest, wouldn't she? Then, who could say? Maybe Sasha would "fall in love with her baby," and decide not to come back.

Hunter knew she shouldn't, couldn't, rely on this, but oh, it was perfect. Her mother would have said, pray to Saint Bernadette! *I'm not sick, Mam. Saint Bernadette is for when you're sick.*

When Hunter went to bed that night, she was glad for the extra space in her California King.

———

The next morning, unencumbered by hangover, Hunter started early. She knew better than to create a new budget that included a future salary, so she continued to work her way through her list.

But a strange thing happened as the week went by. Fewer people were available to talk to her. The people who had promised, on Monday, to call back, never did. She hadn't expected that everyone would. How often did she break that same promise?

But . . . no one?

She made follow-up phone calls. She sent follow-up emails.

Was something wrong in the entire gym industry? Perhaps Energy-4-All's collapse was symptomatic of a larger problem.

The stone of fear in her stomach had come to life. It was now a wild animal, prowling outside her front door.

She shoved Peter's keyboard out of the way and put her head down on his desk. She read stories about homelessness all the time. She didn't actually *read* the stories, just the headline, and sometimes the first paragraph, before clicking her tongue and putting the newspaper in recycling or alt-tabbing out of the article. There was a homeless encampment now, under a freeway overpass, not far from her own place. She saw the complaints on Nextdoor (Hunter thought of it as "GetOffMyLawn.com"): "I moved here from San Francisco to get away from this!" Hunter had pity for the "unhoused," with their beards and plastic bags and Rollaboards, but only in the abstract. That couldn't happen to her, because she had friends.

But no, she didn't. Not really. She had people who came to her parties and coworkers who now were also out of jobs. She had family in Connecticut: an eighty-three-year-old father and a much-younger mother with early-onset Alzheimer's. "Home is the place that, when you go there, they have to take you in." But first you have to want to go there. The encampment under the freeway would be worse, but not by much. Haha.

And her PG&E bill was due.

She remembered seeing a "We're Hiring!" sign at a nearby Starbucks.

Which was fortuitous, because on Friday, when she called Galaxy Fitness, Madison Bloom was not available to take her call.

——

Hunter got off to a good start at Starbucks. Preston, the manager, said she was the most capable employee he'd ever trained. She was working the register on the afternoon of the first day and sequencing drinks at the end of the second.

The afternoon that she handed over a venti mocha with rasp-berry syrup, no whip, no foam, and skim milk, Preston tapped her on the shoulder said she had a future there. "Just don't think about taking my job, lol." He spelled out "lol." She smiled while she patted the steam off her face.

She appreciated the praise, but the novelty of the job wore off quickly. The strap of her apron around her head reminded her of a noose.

Teenagers came in, ordered on the app, then picked up their drinks without pausing their own conversations. Sometimes they came back to complain of the wrong type of milk. Even Hunter thought oat milk was a misnomer. She'd heard a comic point out that oats had no tits.

Welcome to the working class. Eight hours with two ten-minute breaks and thirty minutes for lunch. Were millions of people really doing this every day?

Hunter had grown up in a distinctly upper-middle-class family: attending private schools (Catholic, at her mother's insistence) and wearing clothes from the children's department at Saks, purchased on weekend trips to Manhattan. Since she was an only child, there was all the more disposable income for the types of expenses that Daddy Edward would have found girlie and frivolous if they'd had to spread them among the eight children Bernadette wanted.

Life after college had required a big adjustment, and Hunter had been proud of herself for learning to live accordingly. There was always Dad for emergencies—and extras. That was, until Bernadette became demented and Edward became old. And even then they hadn't imagined her pumping flavored syrup for eight hours a day.

———

Hunter was fifteen years older than the next-oldest barista, Caitlyn. There was also Katelyn, so they were known as "the C Caitlin" and "the K Katelyn."

The younger baristas were welcoming and supportive, but kept their distance. Maybe they sensed that Hunter carried bad relationship juju.

Take pride in your work, no matter what it is. And she did. She refined her technique: milk, shots, syrup, finish. Her memory was good, and her hands were fast.

Then Preston asked her to mop.

At home, Hunter mopped the kitchen floor nightly, using two buckets: one for detergent, the other for rinsing. She replaced the mophead every month.

It was more than pride, she knew; it was obsessive. She sometimes got up out of bed after Peter was asleep and mopped it again. He didn't notice; he was a heavy sleeper.

So why did she feel so anxious when Preston opened the door of the supply closet?

Because these mops were ancient. And there was only one bucket. And that was the good part of her day.

Did it have to be when she was mopping, dizzy from the smell of the generic cleaning fluid, and with the knot in her apron (she'd never wear emerald green again) coming undone, that Cindi walked in?

Cindi would be out of work, as well, since Energy-4-All closed. She was a popular personal trainer, and a beauty in the mold of Hunter herself: tall, thin, blonde. She was at least ten years younger, though, probably more.

Hunter pushed her hair off her face using the inside of her arm, because her hands were wet. *Put up a good front*, she told herself. *Plenty of women have been divorced. You might trade up.*

"How's your job search going?" she asked Cindi, after they exchanged awkward greetings. Much as she didn't want to see Cindi for other reasons, she might get some insight into her own troubles from her. Hunter's latest theory was that the Federal Trade Commission was investigating predatory practices by fitness centers, like those, "join for five dollars a month" offers that morphed into $300 a month while you weren't paying attention.

"Oh." Cindi shrugged one shoulder. "I'm going to go out on my own. Go into people's homes, you know? That way I don't have to split the money with corporate."

"I sure wish Energy-4-All had given us some warning."

"Tell me about it." But Cindi's expression was distinctly puzzled.

Hunter positioned her hands on the mop handle as if it were a bass. She was uncomfortably aware of that ten-ten-thirty rule, and underneath Preston's friendly manner (he, too, was younger, by at least ten years), Hunter heard the clicking of a stopwatch.

But something was amiss. She tightened her grip on the mop handle.

"Well, I'd better get my order in!" Cindi said. "I have a lot of special requests."

Don't we all, Hunter thought. But she wasn't going to let the moment pass. "Have you talked to anyone else from Energy?"

Now Cindi looked nervous: she cast glances up at the menu board behind Hunter. "I wish they didn't use pork in so many of their sandwiches."

"Cindi . . ."

"Oh, listen! I love this song!" Frank Sinatra's "One for the Road" was coming from the speaker. "I've got to Shazam it."

Cindi had her cell phone in hand and was heading toward the speaker, but Hunter called after her, "What's up?"

"Well, a couple of my friends have read *Jesus Warned Me He Was a Jerk*." Cindi blurted. "You've read it."

"I haven't yet, no."

"I guess maybe you should." Cindi took a step sideways. "I want you to know I really enjoyed working with you." Then, "Hey, do you get a discount here? That would be a perk! Perk, get it? Perk?"

"I get one free item a day." Hunter looked back to see if Preston or one of the others was looking at her. "What's in *Jesus Warned Me* that I should know?"

Cindi's pale blue eyes quivered. When she still didn't respond, Hunter prompted her, "Tell me."

"I haven't finished it yet," Cindi said. "But Landon gave me a copy and said to read the first four chapters. Angelica St. Ambrose says things about you that I'm sure aren't true."

Landon had been a senior manager at Energy-4-All. She and Hunter had been in line for the same promotion, the one that Hunter got. She might not be crushed if Angelica had bad things to say about her.

"Damn, that line is getting long," Cindi said. "Gotta run!"

———

Hunter reluctantly spent $14.99 on the Kindle version. She swiped left and saw blurbs from reviewers at prestigious publications, including *The New Yorker* and *The Atlantic*: "raw," "unfiltered," "a look inside

the mind and heart of an alcoholic clawing her way up and out." The
cover was a black-and-white photo of a younger Angelica, holding
a bottle of Glenfiddich.

DEDICATION
To all my friends at AA, who I can't name,
for reasons that should be obvious.
And to Jesus, who laughs at all my jokes.

Hunter swiped a few more times. She could do a search on her
name, but surely Angelica would have changed it. Except she must
not have, or Cindi wouldn't have known . . .

She swiped a little faster.

There it was: not only Hunter, but Hunter *Fitzgerald*. About
a quarter of the way through the book was the story of how she
and Angelica first met, years before, when Hunter was an aide to a
local congressman.

She went on to describe Hunter as "spoiled, entitled—not her
fault, just a product of her upbringing—materialistic, and cold."

Cold? On what planet was she cold?

Or was she?

> *The night everything changed was the night I needed her most. We*
> *used to go out without buzzbands—have you noticed that married*
> *women always pronounce it like it's spelled with 2 Zs?*
>
> *I was trying hard to get sober but Vijay was being abusive.*
> *You can only be called "stoopid" so many times before you start to*
> *believe it, especially if you believe it already.*
>
> *I couldn't find Vijay's suitcase, so I was sure he'd left for good.*
> *I called Hunter from the closet (aren't we all in the closet about*
> *something?), clutching one of his shirts like Linus his blanket.*
> *(If only I had a blanket!)*

Hunter remembered the night. The story about the suitcase stuck in her mind, as well as its conclusion: Vijay had simply moved it to the basement.

She also remembered that it was the last time Hunter went out alone with Angelica. She was enabling Angelica, she'd told Peter. It should stop. Maybe the four of them could do something together. He might like Angelica, and Vijay was doing something in real estate.

> *It was me and Hunter and it started out as any other night. Wow! That sounds like Stephen King, doesn't it? Well, it's not, because he makes that shit up. This is for real.*
>
> *We go to our favorite hangout, Dive Bars Is Us, except there aren't any dive bars in Marin County. Oh no. If I saved the extra money we spent on Johnnie Walker I'd be living in a house like Hunter's now. Chateau de Hunter.*
>
> *So we're there, and the service is, I don't know, like uze, and now is when I have to come clean because you're only as sick as your secrets, which means that a month ago I was on life support. What I mean is, I have no idea how the service was or wasn't.*

When Hunter inhaled she felt a scratching sensation in her lungs. She skimmed through a few more pages of Angelica's recounting of that evening. She and Hunter had "tied one on like there was no tomorrow." Hunter went back to her car, where she passed out, and Angelica went home with a man she'd call "Bob," to protect his identity (*so* his *identity she's protecting?*).

She remembered, too, that she'd asked Angelica to leave with her, and Angelica had declined, though that had happened on other nights as well.

> *So I wake up with no panties on. Why do panties sound so much more slutty than underwear?*

There's the cum on my leg which is exhibit A, huh? And I'm like, wha—a? And this dude I don't recognize is brushing his teeth. Brushing his teeth! He's a rapist, but he has good hygiene. Whew.

No, I'm not a virgin. What I am is naive. I expected that Hunter, who was the designated driver, would designate herself. Oh, and drive. Instead she went to her Free-Us and passed out like . . . well, like a drunk. Which I am, too, but I'm fighting my way back.

Hunter didn't rape me, because Hunter doesn't have a dick, though if she could buy one on a layaway plan, she'd look really different in a bathing suit. So she didn't do the raping. But she had promised to protect me, because I was her friend.

And I'm still her friend, though this is hard to forgive . . .

Hunter had no intention of forgiving. Not now. Not ever. Angelica continued to refer to the incident as a rape. Hunter would never dare contradict her in public; any nonconsensual sex was a rape. But Hunter hadn't encouraged, let alone forced, Angelica to go home with this man.

She remembered that his real name was Blair. And she remembered that, far from passing out in her Prius, she hadn't even brought her car.

Chapter 3

Treasure Island Treasure

HUNTER

Hunter forced herself to read all of *Jesus Warned Me* straight through. While humbling herself at every turn, Angelica managed to portray herself as heroine. Survivor. Advocate.

There were people in her world to admire, like Angelica's sponsors, who were available to talk at 3 a.m., and who, at the slightest hint there was need, would come running with food, DVDs, board games. Her "medevac team," she called them. But they had to remain anonymous, while Hunter was named each time she appeared, as she did in later chapters, moving through Angelica's life like an evil spirit rattling chains.

Hunter tried (and failed) to console herself that Vijay, Hunter's ex-husband, came out looking as bad as she did. He was verbally abusive. He withheld his "favors," as she described their sex life ironically, when he was irritated with her, or with his life in general.

But Vijay was safe in Mumbai, where, apparently, he had a wealthy family and a new wife. Would *Jesus Warned Me* be translated into Hindi? It seemed likely. Hunter didn't go looking for news of the book, but so-called friends (former party guests, coworkers, and sorority sisters from decades before) didn't hesitate to alert her to its rise on the *New York Times* bestseller list. Some were sympathetic. Like Cindi, they said that they didn't believe all of what Angelica wrote.

For a woman who portrayed herself as uneducated (she'd dropped out of Marin City College "thanks to demon drink"), Angelica was clever. She depicted Hunter as a high-functioning alcoholic, condescending, exploitive, vain (say "narcissistic") and materialistic (say "greedy"). But in those chapters in which Hunter appeared, and the conversations that Angelica reconstructed, there were never any witnesses, no one who would speak for Hunter and say, *no, that never happened.*

———

Hunter made Peter's home office into her own, replacing his selfies and sports trophies, which included some from high school, with flowers, and photos in which he did not appear.

She received her first paycheck, but it only covered about half of her monthly expenses, and the nest egg she'd collected before Peter's defection was dwindling quickly, a fresh cookie crumbling in her hand.

She'd confronted Peter about the Visa bill via email, though it required several drafts before she replaced language like "how could you do this to me" with "I'd appreciate you taking care of this."

It was Angelica who replied, "Pierre is working the steps to become more responsible for his past actions. He'll get back to you soon."

Credit card debt was unsecured. Visa couldn't come after her car, or her house (especially since it wasn't her house) or the skis in the gardening shed if she didn't pay it off. But say goodbye not only to cars and houses, but to starting a business of her own, and she'd dreamed of that for years.

Hunter contacted Visa about a payment plan. She dangled the threat of filing bankruptcy, which would eliminate most, or even all, of the balance, and that made them more open to negotiation.

But she still needed to raise some cash to cover groceries until the next paycheck.

She was massaging her forehead when she remembered Chad's disparagement of the Ingraham clock.

Sell it!

No, no, not the clock—she'd have to hire a professional to remove it from its case to determine its value, and that was assuming that it *was* real—but Treasure Island Flea, the monthly event held on the island of the same name, was scheduled for this very weekend, and she could grab some of their more esoteric collectibles and head across the bridges. She only needed to sell a few small items, like William Shatner's Christmas album, to raise enough for a trip to Costco for bulk groceries and cheap gas. It would be faster than advertising them on Craigslist or eBay, and not only did she love the bargaining, but the flea market buyers and sellers were her peeps, and she missed them. Perhaps Peter's lack of interest in visiting flea markets and scoping out garage sales in recent months should have been her first clue that something had changed.

Hunter assumed that the flea market collectibles, as she thought of them, were community property, but no matter: Peter didn't keep a record of their purchases (he explained that he needed to put all his accounting skills to work managing his real estate investments). She did. If he noticed that the Shatner album was gone, she'd tell him that the Klingons stole it.

———

Treasure Island was a platter of fake land attached to Yerba Buena Island, which was real, but useless, except for preventing the Bay Bridge from falling into the water.

The flea market was held on the western side of the island: Card tables covered with blue umbrellas sold picture frames, tube socks, posters, paintings of the bridges and seascapes that belonged in motel rooms, and paperback books sans covers, liberated from bookstore recycling bins.

There were regulars who showed up each month with the same bulk inventory, but it was the one-timers who'd interested Hunter and Peter: the people who had just cleared out Grandma Shirley's attic. They were amateurs, as Peter described them, who wouldn't know a Jackson Pollock from a five-year-old's spin art. "And people who don't know what they have don't deserve to keep it," he'd said.

But the next morning, when Hunter descended from Yerba Buena to Treasure, she was in for a surprise. She followed the orange-jacketed attendants waving marshaling wands, as always, and as always, they directed her and the other autos through lanes created by orange cones into a large parking lot.

Something was different, though. The virtual lanes now led not to the western side of the island, but to the east. The hand-painted "Treasure Island Flea" signs were gone, replaced by smooth, professional ones announcing, "Welcome to TreasureFest," with the graphic of a pirate chest.

Hunter parked near a shabby building covered with splashy colors that were halfway between murals and graffiti. Once she got out of the car, she saw that fake tree trunks created a makeshift, but clearly official entrance.

A nearby poster promised,

A Day of Fun Food and Frolic!
Music from top up-and-coming artists!
A rotating lineup of 40 food trucks!

There were colorful graphics of T-shirts and pants below, and all this superimposed on a stylized Golden Gate Bridge, hovering midair, although from where Hunter stood, the Bay Bridge dominated the view.

So Treasure Island Flea had gone commercial. There were only sellers, no buyers.

She thought of going home. But only briefly, because, as little as she had to spend, there might be something she could buy and resell at a profit. The secret to finding collectibles was persistence and curiosity; in other words, the willingness to plow through a lot of junk.

A young woman took her money and stamped her hand. "Children under twelve are free," she said. What, did she suspect Hunter of smuggling a child in under her shirt? It was true that Hunter could almost have fit one underneath, baggy as it was from the weight she'd lost since Peter's defection.

Others had taken advantage of the promotion. The place was infested with children: riding on daddies' shoulders, squirming in double strollers. Hunter had wanted children, but Peter hadn't, and it didn't feel right to force the issue. Now it was too late, and since she'd never plugged into the world of children, she didn't want to be surrounded by them. Nor did she care for the abundance of dogs, many larger than children themselves, and many who bounded around without benefit of leash.

A row of temporary booths stretched ahead on either side of her, creating a long aisle. Those booths, constructed with collapsible poles and cloth awnings, featured handmade crafts: knit hats, tie-dyed T-shirts, jewelry, and vials of herbal potions that claimed to cure insomnia, constipation, and acne.

She walked the long aisle slowly. The sellers had handheld devices that would allow them to slide a credit card and even to spit out a receipt—that was, the ones who weren't already equipped with Apple Pay. In the days of Treasure Island Flea, not only was payment cash-only, but haggling had been half the fun, at least if you were good at it. Hunter was good at it.

After a while, though, she not only abandoned hope of finding anything for herself, she stopped even glancing at the merchandise she passed, since it invariably resulted in the seller shouting at her to come have a closer look.

Hunter had always been a consumer. She saw nothing wrong with taking money that she and Peter had earned and spending it on items that gave them pleasure, whether it was a kayak for weekend trips, or granite countertops.

But today this all seemed like excess of the most shameful kind. Not conspicuous consumption, but worse: nothing worth wearing. Nothing worth displaying. Not even anything worth giving away. This wasn't self-indulgence: it was waste.

The crowd was thickening. She bowed her head to watch the pavement, and to avoid the loose-running children and dogs, though some of each species banged into her legs more than once.

She was almost at the end of the row of vendors when a loud, unpleasant noise assaulted her: the sound of a band tuning up.

A few steps later she found herself in what must be part of a parking lot on weekdays, from the pattern of white lines painted on the pavement. Now it was a food court, with the trucks forming a circle. As for the food trucks, they were the usual suspects: tacos, frozen yogurt, curries, doughnuts, churros, espresso, Korean barbecue. The mix of cooking pork and deep-frying dough was nauseating enough, but mixed with car exhaust and the briny smell from the water, Hunter was ready to vomit.

Then the musicians, off on a bandstand to her left, burst into "Don't Stop Believin'."

Hunter was going to get the hell out of there, and the fastest way was forward.

Surrounding the circle there was a makeshift fence: a series of plastic orange poles, set close together, and connected with yellow tape. Hunter was wont to respect boundaries, metaphoric as well as literal, but increasingly these days she asked herself, where had following the rules gotten her?

So she hustled through the gathering families, improvising a game of hopscotch in order to dodge not only the children and pets, but the adults carrying obscenely large cardboard trays of greasy food. Even in her hurry, she tried to avoid stepping on the lines bequeathed from the parking lot. *Step on a crack . . .*

She turned sideways to slip through the gap between "Curry in a Hurry" and "Shawarma from the Farma," avoiding the thick power cables on the ground.

Then, "Hey! You can't go out that way!"

She didn't have to look around to know that it was a security guard, and from the wheezy way he shouted, that he was overweight, and out of shape. He would be in a blue uniform, with a cap that had a logo like "All Guard" or "Protect U." She pictured him with a big nose and large pores.

She laughed, without turning around.

"Stop!"

No freaking way, she thought. She measured the distance of the orange poles and the height of the yellow tape, and then, like a well-trained thoroughbred, she leapt over the tape and landed outside the grounds of the TreasureFest.

"Come back here!"—from behind, but the guard's wheezing nearly obscured his words.

She kept laughing, as much as *she* could. Hunter ran the Bay to Breakers, the popular San Francisco 12k, every year. She hadn't been out running since Peter left, but it all came back to her now: the strong muscles of her legs, the accompanying pump of her arms, and the bounce from the soles of her best running shoes, as she delightedly left the TreasureFest with all its tacky and touristy merchandise.

Finally she had to stop. She crouched, resting her hands just above her knees. She was panting, and panting hard, but it was victory panting.

———

As she caught her breath, the euphoria faded. Her diminishing joy coincided with the invasion of the fog. Invading fog was typical of the San Francisco Bay, but the rapidity with which the dark gray droplets gathered took her by surprise: It was like watching a time-lapse video. She hardly had a moment to look at her surroundings before they were obscured past a short distance. She could see as far as a chain link fence and a couple of fuel tanks behind; the buildings beyond that were already hidden.

It was time to go home.

She didn't want to encounter the security guard, or any of the TreasureFest crowd, so she walked west; her plan was to hit the edge of the island and then circle back to her car incognito.

She wasn't sure how long she'd been walking when she realized that she must have headed in the wrong direction. The strains of "Don't Stop Believin'" had faded, replaced by foghorns. She hadn't noticed when they had started up, but they were irritating her now, while usually she found them comforting. At night, when she was at home.

She did know she'd been walking a long time because her feet hurt, even in her running shoes.

She'd wandered into a residential area, though the description was generous, since it consisted of cheaply built, two-story blocks of stucco apartments in a faded coral. She remembered hearing that people actually lived on Treasure Island, and that she'd wondered how that happened—were the apartments "affordable"? Or were they condos? And how did people get them? Then she'd filed it under Things That Didn't Affect Her.

Tentacles of fog reached between the apartment blocks. Tule fog! She'd heard of it, but never seen it, and if this was what it was, she understood why it was responsible for so many auto accidents. She'd crossed the Golden Gate Bridge when it was an act of faith comparable to taking communion, as the red tower ahead was completely invisible. This was something far creepier. Was it possible to have tule fog and regular fog at the same time? Apparently it was. Too bad there wasn't someone to ask.

Which thought made her realize that she hadn't seen another person for a while. The sidewalks were deserted, and she couldn't remember when she'd seen a car, at least not one in motion. At first it had been a relief from the horrors of TreasureFest, but now it was unnerving.

As embarrassing as it was, she might have to call someone. Who? Peter? No, God forbid. Right! Katie, her former assistant manager . . .

Her cell phone said, NO SERVICE.

Hunter shivered, mostly from cold; a little from fear. Hadn't she seen part of a hand move one of the aged curtains? She wasn't sure. She made out the occasional *beeee* of a seagull, and sometimes she thought she heard people cheering, only to recognize it as air currents rustling through the wind tunnels created by the apartment blocks. The smell was of fish and concrete dust.

There were little metal mailboxes grouped together on posts in front of individual apartment blocks. Someone would come out to get the mail at some point!

Then she remembered that it was Sunday.

She walked.

And walked.

At the end of each block she turned in what she thought was the right way, only to find herself on another identical street.

Damn, why hadn't she just retraced her steps? Who cared about a security guard? But it was too late for that now.

Finally, with thumping heart, she knocked on a door. No answer. She didn't knock again, but went to another door, and this second time she gave it two tries.

She stopped after the third door.

Then she saw, up ahead, that what appeared to be a single apartment block actually had a narrow gap between the two sets of doors. It led to an alley.

Hunter Bernadette Fitzgerald did not go down strange alleys. But Alice didn't hesitate to follow the white rabbit, and besides, what was the alternative?

At the end of the alley was an old Airstream trailer. The logo was worn down, but the shell was shiny. There was a stucco wall behind the trailer, with two boarded-up windows.

Hunter approached slowly, but she'd only taken a few steps when the trailer door opened, and a woman descended the drop-down stairs. She was blonde, with large, dark brown eyes, and she was wearing a white bathrobe of a material so thick that it could have hidden a person who weighed ninety pounds or three hundred.

"You here for that lousy TreasureFest?" the woman asked pleasantly.

Hunter took a step backward. "H-how'd you know?"

"Once a month the yuppies come out."

Hunter was undecided as to whether this was compliment or insult.

"Too bad what they did." The woman stuck her hands deeply into the pockets of her robe. "I hate to see these industrial sites turn into pop-up Walmarts for the handicraft set."

"That's just how I feel!" Hunter exclaimed. She took a longer look at the woman. She was shorter than Hunter, but appeared to be about the same age, though her tanned skin showed some of the signs that tanned skin will show by forty: the fine lines not only around the eyes but the mouth. "Do you live here?"

"No, I go everywhere in my bathrobe." The woman pointed with her thumb over her shoulder, to the trailer. "Yes, I live here. And I used to sell at the flea market, when it was a real flea. I had *use-ful* inventory, not single-use knickknacks making a pit stop on their way to landfill."

"Really?" Hunter was always interested in what vintage items people had to sell, and for a moment she forgot to be scared. "What kind of inventory?" Longshot it might be, but perhaps this eccentric woman, though not wealthy, was also a collector, and would want to buy one of the items that Hunter had brought to sell, and stashed in her car.

"Well, I have a lot of things. But here's what I'm most proud of." The woman posed like Vanna White presenting the old trailer as the grand prize. "The dishes from discontinued patterns. Like, Grandma Tiffany dies and the serving for four is missing one salad plate. We'll keep Grandma Tiffany alive in the hearts of her descendants and stop some couple from buying a whole new set. I'm fighting the good fight against consumer culture."

"Grandma Tiffany?"

"It's only a matter of time. I'm Zelda, by the way."

"Hunter Fitzgerald." It was an automatic response.

The woman—Zelda—tilted her head. "Really?"

"Yes, really—why would I . . ." She stopped. It wasn't possible, was it? That this woman who lived in a trailer on Treasure Island had read *Jesus Warned Me?* Hunter had imagined this happening (though neither this soon nor in this situation), so she was ready. "I mean, I'm not that Hunter Fitzgerald."

"*Riiight.*" Zelda put her hands back in her pockets. "And just how many female, or even male, 'Hunter Fitzgeralds' do you think there are in the Bay Area?"

Damn. But it was also a relief. To get it out of the way.

"What are you interested in?" Zelda asked. "Collection wise?"

"Oh, lots of things. Bakelite?"

"Bakelite? Hello, I've got Bakelite. Come in, I'll show you."

Hunter remembered to be scared.

"What, do you think I'm a serial killer? How would I get blood off this bathrobe?"

That was the deal-closer. Hunter would risk her mother's life for a chance to add to her Bakelite collection.

She followed Zelda up the two stairs into the Airstream.

The interior was just what she would have expected, if she'd stopped to expect anything: the tie-dyed curtains hanging from wooden links, strings of beads partitioning off the back; retro decals honoring surfing coves along the California coast . . . and a vintage vinyl record player! Hunter's fingers itched at the sight.

"And here's just a sample of that Bakelite."

Zelda pointed to a table, and Hunter froze in place. There were displayed a lamp with a flamingo as a stand, a Tintin lunchbox, and what appeared to be a Bakelite radio. Maybe this was how an archaeologist felt, when the first shards of crockery from an ancient civilization appeared.

"This is what I was talking about." Zelda picked up a china plate with pink flowers. "It's a discontinued pattern. We like filling the holes in people's lives, don't we, Kitty?"

Zelda was talking to a gray tabby, asleep in a basket; Hunter had assumed that both cat and basket were ceramic. At the sound of its name, though, the cat raised its head.

"Jay Catsby. A girl, but I couldn't resist."

"I can't believe you really live here." It was rude, but it slipped out. "Where do you sleep?"

Zelda patted the table. "This converts to a bed."

"That table? How—"

"I'll show you." Zelda reached for the table's edge.

"No, no, I believe you. Just—the radio, does it work?"

"It needs batteries." Zelda slipped into one of the banquettes. *"Setz dich hin, meine Frau."*

Some words don't need translating. Hunter sat on the booth opposite Zelda. There, for the first time, she noticed a small branch, brightly painted, and with beads and feathers attached at one end. "What's that?" It was about eighteen inches, sanded smooth.

"Oh, that?" Zelda's remark was exaggeratedly casual. "That's just a talking stick."

"Is it 'found art'?" It looked like something one of the TreasureFest vendors would try to pass off as such: She'd registered one display of seashells with happy faces painted on them.

"Quite the opposite. It has a long history." Zelda held it up. "This is a true Native American talking stick. It was given to me by a woman I knew in an artists' colony in New Mexico. It's been passed down from mother to daughter and used in female-only groups. Sometimes to settle a dispute among the women."

"Hah. We used a 'talking three-pound dumbbell' in our team meetings." Hunter mimed pumping an invisible dumbbell, and felt sad. Turnover at Starbucks was high, so it was difficult to make friends. She wasn't sure she remembered how.

Zelda pressed a forefinger on each end of the stick, then raised it to eye level. One end was round, while the other had a small, forked protrusion, from which the beads and feathers dangled. "Talking sticks have been completely appropriated. We shouldn't even call them talking sticks. Maybe communication facilitators."

Hunter tried to catch herself before rolling her eyes, but Zelda smiled. "I saw that. I get it. It's okay to call *this* one a talking stick." It was from a very old oak, she told Hunter, and each daughter added something of her own: like the feathers, or beads, but most often she painted her name or a secret symbol. The beads and feather didn't stay on long, and had to be replaced; the paint lasted longer, but that, too, faded away. "Also, I messed up. It's important that we don't call it Native American. The woman who gave it to me was enrolled in the Navajo Nation, but I think she was part Apache."

"Why didn't she give it to her own daughter?"

"She didn't have any children. But think of all the energy that's rubbed off over countless generations."

This time Hunter did catch herself before rolling her eyes.

Zelda angled the stick, then stroked its torso as it if were a cat. "Here." She held it out to Hunter the way one hands over a knife, pointing the rounded end toward her.

When Hunter's fingers closed around the wood, a tingling sensation ran up her arm. She opened her fingers and let it fall to the table.

"It's still cultural appropriation," Zelda said, "but if you treat it with the respect it deserves, it's okay."

"Are you giving it to me?" *And what am I supposed to do with it?*

"Maybe. Anyway, I'm going to give you some tea and you're going to give me your side of the Angelica St. Ambrose story."

———

Zelda took down some knitting from one of the cabinets near the trailer's ceiling, then poured tea for Hunter from a pot with Mickey Mouse painted on one side, Minnie on the other. "Something wrong?"

Hunter was staring at the hot brown liquid in her cup.

"Okay, be that way." Zelda took another cup off a hook above the sink, and placed it on the table. "See? I'm pouring mine from the same pot."

"I'm embarrassed, but—"

"But this trailer could be a front for the white slave trade, right. Wait!"

Zelda took several swallows from her cup she'd poured for herself. Then she collected the lunch box, lamp, and radio, but left the talking stick.

Hunter tucked one leg up under herself. Zelda didn't seem to be in any hurry, so Hunter told her how she'd met Angelica, several years earlier, at a fundraising event for the congressman whom Hunter had worked for when she first came to Northern California. Angelica kind of glommed on to me, Hunter said, and I felt a little sorry for her, because she obviously had a drinking problem, or she was drunk that night, anyway, and she was in this unhappy marriage, so I'd go out with her every month or so.

Angelica would get drunk, and Hunter would go home to Peter. Vijay, Angelica's husband, had come to California to get rich in real estate, so Peter and Vijay could talk about debt service and balloon payments.

Then Angelica got sober and for a short time they were a four-some: the Fitzgeralds with Angelica St. Ambrose, who had changed her name to "Koka," though she later changed it back. After Vijay left, that was.

"I mean, what was she doing at that fundraiser anyway?" Hunter asked herself aloud, because Zelda couldn't know. Absently, Hunter reached to touch the talking stick. The tingling again. She pulled her hand away.

"You okay?" Zelda asked, tilting her head, birdlike.

Immediately, Hunter remembered exactly what Angelica was doing there: asking Hunter for a job. In the congressman's office. Angelica had no college degree, which Hunter could overlook, but she also had no experience in fundraising, which for a congressperson was the main focus of the job. Hunter hired someone else.

How did I forget that?

She didn't realize that she said this aloud, but she must have, because Zelda said, "Obviously, Angelica didn't."

Hunter stared out the window. On this side, her only view was of the stucco wall and a clothesline, from which a single white sheet hung. For another minute, she only heard the click of Zelda's knitting needles.

Finally: "She wrote about that in her memoir," Zelda said. "Have you read that part?"

Hunter untucked her leg, then tucked up the other one. "I fell on the grenade, yes."

"Then you know that she made an effort to stay sober the whole day so that when she met you she'd make a good impression."

"Boo-hoo! How is it suddenly my fault that she didn't get a job she wasn't qualified for?"

"Relax, Jax." Zelda sighed. "She does have a gift for turning things around." *Click click.* "Anyway, now you need money."

"Badly."

"What about Starbucks?"

Hunter pushed renegade hair off her forehead. She'd told Zelda about the Starbucks job and her original motive to journey to Treasure Island: to sell some of the Fitzgerald collectibles. "What about it?"

"Wouldn't they have some kind of executive training program?"

"They do, but . . ." She thought a moment. "Energy was a chain. I don't want to work for a huge corporation. I want to start something of my own." She folded her arms on the table and looked out at the old stucco wall. "Once upon a time I had fantasies of starting a winery. Now anything with alcohol is tainted. When I was at Energy I was saving to start my own gym, but it's all moot now." Visa had come back with a payment plan that she could manage if her car never needed major repairs, but she'd be in debt for a long time.

Zelda gripped her needles with one hand and used the other to pat Hunter's. "Don't go down that road, girlie girl. Self-pity leads to a cliff."

Which made Hunter think of the top of Mount Tamalpais. She gazed out the window of the Airstream and watched the lone sheet flapping in the wind.

Zelda held up her knitting. Bands of gold, pink, and scarlet re-created a sunset. "Damn." She unraveled a few stitches.

"What's that going to be?"

"A blanket. There are enough scarves in the world, but people always need blankets." She bowed her head over her lap again. "May I make a suggestion?"

"Sure."

Zelda didn't look up. "From what you tell me, you not only have a passion, but an eye for . . ." She freed one hand and made a circle in the air, indicating the contents of her trailer. "Things that people might just give away, that are actually valuable, if you know what you're doing."

Hunter admitted with ill-disguised pride that yes, she liked to think so.

"So, start your own business. You already have inventory in that—what did you call it?"

"The Margaret Keane room."

Zelda emitted a half-laugh. "She had a good run, didn't she? The point is, make a career out of doing something you love: doing what I do, but—what's the expression they use now? Scale it."

She'd had that idea herself. She'd even thought of how she might play on her name: Hunter Does the Hunting, Inc. Or LLC, or whatever. She'd thought a lot about it, but she realized now that she'd feared going into business with Peter, given his lack of money management skills, and he would have wanted to be part of it.

She returned her gaze to the window, where a sparrow perched for a moment on the clothesline before flying away. "Does anyone make money at that?" Peter had never made that big score: a Vermeer under a clown on velvet.

"You will."

There was surprising power in those two words.

But abruptly, Hunter shook her head. "Not soon enough. I need money fast—I mean, a big chunk right away."

Zelda was quiet for a while. "Well, then, what did you learn at Energy-4-All that you can pass on?"

Hunter knew the answer immediately. "I want to help people get healthy."

"I like that."

Hunter felt warm under the sun of Zelda's approval. "I've learned a lot about nutrition and exercise just by working at the gym. By osmosis." She started to reach for the talking stick, just to have something to fiddle with, but pulled back. Instead she twirled her cup around. "It's a great idea! We can meet at my house—"

Without looking up, Zelda smiled; perhaps she was thinking about how it wasn't really Hunter's house. "—that'll keep overhead down. And it won't be just about eating, it'll be about exercise. I have strong opinions about that. I want to help people de-cathect from food."

Zelda smiled again: a knowing, sly smile. "That's a big word. 'To withdraw emotion from.'"

Hunter preened. "And get healthy in the process." She boasted, "You see how I didn't call it 'Get Thin.' If you're healthy, you'll be at a good weight, and I'm tired of hearing people—women—obsess about their bodies." Angelica was one, but Hunter had said enough about Angelica that day.

Zelda listened, with that same knowing half-smile.

Hunter babbled on, brainstorming, randomly describing scenes from the gym ("I saw people come in and do an hour of exercise and then eat a bag of potato chips!") and generally ruminating on the world of food and exercise. She knew that she was blessed—yes, blessed, and she didn't use that word lightly—to escape the cycle of dieting and food fears that plagued so many women (and some men, but she couldn't solve all the world's problems). "And you know, they have these ridiculous apps that tell people how many calories they burned, so how many calories they can eat now."

She'd form a group. She'd have no trouble recruiting members. Women only: They'd speak more freely that way. And it was women who let weight issues get in the way of health. She'd known women who would keep smoking rather than put on ten pounds. And she'd take them on field trips, and start them with little bits of exercise, but they'd build up. And—and vision boards! First night. They could post pictures of what they'd like to look like. But it wasn't about appearance—oh, no! It was mostly about health.

She'd hammer out a four-week—six-week? eight-week?—program. And! This was the best idea of all—the first meeting is free!

Zelda tied off the end of the yarn.

"And I'll have the women—don't you think it should be all women?—keep a journal of what they eat and how much they exercise. Oh, I'm excited!"

"I can see you are." Zelda wrapped what she had knitted around the talking stick. "Take this. To keep order in the group. It's better than a dumbbell."

Hunter protested, but Zelda insisted, "It was meant for you."

"But it should go to your daughter," Hunter protested.

"Define daughter."

Wasn't the blanket meant for a hospital or homeless shelter or other worthy destinations?

"It's not finished anyway."

"What about the talking stick?"

"You'll have it as long as you need it."

When Hunter left the trailer, the fog had dissipated. It was getting dark, but when she got to the corner, the Bay was visible, and all she had to do was turn left.

Chapter 4

Fly Away

HUNTER

Hunter returned from Treasure Island so full of ideas and plans that her muscles strained to escape from her skin.

The screensaver showed a picture of herself and Peter wearing leis. *I really have to change that,* she thought, and the moment she touched the mouse, the budget she'd been working on reappeared.

She wasn't that bad off. If she defrosted some of the food Peter had left behind (much as she disliked ravioli, even when fresh) and went through all his pants pockets, she'd be okay until Starbucks Corp coughed up.

Hunter had a reputation for her skill with social media. Or at least, she deserved one. She was responsible for the 2,334 likes (and follows!) on the Energy-4-All Facebook page, their Instagram following (she'd lost count), and their nearly ten thousand Twitter— now "X"—followers. And obviously, it was through social media that she would launch her new health coaching business. Diet and exercise were the main components, but she would cash in on the psychological aspect as well. Even astrology, if that's what it took. Or the Enneagram, though she didn't know anything about that—*yet*.

She simply had to start with the membership of Energy-4-All. She'd have more than she could handle. Cap the group at—what? Maybe twelve. They'd fit comfortably in the great room. Chardonnay Heights had accommodated fifty guests easily, but that was with people wandering through the house. They kept the Keane room locked.

Since Peter had left, Hunter had been too depressed to open Facebook. But now she metaphorically held her nose, opened her personal page, and changed her status from "married" to "it's complicated." Let Angelica, whom Hunter still counted among her two-thousand-plus friends, make of that what she would.

She discovered that a long list of these supposed "friends" had been posting syrupy sympathy on her page about both job-and-husband loss. "It's a growth opportunity," was typical, while others were more specific: "I can only imagine what you're going through since Hikaru and I haven't faced these issues."

She exited Facebook. Facebook=FB=Full of Bullshit.

She recorded all the ideas she'd had since meeting Zelda, wishing she could type as fast as she could think. They'd meet weekly. Accountability! How many weeks? Keep it open until the first wave of interest came in.

But how much to charge? She wouldn't offer sliding scale—just because she was doing good in the world didn't mean that she had to be a charity. Psychotherapists charged . . . what? $400 an hour, some of them? And without promising concrete results! A group such as this would be a cheaper alternative to therapy.

Then she remembered one of her best marketing tools: first meeting free.

After that, she'd feel them out. Let them put down the first number. Ask what they were paying in dues to their gym. Oh, this was it! Tuesday . . . Tuesdays were good. Tuesdays or Wednesdays, in case people wanted long weekends.

She set a date: a week from Tuesday.

She opened Facebook again, and created a new, public page: GET HEALTHY WITH HUNTER! She had fun choosing a picture of herself in a two-piece bathing suit, as skimpy as good taste would allow, so as to send the message: join my group and wear a two-piece!

Then she posted inspiring stock photos that didn't look too stocky, of bike-riders and mountain-climbers. Not only can you wear a two-piece swimsuit, you can climb a mountain at the same time! She even added a real photo of Peter on skis, since he cut such a seductively athletic figure. Join my group and attract an athletic man!

Marketing: you did what you had to do.

She'd return to boost the living daylights out of the page, but first onto X. Her handle was @HunterBFitzgerald, because she'd had the foresight not to tie herself to Energy in her promos, using instead #Energy4All. As business took off, she'd create something jazzier, like @GetHealthyWithHunter or @HunterzHealth. She'd need multiple accounts, but she wanted to wait until she could use her initial clients as a focus group.

Her first (pinned) tweet read:

> Are you struggling with #weight issues? Have trouble sticking to an #exercise routine? If you're ready to #getHealthy, DM @HunterBFitzgerald Time to #ChangeYourLife!

On both X and Facebook, motivational posts exploded from her fingers. She started with a few teasers ("Are YOU ready to commit?") but moved on immediately to psychobabble that she lifted happily from other, similar programs. She went back to boost the Facebook posts, paying careful attention to demographics (women only!) and geographics (a twenty-five-mile radius). Then she created an event page for the first meeting on Facebook, adding testimonials. She had plenty from her performance evaluations at Energy. Would Boss

Man care that she was quoting him? Possibly, but since he, too, was out of a job, he had more immediate problems, and she'd replace his praise with more current, and relevant, quotes, before long.

———

She checked the Facebook event site hourly at first, and then every five minutes. Someone whose name she didn't recognize wrote "sounds like fun good luck! ☺"—but they did not click "attending." Or even "interested." No one did.

Her expectations had been unrealistic. That was all right: it was good to aim high.

It only meant that she had to work even harder.

She began the long process of individually messaging friends. She crafted a standard message that included information about dates, times, and her address, and then personalized the notes where she knew something about the recipient. It was labor-intensive, but this was when the women got separated from the girls.

She posted pictures on Instagram, with flamboyant captions. And TikTok! How had she overlooked TikTok? She was just getting started on a TikTok Energy-4-All promotional campaign when the company collapsed. Now she created a personal account, and did her best, with her yoga mat and a medicine ball, to create a few videos.

When the morning dragged on with no takers, she dismissed her rising anxiety easily: It was the end of the weekend. People (and when she said "people," she meant "couples," and when she said "couples," she meant "affluent couples") were coming back from the wine country, or Tahoe. Give them time to settle in.

But two more days of relentless, coffee-fueled, posting, boosting, and tweeting generated nothing. Unless one counted a handful of additional generic comments on Facebook, "Sounds gr8☺!" Meanwhile, #EnergyClosed had stopped trending.

More coffee. Emails to friends, starting with the ones who'd written on her page.

Finally! The profile pic was of a sunflower, but the name was EmmaLee:

```
Hi Hunter can you help me pay off my
car loan Othrwise bank will take it
☹. I'm only asking $5,000. It will
bring good things back to you.
```

Hunter shoved Peter's mouse pad and pencil holder to the floor, to make room to lay her head down. Zelda, a woman in an Airstream trailer, had recognized her name, so why should she be surprised that Angelica's memoir had turned the entire internet against her?

When all else failed her, Hunter turned to cleaning.

———

She had her water bottle in one hand and a can of Pledge in the other when she came into the great room, intent on polishing the cherrywood table that she and Peter had used to spread out buffets for their guests.

There was Zelda's talking stick, propped up against the chair at the head of the table.

Weird. Hunter was pretty sure that she'd put it away, in the drawer where she kept her tank tops, still cocooned in Zelda's mini-blanket. But she'd been so excited when she came home that she might have dropped it on the table. Somehow it had fallen on the chair. Somehow its knit covering had disappeared.

Clearly, Get Healthy wasn't going to happen. What should she do with the talking stick now? Return it to Zelda? No, after that lady had been so kind to her, the last thing she was going to do was show up to announce that she had failed.

Zelda's original suggestion had been that she become a collect-ibles trader. If it was an authentic Navajo-Apache artifact, it might be worth a lot of money. Was it possible that Zelda, who was so intuitive, and who knew that Hunter was passionate about such things, have given it to her as a safety net, something she could sell if desperate?

She stroked it as Zelda had. Up close, she could see traces of white paint that had once been words, or symbols, but which were now indecipherable. It was smooth, from decades—centuries, if Zelda were right—of the evolving materials used to preserve wood. She couldn't tell, though, exactly what the finish was, so she didn't want to spray Pledge, not even her Pledge Multi-Surface Furniture Polish Spray, on it without further research.

She hadn't examined it closely inside the trailer. Now she saw how exquisitely detailed it was, not from fancy-schmancy woodworking or the materials themselves, but from the work of so many hands. And while much of the painting was white, there were dots of gold, pink, and scarlet, the same colors as the cloth that Zelda had knitted. The little fork at the end held plastic beads that could have come from a kid's toy, but they seemed to fit with the white, black-tipped feathers.

She couldn't sell it, and she couldn't bring it back to Zelda, so goddam it, she was going to use it as a talking stick. Hunter Fitzgerald was not a quitter.

———

She trespassed on her neighbor's yard, then used a telephoto lens to get a good photo of her house. It made Chardonnay Heights look castle-like, with its gable on the south side. Above and beneath the photo, she typed the salient information: her address (she had qualms about that, but some risk-taking was crucial now), the meet-ing time of the group, and the title: GET HEALTHY WITH HUNTER! For the rest of the text, she brazenly lifted inspiring phrases from the websites of diet and exercise programs.

She omitted any reference to money, or to the duration of the workshop, but at the last minute she remembered to add *First Meeting Free*.

She printed the flyers on photo paper. The colors were crisp and vibrant and she was reinvigorated. She put the flyers in a padded mailer envelope and launched the Prius.

———

Moving north on 101, the spine of the county, through intermittent showers, Hunter stopped first at Mill Valley Town Square, and then at Strawberry Village.

But she had no luck with posting her flyers. One by one the restaurants, the shops, the art galleries, and even the bookstores, turned her down. Employees and managers alike responded with indifference, irritation, and sometimes hostility.

Apparently, community events were acceptable for bulletin boards and windows ("That's to support a high school production of *Rent*." "That psychic reader is raising money for an urban garden.") but for-profit enterprises such as Get Healthy! were radioactive.

She left Strawberry Village feeling discouraged. But she'd reached the twenty-fifth mile of the marathon. Larkspur Dock—that was the place! It was the most upscale and stylish shopping area in Marin. *They* would see the value of her enterprise.

———

By the time she arrived at Larkspur Dock, she was tired, wet, and contemplating how much better the world would be with stricter gun control laws.

Then, just as she cut her engine, thick clouds exploded, pounding her Prius with the wrath of God.

This was nothing like the sporadic rain of her expedition up until now. It was odd, too, in that there had been no rain predicted, at least not according to her weather app, and so she'd taken little notice. The wind picked up, too; through her windshield, she saw trees waving their limbs like hula dancers.

She'd only brought a light jacket, but she wiggled into it, difficult as it was in the confined space of her Prius, then tucked her envelope underneath. When she ventured out, her blouse fluttered at the placket and her hair blew in front of her eyes.

She protected her flyers with the ferocity of a mother bear.

The mall had a neo-frontier look: one-story buildings, with gray wooden siding, and storm windows. The landscaping was too elegant for any real frontier, and each store, restaurant, and personal service had a one-word name: Hush for the pillow store, Cones for the dairy-free frozen yogurt shop, Train for the gym. (*That* franchise was thriving, but they weren't hiring.)

At Bites, the dog biscuit bakery, a young man in a black turtleneck responded to her request with, "We don't care to validate personal ambition."

At Bulbs, the tulip-only florist: "Our client-base is too sophisticated for this."

And, "This is just real estate porn," a twenty-something salesgirl in Lay, the linen store, dismissed her, indicating the picture of Chardonnay Heights.

It was that last rejection that drove Hunter to shelter under the eaves, waiting for the rain to subside. She held the padded envelope against her chest. Real estate porn? How insulting was that? Perhaps—just perhaps—it was worth going home and reformatting the flyer. Make the colors of the house a little less bright. Make the text larger. She undid the flap and cautiously pulled the flyers out. She'd been smart to use photo paper: it was slick and the water that fell on them now beaded up. She tugged them out a little farther.

They looked professional! The salesgirl was wrong. Gen Z. Hunter felt like returning to tell her that the shop should be called "Lie."

There was a final option: return to Mill Valley and put them on lampposts. That was illegal, but to her knowledge, no one was wearing an orange jumpsuit because they'd advertised themselves as an "Experienced Algebra Tutor."

But, photo paper or no, this kind of rain would destroy the flyers quickly. Even worse, for her, was the sheer tackiness of it. Two months before, at Energy-4-All, there were thirty people reporting to her, if you counted desk staff. Now she was getting insulted by a girl young enough . . . well, never mind that.

Wait—there, across the plaza, was Sheets, the stationery store. She hadn't tried them yet. Maybe this was a test, to see if she would go the last fraction of a mile, or whatever was left of this personal marathon.

And the rain stopped, just that suddenly. So she was still holding the flyers, fanned out like a bad poker hand, when she started her dash across the plaza.

. . . And a forceful, unexpected gust of wind blew the flyers from her fingers. She watched them take to the air and fly away with surprising speed, like paper F25s.

Another gust sent a chill through her. This one carried off the last of her energy and determination.

So much for a "test." She vowed that she'd never again ascribe meaning to anything in this godless universe. She was going home. Hunter Fitzgerald, a quitter.

Chapter 5

You Never Forget Your First

PENELOPE

Penelope Winthrop was very afraid of death.

And Scott would remarry within a month, the lousy bastard.

But all she knew at that moment was that she couldn't go on like this: the pain in her chest was unbearable. When she tried to inhale, the stinging in her lungs would have made her cry out, if only she could draw enough breath.

The room was nearly dark. The only light was from the monitors surrounding her; they produced a faint, insectile buzzing.

"You're just fine, Mrs. Winthrop." The doctor's voice came from everywhere and nowhere at once.

Hand on her shoulder. White coat through her slitted eyes. Then the sound of footsteps receding.

———

A few hours before, the pain had awakened her. It felt as though her heart was being squeezed by a fist.

She'd managed to get out of bed and stagger into Scott's room. There she collapsed across his legs.

"Take me . . . to the . . . hospital," she rasped.

———

It was their second visit that week, their fourth in the past month.

They'd put something into the IV that made her drowsy. If it hadn't been for the pain she would have slept; as it was, she was in an underwater gloaming where she couldn't speak or think clearly.

"Wake up, Penelope, dear," Scott said, patting her hair. She smiled at his touch, though her eyes had closed. She imagined the nurses smiling, too, watching such a tender moment between this long-married couple.

Then Scott's breath was hot in her ear. "There's no frigging heart attack," he said.

Penelope turned her head to the nurse, who was fiddling with the IV tube. "Can I have my handbag?" she asked hoarsely.

"No, no. What do you need? I'll get it for you."

But Penelope could hardly tell her what she needed: a Valium.

It was in this drugged but terrified state that Penelope remembered how it started, fifteen years before.

———

It wasn't as if she'd never heard of Valium. The first time she heard about it in regard to herself, though, was the day that Scott took her to Dr. Schmulewitz, in Greenbrae. Or was it Kentfield?

That Scott was there with her made her realize how serious it was. Scott was never in Marin County during daylight hours, or very often in the evening, either. He rose at 5:30 a.m., went jogging, and headed to the city by 6:30: "The only way to beat the goddam traffic." She might see him before she went to sleep; she might not.

On weekends he followed an identical morning schedule, though he did spend the afternoons in Marin, at the club, where he golfed, but did not drink.

Dr. Schmulewitz was bald all the way back to his collar, where an inch of pure white hair surrounded the bottom of his scalp, like an ermine stole. He had no discernible neck: his white coat reached nearly to his dangling earlobes.

"I'm concerned about her, Fred." Scott put his fingertips on the edge of the desk. Scott had beautiful hands with long fingers and perfectly groomed nails. He never spoke of manicures, so Penelope imagined that he had a secret place he went to, where he paid only cash and used a fake name. A *nom de manicure*.

"It's been a very tough couple of months," Scott continued. "She was sure she had cancer." He described the series of tests: the X-rays, the MRI, the ultrasound, the scopes through every orifice. And would you believe it, doctor, but the blood tests were the hardest of all, since Penelope usually fainted when stabbed with a needle? Sometimes just at the sight of a needle? But no, he took it back—just don't get him started on the MRI. Penelope was claustrophobic.

Penelope tugged on the hem of her skirt. She was in no way reassured that she didn't have cancer, especially not ovarian or pancreatic. There was a reason they were called "the silent killers."

"I just want her to stop worrying so much."

Penelope looked up, startled. Scott's voice had shifted abruptly from frustration to concern. He turned sharply, so that his back was to them, but she could see that he covered his eyes with his hands for several moments. "Can't you help her?" His voice cracked.

She had never heard his voice break, let alone seen signs of tears, not when his mother died, not when he missed that hole in one by three inches.

She thought she might cry herself. She'd been so unfair to him. Suspecting him of affairs . . .

"You betcha." Dr. Schmulewitz had an old man's ragged voice. "All these fancy-schmancy new medications," he said dismissively. "Prozac-schmozac. Lexapro-schmexapro. Buspirone-schmusmirone! I'll tell you what's worked for my patients for years: Valium." He leaned over his desk, where there were several stacks of papers cantilevering over each other.

"But stay away from the generic. Generic-schmeric. I have to write a special prescription to satisfy those damn insurance companies."

He scribbled on a prescription pad as he spoke; then he handed it to Scott. "Nancy!" he shouted.

The nurse-receptionist came in. She was a young woman, with a large cross tattooed on her chest where a three-dimensional one might have rested. "It's actually Brittany," she said to Penelope and Scott. She added, with a mix of rue and amusement, "He likes to call me Nancy—that was my predecessor's name."

"I remember Nancy," Scott said.

"She was a nice girl." Dr. Schmulewitz sighed. "But she retired."

When they left Dr. Schmulewitz's office, Scott drove straight to the pharmacy. Penelope protested, "I'm perfectly capable of filling my own prescription." But she rubbed his thigh to demonstrate her appreciation.

"Let me do this for you."

Didn't he have to go back to the office?

This was more important, he said.

She hadn't felt so cared for in a long time.

He pulled into the mall. It was a giant mall, close to their freeway exit. All the malls of Marin were close to Highway 101. Once upon a time people settled near lakes and rivers; now they occupied the land next to the freeway.

"You stay here," Scott said.

It seemed like a long wait. The car was hot, and Scott had left the child lock on: a bad habit of his, since they had no children. She thought he did this with her safety in mind, so she couldn't be irritated, but she might have a hot flash if she had to wait much longer, and without her reading glasses, she couldn't be sure which button to press.

"Here."

Scott held out his palm. There was a light turquoise pill there, very small. For all she knew it could be cyanide, but she swallowed it before he could even hand her the bottled water he'd brought. Then she chugged the water down anyway. "What took you so long?"

He looked hurt. "I pushed my way to the head of the line. It's only been ten minutes." He smiled sheepishly. "Or so. I wanted to grab you some ginger ale, because I know it's your favorite, but there wasn't any that was cold."

It was only after they passed the Marina that she began to feel it: the sensation of something lifting inside her, the way bread rises. Or even . . . Penelope was terrified of flying, but this was like the moment that the landing gear parts the runway, and you know that you're going to reach the sky after all.

And when she thought ahead, to the rest of the afternoon and the evening that lay before her, it wasn't with the usual dread. Rather, all the quotidian tasks (watering the plants, removing her makeup, bathing, brushing her teeth) that usually oppressed her, seemed so easy, so doable, so pleasant . . .

And then a blessed peace settled over her. A peace she hadn't known since she was a child in church, knowing they'd go to her grandmother's house for Sunday dinner afterward and have roast beef . . .

She wasn't high. She was just *okay*.

When they pulled up to their front door, Scott kept the engine idling. "Are you all right to make it inside? I can see that the pill has had, let's just say, the desired effect."

"You aren't—" She stopped before finishing, *coming in?*

"I have to get back to the office."

"But—" She stopped again. It had to be 4:30 by now.

"I'll call to check on my little wifey."

When she got out of the car, she swayed on her heels.

"You're not going to fall on me, are you?" Scott laughed.

She wasn't completely confident that she wouldn't, but she didn't want to trouble him further. Then she almost did fall, but she grabbed the loop of the lion's head door knocker in time.

She was searching for her house keys when she heard the car go into reverse. Scott called through the half-open window, "I knew Dr. Schmulewitz wouldn't let us down."

————

The appointment with Dr. Schmulewitz was many Valium ago. Here she was in the emergency room, fifteen years later, as worried as ever.

Even without "a frigging heart attack," they spent another hour at the hospital before the doctor said she should go home.

The nurse said that Penelope had to be wheeled to the car. Scott insisted on pushing the wheelchair; the nurse insisted that *she* should; and the two of them flirted until the nurse—a young Asian woman—demurely relented.

Scott had that effect on women, even at seventy-four. A year older than Penelope. It was one of life's great injustices that men aged so much more attractively than women, or at least some did, and Scott was one. He was tall, trim, and had a full head of hair, graying, but still with a few streaks of black. His skin was leathery from years of playing golf and tennis, but a man could pull it off. Penelope had similar coloring and height, but somewhere along the way she'd lost an inch. Or two.

When they got to the loading zone in front of the hospital, Scott turned control of the wheelchair back to the nurse while he went to get the car.

"He's charming," the nurse said. "You're lucky. They don't make men like that anymore."

The sedative they'd given Penelope when they'd first come into the ER was wearing off (and all right, she'd needed one; maybe she had shouted a few obscenities about how no one cared about her suffering), which was unfortunate, since now that the pain was gone she could have enjoyed the sedative.

When Scott returned, he first put both her arms around his neck, and then, after sliding his own arms under her knees and back, lifted her bodily from the wheelchair. The nurse drew a sharp intake of breath.

"How is that, dear?" Scott asked more than once as he gently set her down in the passenger seat and drew the seat belt across her chest.

Penelope's last sight of the hospital was in the vanity mirror: the young nurse waving as if they were departing on an ocean liner.

A moment later, Scott slammed on the brakes at a red light. Penelope fell sharply forward; the seat belt locked. "This is the last time I'm doing this," he barked. "You expect me to go to work now?"

They'd gone to the hospital sometime in the so-called wee hours. She didn't know what time it was now, only that it was early morning: the eastern sky was still pink, and the rising sun was setting the windows of the houses on the hills aglow.

"Do—do you have to go to work?" she asked, though God knew she didn't want him to stay home.

"Yes."

Silence between them.

"I. Have. Tried. So. Hard. To. Help. You."

He slapped one hand against the steering wheel after each word. Then he turned on Bloomberg News.

". . . the euro is at a six-week low against the dollar . . ."

Through the window, Penelope watched the storefronts of San Rafael pass. The sidewalks were empty.

". . .says he's unsure what the Fed will do when they meet next week. . ."

Then something about an IPO and Spotify.

Click.

"I cannot keep this up." Scott spoke as if talking to himself, but the next remark was aimed at her. "I'm going to hire you a nurse."

"I don't want a nurse," Penelope whimpered. "Just get me home so I can go to sleep."

"Sleep. Aaaaah." He stage-yawned. "Wonder what that's like."

Penelope did feel guilty about keeping Scott up much of the night.

But what could she have done? Her father had had a heart attack when he was sixty-eight. He survived, but eventually died of cancer. She had a cousin who had died in her fifties. Under mysterious circumstances, but that wasn't the point. It was just a matter of time before it happened to her. She had sixteen bottles of cologne in her bathroom; most of it would outlive her.

Penelope leaned her cheek against the window, seeking the coolness of the glass, but there wasn't any. It was sticky and warm.

She'd had other health worries over the years, such as the moles that looked exactly like pictures of malignant tumors. Then there had been the lung cancer scares: She'd been a smoker as a young woman, for many years, too. Everyone smoked back then. She kept it up even after the club made it verboten to smoke on the grounds, and when she hid behind the pool cabana one of the attendants inevitably ratted her out.

Then Quinn Loveland got lung cancer and died and Penelope finally quit.

There was a dot of bird doo on the otherwise clean windshield. Penelope found a crumpled Kleenex in her purse, rolled down her window, and reached around to see if she could wipe it off.

"For God's sake, you're going to fall out of the car!"

She released the Kleenex into the air and watched it, again in the vanity mirror, as it sailed away.

"This is it," Scott said. "I can't leave you alone."

Chapter 6

Retail Therapy

PENELOPE

A few days later, Penelope woke early because of back pain. She'd had back pain off and on for twenty years now. It meant that she'd had to give up tennis, which broke her heart—she was such a good player! Twenty years and she had yet to find a chiropractor who could help.

She was plumping pillows, trying to give herself some support, when Scott came in. He kept some of his wardrobe in her room, since that was where the walk-in closet was.

"I see you're ready for the day." He was tying his tie, but the full-length mirror on the inside closet door gave him a view of the room behind him: the half-empty glasses of cloudy water, the wadded-up Kleenexes, the paperbacks split open and laid upside down, along with a few *US* magazines that she hid from view when she had the energy, and the Kindle Fire he'd bought her but that she'd never figured out how to use. Most of all: the myriad dark orange bottles of pills on her nightstand.

She wanted a clever comeback, but they deserted her at such times. She unwadded the Kleenex in her lap and pressed it to her nose.

Scott snapped his suspenders into place. Today's were a red-and-black argyle. The brightly patterned suspenders, along with his fedora, were two of the affectations that made him recognizable in court where, from his success at representing white-collar defendants, he'd earned the nickname "Scott-free." Then he turned from the mirror. "Now, darling, don't sulk. I have a surprise for you."

This time she had her riposte. "Moving to Bora Bora with your latest girlfriend?"

She rarely mentioned the girlfriends, but they were no secret. Not anymore. The unspoken understanding between Penelope and Scott was that the girlfriends pass through his (and therefore her) life very quickly. As long as they could be bought off with a diamond bracelet, instead of a diamond ring, there was little to fear.

"I told you I was going to hire . . ." He sang Cole Porter in his melodious baritone, changing one crucial pronoun: "Someone to watch over you . . ." He leaned out the bedroom door. "C'mon in, sweetheart."

A short, buxom Asian woman in a white uniform stepped in.

"I was going to wrap it in Christmas paper and put a pink bow around it but, darn, we're all out of Christmas paper, and I thought a pink bow would be overkill."

Penelope drew the covers up higher.

"This is Reyna," Scott said.

"Hey!" Reyna greeted her with a huge smile. She had a mouthful of large, magnolia-white teeth.

Scott put his hand on the woman's—what was her name again?—shoulder and gave her a gentle shove forward. "I do wish I could get up in the middle of the night whenever you had a hankering to get hooked up to an IV." Scott coughed into his fist. "But someone has to keep all this in motion." Now he used his fist to make a circle in the air above him. "So unless you want to study for the bar exam this summer, I guess it has to be me.

"Reyna is an LVN. If it weren't for the white male patriarchy, she'd be a registered nurse."

Reyna refreshed her smile. "I don't know if we can blame the patriarchy for this one. I'd like to be an RN, but you know, money, at least for now."

Scott looked down at Reyna, who was a good foot shorter than he. "As for Penelope here," he said, "I don't think she could turn on a light switch if the directions weren't written in English. You know I'm kidding, dear. It's good that you're not sensitive."

Penelope was unabashedly studying Reyna. She had brown eyes with those little folds, but Penelope was no longer sure that she was Oriental. "Where are you from?" she asked.

"Stockton. Bright lights, big city!" Reyna laughed. Her laugh was full, and throaty, and—and generous, Penelope thought. She had to be generous, to laugh about Stockton. The name was synonymous with gang- and drug-related crime.

"And it gets better!" Scott mimicked the narrator of an infomercial about a new blender that mopped the floors when you turned it upside down. "She's moving in with us next week."

"But where—"

"I'm giving up the home gym." Scott clamped his hand over his heart in a gesture simulating piety. "This is how much I love my wifey-pifey. I have movers coming for the treadmill and the Stairmaster." He looked at Reyna with unmasked fondness—or was it, just possibly, respect? "Reyna says she doesn't mind if I leave the stationary bike there."

"No worries!" Reyna said.

"Also, I took your driver's license out of your wallet," Scott said. "That's another reason Reyna is here."

"But—"

"But nothing. Your fender-bender average is increasing to where the probability of a fatal accident is approaching—*has* approached an unacceptable level." Scott capped his head with his fedora, pinched the brim, and tugged it an inch lower. "I'll leave you two alone now."

But with whom was he leaving her, really? A nurse? A maid? A caregiver?

A babysitter?

———

Now Penelope and Reyna were on their way to Larkspur Dock, the open-air mall. There was a spa there, where Penelope could get a decent massage.

Penelope let Reyna drive. She was wary about that, because Orientals were supposed to be bad drivers, but she didn't have much choice, not without a driver's license. Meanwhile, Scott had told her that she was a bigot and that she should say "Asian American," not "Oriental." And by the way, if it came up, and Penelope didn't want to sound like a moron, Reyna's ancestry was Filipino.

Penelope didn't know how to do anything fancy on the internet, like finding out what the safest traffic routes were. She'd only learned recently that such a thing was possible. But she knew that, although it went against reason, the freeway was safer than surface streets, so she instructed Reyna to take 101. Penelope measured distance in freeway exits, and from their San Rafael home to Larkspur Dock was only three.

She watched Reyna closely as she drove, and for the most part she was careful. Of course, Penelope didn't want to be too bossy or to seem like a fussy old lady, so she concentrated on staring straight out of the windshield, and only sneaking glances when she thought Reyna wouldn't see her. Two hands on the wheel? Yes. Eyes on the road? Hmm—not 100 percent. Riding the brake? Penelope couldn't see down there. She needed to get to the eye doctor to check about a new prescription for her glasses.

But then it started raining.

Reyna set the wipers to medium. Penelope gripped her seat belt, but let go when she realized that might cause it to malfunction. She held out her hands as if blessing the dashboard, and noticed the brown spots. They'd been there for a while, but could they turn cancerous?

"Do you want me to turn around?" Reyna asked.

Penelope considered it. They were only one exit away and Tanya would charge her if she canceled at the last minute. Penelope didn't care about that part, but she did care that Tanya would be annoyed, and maybe not fit her in next time Penelope tried to make an appointment.

These thoughts prompted Penelope to reach discreetly into her purse for a Valium. They were small enough that she could swallow them without water, and she didn't want Reyna to take note. "No, let's keep going."

Reyna made the necessary lane changes smoothly. The Larkspur Dock exit was the same as the one that led, if one headed west, to San Quentin, the state prison, where they still executed people. Or did they? Penelope couldn't recall whether the death penalty was on or off these days, but she felt uneasy at the proximity of such dangerous men. Women, too. They'd gassed poor Barbara Graham there.

But Reyna took them down the off-ramp as smoothly if it were a playground slide and turned the Mercedes back under the freeway, away from crime and punishment. "I saw online that they have valet parking here. Let's do that, what do you say?"

Penelope was grateful that Reyna had suggested it, so that she didn't have to. She worried about catching cold in the rain.

The valet parking spared them the endless, dizzying search for a parking space, but when they got out of the car, a chilly wind stung

Penelope's neck. She should have wrapped a wool scarf around it, not just the satin Hermès.

"You should have taken a warmer scarf," Reyna said. She lay her hands upon the lapels of Penelope's suit jacket, pulling them closer together, giving her chest a little added protection.

They took a few steps in the direction of Rub, the spa. It seemed very far away.

"Valet parking isn't much good if it can't get you any closer than this," Reyna said, and Penelope started. Reyna was like that character on *M*A*S*H* who always knew what people were thinking.

"Give me your arm." Reyna extended her elbow, but Penelope hesitated. Hanging on to a nurse's arm? She wasn't ready for that. Maybe if Reyna were in street clothes instead of the white uniform . . . they couldn't look like relatives, obviously, but maybe like friends? Penelope was not a racist. She didn't mind if people thought she had a Filipina friend.

"I'm okay for now," Penelope said.

Inside Rub, the atmosphere was calming: soft Celtic music played, something that sounded like whale songs, which harmonized with the prints of dolphins and baby seals on pale blue walls.

Calm wasn't meant to last long. "Hello, Mrs. Winthrop," the receptionist acknowledged her, but without taking her eyes off the slender computer monitor in front of her. She was wearing a formfitting sheath dress in an aqua that matched the Valium in Penelope's purse. "I'm sorry, we tried to get ahold of you, but Tanya had to leave for a family emergency."

Penelope was not the kind of person to lose her temper, but at this news her lower back burst into flames that traveled to her shoulders. "Why didn't you call me?" she demanded.

"We tried to get ahold of you," the receptionist repeated serenely. She still didn't look in Penelope's direction. She leaned a little closer to the monitor, and recited a number. "Isn't that right?"

She'd read the number of Penelope's new cell phone. "That's my backup phone number! You should have called my landline!"

"Oh, you mean . . ." The receptionist recited another number, then shrugged. "I guess someone reversed them. You know, most people use their cell phones these days."

"Ma'am." Reyna addressed the receptionist, who started, before looking up at them, finally. She looked barely old enough to drink: Perhaps it was the first time that someone had called her "Ma'am." Well, she'd better get used to it. "It would have been more professional if you'd called *both* numbers, don't you agree?"

Penelope had been near tears when she heard about Tanya's abandonment, but she felt better already, with Reyna at her side.

"Tanya's mother . . ." The receptionist began indignantly, but faltered.

"I understand you assess a cancellation fee within twenty-four hours," Reyna went on. "How do you compensate the victims?"

"Victims?" the receptionist echoed.

"My client and I made a long trip in inclement weather." Reyna squeezed Penelope's arm. "We deserve twenty-four hours' notice as well."

"That's not our policy." The receptionist reglued her eyes to the monitor.

"I'd hate to see my client and myself posting one-star reviews on Yelp."

Penelope appreciated being referred to as a "client," rather than a "patient."

"We have a four-point-eight Yelp rating!" The receptionist's formerly melodious voice had a sudden, defensive squeak.

"A discount on our next appointment might cause us to reconsider."

The receptionist tapped a few keys. Penelope imagined two gunslingers facing each other on the dirt road of an Old Western Town, gripping the handles of their six-shooters.

"Would tomorrow at 2 p.m. be convenient." A question without inflection.

Reyna turned to Penelope. "What do you think, Mrs. Winthrop?"

"Huh? Tomorrow at 2:00 . . ." She had nothing planned. "Sure, I mean . . . sure."

"We'll be back," Reyna said as they exited. "And please make sure you have the landline phone number listed first."

––––

Outside, the rain had stopped, but the wind was stronger than before.

"I hate to think of coming all the way back here tomorrow," Penelope said.

"Then we won't. And if we do, these guys are giving you at least a 20 percent discount. Make that 50 percent," she added, after forming her lips into a thoughtful pucker.

Thwap.

Someone slapped Penelope—so hard that she was blinded.

"OMG!" Reyna cried. "Where did that come from?" She pulled off the sheet of paper that had stuck to Penelope's face. "Are you all right?"

Penelope was still shaking. It *was* a sheet of paper—had someone thrown it at her? She had felt its sharp edge scratch one cheek. "It's so windy. Let's go home."

But Reyna didn't move. She was staring at the printed side of the page.

Penelope tugged on Reyna's white sleeve, yes, like a little girl. She was cold and wanted to be back in the house. Scott hadn't said when movers were coming for the gym equipment, or anything about a bed. Would it be a queen, or a king, or maybe only a twin? She had to ask him, and to check the linen closet for what they had that was freshly washed.

"Look, Mrs. Winthrop."

"Call me Penelope."

"Look, Penelope." Reyna tapped the paper. Her fingernails were unvarnished, but smooth and clean.

"Can't we get the car?"

"Yes, but—" Reyna thrust the paper under Penelope's nose. When Penelope finally got her readers on, she saw the line that Reyna was pointing to: IMPROVING NUTRITION CAN RESOLVE MANY HEALTH PROBLEMS.

"Doesn't this sound like something you could—something that would . . . would be fun?"

It did, though she wasn't sure she wanted to commit. It meant yet another trip outside the house, and each of these forays was burdensome, as she refused to lower the bar: going out meant panty-hose, and always would.

Reyna had Penelope's elbow, and was guiding them back to the valet station. "I'll take you," she volunteered cheerfully, with one of her toothy smiles. "And I'll come pick you up."

And Penelope remembered going down the list of titles: nurse, caregiver, maid . . .

How about "friend"?

Chapter 7

The Most Awful Time of the Year

DANNIKA

This was the worst day of the year for Dannika, and always would be. So she hardly needed more bad news.

But there it was, in the email:

```
Dear Ms. Arenescu:
We regret to inform you that we
cannot offer you a place in the
fall class of 20 . . .
```

Dannika wanted to delete it immediately, but she was keeping a list of the schools she applied to and their responses (ten applied; eight no's). She couldn't face adding this one to the list, so she simply moved it to "old mail."

Who would have expected that the next email would be worse?

```
Hi Dannika,
In case you forgot today is the third
anniversary of your mother's death.
```

As if she could forget!

> She was one of the bravest, kindest
> people I ever knew, not to mention a
> great artist.

Dannika's mother had been a jewelry maker.

> I hope you've moved on. I've kept my
> part of the bargain and kept my secret.

What was Bronwyn talking about anyway?

> Anyway, just wanted you to know that
> I'm thinking of you this day. I'm
> about to leave on another one of my
> world travels. Now that I've vis-
> ited every continent (well, except
> Antarctica!) I want to visit every
> state in this "great" nation of ours,
> lol. So by the time you read this
> I'll probably be gone. Jethro and
> I are taking the RV on the road now
> that she's had to retire from quilt-
> making due to her arthritis. ☹☹

If Jethro's hands were too crippled to sew, Dannika hoped that Bronwyn was committed to doing all the driving.

> Bronwyn Laramie Layton, MFT, PA, HAL
> PS I'll be traveling and so can't be
> reached after today.

```
PPS "ps's" aren't necessary in the
world of computers, but I'm old and
can't break the habit. LOL!
PPPS It's thanks to your mom that
I'm doing volunteer work with
hospice now.
Treat everyone you meet as if they
are God in drag. —Ram Dass
```

Bronwyn was a stout, cannabis-loving woman with the hint of a moustache. She was one of Dannika's mother's closest friends, a member of the Craftswomen's Circle, and she'd been with Mosi (Dannika's pet name for her mother, in the tradition of the March girls' "Marmee") much of the time during her final weeks.

One afternoon, not long after Mosi's death, Dannika, exhausted from three nights of punishing insomnia, had crawled under the duvet in her mother's room, which still smelled like her mom, a mix of sage incense and fresh bread. It was the scent of her mother's bath-robed arms around her, and it lulled Dannika to sleep.

An hour into this much-needed nap, Bronwyn shook her awake, crying, "What are you doing?"

Bronwyn, for all her claims of "centeredness," was a big, fat drama queen.

((pop))

A new email came in. The extension read ".edu." That was all Dannika needed to see. Her stomach did a few flips, and she almost slammed the laptop closed, but her finger twitched on its own.

```
We regret that we cannot offer
you a place in the graduating
class of 20 . . .
```

This time she did click *DELETE*.

She had to get the hell outta there.

———

Dannika fled to the Café Ravi.

The Café Ravi was in "downtown" Fairfax: a half-mile strip of funky, family-owned businesses. Walking distance.

The Café Ravi had no Wi-Fi, which was one reason that it was usually deserted, or almost. Today the only other customer was the man with Einstein-like hair who sometimes complained to the owner, in a reasonable manner, that there were microphones in the cinnamon buns.

A little bell dinged as she walked in. Then there was the smell of stale oatmeal raisin cookies, and the yellow walls with the chipped paint, and the single fly that was always there. Dannika imagined it had been granted eternal life. It inspired her private nickname: "Ravi's Fly by Night Café."

But the espresso was drinkable.

She brought her journal. She would write a poem for Mosi in honor of this day.

She was flipping to a blank page when a clatter announced the appearance of a large coffee cup and saucer in front of her, close enough to her journal that a few drops of foam spilled on the paper.

"M'lady."

Dannika looked up.

Fuck.

It was that little barista, or waiter, or whatever he was. Mostly he was the floor-sweeper. His name was Howard. She knew that because the owner, Ravi (who was a weird-looking dude himself, with eyes that bulged out like that friend of her mother's who had that thyroid problem), was so often shouting at him, "Howard, we're out of soy milk!" "Howard, take out the trash!" But most often, "Howard, you need to sweep now!"

"What's this?" she asked.

"It looks a latte like a latte to me." He tried to deliver this dead-pan, but had to stifle a chuckle.

"I was just about to order," she said irritably.

"And what were you going to order?"

He had her there.

"I need sugar." She started to get up.

"Three sugars, right? I put them in already."

She was creeped out and pleased at the same time. "Whole milk?"

"Whole milk, m'lady." He put his hands together in the "namaste" position.

She twisted around to reach for her messenger bag, which she'd hung on the back of her chair.

But he held up his hand. "All taken care of." He motioned in the direction of the cash register.

"Well, thank you." Probably no one had ever traded sex for a latte, even a six-dollar one, but what he did expect was almost worse: conversation.

The legs of the chair opposite her emitted a teeth-clenching grind as he dragged it away from the table. Then, in case that wasn't enough to make her brain explode, he turned it 180 degrees, and sat down facing her, arms resting on its back.

She didn't want to let herself think it, that this was the kind of guy that her mother's friends from the Circle were always trying to fix her up with: short; not fat, but dumpy; thick glasses that made his brown eyes owlish, red high-top sneakers, and tight curls peeking out from under his baseball cap, which he had on backward, as if it would make him look cool. It was only after Mosi died that she felt like she could say no Mosi's friends. Before that, there was the one who drove the Ford Fairlane and the dude who tried to convert her to Mormonism. The Mormon dude came out to his parents the next day.

"I guess you're a *Twilight* fan, huh?"

She got that sometimes, even though *Twilight* was ancient history. She dressed all in black, leather when possible, and she had dyed her dark brown hair ebony, except for a patch in front, where she'd shaved several inches above her right ear. She wasn't going to tell Howard the story behind her look: She'd worn black to her mother's funeral, and for days after. Instead of giving it up, she'd added black boots, and painted her fingernails to match.

"No." She uncapped her silver gel pen as a hint.

"Why black paper?" His fingers walked a few inches closer to her journal.

She pulled it a few inches back. "I like the way it looks—the silver against the black." She hesitated before adding, "It makes me look more talented."

"So black is your thing, right?"

"Right." She contemplated the latte. Sipping it now would increase her level of commitment. Should she just get up and leave? Mosi never wanted her to be rude.

"Hey!"

She started. Howard was looking past her.

"You wanna go hear the Pink Elephants?"

She followed his gaze; he was staring at the community corkboard. Every local café had one, but Café Ravi's hosted announcements by the bottom of the desperation barrel: readings by unknown local authors and performances by unknown local bands.

"I've heard them. They suck." They probably did.

"Too bad." He tugged on the bill of his cap. "Do you like the movies?"

"No," she lied. Who didn't like the movies? But even this didn't drive him away. Where was Ravi, all bulgy-eyed and short-tempered, to demand he get back to work? For once she wished the other habitué would come in: the guy in the baggy trench coat who would shout about how income tax was unconstitutional. Then it would be Howard's job to get him out, usually after the bribe of one of those godawful cookies. She put her thumb against the edge of her notebook and snapped the pages.

"So are you just a lady of leisure? I mean, I see you in here in the middle of the day. Do you have a real job?"

"No." She had nine cats, the care of which was a sacred trust, inherited from her mother, and she read a lot, but most of her time, these days, was occupied preparing a new round of college applications.

"So, what do you do?"

"I'm *trying* to write." She held up the pen like the Olympic torch.

"So, what are you writing about? It isn't about a handsome young waiter, is it?"

That did it. "I'm writing about my mother. She just died."

Three years wasn't "just," but it felt like that to her.

"Can I see?"

She would have liked to show her poetry to the right person. But everything touching her mother was private, almost holy. And she also sometimes wrote poetry about Rafe, Last Name Unknown, a drummer with his own band (*not* the Pink Elephants, or any of the other wannabes who had to advertise on the community corkboard), whom she'd met at his day job as a checker at Safeway.

"No, you can't see." She closed the notebook. Tapped the pen against the table.

"How'd she die?"

The nerve of this socially challenged dweeb! He didn't deserve to talk about her mother . . .

But *Dannika* wanted to talk about her. She wanted to talk about her badly. And there was no one else. Except for Bronwyn, soon to be ensconced in an RV somewhere in the desert, where T-Mobile had no coverage, the women of the Craftswomen's Circle had moved on.

"Breast cancer."

"So . . . are you worried about inheriting it?"

That was the furthest thing from her mind. If she hadn't been so irritated, she would have felt sorry for him, the way, in the end, she'd felt sorry for the dude with the Ford Fairlane. She knew what it was like to spend Saturday nights binge-watching comedy specials on Netflix. Her high school friends had gone on to college, graduated, found jobs. Some were in graduate school. A few had married. No one lived nearby.

"It's not that," she said. Her chest was tight. "I didn't go to college because she got sick. Then before she died, I promised I'd go back. But I haven't."

The fly-in-residence lurched across the table. Howard batted at it.

"So, where were you going to school?"

"I was accepted at UCLA." She raised her chin.

"UCLA. Wow. That's a tough school to get into." He used his heels to drag the chair closer, which meant another screech from the floor. "Wow. I graduated from SF State. And I have the student loans to prove it."

He thought that was clever, but when she didn't respond, he kept talking, about some kind of boring BS, until his voice merged with the buzzing of the fly. She looked down at the latte, where all traces of foam had dissolved.

And thought about Mosi. She could have told Howard much more: That the cancer, when discovered, was Stage Four. The doctor said she'd only live a few months. But then, after the double mastectomy, she was pronounced cured, and she told Dannika, "Go! It's an hour's flight away!" It wasn't too late; Mosi had been diagnosed before Dannika's high school graduation and UCLA was on the quarter system and classes didn't start until late September.

But by August the cancer was back.

After that it was a waltz: *one*, two, three, *one*, two, three: chemo/radiation, remission, recurrence. *One*, two, three.

There were good, hopeful periods at first, but each remission was shorter than the one before and then there were the final, agonizing months, the flame of hope burning on dwindling fuel.

During the entirety of Mosi's illness, Dannika had reassured Mosi that she would return to school. They finished that sentence, "when she was well," until hospice came in.

Howard must have sensed that she wasn't paying attention to his story about Professor Who Gave a Shit, because he changed the subject back to her. "Wow. Three years. What have you been doing since then?"

The dude was obsessed with her schedule! "I keep busy." But then she blurted out, "I *am* going to go back to school."

"Cool. School is cool."

He grinned as if he were T. S. fucking Eliot.

But failure burns.

And it begs to be shared.

"See, like I said, I promised my mom I'd go back to school, and I finally started applying, but I keep getting rejected everywhere. And I feel like the whole county knows."

"So, maybe someone will put up billboards that say you've been rejected. Like that movie!"

"What movie?"

"The movie about the mom who puts up billboards to make the cops find out who killed her daughter. It's an old movie."

He started to tell her the story of the movie. She didn't listen, just uncapped and recapped her pen until she heard him ask, "So, why don't you go to Marin City?"

Dannika shook her head. "I promised her I'd go to a four-year college." Then she shook her head again, harder, trying—failing—to keep the memory from coming back.

The day before the end.
The loose hold of Mosi's clammy hand.

> *"It has to be a four-year college."*
> *"Of course, Mosi." Dannika's voice shook.*
> *The day they received the email acceptance to UCLA was a*
> *day of over-the-top joy. They relived it over and over, dancing*
> *around the worktable, Mosi in her fleece jumpsuit with the tuxedo*
> *cat pattern. They were going to frame the acceptance, but they*
> *didn't get around to it, only stuck it on the refrigerator with a Big*
> *Bird magnet. Just as well.*

"But Marin City takes anyone."

Mosi would have said, "He knows how to make a girl feel special, doesn't he?" and they would have laughed together.

"It just seems like you could save time that way," Howard said.

"My grades and scores were good enough to get me into UCLA six years ago." Dannika stuck the tip of the pen in the corner of her mouth. "You know . . . I think my problem is the personal essay." No one could fault her for caring for her mother—she could present that as a plus—but what about the three years since? How to convince a university that brushing her cats, and four weekly visits to the cemetery, made her as good a candidate as when she was a high school senior? "That's my stumbling block."

Howard perked up. "Let me come over and help you with it."

The table started shaking. WTF? She peeked underneath: he'd been bouncing his knees against the bottom. He stopped the moment she looked, but she had looked, and the underside of a table in the Café Ravi was something you could never unsee.

"I don't want to brag, now, but I was an English major, and I'm pretty good—"

"I don't think so, dude." She shook her head and spoke with the pen still in the corner of her mouth.

"C'mon. I'll bring the wine."

"No way, Hervé." That was a Mosi twist on "no way, José."

"Howard!"

Finally! Ravi to the rescue.

"That's my name, don't wear it out." Howard said under his breath. His chair scraped against the floor; she clenched her jaw yet again. "Sure I can't help you?"

"I'm sure."

"At least tell me your name." He tilted his head in the direction of his boss. "I know you know mine."

She would have lied, if she'd been able to think of a fake name quickly enough. "Dannika."

"Dannika . . . ?"

"Dannika." She flipped her journal closed.

"Dannika Dannika?"

Imagine spending a full hour, let alone an entire afternoon, with Howard-the-floor-sweeper. It made her want to give another chance to one of the guys her mom's friends had fixed her up with. Preferably one of the gay ones.

"Well, call me Howie, not Howard."

"Okay." *As if that makes you any less of a wimp.*

Chapter 8

Swept Away

DANNIKA

Dannika was driving to the farmers market when the first drops hit her windshield. She'd checked her weather app before she left, though, and no rain was predicted, so this was just God squeezing the fog.

The drops fell sporadically until she reached 101. Then the skies opened up.

The vendors would throw tarps over their produce and pack up. It pissed her off, but there was really no point in turning around. The farmers market was right below Larkspur Dock, an overpriced, elitist, the-one-percent-posing-as-hippies "outdoor gathering space" that she despised in theory, but which was also home to an independent bookstore, Leaves. The last independent bookstore in Fairfax had closed when she was still in high school. Dannika loved bookstores: It would be worth the trip if she could browse there.

By the time she parked the rain had whipped up into a full-fledged storm. Now it was personal. She pulled the collar of her leather jacket up to her ears as she walked to the bookstore. Still, the wind found its way through the gaps, blasting at her throat, while the raindrops were tiny needles against her face.

Ahh, but the bookstore was close by: inside, it would be warm, and she would be surrounded by the smell of croissants and espresso. Dannika refused to go Kindle: she loved to put her nose up close to the binding of an old paperback, and commune with the tree that gave its life.

Damn it!

From just a few steps away, the bookstore had looked the same as always: popular, newly released novels facing out in the window, and even the announcement for a recent poetry reading. But another sheet of paper, on pink stock, faced out: LEAVES MUST CLOSE. The date was today.

There was a dense block of text below the announcement. The owners were "grateful for the support of their loyal customers," but what followed was rather thinly disguised rage:

WE FIND IT IRONIC THAT A GENERATION THAT ENJOYS TWISTING THEMSELVES INTO POSITIONS THAT NATURE NEVER INTENDED (*they must mean yoga*, Dannika thought) CAN'T BESTIR THEMSELVES TO RISE FROM A SEATED POSITION, AND PREFER TO MAKE THEIR LITERARY CHOICES BASED ON ALGORHYTHMS (Dannika wondered what spellchecker didn't catch that) RATHER THAN ON THE WELL-CONSIDERED ADVICE OF A TRAINED PROFESSIONAL.

Now it was *really* personal.

There was more about "the changing marketplace" and "evolving demographics." Dannika did order from Amazon, but when possible (and it was almost always possible), she only bought used books from them. She reached into her messenger bag for a pen and wrote, "See you in Hell" at the bottom of the poster. The weather had driven away enough shoppers that she thought she was safe, although these days there were so many security cameras around, it was like Winston Smith's Airstrip One.

Since she'd come all this way, she thought of maybe looking in the window at Beads, the craft store. But the wind, almost unbelievably, had kicked up even harder. Dannika was a native of Marin (technically born in New Mexico, but she had no memory of that, since she'd arrived here as an infant) and so had no experience of hurricanes or twisters or any of that *Wizard of Oz* stuff. She supposed, from the footage she'd seen online of cars flying through the air, that winds could get much worse than this, because though she did not feel like she was about to take to the sky, many other things had: sales receipts (who got those anymore?) and candy wrappers—and holy shit, a plastic bag!—were flying like the Wicked Witch's monkeys. You'd think that Marinites would know better than to litter.

She stomped back to her car.

A piece of the flying debris had been trapped under the tip of one of her windshield wipers, where it now clung for its life. She yanked it out, and almost let the wind take it, but she knew how her mother would feel about that, so she went looking for a trash can, and found one shaped as a tiny concrete whale. But its mouth was wide, and twice when she tossed the paper in, it blew back onto her chest.

If you love something, let it go was the corny-as-fuck saying her mother's crowd liked.

It was a poster of some kind. Her first thought was that it had to do with the bookstore. But no, there was a picture of a house on it: creamy stucco with white trim, and a wide wooden door, and a side-steepled roof.

She intended only to glance at the text below, and then to stuff the damn thing all the way down the whale's throat, if necessary, and get out of the wind (the rain had stopped, almost weirdly suddenly, but the sky was an apocalyptic iron dome that was going to let loose again soon)—still she couldn't avoid seeing the heading, which was in a bold, *New York Times*-y font: GET HEALTHY! In smaller font, below: *IN BODY, MIND AND SPIRIT.*

It was the word "spirit" that intrigued her. And then, LOVING, SUPPORTIVE ATMOSPHERE.

There was more text, most of it illegible, but she thought she saw, HEALTHY WOMEN HAVE HEALTHY RELATIONSHIPS.

Rafe. The drummer. She'd seen him at Safeway just a few nights ago, and he'd complimented the new garnet stud on her left ear.

At the bottom, bold-faced: FIRST MEETING FREE.

Bronwyn, Dannika's mother's sculptor friend, was still road-tripping across the Southwest, but Dannika knew what she'd say if she were here, since she never missed an opportunity to tell Dannika that she had to get out of the house more often. And, as Mosi used to say, "Even a stopped clock is right twice a day."

Chapter 9

Summertime, but the Living Ain't Easy

ALICIA

Alicia Lieberman, MD, knew how to clear a room of all available men with a simple statement. "I'm a single mom with a teenage daughter."

Not that she was in a room with available men very often. The dating pool shrinks for all women when they reach thirty-nine, and Alicia didn't consider herself particularly attractive, not with early middle-aged spread, and a flat-bridged nose. She had only a few strands of gray, but she dyed them to match her black hair as soon as they became noticeable, or, if she were too busy to get to the hairdresser, she wore a scarf. She liked scarves anyway.

That wasn't what kept her from dating apps, though, where she'd be able to say that she was a doctor, and post a flattering picture from five years earlier. No, it was that teenage daughter: Summer, fifteen years old (no dad in the picture) whom she needed to protect. What if Summer got attached to a man who abandoned them? Or what if Alicia invited a man into their lives—a smooth-talking, seductive man, who secretly abused Summer? It simply wasn't worth the risk.

As for Summer, she was a good girl, if being "good" meant staying out of trouble. Alicia, as a board-certified OB-GYN, knew the signs of drug abuse: sleeping at odd hours; bloodshot, dilated eyes. Or the marks that resulted from cutting, or—God forbid—needles.

This was how Alicia consoled herself on a typical evening, when Summer passed hours behind her closed bedroom door, with the Top 40 station playing loudly enough to make Alicia's own work or entertainment (did she really not deserve an hour to read a little Doris Kearns Goodwin?) impossible. And since Summer had started high school, the music had gotten even louder.

Then, late one night, Alicia walked into an empty house. Empty and dark.

She was rarely late coming home. "Babies come when they're ready!" was the cheerful adage she used to reassure expectant mothers. But that didn't make it any less inconvenient for Alicia when she couldn't avoid being the obstetrician on call. She'd joined a big practice to minimize the times that would happen.

But it had happened that night. She had texted Summer throughout the evening, but these days Summer didn't respond to texts. (To texts, to voicemails, to emails, or to shouts from outside her door.) Instead, Summer would order from Uber Eats, watch Alicia's TV, and put herself to bed.

For as long as a full two seconds, as Alicia stood in that empty and dark kitchen, she indulged in the fantasy that Summer was acting out. Chilling with new friends! Forgetting to call! Just like she overheard the other moms complain. Then she went from room to room, turning on lights, shouting. Summer would be hiding under the duvet of her own, or the guest room, bed, having descended another rung on the teen moody ladder.

When Alicia came back to the kitchen, she saw that there was a voice message on her machine. It was from the school.

"Your child (pause) *Summer Lieberman* (pause) was marked absent this morning. Please let us know the reason for this absence as soon as possible to avoid . . ."

Alicia didn't listen to the rest. It was a robocall, with the voice switching to allow someone to insert Summer's name.

Why the fuck didn't they call her at work? Why didn't they call her cell?

The reality made Alicia sway on her feet. The first few hours after a person went missing, especially a child (and Summer was more a child than most fifteen-year-olds) were make-or-break. Alicia lowered the receiver as this sank in.

She called the police.

They took the information. She emailed them a picture of Summer.

She pulled a class roster from the drawer below. It was from Summer's K–8 school, but it was the most recent class roster she had: Rosters had ended when one demented troll had harassed another parent. No more sending out names, emails, or phone numbers. Then she worked her way down the eighth-grade class roster, until the third dad yelled at her for waking him up.

Then she called hospitals. No one complained about being awoken, but no one could help her, either.

Her next step was digging through Summer's room. She emptied Summer's drawers, throwing each item singly over her shoulder to make sure she didn't miss anything. Hidden among Summer's socks and underwear, she found *The How to Be Yourself When You Don't Know Who You Are Workbook;* she flipped through, but the "workbook" pages were blank.

She went through the pile of jeans, T-shirts, sweaters and blouses on the floor of Summer's closet that went halfway up to Alicia's knees. Then she looked under the bed, where dust bunnies reproduced like real-life bunnies.

Finally, she stuck her hand between the mattress and the box spring. Her fingers touched metal. She pulled.

It was a spiral notebook. The cover was unmarked, but the first page bore the handwritten title, *Journal*, with the year below. She didn't hesitate before turning to the next page. She wouldn't have, under ordinary circumstances. She respected Summer's privacy. Also, she would have been terrified of what she might find out. She *was* terrified of what she might find out.

The first entry was dated in late March, only a few weeks earlier.

> I don't know why I thought this year would be different. Deadwood High still sucks. There are the kewl kids and the rest of us. Once a lozer, always a lozer. It must be in your DNA. I don't want to leave KC on her own, besides, I need someone to have lunch with. Lozers have to stick together.

There was more of the same for a couple of pages, description that made Alicia squirm. Alicia's own high school years weren't the happiest of her life. Kids called her "nerd" and "four eyes." She'd survived because she already knew that she wanted to be a doctor, like her dad.

She touched her finger to her tongue, the better to flip the pages.

> Now that I'm hanging out at the park, school is a lot more fun! I'm one of the kewl kids now, not a lozer. And I don't know why I was scared of weed! It makes everything better.

Two days later:

> His name is Prophet John. He's had his eye on me since before winter break. He said he had to work up

the nerve to talk to me!! He's so handsome, and he's 19!
I can't believe he'd be interested in me, but he says I'm
smart, and that that's more important than being hot.

Alicia closed the notebook for a moment. When she pulled herself together, she read on about how Prophet John earned that
soubriquet because he was psychic: he regularly predicted earth-
quakes in South America and which local band was going to get
a recording contract. He was from a rich family, but he'd run
away because he hated their values. After school, during lunch
break, *and sometimes during class time*, he held court (Summer called
it "hanging out") at the far end of the park, under a giant oak,
surrounded by admirers. Alicia pictured him with a scanty beard
and red bandana.

The last entry, dated only the day before:

He's made up with his family and he's going home.
(Summer had drawn a simple face with tears falling
from one eye.) I just want to be with him forever.
I can't live without him.

The journal ended there, mid-page.

None of this sounded like Summer. Not at all. That was how
little she knew her own child.

But all she had to do was to get in touch with KC's parents,
and . . .

Who was KC?

Guilt slammed into her so hard, she almost fell backward. Come
Monday, she could get ahold of the school administration, but by
then Summer could be in the cargo hold of a 777, on her way to
Saudi Arabia.

Alicia had no more information than before—what, did she think
that the name "Prophet John" would appear on any roster? But it wasn't

the outdated roster. It wasn't Summer's secretiveness, or sulkiness. It was Alicia herself. If Summer was a loner, well, Summer was a loner. She probably had more friends than Alicia knew about—Alicia *hoped* that she had more friends—some friends, any friends!—but Alicia didn't know any of them. She'd made it to the parent-teacher conference back in September and almost gave herself a freaking medal, simply for doing what every parent did. If she'd been more involved in Summer's life, if she'd volunteered at the school . . . but when the requests came home for field trip drivers and shifts managing the library, she tossed them in the special circular file, *because she was a professional woman with no partner*, so wasn't *she* important! If she'd done some of that, if she'd done *any* of that, she'd know the high school parents, *some* of the high school parents, and she'd know whom to call! She didn't even know which park was "the" park, or where it was!

But she could start again. Summer was only one semester into her high school years. She could switch schools, and they could both have a fresh start, mother and daughter, if only she came back. *Knock on the door, sweetie, I don't care if you lost your key again.*

Alicia had to call her own parents. Her throat closed up at the thought, but they might hear from Summer. Or what if Summer had gotten to them, somehow, but didn't want them to contact Alicia, or invented some story about how Alicia already knew she was there, so there was no need? Summer had left sometime early that day, so she could be in the Boston area by now . . .

Their immediate hysterics were the unavoidable price. It didn't help that, back in Brookline, it was 3:00 a.m. After that, she couldn't really be angry with them, could she, for calling her every five minutes?

Now what? She wanted desperately to talk to someone. There was no one. When Summer was little there were a few other single moms with whom she could share the hardships: lack of a second income. Lack of family to babysit. Lack of companionship. Lack of sex.

But Summer had outgrown the Mommy and Me Playgroup stage. Now Alicia knew many people, from her colleagues and support staff (she tried not to think of them as "subordinates"), and she was part of a wide network in the gynecological and obstetrical fields. But friends? Confidantes? Nary a one.

She paced the house, grabbing at the roots of her hair and tugging until strands came loose. She turned on water for tea and then forgot about it until the smoke alarm went off. She put a head of lettuce in the dishwasher.

She imagined Summer lost in the sketchiest part of San Francisco, too shy to ask for directions . . . but that was good, because if she did ask for directions, and someone offered her a ride. . . . Ariel Castro had lured three young women into a car and held them prisoner for eleven years. What if . . . no, Summer was too smart to get into a car with a stranger. Wasn't she? *Wasn't she?*

Alicia had been raised in a Jewish family that belonged to a synagogue, where she'd become a bat mitzvah, but by the time she got to college she'd left that behind. She was proud of her heritage-as-heritage, but it stopped there.

Not that night. There were no atheists among the parents of missing children. She fell to her knees, clasped her hands, recited the *Shema*, which was the only prayer she remembered, and then defaulted to English, promising God that she would never be disappointed in Summer again for mediocre grades, would never criticize her for taste in clothes—would never criticize her at all! *Just let her come home.*

When the phone rang at 7:30 a.m., Alicia had fallen asleep in front of the television. She woke to see a reporter describing a motorcycle crash in the East Bay. Then she answered.

A sharp-eyed policewoman had noticed a teenage girl traveling alone at the Greyhound bus station near the Las Vegas Airport. They sent a photo to her cell phone. It was Summer, all right:

pasty skin, mouth hanging slightly open to reveal the braces on her upper teeth. Plaid shirt with a dark stain on the front. Alicia had the odd thought that if Summer had succeeded in reaching whatever her final destination had been, how would she have found an orthodontist?

"If she's willing, we can release her to your custody, but it has to be within twenty-four hours."

"Oh, I can be there in—" Alicia's voice was squeaky from giddy relief. She was already looking at Southwest flights on her computer, while she held the phone between her shoulder and ear. Putting the policewoman on speaker would send the wrong message.

"Hold," the policewoman said, and the next thing Alicia heard was a different, even more officious female voice. "Are you Mrs. Lieberman?"

"Doctor Lieberman, yes." Later, Alicia told herself that she added "doctor" to reassure them that they had the right person. "I told your colleague that I'd be there in a matter of hours."

"I'm from social services. I have a few questions for you."

Alicia tensed.

"We need to rule out child trafficking."

"For God's sake—" Alicia stopped, thinking of Summer's diary.

"There are no bruises or marks on your daughter's body, and she looks healthy enough. No narcotics in her possession."

"Just let me come get her," Alicia begged. *I don't need this tsuris!* Her Yiddish vocabulary was an invasive species that sprouted when she was under stress.

"Just let me do my job," the woman said, and Alicia saw that there was no way around this, no matter how many degrees she had. "We also need to rule out sexual abuse."

Just be grateful, Alicia told herself. *Just be grateful.*

———

Alicia had last been to Las Vegas ten years before, for a medical convention. She remembered being startled by the uber-tackiness of the airport, the rotating lights of advertisements for casinos and their shows, including half-naked women.

Before Alicia walked into the police station, she clamped on her hospital ID badge. She wanted them to know that she wasn't some trailer trash tramp who got knocked up, even if she was a single mom. She had admitting privileges at two hospitals.

They were keeping Summer in a break room, with vending machines and ominous notices about CPR and other, still-missing children. Sitting next to Summer was a petite policewoman, who looked barely out of high school herself, and whose dark blonde ponytail stuck out from under her cap. They were deep in conversation.

There were several other officers milling around, and neither Summer nor the policewoman—her name tag said "Tawny"— noticed her. Alicia slid closer to the soda machine.

To look at them they could be girlfriends. Summer was smiling.

Summer was asking the policewoman, how real was *Special Victims Unit?* Alicia detested that TV show, and was unhappy with its popularity. She didn't understand why people were so gripped by stories about infanticide and spousal abuse.

"I stopped watching it when Christopher Meloni left," policewoman said, but then, she rolled one shoulder back. "It's pretty accurate. They have consultants on the show to make sure."

"Would you like to be a consultant like that?"

The young woman scratched the back of her neck. "Might be fun."

"The Olivia Benson character is the child of rape."

"Well, better that than her mother having an abortion!"

Summer hesitated. "I guess." Then she registered Alicia's presence. And, at the sight of her mother, her face drooped, and suddenly she looked older, not younger, than fifteen.

Alicia approached them with long, casual steps. "I'm surprised there aren't slot machines here," she joked. The Las Vegas airport was crammed with them, starting at the end of the jetway.

Summer and her new BFF, Tawny, stared at her like the uninvited guest she was.

"I guess this is my ride," Summer said. "It was fun meeting you."

"You, too." Tawny pushed her chair back. "You've got my cell, if you need to talk some more."

After that, it was only paperwork. Alicia could not have imagined that paperwork could be so humiliating.

———

Alicia thought that when she had a baby she'd get a lump of clay that she could fashion into whatever she wished. And what she wished for was a studious, politically aware, very secure daughter: one who would be indifferent to the opinions of others.

It didn't happen that way. Her mother told her, "That's the drawback of having one kid. If you had another one"—throat clearing—"you'd see that they're born with their own personalities." Alicia had one sibling, an older brother.

But Summer-two-point-oh was moot. Alicia would never have another baby. She'd missed a little of Summer's first year, but what she saw of it was enough to make her consider a tubal ligation. Her mother assured her that Summer was a typical infant, but if so, then Alicia wouldn't survive *any* baby's nonstop, insistent needs. Just not being able to leave the house without a diaper bag drove her close to panic attacks.

———

On the flight back, Alicia got stuck in the middle seat, between Summer, to whom she'd given the window, under the preposterous delusion that Summer would appreciate the gesture, and a man with a BMI of twenty-seven, who smelled of gin.

"You'd think they were doing me a big favor by letting you go."

Again, she'd meant it as a joke, but Summer didn't laugh. "Sorry for the inconvenience."

Alicia squeezed her plastic cup, which now held only ice. She'd been perspiring heavily since they reached the airport, and the man who'd scored the aisle seat wasn't doing much better. Alicia suspected he hadn't done well at the airport slot machines, the lights of which, along with those glaring advertisements, she feared had done permanent damage to her retinas. Or maybe her slightly blurred vision was the effect of getting only two hours sleep. She'd been running on adrenaline, but now, in the air, she felt the whole plane swaying like Foucault's pendulum.

"At least you didn't have to cancel any patients." Summer had her nose pressed to the window. "Since it's Saturday."

Alicia went on the offensive. "Well, guess what. You're switching schools."

Summer didn't look away from the window, though all there was to see was a floor of white.

"Wow. You just got that genius idea now?"

"Wh-what do you mean?"

"I hate Deadwood!" Summer raised her voice, enough so that nearby passengers turned to look. "I told you I didn't want to go there in the first place."

Deadwood was what Summer called Redwood High.

"No, you didn't." Alicia made a downward motion with her palm, to convey that Summer needed to quiet down.

"I did so! And I've been telling you every day since high school started!"

Louder this time, and Alicia looked around with an expression of, *you know kids! Haha!* "What about . . . what about . . ." She felt foolish saying the name.

"I've never even talked to Prophet John. He's mentally ill." Summer bestowed a familiar smirk on her mother, then turned back to the window. "I picked him to write about because he's the scariest dude who hangs out around the school. I knew you'd find that 'diary.' You're not as dumb as you look."

It took Alicia some moments to absorb this. "You wrote all of that just for me to find?"

"Most of it." Pause. "Who uses a spiral notebook as a journal?"

"What about KC?"

"She's real. She's a loser like me."

"But you're not a loser," Alicia protested, without sounding very convincing. "The—the marijuana?"

"It's called 'weed,' and I did try it once. The kids who smoke every day are so stupid, they can't remember their own names."

"Why did you run away, then?"

"To get away from you!"

"But why Las Vegas?" Maybe Summer got that far and ran out of money. Or maybe she got on the wrong bus. Or maybe . . .

Alicia spent the rest of the flight pondering this and other possible explanations, which was all she could do, since Summer was through with talking to her.

Chapter 10

All How You See It

ALICIA

Alicia would not let a little rain stop her. This was more than a little, but after the last few weeks, and especially that afternoon, she deserved a smoothie, and dammit, she was going to get one, no matter how fast the waiting room filled.

Larkspur Dock was right off the freeway. She could hit Squeeze, the juicery.

Now that Alicia knew that neither Prophet John nor marijuana were imminent threats, she'd wanted Summer to wait for the new academic year before starting a new school. But Summer was adamant. Voices were raised. A door was slammed.

Alicia gave in.

Then she spent hours on the internet, looking at every private school within reasonable commute time. There were schools for the supposedly gifted, and Catholic schools, and one Jewish school, and progressive schools that didn't give grades but that did sponsor beach clean-ups. Alicia thought, yeah, that was nice for the beaches, but, "abandon hope of college, all ye who enroll here."

She narrowed her search to New Horizons. It was the website with the most euphemisms (a.k.a. "BS"): "diverse learners;" "unlocking potential;" "a whole student approach." Alicia tried, but failed, to stop herself from thinking that in such a challenged pond Summer would be a smart fish.

In order to finagle Summer into New Horizons midyear, Alicia had to meet with the school counselor, Dr. Olivia True. At least she wasn't supposed to bring Summer to this confab. "That way we can speak openly," Dr. True had said.

A PhD did not make one a real doctor, and Alicia was expecting "Dr." True to be exactly the type of condescending professional who'd been telling her how to raise Summer from day one. Given the cost of a private vs. public school education, Alicia should be interrogating *them*.

She had gone to the meeting with her lab coat on, to cover the sagging rear end of her jeans, and she had a floaty mauve scarf to tuck under the notched collar of her moss green blouse.

Surprisingly, though, by the end of the interview, Alicia had warmed a little to Dr. True. That began when she described Summer's taste in books: YA novels with bubblegum pink covers, about girls named Emily or Britney, who inadvertently become rock stars. Dr. True said, "At least she reads something in print. And for pleasure. That's more than I can say for a lot of our students." And, "The tall girls always get teased. It's from envy, really. Down the line, height is a plus."

But most powerfully: "The important point is that you have to start with where Summer is, not with where you want her to be."

The last part hurt, but by the time Alicia got to Larkspur Dock she admitted that Dr. True just might have a point.

The rain had stopped, and Squeeze was in sight.

Dr. True then made a suggestion that Alicia didn't think much of, since (1) it was obvious and (2) Alicia had tried it. "Summer needs to engage with her peers."

Alicia had proposed at least a dozen ways to give Summer that opportunity, including volunteering with other teens at the SPCA, or as an Exploratorium High School Explainer. She'd even offered to join the local synagogue (although the dues were exorbitant) so that Summer could check out the youth group.

Nonstarters, all.

At Squeeze, Alicia ordered a Pomegranate Passion Parade. Awaiting her at the office, in addition to a couple of patients, was a stack of forms to fill out, all intending to appease the insurance companies. The patients would just have to wait, and the forms would all boomerang anyway, so what was the rush on them?

She'd wanted to sit for just a few minutes at one of the outdoor tables, but they were deserted now, sporting only giant polka dots of water. So she headed back to her car, Pomegranate Passion Parade in hand. It was more "gluey" than "smoothie," and, as it slid down her throat, it left the occasional pomegranate seed stuck between her molars. But she focused instead on Olivia True's parting words: "Summer has strengths she hasn't shown you yet."

Up ahead, an old man sitting on a bench got slowly to his feet. There was a piece of paper stuck to his rear end: He must have sat on it, and then the rainwater caused it to adhere.

Alicia took the straw out of her mouth long enough to shout, "Excuse me, Sir!"

He didn't hear, and she shuffled ahead to catch up, splashing puddle water over the cuffs of her jeans. As slowly as he was moving, with his tripod cane, she only gradually closed the gap.

"Excuse me, Sir!"

When he didn't respond, she tapped him on the shoulder.

"What?" he growled, when he turned around.

She held out the paper by way of apology.

"So? Throw it away!"

He thumped on.

Well, fine, Alicia thought. She looked around for a trash can. The paper was soaked and the photo becoming blotchy, but she zeroed in on a few words that were still legible: PEER SUPPORT AS YOU CREATE BALANCE IN YOUR LIFE: BODY, MIND, AND SPIRIT.

Alicia wasn't a joiner. She looked down on women who needed groups, even book clubs, let alone therapy. But it gave her another, better idea.

Alicia had joined the big practice that was Whitewater Obstetrics and Gynecology not only to have other physicians to cover for her, but to work with older practitioners who might mentor her. And there had been, if not a single, life-changing mentor, then older doctors who were resources.

She'd once suggested to Summer that they look into the Big Sisters program; she should have worn a Kevlar vest for that encounter. But! This group was clearly directed at older women, and perhaps among them would be someone to become that de facto big sister/mentor. The flyer had probably looked more impressive before a month's worth of rain had fallen on it.

At that moment, Alicia made out the words, FIRST MEETING FREE.

Alicia wasn't so naive that she'd ask Summer to accompany her to this meeting. What did she think, that they'd put on matching, mom-daughter sweaters? And it wouldn't be fair to ask Summer to go on her own. But Alicia could go. Anyone showing up, by definition, was likely to have some level of maturity, by virtue of caring about her health, not just her body image. Perhaps even the facilitator herself.

Nothing to lose.

Chapter 11

First Meeting Free

HUNTER

Hunter stood in front of her west-facing, floor-to-ceiling windows, waiting for the sun to dip low enough that she could raise the mesh shades. She'd made a cup of tea just to have something to hold.

Now that she might have to leave Chardonnay Heights, she regretted every night she hadn't stood here to watch the sky fill with pink, orange, peach, and salmon.

A full-time Starbucks salary would keep her out from under the overpass, but it wasn't enough to keep her in this, or in most parts, of Marin. Granted, if she held tightly to the corporate beanstalk, she might eventually (*eventually*) climb back to mid-level management, and a salary equivalent to what she'd earned at Energy-4-All. To say that she'd been passionate about her job was an overstatement, but at least a gym was a positive force in the world—more or less.

Passion for a career was a First World luxury. For now, she had to find some sort of gig work, maybe twenty hours a week. Packing groceries at Whole Foods. Walking dogs. Cleaning other people's houses. Every job had dignity, but when you were up to sixty hours, you had to dig deep to find it, or dig up a few psilocybin mushrooms to create this "dignified" reality for yourself.

That rainy afternoon at Larkspur Dock, after the flyers disappeared into the clouds, she'd had one last idea: *Sue Angelica! And the publisher!* It couldn't be legal to accuse her of allowing Angelica to be raped! Especially not when it made Hunter unemployable. That's what lawyers called damages. Hunter wouldn't get greedy: a year's salary . . . maybe two . . .

So, once home, and changed from wet clothes, she called Stanley Butler, the congressman whom she'd worked for when she first moved north, after college in Southern California. She'd had her own fantasies about running for office: She figured that it couldn't be more brutal than sorority politics, and it wasn't, in many ways, but when she got up close enough to see its inner workings, she left that idea behind.

Stan himself declined to run for a third term, exhausted from the 24/7 fundraising required by the two-year election cycle, and had gone back to practicing law in San Francisco.

No, he hadn't read *Jesus Warned Me*. His wife was reading it (and loving it, he admitted). Karen loved stories of redemption.

Still, when Hunter mentioned a lawsuit, Stan's voice went from congressman-raising-money to lawyer. Baritone to bass. Start with that little thing called the First Amendment, and then add that the burden of proof in a defamation suit was on the plaintiff. Would any of those potential employers from the fitness industry, if deposed, say that they didn't hire her because of what they'd read—or, at this stage, most likely only heard—about her from Angelica St. Ambrose? No, they'd say that there really wasn't a job opening, or that it had been filled. Legal fees would be enormous, and she'd only be calling attention to the book.

Sue the publisher? He hoped she was kidding. A big press with a bigger team of lawyers? They hadn't paid anything out on behalf of that rock-climbing guy who raised money to build schools in the Middle East and spent most of it on family vacations, and he invented stories J. K. Rowling would envy.

Besides, it would achieve the opposite of what she wanted. So what if the memoir was on the bestseller lists? Maybe her crowd read those books, but ask the next customer who came into Starbucks, when was the last time they actually bought a book? Meanwhile, get Angelica in front of the *New York Times* and a TV camera, and she'd send so many of the semiliterate to Amazon that the website would shut down, as surely as the Bay Bridge after a propane tank explosion.

Stanley did have one suggestion. There was a lawyer in his firm, one Will DeWitt (specialty: environmental law) who was also all het up about *Jesus Warned Me*. Something about a lie Angelica told about one of his relatives. Stan had given Will the same advice, to let it blow over. Maybe Hunter would like to meet Will, though. Full disclosure: Will was a quirky guy. He lived on a houseboat in Sausalito, but he was one of the few male attorneys who wore a suit to the office. The women, now, *they* were all in pantsuits. It was some sort of political statement.

———

Hunter's mug of tea was cold in her hand. The sun had hidden itself behind a thin strip of clouds, so she decided it was safe to raise the inner shade. She pressed the remote and filled the room with light, just as the doorbell rang.

It must be another realtor. She'd ignore it, and wait for the pair of eyes to peer through the window, trying to spot her.

Second ring. She ignored that, too. Let the pushy broad—for it was almost certainly another woman—explain to her clients that they'd made the trip for nothing.

Then came a series of fierce knocks.

At my chamber door. So this was how Edgar Allan Poe felt: They were trying to bury her, but she wasn't dead yet. She was going to hand this realtor's ass back to her.

Again, even harder: *Knock, knock. Pound, pound, pound.*

She flung the door open. But the young woman outside was like no realtor Hunter had seen before. She was all in black: leather mini-skirt, black bustier, black over-the-knee boots, black eye shadow and lipstick. The left side of her head was shaved, revealing a multitude of piercings on that exposed ear, and a nose ring finished her look. "Is this the place?" she asked, a tiny, timid voice belying both her juvenile delinquent appearance and loud knocking.

"The place for what?" The girl had a messenger bag across her chest—incongruous with the bustier, but maybe she was here to distribute her own flyers, promoting a junior college production of *Dracula's Granddaughter.*

What the girl pulled out, though, although it looked quite the worse for wear, was one of Hunter's flyers. The color photo was muddied in patches, and the only letters intact at the top of the page were HE Y!

"Isn't it today—tonight?" The girl pointed to the date and address, which were still legible.

Hunter had completely forgotten that it was the evening—supposedly—for the first group meeting. "Not happening," she said. She was embarrassed enough that she was going to close the door without further niceties when a Mercedes came crawling up, shoving aside the bushes that, without benefit of gardener (she'd let Vicente go), had begun closing in on the already-narrow driveway.

The passenger door opened and one female leg stuck out, with an elegantly shod foot at the end. Limb by limb, the rest of the woman emerged, until she was hanging on the open door of the car, legs spread at hip-width for balance. The woman was big-boned, but slender for her height, in a tweedy suit that had a Chanel vibe. She was panting slightly, apparently from the exertion of debarking the car.

Another, much younger, woman, in a white uniform, jumped from the driver's side, then raced around to ease the first woman off the car door. "Are we in the right place?"

"I don't know," Hunter said. "Where are you supposed to be?"

The tall woman produced a rolled-up sheet of paper from a pentagon-shaped handbag with a large buckle. "Read it, Reyna. I don't have my glasses."

"Never mind," Hunter said.

"Call me if you need me!" The woman named Reyna jumped back into the Mercedes before Hunter could shout that she needed to take the tall woman with her.

"Damn," Hunter muttered. Louder: "Someone's playing a practical joke on me."

Suddenly, the tall woman clutched her throat. "I need to take some medicine—a pill," she squawked. "Can I come in for some water?"

What could Hunter say to that? The older woman (she looked at least seventy) might collapse in her driveway, then sue for the few bucks Hunter had squirreled away. She stood back and motioned her in.

Goth Girl looked hesitant. Hunter was about to shoo her away, but then thought, it might be good to have a witness if anything untoward transpired.

The kitchen blended seamlessly into the open plan of the main floor, with only a breakfast bar demarking the two. The Chanel woman put her purse down there, then groped at some length inside. She mumbled, "They're here, I know they're here, did she take them out of my purse?" with increasing urgency.

"Let me help you," Goth Girl offered.

Chanel pulled her purse back toward herself, but then relented. Goth Girl took it, then emptied it item by item: a pack of tissues, Advil, disinfectant wipes, lipstick, breath mints.

"Oh, God bless you!" the old woman exclaimed when Goth Girl produced an orange prescription bottle. "Can you help me open it? I tell them I don't want the childproof cap, but . . ."

Goth Girl popped it open; Chanel tipped two small pills into her hand and swallowed them with the water that Hunter provided.

"Are you okay now?" Hunter asked hopefully.

"Give me a minute. Do you mind if I sit down?"

"Of course not!" Goth Girl answered for Hunter.

There were only two stools at the breakfast bar, and Goth Girl eased Chanel into one and helped her prop her legs on the footrest of the other.

That was when Hunter, and most certainly the others, heard the shout. "Is anyone home?"

It was a low-pitched, aggrieved, and very loud voice, accompanied by heavy footsteps that moved in the opposite direction from where Hunter and her unwelcome guests sat. "Helloooo?"

"We're in here!" Chanel shouted back, sounding very much like someone who had no intention of leaving "here" anytime soon.

The footsteps stopped. "Hey, is that an Erté?" Then the footsteps started up again, now moving toward them. From her heavy tread and her booming voice Hunter was expecting a plus-size person, but the woman who appeared a moment later was, if anything, smaller than average.

Still, she was a woman who took up a lot of space. She was a doctor: Hunter's first clue was the lab coat with her name, *Alicia Lieberman, MD* in red stitching, though the top of the letters was obscured by an infinity scarf. The heaviness of her stride came from her stacked-heeled loafers. "Can I have some water, too? I can't believe I left mine at the office. So stupid." She banged her head with the heel of her hand. "And someone is going to have to help me back down this driveway."

Hunter instinctively looked for the flyer. There it was, or what remained: a dog-eared corner peeking out from a doctor's bag that the woman had dropped, and that had landed on the floor with an unsurprisingly loud thud. "I'm sorry, what?"

The doctor grunted her amusement. "Water? Comes out of the faucet? But I don't want it from the faucet, not with that fluoride. What bottled water do you have?" Before Hunter could process this request, the woman went on, "I'm not staying long. I'm actually here for a friend. Have you started yet? Is this it?" She looked quickly from Goth to Chanel, but then she addressed Hunter directly, "Is this your deal? Do you have a degree or what?" Happily, she didn't wait for an answer. "How about you?" she demanded of Goth. "What's your story?"

"I'm just . . . interested."

"I'm feeling a little better," Chanel said, putting her hand on her heart. "But I'm getting cramps in my legs." She leaned over to massage her calf.

Hunter was about to demand that all three women get the hell out, when the sun dipped below the level of the cloud barrier, sending beams of colored light on the opposite wall, and casting a holy glow on the wall opposite her. Hunter did not hear angels sing, but the reflection of the setting sun reignited in her the fire of previous weeks. These were hardly the women she'd imagined as clients. But they were there. Perhaps—just perhaps—it was still possible to salvage her dream.

"I'm glad you came." Who knew—maybe she would be. "I was hoping for a small group," she lied. "Let me introduce myself. I'm Hunter Fitzgerald, a professional lifestyle and health coach." She'd learned this in politics: the more BS, the more believable.

The Chanel woman was Penelope. Lab Coat was Dr. Alicia Lieberman.

Goth Girl was Dannika. She was also the buzzkill. "Are you the Hunter Fitzgerald that Angelica St. Ambrose wrote about? Was she, like, your mentor or something?"

Dannika hadn't read the book; that was a relief. And what was that twelve-step saying? Fake it till you make it? "Not exactly, but I'll tell you all about how my experiences with her indirectly helped me get healthy."

Now they were intrigued, especially the two women who knew nothing about the story yet; and when she asked, calmly and authoritatively, "Shall we begin?" they silently agreed.

———

Easing Penelope off the barstool was a team effort, but then Hunter herded them into the great room, where there was a small seating area in front of the west-facing windows. Penelope leaned on Dannika's shoulder, while Alicia warned the latter, "Be careful of her spine!"

"I'm going to lay out some ground rules," Hunter announced. She'd put on a tracksuit when she came home from work, hoping it would motivate her to resume her running schedule. It hadn't, but now it looked perfectly appropriate for leading a group called Get Healthy. The three women were looking at her expectantly. She was in charge again, after too long a time.

It didn't last. Penelope asked Dr. Alicia a question about menopause—and why did the symptoms never end? Alicia didn't want to give medical advice to someone who wasn't a patient. Penelope wondered why she had to pay thousands of dollars for health insurance when poor people got it for free. Alicia said she had her facts wrong.

Dannika thumped the arm of her chair when she said that health care was a right, not a privilege. Voices rose as each woman attempted to be heard above the others. When Penelope didn't get her initial questions answered she made a semi-audible remark about how wearing a scarf with a lab coat was "an interesting fashion choice."

Hunter had to shout to be heard. "Hold on! Don't move."

She ran for the talking stick. After finding it in the great room, she'd placed it in the Margaret Keane room, in honor of Zelda's generosity.

She returned, waving it in front of her like a scythe.

Maybe it was mere curiosity that quieted them, but they all shut up and focused on this new object, with its feathers and faded paint.

Hunter explained its function, while gripping the bottom with both hands. The feathers at the top tickled her nostrils. Zelda said that it was a symbol of authority, but it was more than that: It *granted* her authority. She imagined the power of generations moving through her body.

Dannika interrupted to say that her mother's group—the women's Something Circle—didn't need a talking pillow, or a talking stuffed teddy bear, even a handmade one, because they respected each other.

"So you must know that you're not supposed to talk while I have it."

"Okay, okay, we get it."

After Hunter had created her first social media posts, while she was waiting for the tidal wave of responses that never arrived, she'd rehearsed an opening speech, and almost magically, still holding the talking stick with both hands, it came back to her.

They would exercise daily. They would eat better. And it would be easy, because . . . because they would gain insight into themselves, and why they ate . . . inappropriately . . . counterproductively . . . Health wasn't about being skinny ("easy for you to say," she heard from one of them, but ignored it): health was balance. An attitude. "Start with a journal. A daily journal. No judgment! I mean, no judgment from me or from yourselves. Write down what you did for exercise and what you ate. Exercise is anything you do to move your body. Put on music and dance! Take the stairs instead of the elevator!" *Think, think, Hunter* . . . "Weed the garden!"

"I don't have a garden," Alicia said.

Hunter overlooked that, too, but told herself to move it along. She knew how informal, how unorganized, how *unprofessional* this so-called group was. She hadn't even offered them any refreshments, unless you counted water for Penelope's pills.

But. She had the talking stick, and they were still here. Restless, from their body language, appraising each other warily, and sitting uncomfortably close. It was purely luck that there was a love seat with two armchairs. Also luck that Alicia and Dannika were both on the short side. Penelope was in one armchair, leaving the other empty for Hunter. Now was the time.

"Tell me about yourselves!" Hunter had already chosen Dannika, and she was about to reach out to hand the talking stick to her . . .

. . . when a tingling went up her arm, as it had in Zelda's trailer. This time, though, a light, as from a camera's flashbulb, went off in her brain. Then a short film played in her head, like a dream freshly remembered upon waking: blurry around the edges, and strangely tinted, with reds and oranges where reds and oranges didn't belong.

> *It's one of their parties. A big party. The people are ghostlike, not fully formed, but she can name those standing close to her: Larry Proudfoot, June Fern, Atwell Barnes. And Peter. He's swaying. He's halfway to drunk. He'll get the rest of the way soon. "He was confused about anti-deficiency statutes," she hears herself say. "Someone forgot to tell him that they don't apply if you're trying to unload three houses at once."*
>
> *Laughter.*
>
> *"That's how he lost the last half mil."*
>
> *More laughter, less enthusiastic.*
>
> *Same night. She wakes to a trembling in the bed. Earthquake? Every time she feels a shaking she thinks, uh oh. This was why her mother didn't want her to come out west.*

*But no. It's Peter, crying. He doesn't say anything, but she
knows that he's ashamed: ashamed he lost so much money on the
house he had to sell, embarrassed that everyone knows it, embarrassed that they know it because his own wife told them.*

Should she hug him? Tell him she's sorry?

*She stares at the ceiling. She's only ever heard a man crying in
the movies. The sound embarrasses her.*

She rolls over slowly so he won't know that she woke up.

Closes her eyes.

"Are you okay?" Alicia's face showed a deep frown line. "You're
not—do you have a seizure disorder?"

"No," Hunter said. "I just . . . I spaced out for a moment. Uh . . .
uh . . . Dannika?"

Hunter was relieved that she remembered the girl's name, but she
had to pretend to listen to her. She absorbed the fact that Dannika's
mother had died after a long illness.

When had this happened, this memory she'd just recovered, of
Peter weeping over her remark? She did remember. She remembered
the house he was going to flip, *did* flip, just not the way he planned.
It was in Hillsborough.

Then Dannika, who had been shedding tears while she spoke of
her mother's death from cancer, shuddered.

"Are *you* all right?" Penelope asked her.

Dannika didn't answer right away, but then, "Yeah, yeah. What
was I saying?"

"Can we tell her?" Alicia asked archly.

"Never mind, I remember." Dannika shook the hair on the side
of her head that had hair. "So, hospice came in—"

"You told us that already," Alicia said.

"Don't interrupt!" Penelope said.

When it was Alicia's turn she first said that she was really
here for her daughter, so she didn't need to talk about herself.

Then, with no prompting, she told them about how her daughter had run away, and only her quick action had saved her from possible abduction.

But she, too, froze in the middle of her story. It wasn't the way people lose the thread of a tale. It was a hiccup of the face and body, and it reminded Hunter of how Alicia had asked her if she had a seizure disorder.

Then Penelope's turn came around, and Hunter was able to listen a little better. Penelope's voice was shaky, and her story meandered, but she managed to communicate that she had a variety of physical challenges that eluded diagnoses, so a group called Get Healthy seemed a good fit.

Then her voice trailed off and she lowered her chin to her chest. Hunter was afraid she'd dozed off, but a moment later she snapped to attention. "Sorry," was all she said.

———

It was 7:00. Hunter remained a little distracted by her memory of Peter, but buoyed by the hope of reviving her plan.

Which reminded her of why she'd made this plan, which in turn reminded her to raise the issue of money.

"First meeting free," Alicia said.

"Right, but next week—" *Let them put down the first number.*

Dannika did. It was very low. Hunter doubled it.

They agreed! Hunter wished she'd tripled it.

"On a weekly basis, though," Alicia qualified.

"Fine. Just bring your journals next time."

She reviewed their assigned daily practice (people loved the word "practice" these days) of recording food intake and exercise. "No judgment," she repeated so frequently that it sounded judgmental. "We take you as you are and make adjustments. And you are not competing against each other."

After they all left (Penelope aided by the young nurse), Hunter realized that no one had taken her up on her promise to explain her role in *Jesus Warned Me*. Stanley was right. Maybe they were being polite, but maybe—just maybe now—Angelica had left room for her to have a life of her own.

Chapter 12

All Downhill from Here

PENELOPE

Penelope called Reyna when the meeting was over, and, as promised, Reyna came to pick her up. "How did it go?" Reyna was backing down the treacherous driveway with only one hand on the top of the wheel. Instead of relying on the camera, she twisted around. But she did everything with that big smile.

"Well, it started out okay." Penelope was shaken up. How to tell Reyna what had happened to her?

"Who else was there?"

"Three other women." Penelope described them briefly: the bossy doctor, the girl dressed in black with all the piercings, and their hostess, a skinny, take-charge blonde. "We used a talking stick."

"That was a good idea."

Penelope wasn't so sure about that.

It was Dannika who had handed it to her. At first, Penelope was only aware of how it was warm from other holders, and she worried about what germs she might be picking up. She removed one hand, fumbled for her tissues, and wiped it down.

"What should I talk about?" she had asked.

"Anything for starters." Hunter shrugged. "Introduce yourself."

Penelope couldn't remember what she rambled about. Probably that last ER visit that had led to Scott hiring Reyna.

But she'd been so nervous when she first arrived at Hunter's, that she'd taken two Valium instead of one, and she was feeling it. Usually two didn't affect her much, but for some reason she felt herself drifting, the way she did when she was falling asleep (if she'd had *enough* Valium) and images from dreams-to-come appeared and disappeared, and then . . .

> She was standing in a circle of light from the Shell station sign.
>
> She kept looking at her watch. 8:10. 8:11. The man she knew only as "Kansas City Bob" was supposed to meet her here at 8:00.
>
> Penelope had told Scott that she was getting together with a friend. She was prepared to say that it was a friend he didn't know, but he didn't ask. He didn't ask when she'd be home, either.
>
> If she didn't come home at all, would he notice? He'd have to notice eventually, if only when his shirts needed to go to the laundry. And then, would he call the police? She should have gotten one of those new cell phones that some women had for the sake of safety.
>
> Trish from the tennis club had a prescription to refill, and she'd sell half of them to Penelope, but Trish's mother was sick, and Trish had to go out of town to see her. At first, Penelope tried not to hate Trish or her mother for it. Now she didn't have the energy to hate anyone, not with her skin prickling and the heart palpitations and the sweat on her forehead.
>
> The young man who took over Dr. Schmulewitz's practice, some Ivy League frat boy who thought she was just a middle-aged hypochondriac, wouldn't prescribe Valium. He told her to try meditation.
>
> 8:14.

She tried other doctors, but none of them understood why she needed it. The women doctors were meaner than the men: The men were harsh, but the women were bitches.

Finally she found a doctor who agreed to give her a prescription for 10 mgs a day, as long as she saw a psychiatrist once a month. Penelope thought that was pointless, but she wasn't going to argue. 10 mgs a day wasn't nearly enough, but she knew instinctively that if she begged for more he'd cut her off entirely.

8:16.

Penelope was bouncing on her heels when a dented white pickup truck pulled up, stopping just short of the circle of light. She could just make out a male figure inside the cabin. He had a beard and a Giants baseball cap, but she could see that he was white.

She stood by the door of the truck until she realized that Kansas City Bob was not going lean over to open it. She pulled a handkerchief out of her purse and wrapped it around the handle. Then she had to take a giant step to haul herself onto the cracked leather of the passenger seat. There were potato chip crumbs littered across it. More crumbs of a less certain origin lay on the floor below. The smell of cigarette smoke made her queasy. Funny how she'd thought that quitting smoking was hard.

When they got on the freeway she worried that he was going to kidnap her. But Tennis Club Trish knew him. Didn't she? Or she knew someone who knew him. But maybe it was part of a larger plot that involved other people.

They got off at the Marin City exit.

Then they drove to a dark street. If there were any nearby lampposts, the lights were burned out. She handed Kansas City Bob an envelope with cash, and she could just make out that he went inside a house, which was dark except for one light in an upstairs window. And it was strangely quiet: she expected music blaring, and shouting, or at least people talking.

She checked to make sure her door was locked.

She was still scared that someone might force his way into the truck, or shoot a gun through the windshield, right into her face, but with passing seconds, and then minutes, her focus narrowed to a pinpoint. She was only scared that Bob might not return, or return only to say that there'd been a problem. They were keeping the cash but there were no pills.

She didn't care about the cash.

When he walked back out, she floated to the ceiling of the cab. Although, no, he might still not have . . .

But he handed her the ziplock bag. She closed her fist around it, feeling the plastic crumple, but not squeezing so tightly that she might damage the pills. Once they'd been around a while they got chalky and crumbly. She wanted to take two right away, but now that they were in her hand, her withdrawal symptoms receded enough that she could last until they got back to the gas station.

When they did, she did not wait for Kansas City Bob to open any doors. She leapt out, hitting the pavement hard, sending the sting of invisible needles up her legs.

In her own car she held them up to the dome light, then took two. Relief was instantaneous.

She'd forgotten that that had ever happened.

Forgotten, yet she had learned from it. Since then, she'd found other sources to use as backup for Trish. It was easy to bring up the subject in casual conversation: "I'm flying back East next week, and I get so nervous on planes." (She hadn't been on a plane in years.) "It's funny you say that, because Valium is the one thing that can help me sleep." She developed a sense for when to pursue the subject and when to drop it.

Penelope wanted to tell Reyna about it, but Reyna would think so much less of her.

"You okay?" Reyna asked.

"Oh . . . my mind was wandering." She leaned her head against the window. They were passing the mall where Scott had filled her first prescription.

Now that she had recalled her night in that dark neighborhood, it was hard to deny that she was an addict. The word itself was like the click of a German officer's boots. *Du es eine addict.* She'd been saying to herself for years that she simply needed it, the way that diabetics needed insulin.

It was like a tennis match in her head: She hit the ball: *I need it!* It came back over the net: *You risked your life to get it!* Hit it back, hard: *I never risked my life—if anyone was in danger, it was Bob!*

Du es eine addict.

Chapter 13

You'll Be Fine

ALICIA

Thanks to the evil empire that was known by the euphemism "managed care," Alicia had a ten-minute block of time to devote to her current patient, Schuyler Applegate. Schuyler was carrying twins. Alicia had not been involved in their conception, and Schuyler's husband only remotely so, as they were the result of IVF. Another specialist—a male doctor trained in this once-breakthrough technology that was now so commonplace that there were three sets of twins in Summer's grade alone—had implanted the embryos, and then Alicia took over.

The Applegates had been fortunate in that the first procedure had worked. Alicia knew couples who raided their IRAs, borrowed from their own parents, then mortgaged their homes to the foundation, before they got a baby—if they got a baby at all.

Schuyler was complaining of heartburn. "I can only sleep upright in a chair!"

"Try Tums," was Alicia's reply.

"They don't help!" Schuyler pouted. "I wanted a female obstetrician because I thought I'd feel more nurtured by a woman."

Not this woman, Alicia thought. *At least not for this patient.*

One reason that Alicia became an OB-GYN was that she wanted to have women patients only. She was unprepared for the Schuylers: a woman who waited until she was forty-one, and then expected instant family (and yes, her twins were a boy and a girl); a woman who had money to spend on IVF, and then complained because she'd have to deliver in an operating room, instead of the luxurious, mauve-painted, labor, delivery, and postpartum suite. "Twins are considered a high-risk pregnancy," Alicia had explained, as patiently as she could. (Was that why they called them "patients"?)

"I don't want to sleep in a chair," Schuyler whimpered now. "I want to be sleeping next to my *husband*."

Alicia had never had a husband. When Summer was five—a precocious five-year-old who knew that a mommy and a daddy made a baby—she'd explained that Summer's dad was another medical student who'd broken up with her when he learned that she was pregnant and intended to keep the baby.

"It had nothing to do with you," she'd said to her daughter. "He just didn't want to be with me, and he didn't want to be a dad. I didn't even know if you were a girl or a boy yet." She particularly wanted Summer to know that she hadn't been rejected because of her gender.

Alicia conceived Summer during her fourth year. It was the highest achievement of an already high-achieving life, to have a baby while in med school. Granted, her due date landed neatly during the summer, which in turn inspired her daughter's name. "Summer" was a bit New Agey, but Alicia loved its associations of light and freedom, beaches and fresh fruit.

The med student was Joshua Goodman. He had not broken up with her. She had broken up with him.

It all came back to her during that first talking-stick meeting.

She sits down in the cafeteria, ready to tell him. He's rearranging
his plates. He always eats one item at a time: the pasta salad, the
green salad, and only then the sandwich. It annoys the hell out of
her. She asked him about it once and he said cheerfully it was just
his "thing."

It's funny how she likes the disinfectant smell of the hospital,
but the cafeteria smell, especially anything with tuna, makes her
want to puke.

She's afraid he'll try to stop her from having an abortion.

"I'm going to check your cervix." Schuyler was already in the stir-
rups; Alicia rolled her stool into the embrace of her patient's legs.

Schuyler bit her lip in anticipation of pain that wasn't coming. "Can a woman who has twins ever get her body back? I had
a perfectly flat tummy before I got pregnant. Almost nonexistent!
Convex!"

You mean concave.

". . . and I've already gained 38 pounds!"

Don't come kvetching to Alicia Lieberman about weight gain.
Just stay away from carbs.

Under the canopy of tissue paper, Alicia smiled. "You're like
Mark Twain's aunt."

"What?"

"A sinking ship with nothing to throw overboard. I never had
a flat tummy, myself. So you see, I had nothing to lose by having
a baby."

"I didn't know you had children, Dr. Lieberman." Schuyler
sounded amazed.

"Because my personal life is none of your business."

"You used to be much nicer, Dr. Lieberman."

"No, I wasn't. You're pregnant. That makes you sensitive." If
Alicia offered "concierge" service to her patients, she'd at least be
better compensated for putting up with the Schuylers of Marin.
But she needed to wait until Summer was older and went away to

college, *kine abora.* (*Kine abora.* Those words were intended to ward off disaster, but they were Old World, embarrassing, and she never said them aloud.)

Then she regretted her harshness. "You know, for a multiple, you're having a pretty easy pregnancy." There were plenty of possible complications: non-vertex fetuses, preeclampsia, edema, gestational diabetes. The worst was when the results of the amniocentesis revealed that the fetus had Down syndrome or spina bifida. Devasting news. Tough choices to make.

Thankfully, a bad amnio was rare. What was common were miscarriages. They'd always been common, of course; it was just that women were a few days late and didn't think much of it, or, if they did, they were either disappointed—or relieved. And it was yet another patriarchal myth that most women had regular twenty-eight-day cycles. Alicia herself had a forty-two-day cycle (on average), and often missed periods for no discernible reason.

Which was how she got pregnant with Summer. That, and that in the rush of a last-minute opportunity to have *actual sex* she'd neglected to put the spermicide on her diaphragm. A medical student, and one hoping to specialize in gynecology and obstetrics. . . . What would a psychologist say about that?

> *Watching Joshua start on the sandwich, she thinks, I'll tell him.*
>
> *No, I won't tell him.*
>
> *I might miscarry anyway.*
>
> *Then the smell of the tuna incites a new wave of nausea, and she knows that she's not going to miscarry. The nausea is a sign of the hormones doing their job.*
>
> *He uses his napkin to pat up the ring of moisture beneath his water glass.*
>
> *Tell him.*
>
> *Don't tell him.*
>
> *I don't want a baby. Can he make me have the baby?*

No!

But the world is tilted against women. What if Joshua finds a way to stop her? Joshua's going into pediatrics—that's how much he loves kids!

She doesn't know if she wants kids at all. She sure as hell doesn't want one now.

She'd better terminate soon. Dr. Chang will do it, and keep it to herself. And Alicia has to hurry; she's at least eight weeks.

So she tells Joshua, "I think we should take a break."

"What? No! Why?"

He looks so startled. She's startled to hear herself say it.

Her mother wants to know why the father "can't take some responsibility," but Alicia got her to shut up when she pronounced, "He dumped me when I said I was pregnant."

That's what started the lie, and maybe because it was so much more convenient this way, after a while, Alicia believed it.

Until a few days ago.

When it was her turn, Alicia had merely let the talking stick lie across her lap, until Hunter prodded her to hold it, as the rest of them had.

She ended up telling them that Summer had run away, though she hadn't planned to. She kept the story matter-of-fact. No big deal. Teenage girls were always trouble, right?

But then those memories, in flashes, appearing, disappearing, like a skipping film. She tried to ignore them. She kept talking, until she heard how she was nattering.

She hadn't forgotten. Not exactly. She'd photoshopped the memory, with one layer that of Josh, another of her thoughts, another of her fears, and yet another of her later thoughts. The layers merged into one image, the one in which Joshua was the bad guy.

Alicia's hope of finding a mentor, or even a role model, for Summer, when she carried the blurred flyer to Hunter's home, had been naive. She'd go back one more time, partly out of curiosity, and partly to see if she herself had something to offer them.

She rolled back. "You're one centimeter dilated," she said, "and 20 percent effaced."

"Does that mean the babies will come early?"

"We don't want them too early. If we can make it to thirty-five weeks—"

"I know all about that," Schuyler snapped. "But I'm so *uncomfortable.*"

"I know, and I'm sorry."

"When the babies do come, it'll be so much easier," Schuyler predicted.

"Oh, certainly." Babies weren't that difficult. When they were upset, there were limited causes: hunger, fatigue, the discomfort of an unchanged diaper. But when your teenager insisted that you put her in a new school, because that would solve all her problems, and then it didn't, but she came home and refused to discuss the new problems . . . well, wouldn't it be nice to fix it by changing a diaper then?

Schuyler detected the sarcasm. "I'm going to have a full-time nanny," she said smugly. "And one for nights, too. I'm going back to the bank after three weeks. So I should be fine."

"Yes," Alicia said. "You'll be fine."

Chapter 14

In Case You Can't Stand It

DANNIKA

Dannika knew that to sit on Cat Hair Couch was to rise covered in orange, white, and gray fur, but it was the price of having Rodion Romanovich Raskolnikov, a.k.a. Razzy, the orange tabby, in her lap. He was purring, and he conformed to her thighs like cheese melting on a burger.

She stroked his back. She felt guilty about having a favorite, but she couldn't help it. "He's my lover and my friend," she joked once, but the women of the Circle weren't famous for their sense of humor. "What do you mean?" Jethro asked, and Dannika quickly bailed out of that convo.

Razzy was the first cat that Mosi had let her name. Mosi named her cats after old-time movie stars and titles: IClawdia, and Tim Purry. Dannika named her cats after characters from novels, like Miss Havisham and Pumblechook, from *Great Expectations*, and Katerina Ivanovna from about four of Dostoyevsky's novels. Dostoyevsky really liked that name for some reason. Maybe it was the Russian equivalent of "Jane Smith."

Razzy's purring faded. That meant that he was asleep.

Dannika needed to pee badly, but she wouldn't move until Razzy did, or until she couldn't stand it, and she could stand it a little longer. So, sitting there, though she tried not to, she went back to thinking about the meeting at Hunter's house:

When Dannika first took hold of the talking stick, her arm tingled, the way it does when you hit your funny bone.

After that, it was like watching a movie.

She thinks she has the right amount of pills.

She's been taking them out for a long time. She does it the way her friends steal gin or vodka from their parents, adding water to make up the difference. With the pills, she dumps the whole bottle, takes out a few, then replaces them with something like Tylenol, or even SweeTARTS, if she doesn't have anything else. She doesn't want to deprive Mosi of what she needs, but Mosi has always been so antidrug that she won't take as much as they'd let her. Besides, no one is going to mistake a purple SweeTART for a narcotic.

She's been telling herself all along, "This is just in case you can't stand it." When Mosi's gone.

She did a lot of research on the internet. There are sites for people who want to commit suicide, though they never use those words. It's "death with dignity."

She's finally asleep. Then she feels the bed rocking, and hears someone calling her name. She doesn't answer until the shaking gets worse. She rolls over and opens her eyes.

"What were you doing?"

It's Bronwyn, yelling.

"I knew something was wrong. Your Mother's spirit communicated to me that I needed to save you."

Dannika is having trouble talking, she's so out of it. She knows that yeah, she took a bunch of pills, and followed the instructions on the website to make sure she didn't take too many, so that she threw up, or maybe choked on her own vomit. That would be okay, if she just died, but the worst thing that could happen is that she ends up in one of those comas where you live for years on a ventilator.

"I was just taking a nap," she manages to groan through the heavy invisible blankets on top of the real one. "Stop being such a drama queen."

"Don't lie to me, young lady. I'm going to call the police—"

Dannika might throw up now. The police will lock her up for seventy-two hours. That happened to a couple of kids she knew in high school.

"No!"

"Listen," Bronwyn says, "either I call the police or we do our own suicide watch."

That thing about the police was just to manipulate Dannika. Bronwyn wants to call the other women to come over to watch Dannika in shifts. Dannika thinks, no way, Hervé—if that isn't reason enough to lie, she doesn't know what would be.

She has to try harder to focus. I said I was just taking a freaking nap, okay? I haven't slept in days. So maybe I would have stayed asleep for a buncha hours if you'd left me alone. So what? Oh my God, I needed some sleep so bad, why did you wake me up? Look around if you don't believe me. Do you see any empty pill bottles? No? Okay, then! That? That's a freakin' SweeTART! Are you going to call the police because I had some candy?

Finally she convinces Bronwyn. And Bronwyn's hysterics are making Dannika realize that she can stand it, that Mosi doesn't want her to be with her just yet.

And later, Dannika thought she'd been telling the truth. It was like reading a book, and then seeing the movie version, and later thinking that scenes they added to the movie were in the book, too. Like, in the movie version of *The Help*, there was a scene where Celia Foote makes dinner for Minny, now that she knows how to cook, and Dannika kind of remembered that scene from the book. But then she reread *The Help*, and saw that no, it wasn't there.

When the memory of Bronwyn waking her up came to her at Hunter's house, she felt her whole body jerk. But no one noticed.

Now she clutched the fur on Razzy's neck. He lifted his head and meowed. There were other cats in her Kitty Kollection who would have howled and scratched her. Not Razzy. He looked over at her in his lazy, loving cat way and understood that she hadn't meant to disturb him, let alone hurt him.

Since she'd left Hunter's, she'd remembered more.

After Mosi died, the Craftswomen's Circle hovered for three weeks. They brought her casseroles, mostly inedible vegan shit (she was a vegetarian, but give up cheese, and eggs? How does laying an egg hurt a chicken?), but she managed to eat them anyway, at least sometimes. They did laundry. In between visits, they emailed, and they even called on the phone.

Then they fell off, one by one. Bronwyn was the last to go, but she returned to her own life, too.

One day Dannika looked in the refrigerator and there was nothing there but protein bars and Diet Dr. Pepper.

That was when she couldn't stand it.

It was just luck that Bronwyn came over the afternoon of the so-called "nap."

Or was it luck?

———

Dannika had been raised by basic cable, and a few Hallmark specials taught her all she needed to know about America's dominant Protestant culture.

When Dannika was eight she read Hans Christian Andersen's "The Little Mermaid." (She'd overheard Mosi brag that she was reading at a ninth-grade level.) Dannika had already read all the Laura

Ingalls Wilder books, which was good, because a few years later, Mosi banned them for their negative portrayal of indigenous people.

Disney completely ruined the Andersen story! The Little Mermaid didn't want some stupid prince to marry her.

The Little Mermaid wanted an immortal soul.

That was the beginning of Dannika's longing for God. Thinking about God gave her a feeling that overlapped a little with sex, but had its own distinct boundaries, too. And she was fascinated with thoughts of an afterlife. Here on Earth, you had to look for God in Baby's First Smile or something. But the thought of actually *being* with God made her chest tight. In a good way.

It wouldn't be like "being" here, but how could you imagine what it would be? For now, the closest she could get was that feeling from a vivid sunset, when a layer of gold shone through between two layers of pink. Behind the gold was something that moved her wordlessly. Something that made her feel scared, but loved and safe.

Going to church didn't cut it for her. The one time a year Mosi took her, on Easter, Dannika didn't get any feeling of God's presence from singing hymns or by reciting psalms, with their old-fashioned language. The last thing she wanted to hear was some middle-aged man in a dorky white gown tell her how God wanted her to behave, and it creeped her out to shake a stranger's hand and say, "Peace be upon you."

Dannika did not think of herself as arrogant, but she was sure that she knew as much about God as anyone else. How could anyone else know more, unless God, or maybe an angel, talked to them, and all that would mean was that they were crazy. People had different beliefs, and she totally respected that, the way Mosi taught her, but anyone basing those beliefs on stuff written by—no joke— God knew who, was relying on other people, not God. You had to feel in your heart, in your gut, what was right, what maybe God wanted, and what *you* felt was as true as what anyone else preached or claimed.

She also knew that God didn't need praise. He created the universe and now He needed compliments for it? It reminded her of some of her friends' boyfriends, who needed to be told over and over what good football players they were.

Then there was the one about how God made the universe, or let's not get greedy and just say that God made the world, and now He lets people run it, so that when they hurt each other, or when someone dies of cancer, he's *upset* for them? That. Was. Just. Plain. Nuts. The Creator of the universe, the force that sustains all life, has tears in something that correspond to human eyes.

Dannika never talked about this with anyone, though. Her feelings about God were exquisitely private. She didn't even talk about it to Mosi.

But when she was alone, she talked to God frequently, thanking him for good grades, reproaching Him for the drought. She didn't know if He heard her, but it was possible, wasn't it? Maybe He was only her imaginary friend, but she liked thinking that maybe, after all, maybe . . .

Raskolnikov raised his ass, and then his legs, then stretched his whole body. Like it or not, for now, Dannika had to stay here to take care of him.

Chapter 15

No Place Like Home

HUNTER

The driveway was steep. Hunter pumped her arms hard. She could stop, catch her breath, walk the rest of the way. But no. From their first day in Chardonnay Heights, the driveway had represented not giving up.

"Look at you!"

Angelica. At the top of the hill. Getting out of her Tesla, from the driver's seat. Peter from the other door. "You're like Flo-Jo!"

Hunter concentrated on the last few yards. She'd pushed herself to start running again, finally. She found that she'd lost a great deal of speed and stamina, but she was determined to rebuild both, and the burning in her hamstrings was encouragement, not pain.

She stopped next to Angelica's car, then bent over to grip her calves and stretch her quads. Whenever she thought of Angelica, Hunter pictured her in one of the private school uniforms of her own youth: plaid skirt, knee socks. But here she was in her characteristic blend of cowboy and Native American look: a Western shirt over a pair of jeans. Fringed boots.

"The film option didn't get renewed after all." Angelica flicked her hand toward the front door.

"How dare they." Hunter had thought about this moment. Seeing Angelica again and yelling, *you have fucked up my life big-time.*

However, she stayed silent. Angelica could make her homeless.

Then she looked up and saw Peter, as his head rose from above the passenger door. Heartbeat one: He's so handsome! Heartbeat two, three, four: *shame, shame, shame.*

After the three women from Get Healthy had departed, Hunter had a brief respite. The group was small, but it was something she could build on.

But then, a few hours later, in bed, she relived yet again how she had embarrassed Peter in front of their friends. No, call them guests, since the "friendship" of this cohort had proved of little value.

Call them by any name though: the first memory opened a sluicegate. In the six days since, she'd be checking for water spots on a glass at home, or at work, adding hazelnut syrup to a latte, when she recalled another cutting remark couched as humor. "Hey, who cares about a negative cash flow?" *Can't-you-take-a-joke-dear?*

If she was passive-aggressive in public, she was sometimes cruel in private. *I told you that it you were paying too much for a house in that neighborhood.*

She'd been unable to count how many times a week she'd done this to him. Once? Twice? Daily?

She owed him an apology, but not now. Not here. After all, he still owed her one, too. Her mother's expression from her own Wexford childhood was, "There's a pair of them in it," and she and Peter were the pair in question.

Peter, oblivious to her thoughts, gazed at her benignly. He reminded her of frescoes of saints from her childhood, but better looking. Angelica was making him happy.

"So you could say that I'm fiscally embarrassed," Angelica was saying. "They don't give these things out with Happy Meals." She patted the trunk of her car.

Angelica shared Peter's tendency to get in over her head financially. "So we might give you an opportunity to practice some Christian charity." Angelica raised her eyebrows very high.

Hunter wondered for a moment what that might mean, and then it came to her: Angelica and Peter were going to take the house back. But she kept quiet; she might be wrong, and if so, she didn't want to give them any ideas. "Aren't you making money from royalties?"

Angelica shrugged. "This capitalist society is rigged against artists." After a pause, "I have to earn my advance back first."

Hunter pushed her headband up a little higher. It was reassuringly damp; perspiration was good. "What about that house in—" Hunter couldn't, or didn't want, to remember the name of the town.

"San Anselmo!" Angelica said. "I'm renting it out. Or I will rent it out, as soon as I can find a nice Muslim couple. I mean, they don't have to be married, or cisgender. But they've experienced so much harassment."

Hunter plucked her key from the little slot in her joggers that was designed for that purpose. The stone of fear had returned to its own home at the bottom of her stomach. Where could she go? She could always work in a Starbucks in Connecticut. *Or shoot myself.*

"Can we come in, or is this like one of those restaurants where you have to have a membership?"

Peter finally spoke. "We could use some water."

"Of course." *It's your house.*

Once inside, Angelica went straight to the refrigerator. "This isn't a good place for someone with an eating disorder."

Peter got each of them bottled water.

Hunter sat on one of the breakfast barstools. Might as well get it over with: "To what do I owe the pleasure of your visit?"

"Welllll." Angelica took a swallow, put her glass down on the counter. "Petey, you take this one."

"We're moving in," Peter said.

Hunter closed her eyes. Small satisfaction in having been right. "I thought—I thought the house was on the market." Though no new realtors had appeared.

"Why do you look so upset?" Angelica asked. "Oh, you're worried that you have to move out, aren't you?"

"Don't I?"

"We're Christians," Angelica said. "We don't do evictions."

"You can stay here," Peter said.

"Are you joking?" Hunter pictured a tent in the now-overgrown backyard. Maybe a doghouse.

Peter took his water to the great room, where he slumped in the love seat. "This is a buyers' market," he said, and Hunter, though she hated herself for it, wanted to say, *oh, so now you know when it's a buyers' market.* "Not a good time to sell."

For a moment, Hunter told herself to be grateful. Then she remembered that it was Angelica herself who'd gotten her in this situation. "You lied about me," she said.

"When?" Angelica kept staring at the inside of the refrigerator.

"In your damn memoir!"

"Oh, that. Don't you have anything that didn't come from Whole Foods? I only wrote my truth, Hunter. I didn't think people would take it that way."

"Well, they did, and now I can't find a new job."

"Maybe you're meant to do something else. Everything's part of the plan."

Save that claptrap for your tweets. But she wouldn't speak her mind until she had another place to live.

"I give up." Angelica closed the refrigerator. "If I've damaged you in any way, I'm truly sorry. I can help get the word out that you're not the person they think you are. But maybe people wouldn't be so quick to believe bad things about you if they didn't have a reason."

"You can have the big bedroom," Peter shouted from the love seat.

"That's right!" Angelica said. "I'm reliably informed that you and Petey had conjugal relations in there a few times. It has Fitzgerald juju. We want a fresh start."

It was weird and creepy, but it was better than working at a Starbucks in Stamford. She barely remembered her bedroom at home—was the Ricky Martin poster still there?

"You just have to clear out the Margaret Keane room," Peter said. "Angelica needs it. You can put the extra stuff in your room."

Angelica joined Peter on the love seat, where she caressed his neck. "I've left AA," she announced. "Don't you have any throw pillows? They help Petey with his back."

"I don't do throw pillows," Hunter murmured. She disliked clutter, and her ivory midcentury modern sofa was bare.

"There are some in my office," Peter said.

She jumped up. He was right: there were a couple still resting on the foldout sofa, but she didn't want him to go in there until she had a chance to shut down the computer. "I'll get them."

Angelica stuffed her hand into Peter's marvelously thick blond hair. "Isn't he gorgeous? I've left AA," she said again.

"I'll be back!"

Hunter ran to what was now her home office, where she closed the open tabs and clicked "shut down." So this would be Peter and Angelica's bedroom? Yes, weird and creepy.

She grabbed both pillows, guessing that she'd be back if she left any behind.

"Aren't you going to ask me why I've left AA?" Angelica asked as soon as Hunter returned.

"Sure. Why-have-you-left-AA?"

"It isn't spiritual enough. A 'higher power'? That could be the phone company. Or the IRS. And aren't you going to ask me what I'm going to do with that room? Where you keep all your . . . um, stuff?"

"Sure.   What-are-you-going-to-do-with-that-room?"   Hunter proffered one pillow, gripping the edge with thumb and forefinger. Angelica tucked it behind Peter's back.

"You inspired me, Hunter! I'm going to start a group." She put her hand on Peter's thigh. "Petey will go to meetings without me for a while."

He smiled vacantly. "Yeah, like a big boy. I call it 'Awesome Alcoholics.'"

"And my group is going to be about the real way to get healthy, spiritually healthy, which is through Jesus."

"Why just Jesus?"

"He's real and really here, and if you deny him . . ." Angelica drew her finger across her throat.

Hunter surreptitiously plucked at the fabric of her sports bra. It was not performing its advertised promise of wicking sweat away. *Steal my husband, my house, and then my idea?* Her "group"—if three people could be called a group—was supposed to gather at six the following evening. Would they bring the journals she'd asked for? Did it matter? Since the memories intruded (*"Wise words from the man who predicted the failure of the Apple Watch!"*) she'd lost her mental momentum.

"How do you even know about my group?"

"Hah! They have this thing now, called Twitter. Oops! I mean X. Your hashtags were trending."

"It didn't get me any takers."

"Aren't you going to ask me what my program is called?"

Hunter sighed.

"Okay. It's called 'the Fourteenth Step.'"

"Why not 'the Thirteenth'?"

Peter explained, "'The Thirteenth Step' is AA slang." He sounded smug about being in the know. And why not? Hunter cringed, thinking how often she'd corrected his grammar, and pointed out factual errors, like the time he'd referred to the Industrial Revolution as "a defining feature of the eighteenth century."

"It's about people who come to AA looking for a hookup."

"Petey's pretty smart."

Hunter remembered, in pulsating images, Peter having his wisdom teeth out. His broad hints that she should accompany him to the surgery, that she chose to ignore. His recuperation, which seemed to take forever. His bleating for water and applesauce. She stayed home one day and then quoted the information sheet from the surgeon that he shouldn't need more time than that to recover.

Of course he fled to Angelica. Angelica might be bossy, but she took care of him.

She put one hand on her forehead. *Begone, Demon Memory.*

"I was thinking of calling it the Jesus Warned Me Workshop," Angelica was saying. "Then people will have to buy the book." When Hunter didn't respond: "Right?"

Hunter brushed her shoulders, pretending that the memories were dandruff, although she didn't have dandruff, and she didn't plan to. "The book is doing pretty well already."

Angelica stayed focused on her project. "I want a place where people can talk about recovery and name names. Really, it's your idea."

"So what is this about, weight loss or sobriety?"

"Both! If you have one you have the other."

Hunter didn't argue. Let Angelica carve out her own niche. This confident woman was unlike the Angelica she remembered, who was flamboyantly insecure, her humor of the most self-deprecating kind. ("My thighs are like redwood trunks! My ass is flabbier than raw pizza dough!")

Abruptly, Angelica gripped Peter's hand. "I'd feel better if you cleaned out that room now. It's making me edgy."

"Edgy?"

"The fifteenth step is purging the excess in our lives, but let's not get ahead of ourselves."

"You can have it all," Peter said, though he looked pained. "It's mostly junk."

"Junk!" After they'd spent hours at Salvation Army stores!

Peter chugged water, then put his sleeve up to his mouth. "I was grabbing at anything when we went to those flea markets. To fill the Jesus-sized hole in my heart."

"You don't want any of it?"

"Well, maybe the baseball cards." Peter looked at Angelica, as if for permission. "Let's keep those. I mean, I'll keep those."

———

Once inside the Margaret Keane room, Hunter took a deep breath, and let the miasma from her possessions calm her. This wasn't the clutter that Crate & Barrel sloughed off, this was history in the form of vinyl albums and comic books.

There wouldn't be space in her room for the three bookshelves on which she'd organized their purchases, but she needed to cull the collection anyway. No, not cull, *curate*. Peter believed that more was more, and he'd bought many things she thought worthless. Fine! She loved organizing, sorting, labeling, *and* throwing out, everything from socks to flatware. She'd get rid of what wasn't worth saving, like the Elvis paperweight that had been mass-produced. Peter also couldn't grasp that the value of an item was related to its rarity. Hunter might be ashamed of how she'd treated him, but her shame didn't make him smarter.

She emptied one of the boxes that Peter had filled with random acquisitions, and labeled it TRASH. All the Elvis memorabilia went there; she'd try to find some worthy charity to give it to. Next were the snow globes and souvenir spoons that you could buy at any airport.

Zelda was right: she did have an eye for this. An eye and a passion.

When the time came to set the baseball cards aside for Peter, Hunter had an attack of scruples. She didn't know anything about baseball, but she knew that Peter had some cards that he thought might be valuable. His strategy was to buy the cards of players in the minor leagues, gambling that one or more of them would become superstars—or (and this was just as good) the subject of a scandal that got them banned from baseball entirely, thus making their likeness more collectible.

Peter kept them in sheets of plastic sleeves, which he'd put in a binder, but in no particular order. Hunter balanced the binder on her knees, and slid out the ten that she knew he had the highest hopes for. Hunter didn't trust Angelica not to lose, or to give, them away, and especially not to sell them if she were in financial trouble—and Angelica would always be in financial trouble.

She hid them, temporarily, in her room, between her mattress and box springs.

"Peter!"

When he came in, Angelica was trailing him, one finger tucked into his waistband, and giggling.

"I'm sorry," Hunter said sweetly, "I need help with the Margaret Keane." Though she didn't need help.

"The—" Angelica stopped. "Petey, you never told me—"

"I want you two to have it," Hunter said. She had dragged the painting out from behind the bookshelf. The girl and the cat with the cavernous eyes were in a cheap frame.

Angelica's own eyes grew big. With greed, Hunter thought, but she might well have been imagining—or even wishing—that. "We can leave it here, then." Angelica pointed to the wall. "Look, it'll be inspiration for my group. She was a Jehovah's Witness, you know. They're crazy, but they're my kind of crazy."

More research had convinced Hunter that the painting was a copy. She hadn't had the heart to tell Peter before (*so you see,* she told herself, *I could be nice to him sometimes*), and she wouldn't tell either him or Angelica now. Let Angelica think that she possessed the most valuable item, and that the rest was junk.

Angelica led Peter back to the great room, and Hunter returned to her task, while eavesdropping on Angelica cooing about Margaret Keane, what a good person she was, what obstacles she'd overcome.

The last items Hunter came to were the vintage Barbies. Peter didn't want to collect dolls. They were "girly." But Hunter had been a Barbie fanatic as a child, and he indulged her, though since he could be prone to snide remarks as well, she'd kept them out of sight, in a box in a corner. Many, she knew, were of more sentimental than monetary value: the costumed Marie Antoinette Barbie. The Lucrezia Borgia Barbie.

But then there was her prize: a doll that she believed was a Joan of Arc Barbie. It was out of the box, but in excellent condition, thanks to the bubble wrap she'd put around it.

Three weeks later, Hunter sold it on eBay for mid-five figures and her career—though sub-, rather than supersonic, and prey to ups and downs—was launched.

———

The next day at her Starbucks shift she overheard the C Caitlin and the K Katelyn talking about Angelica. Hunter looked for somewhere else to be, but skinny vanilla lattes don't make themselves.

"She's a recovering bulimic," Katelyn said. "I follow her on X."

"Oh, me, too!" Caitlin said. "I liked what she said about being of service to Hunter."

"Giving her a place to live! It's awesome."

Then one of them noticed Hunter and shushed the other.

Hunter pictured the steam coming out of her ears at the same time she was forcing it into the milk.

Chapter 16

The Placebo Effect

HUNTER

After overhearing this conversation, Hunter just had time to untie her apron and head home for the second meeting of Get Healthy.

The second meeting would have to be the last. She couldn't imagine the group carrying on with Peter and Angelica in residence. Happily, the Twin Terrors were away for the night, probably racking up more credit card debt at some new trendy restaurant, but by next week they'd be moved in. At least Peter, though he might study the wine list, wasn't going to spend $500 on Bordeaux, even though it had been a very good year.

The three women who'd taken a chance on her deserved an explanation, if they showed up again.

They did.

Penelope got dropped off by Reyna. Alicia brought her own bottled water, a brand called Montana Sky. Dannika was wearing a beret that still left the shaved side of her head exposed.

At the last minute Hunter had retrieved the talking stick. Hunter gathered them in the great room, where they were surrounded by the vast negative space that had once been filled by their many, Gatsby-like parties—and how perfect was her last name, "Fitzgerald"? Too bad she'd had to marry Peter to get it.

She'd rehearsed her opening. She was going to tell the three women that she wouldn't take their money after all.

She also wanted to tell them about her new venture in collectibles. It was a baby step in marketing. The secret to collectibles—maybe the very secret of life—was networking. Dannika lived in an old house, and her mother had been a bit of a hoarder, so who knew what "junk" might be stashed behind an old breakfront? The real treasures weren't to be found in an auction house: they were hidden in the basement.

And that was all she was going to talk about. Hunter was a private person. She didn't gossip about others, she'd never been to a shrink, she'd stopped going to confession in her teens, and she never told anyone about "a weird dream I had last night." She was hardly going to tell them about her recent memories.

"Things have changed since last week," she began. "Since just yesterday, actually, which is why I couldn't let you know before." She rapped the forked end of the stick against her palm.

Faint "mmm's?" rolled through the circle.

It was the third rap that did it.

Instead of continuing her prepared, semi-truthful speech about how she was going to "go in a different direction, focusing on pursuing her new business," she collapsed on the armchair.

And cried.

Hunter almost never cried. She hadn't cried when her mother's Alzheimer's diagnosis was made official. She hadn't cried the day that Peter left. But the story came pouring out: not only the nightmare on Mount Tam, but the memories evoked by the talking stick the week before.

The ensuing silence had the texture of creaking furniture, of the *sssshh* of rear ends shifting against fabric. The air itself seemed electrified, and the dust motes visible in a shaft of light from the window were specks of reproach.

"Whoa . . . your husband left you for your best friend?"

Her dignity lay around her like a bathrobe that had fallen off. She did her best to put it back on, finding first one sleeve, then the other. The three women waited with a mix of respect and embarrassment. "I wouldn't call her my best friend." Someone had handed her a tissue. "To say the least. We'd always had a . . . a fraught relationship." Damn! She shouldn't have put on mascara that morning.

Penelope pronounced judgment. *"Men."*

Hunter was exhausted from her own outburst. She didn't like sympathy, and she despised pity. Yet, in between sobs, she had told them about the memory that had returned unbidden, that it had triggered further memories, and that the unavoidable conclusion was that she was in part—maybe largely?—responsible for the failure of her marriage.

"This isn't how I planned . . . anything," she choked out. Now she only wanted to get rid of them. Never mind what vintage items they might have at home. "But we can't meet anymore, because we don't have a place to meet. Angelica and Peter are moving back in here. Well, Peter's moving back. Angelica's moving in."

The others fidgeted, avoiding eye contact with each other. What did she have to do to shoo them out? Hunter remembered the final words of the Latin mass, *Ite missa est.* "Go, ye are dismissed." Maybe, like saying "Beetlejuice" in the mirror three times, that would have the magic effect of making the three of them *disappear.*

And maybe it would have. Except that Penelope said, "I—I remembered something, too." She opened her clutch. In its maw they could see a prescription bottle without a label, nestling in the black satin lining, next to a compact, a lipstick, and a miniature spray bottle of cologne. "It's Valium," she said hoarsely. "All week I've been remembering things I've done to get hold of it. Sometimes even dangerous things." Her hands shook as she snapped the purse closed. "They make it so hard! Everyone's on their high horse about medication now—after they got us hooked on it!"

"I never prescribe anything like that," Alicia said.

Penelope told them the story of her first appointment with her husband and a now-deceased doctor. The need for increasing amounts. The increasing danger and desperation.

In the early days, Penelope pretended that she'd lost the bottle, or claimed that her housekeeper must have stolen it. But you could only pull that off so many times, and only switch doctors so often. So she struck up conversations with women at her country club, sending out innocent feelers. Guess what? There were women who had refills they weren't using, but everyone can use a little extra cash.

It still wasn't enough.

So then came the conversations with perfect strangers. Uber drivers. Baristas. She'd embarrassed—no, humiliated—herself more than once.

"And you forgot all this?" Hunter asked—intrigued, and also relieved to have someone else to focus on.

"Not exactly." Penelope rubbed the clasp of her purse with her thumb. "Do any of you remember Polaroids? The way the image would rise up in the square?"

"You can get Valium online," Dannika said, "or in Mexico."

"That is *not* helpful," Alicia said.

"Well, it was like that, sort of," Penelope said. "The memories coming back."

Dannika sighed. "I remembered something, too, I told you my mom died, and for a while I thought I really couldn't live without her, so . . ." She stopped. "So, I am hungry! Let's order pizza!"

"This is supposed to be 'get healthy,'" Penelope said.

"So get vegan freaking pizza." Dannika raised her hands in surrender. "You just said we weren't going to have this group. Let's have a two-meeting-only-going-away party."

Hunter did not overlook Dannika's, "I remembered something, too," but was distracted by the temptation of having one final celebration of a sort at Chardonnay Heights. Besides, she was no longer there in any guidance counselor role.

Alicia said she was hungry, too, hadn't Hunter thought about dinner when she scheduled the meeting for six? And Penelope agreed, since Reyna wouldn't be expecting to pick her up for a while anyway.

Then the discussion over toppings began. Penelope was allergic to shellfish, mushrooms, and olives. Dannika was a vegetarian. Alicia said that pizza wasn't pizza unless it had pepperoni.

Hunter solved the problem by finding a restaurant that would customize two halves each of two pizzas. "You can each choose exactly what you want." With a sigh, she added, "my treat." She'd have to dig deep for that, but she'd dragged them all out here with the promise of another meeting. She'd also hoped to collect money from them; she'd even set up a Venmo account for the purpose. But that was before.

———

"We should have gotten sodas," Penelope said.

They were sitting around Hunter's cherrywood table, eating with their hands, using paper towels instead of napkins.

"That stuff is so bad for you." Alicia detached a second slice of her pizza from her designated half. Hers was the one with the most toppings. "I didn't keep a food journal." She positioned the pizza slice perpendicular to her mouth on an invisible conveyor belt. "There are some things you're better off not knowing."

"But you do know what Angelica St. Ambrose would say," Dannika put in. "'Jesus warned me not to get on the scale.'" Dannika snorted. "My mom's friends talk about her memoir in group emails. I don't know what makes her think she has a pipeline to Jesus. Drives me fu- effing crazy."

"I think Summer likes her." Alicia paused between bites. "She's got a dieting app called Praise the Lord and Pass the Pasta." She reached for the garlic bread that someone (probably Alicia herself) had added to their order. "You know, it's funny, I remembered something, too."

"Just now?" Hunter brushed garlic breadcrumbs into her palm.

"No, last week." Alicia went on to describe, interrupting herself with the occasional short laugh, how she'd discovered she was pregnant, but didn't tell the young man who was the father. "And the funny part is that I always remembered it as him breaking up with me, not the other way around. That's what I told my parents, even."

"Did that pregnancy turn into the daughter you said ran away?" Penelope asked.

"Yeah."

"But." Dannika leaned forward. "He knows about her now."

"We didn't stay in touch."

Hunter participated in the collective gasp. "You never told him?"

Alicia swallowed before answering. "No."

They all pounced: Dannika, Penelope, and, after a beat, Hunter. "Tell him!"

Alicia drew herself up. "I told you, we didn't stay in touch. I didn't see the need. And now I don't even know anything about him."

Dannika said, "You can find anyone on the internet. You can find out how much he makes, for God's sake."

"I knew that," Alicia snapped.

"What does he do?" Penelope asked.

"How should I know? He was going to become a pediatrician."

Hunter didn't like to give advice, never had—not even when she thought she had her own life under control and considered herself a role model of self-possession and success. But she cleared her throat of mozzarella and forged on. "The way you describe your daughter—Summer, right?—she might benefit from knowing, um, the truth."

Alicia reminded them that she was the only one in this little group who was a parent, leaving unspoken, *mind your own business.*

A tense silence ensued.

"Maybe I'm not a parent," Dannika said, "but I'm the daughter of a single mom. My mother didn't know who my father was, but she was such an exceptional mom, it was like having two parents. Now that she's gone, though, I wish I had another one. Parent, I mean."

Hunter had to admit that Alicia had reason to be defensive about the none-too-subtle implication that she was not the mom that Dannika's "Mosi" was.

"I'll think about it." Alicia tossed her crust into one of the boxes, where a slice of Hunter's pizza remained. "It's been so many years."

There was something else on Hunter's mind. "I wonder . . . I mean, do you think it's possible . . . that holding on to this—I mean, that—" The talking stick would have made a decorative centerpiece, but Hunter had returned it to her room, where she displayed it on her nightstand. "That it has any effect on us?" She was thinking of the memory she'd had about Angelica, back in Zelda's trailer.

"What do you mean?" Penelope asked.

"Like . . ." Hunter raised her fist to mime holding the stick up. "Like everything we've talked about."

Alicia said, "Probably it has a psychological influence. We feel like we're supposed to open up. It's called the placebo effect."

"Gee, like I never heard of that," Dannika said. "Anyway, if we feel it, it's real. Everything's psychological anyway."

"The difference between real and placebo is that placebo is never permanent," Alicia explained. "Where'd you get that thing, anyway?" she asked Hunter.

"Treasure Island." She left it at that.

"It's real if we think it's real," Dannika insisted again.

"Yeah, but—"

"Let's put a pin in that debate." Hunter folded her hands. For a moment she'd thought, *we came together too randomly for it to be random.*

That was silly, but, "Why don't we keep meeting anyway? No more 'get healthy,' and no money involved. Just to see what happens."

She was too shy to add that she'd enjoyed having company for dinner. Not the usual crowd of managers and brokers and architects and consultants. Just women. No one drinking, either.

"What are we supposed to talk about?" Dannika asked.

Hunter shrugged. "Anything. I guess."

"Why not?" Dannika asked.

Alicia retrieved her pizza crust. "Maybe."

"Although, we can't meet here once my ex and his new lady friend . . . maybe it's not such a great idea."

"We can meet at my house," Penelope said. "Scott's never around. By the way, I'm going to pay for this." She waved her hand over the greasy box that she'd shared with Alicia. Then she caught Hunter's eye, and it might have been Hunter's imagination, but she read in Penelope's glance, *I want to do something nice for you.*

Alicia finally pushed her plate away. "Then whatever we talk about stays private." She raised her right hand. "Sacred oath."

"We have to let Reyna in on it," Penelope said. "Especially if we're meeting at my place."

"Only her, then," Alicia said. "Otherwise I won't feel free to speak."

"And it is important that we feel free to speak," Dannika agreed.

Hunter rose to do what she did best: clean up. "No, stay there," she said when the others moved to help.

Alicia folded her arms over her chest. "There's something about an empty table that says 'go home.'" But she was smiling.

"When are we meeting again?" Penelope reached for her purse, which was hanging on the back of her chair. "I'll give you my address. Hunter, do you have something I can write on?"

"Yeah, just a sec." She was folding the cardboard boxes to recycle. "But by the way, especially don't tell anyone what I said about the talking stick. People will think we're crazy."

Chapter 17

Harder Than It Looks

PENELOPE

The women of Hunter's group were the first people to whom Penelope had ever admitted that she was addicted to Valium. No, they counted as the second, third, and fourth persons. The first person had been herself.

Before they disbanded for the night, Dannika had asked, "what about rehab?"—which prompted Alicia to declare, "Rehab is a multibillion-dollar industry that won't publish their results." She continued in this vein for a while: If their 98 percent success rate was based on who was clean at the end of their stay, it was meaningless. And if addiction was a disease, as everyone seemed to agree it was now, then why were the doctors on staff so rarely board-certified in addiction treatment?

When the others pressed her, she backed off a little, mumbling disclaimers about how it wasn't her specialty of medicine and how it was still probably the best alternative, if Penelope did her research.

But Penelope didn't want to go to rehab. She knew women who'd been in and out four times, and who were still getting soused by the pool. She also didn't want to involve Scott. Oh, boy, did she not want to involve Scott. He'd pay for it, sure, then make *her* pay for it.

"A twelve-step group, at least," Dannika said.

Penelope shook her head. "I want you ladies to help me. I think I can taper off on my own."

Alicia said that was feasible, but insisted, "This doesn't count as medical advice."

But it was one thing to admit she was an addict. Another thing to remember.

Even the next morning, since she woke up at 10:00 a.m., which was earlier than usual, Penelope's first thought was, *Valium is something I need and nothing I can't handle.*

Then she remembered her dwindling supply, and how carefully she would have to ration before her next refill, unless she wanted to seek out Tennis Club Trish sooner than usual.

So she hoisted herself out of bed and went to see Reyna, already at the stove, cooking something for lunch that smelled of tomatoes and olives. Reyna had abandoned her uniform, at Penelope's request, and she was in a peasant blouse and jeans that were snug across her derriere.

"Morning." Reyna turned to pour water from the kettle into a teapot. She didn't use tea bags.

Penelope was grateful that the women had made Reyna an exception to their confidentiality agreement. Penelope wanted to get free, but she needed Reyna's help.

She inhaled deeply. Then she told Reyna the whole story, starting from the first appointment with Dr. Schmulewitz.

"Oh, Penelope." Reyna stirred sugar into her own tea, and for once her big smile was missing. "Do you think I didn't know you were abusing it?"

That made Reyna the fifth person to know.

"Why didn't you say anything?"

"It was none of my business."

"Will you help me, then?"

Reyna shook her head. "What about rehab?"

"They're just revolving doors." Either Hunter or Dannika— Penelope couldn't remember which one—had summed up Alicia's skepticism about the industry with that image, which Penelope liked. It made her think of old hotels and department stores.

Reyna half-heartedly pushed the idea a little longer. She knew people whom various programs had helped. But in the end she didn't disagree. She had many friends in the health-care profession, including some who worked in rehab facilities. "It's like, they hear people say, 'I can't sit in this circle of chairs again.' Besides," she concluded, tapping her spoon against the edge of her cup, "I don't see you petting horses."

Equine therapy was very big in the rehab world.

"So, all right, let's see how it goes." And no, she didn't need to discuss this with Scott.

Reyna believed in the laws that were dictated by your heart, not printed by the men in power.

————

"You can trust me to follow the plan."

"No, I can't," Reyna said, but her big smile softened her words.

Penelope still hesitated, but when she handed over her two bottles (she separated the five-milligram yellows from the ten-milligram blues) she felt liberated.

The first two days were easy. She was awake and alert in a way she couldn't remember being in years.

The third day was tougher. "I feel so anxious."

"We're going very, very slowly," Reyna said. "Ten percent a week."

"It's not *having* them. Maybe I should keep some."

"If you really want," Reyna said, but she sounded so disappointed that Penelope said, no, she'd be fine. Penelope did not like confrontations and fighting. She couldn't shake her mother's many admonitions against "behaving like a badger."

The next morning, she told Reyna that she hadn't been able to sleep.

Reyna pursed her lips. She had a lovely mouth, with full lips. Penelope had always hated her own thin lips: It was almost pointless to put on lipstick, though she did. "Penelope, I think it's psychological? Because, really, we're reducing it so slowly."

"I might have been mistaken about exactly how much I was taking. You might have cut me down by more than ten percent."

What was the rush with all of this? She'd admitted she had a problem. Supposedly that was "half the battle." Couldn't she get some credit for half the battle and do the other half later?

Yes, she'd had to hustle. Yes, she had to humiliate herself with Tennis Club Trish, who liked to play games with her: "I thought I could pick up my prescription today, but it'll be next week." But still, she didn't have to quit *now*.

Reyna went out that night. That was only fair. She wasn't an indentured servant. Living in was pressure enough, though Scott must be paying her accordingly. (Penelope would never ask how much. She didn't want to know.) Reyna had a right to her secrets. It was strange, though, that Reyna told Penelope so much about her family—her three much-older brothers and her aging mother, in long, detailed, and highly amusing stories that revealed her affection for all—but nothing about her current, if inevitably limited, private life.

Maybe it was only the movies. Alone.

Penelope stayed in her own room, watching TV. When she was growing up there were three channels to watch—four, if you counted the educational one, which her father said was run by Commies, so she wasn't allowed to watch it (not that she wanted to). Now there were more than she could keep track of, literally hundreds, and there was still nothing on. She landed on something

called *Trial by Marriage* that matched couples with a giant spinning wheel then followed them through an-all-expenses-paid visit
to a romantic destination in Greece. "Our cameras have once-in-
a-lifetime access to what goes on behind the scenes at a honey-
moon!" the narrator boasted, and Penelope thought that the Arabs
who perceived America as decadent beyond redemption were on
to something.

Penelope needed another pill. That was all there was to it.
Reyna was making her go too fast. Her chest had tightened.
It wasn't a heart attack; her recent echocardiogram, to which
Reyna had accompanied her, was normal, and Reyna had more
or less convinced Penelope that her chest pains were the result
of anxiety.

But what about that prickly sensation? Like ants marching up
her arm?

When would Reyna be home? Did she even think of it as home?
Never mind that. As soon as she did come home . . . Penelope paid
attention to when Reyna came in. She would lie awake and listen
for the rumbling of the garage door. It was always after midnight,
sometimes after 1:00 a.m.

She could not wait that long. She tiptoed to Reyna's room. Scott
was out for the night; she didn't care where anymore. She tapped on
Reyna's door, just in case Reyna had come in and Penelope hadn't
heard her. That was silly, of course. She tapped more firmly, and
then knocked.

When Reyna didn't answer, she opened the door.

Reyna's laptop was open on her desk. Streaks of colored light
dashed across the screen. Penelope knew that touching any key
would reveal what Reyna had been looking at, but she wasn't here
to snoop. She only wanted to take one yellow pill, to remove the
crawling sensation, then she'd go back to bed. Besides, Reyna was
still her employee.

The room held only traces of its former life: indentations in the carpet led to the stationary bike, dragged out of the way, and in one corner there was a closet that afforded space for a set of adjustable barbells, weightlifting gloves, and grips. The furniture was motel-issue, pieces that Scott had purchased on short notice, but Reyna had brightened it with hyacinths in a vase, and a few black and white photos.

If the pills were in plain sight, Penelope would take one and leave. Or maybe the whole bottle. They were hers, after all.

But the pills were nowhere on the surfaces of Reyna's room. *She knew I'd be here*, Penelope thought.

That made her angry. Who was Reyna to control her?

Penelope opened the top drawer. Here there was lingerie: She saw lacy thong underwear in one corner and cringed with embarrassment. Obviously, Reyna did have a boyfriend in the city. At least, Penelope hoped it was a boyfriend in the city, and it wasn't that she was sleeping around.

She forgot about Reyna's sex life when she dug deeper into the pile and didn't find what she needed, not under the cups of brassieres, nor tucked into the folds of tights.

In the drawer below were folded sweaters. Below that, jeans, and one pair of black silk pants. Penelope lifted everything up one by one, neatly. At first. Then, as she excavated additional layers and still found nothing, she became less careful, and even, at the end, tossed two pairs of jeans over her shoulder, onto the bed behind her. If she could find *just one pill* she'd have no trouble putting them back.

When she'd emptied the drawers, she sat on the bed to rest. She was shaking from frustration and Valium withdrawal—Reyna would take pity on her if she saw her now. She took a deep breath, and gazed at the photos on top of the dresser. One was of a middle-aged woman who must be Reyna's mother. The other photo was of a younger woman. A sister? No, Reyna didn't have any sisters. A cousin? Penelope couldn't see if there was a resemblance. She held the picture up, holding it by its frame so as not to leave fingerprints, and looked closely. The woman was white, Penelope thought.

The closet. Reyna's old uniforms hung there, as well as a few rather short dresses. There was a bankers box on the closet floor. Penelope lifted the lid but found only old plastic containers with costume jewelry and nail polish.

The bathroom!

Things were in slightly more disarray there: lots of tubes and jars on the counter, though all neatly capped. A smear of something red, probably lipstick, on the tile. What did Reyna need makeup for? Her skin was flawless, a smooth light caramel without ridge or pores.

The medicine cabinet! Maybe Reyna took some kind of medication. So many people did. And then, when Reyna knew that Penelope knew about that, Reyna would have to be less judgmental.

But the only drug there was Midol.

Here, too, there were drawers, and Penelope rifled through them, thinking that this must be where Reyna would have hidden them, in the last place that Penelope would look, but Penelope was smarter than that!

She heard something. Scott coming home? She froze, holding a jar of moisturizer midair. The clothes strewn on the bed!

The sound did not recur. Penelope figured that she was safe a little while longer, but she rushed back to Reyna's room, and reloaded underwear and jeans as quickly as she could, and told herself that they did not look as though they'd been disturbed.

One of the drawers wouldn't close all the way. Penelope shoved and wiggled, wiggled and shoved, trying to get the runners back on the tracks, but the drawer kept bumping against something. Penelope pulled out the drawer immediately beneath it, and confirmed her suspicion that she'd caused something—it was an unopened package of pantyhose—to stick up, and block the closing of the drawer above.

Penelope reached for the package, squeezing her arm into the space between the drawers. The tip of her middle finger touched the cardboard, but she couldn't grip the sides. She stretched a little farther. No. Not quite.

She pulled her arm back out. Or tried. Her elbow wouldn't go over the lip of the drawer. She pulled again, scratching her skin against the wood.

Her arm was stuck.

That was when Reyna came in.

Chapter 18

It's Been a Long Time

ALICIA

Since the new school hadn't done the trick, Alicia was officially out of ideas.

Meanwhile, Summer came home daily only to disappear behind *The Hunger Games* poster on the door of her room and blast the easy listening station; it was the same music they played at Alicia's office. She would have preferred hip-hop: rappers had a right to be angry.

One evening, she pressed her ear up to the door and overheard Summer talking to KC, her friend from Redwood High. ". . . then she said, 'Cher called. She wants her hair back.'"

A pneumatic tube sucked Alicia back to her own high school days, when everyone had the Rachel, but Alicia's hair was too thick and wavy.

"Who's Cher anyway? She thinks she's a riot." Summer tried, failed, to laugh it off. "'Then she said, 'It's called Head and Shoulders. Look into it.'"

Alicia threw open the door.

"Mom! I need my privacy!"

"Hang up that phone and talk to me!"

More shouting. Tears.

When the volume went down and the sobbing stopped, Summer told her about the girls who lay in wait in the halls, and sometimes followed her to her next class, the better to taunt her.

They told her she was cross-eyed. "From looking at your nose too much."

"You are not!" Was she? Summer had big hazel eyes. No, they looked fine to Alicia. Mournful, perhaps, but straight.

"And, 'Old Navy called. They want their clearance table back.'"

Nothing new under the sun. Only the names had been updated.

What, should she have Summer change schools again?

What if the fault wasn't in the schools?

———

Alicia called the principal of Summer's new school and demanded a team meeting with him and all of Summer's teachers. Supposedly they had zero tolerance for bullying, didn't they?

The principal ventured that any school was challenging for a new student at this age, especially one who joined midyear; one teacher suggested that Summer have a party and invite the girls who excluded her; another ventured that Summer could "send out more confident vibes."

Alicia threatened a lawsuit.

The meeting was private, but in the days of social media, the concept was obsolete. Someone—Alicia would never know who— must have said something to someone, who posted something to somewhere, and it was all over the school in two days.

Which was when Hurricane Summer made landfall. She was now the daughter of the crazy bitch doctor. Couldn't Alicia have left bad enough alone? The girls still lay in wait, only now they had a new song to croon: *someone needed her Mommy to scare us. Ooooh, we're so scared.*

I was trying to help, Alicia said, but Summer slammed the door to her room, and didn't speak to Alicia until two days later, when she needed a ride to the mall.

———

That night, Alicia was at her computer, obediently typing her weekly email to her parents, when she remembered how the other women had insisted that she contact Joshua Goodman.

She had no intention of doing so. What could it bring into their lives except more tsuris?

Tap, tap, tap. *IT WAS A GOOD WEEK.*

Liar. But the Liebermans didn't need to know more.

Alicia caught herself staring at the takeout menus by the phone. Blue Barn. Amici's East Coast Pizza. Uncle Wing's. The menus had been made obsolete by Uber Eats, but she'd never gotten around to taking them down.

Joshua wouldn't want to hear from her after all these years. He must be married and have a family of his own. She pictured three children: two boys and a girl.

But it was like a pebble in her shoe, the curiosity. Here she hadn't thought of him in years, but now, no matter how she tried to get back to the email, her finger kept opening up Google. And she *was* curious.

Dannika was right: he was easy to find on the internet.

He had become a pediatrician, which she thought spoke well for him, and, like her, was part of a large practice, only in the Boston area. The practice's website had individual profiles of each doctor, and his picture showed him having aged only a little, with the line of his curly black hair having barely receded, and a nose you had to call "prominent," yet one that fit his face.

She saw the resemblance.

Joshua listed his interests as gardening, cooking, and travel. And while all the other doctors had mentioned family, his did not.

No, Alicia, he hasn't been waiting for you. Still, she had that creepy, otherworldly feeling that the others spoke of, and which she always wanted to shake off, that somehow this was meant to be.

There was a contact button, but that would be visible to the office staff, so instead she went to LinkedIn, where she also found him easily, since she now knew that he lived in the Boston area (and of course there was the "MD" after his name). He had a different picture there, and she wondered how recent the photo was. The one she used online was ten years old.

She spent an hour watching YouTube videos about the Civil War. Then she sent him a message.

```
Hi, Remember me?
```

Like a drug addict in the making, she told herself she could stop anytime she wanted. Let him respond that he was busy planning his triplets' birthday party, and did she know any magicians for hire?

He didn't reply.

Just as well! She could tell the others that she tried, and he never got back to her, and they could stop with the noodging.

But the next day,

```
I didn't expect to hear from you.
It's best that we don't keep
in touch.
```

He was right.

But he had responded. If he really didn't want to her from her, he would have ignored her, and possibly blocked her.

Pebble in her shoe again.

He has a right to know, they had said.

He'd think she was asking him for child support. Or maybe that she was a Nigerian prince.

She put her head down on her keyboard, setting off a frenzy of Ys and Ts.

Several YouTube videos later, she composed a message, in which she invented a story about having discovered that she was pregnant after she broke up with him.

She deleted that. She couldn't start off with yet another lie, even if the first "lie" had been one of omission.

She composed a new letter, in which she apologized to the point of groveling, but then proceeded to document the challenges of being a single mother, concluding, "I think I've suffered enough."

She deleted it all.

She wrote three more that she deleted.

Finally, she typed,

```
You have a daughter. Her name
is Summer.
```

She clicked "send."

Then spent the next half hour frantically searching for an "unsend" button.

```
If this is a scam to get my bank
account #, it's not going to work.
```

No turning back now. She wrote back with more details, describing the cafeteria. She omitted the smell of tuna.

Joshua:

```
How could you do this?
```

She wrote an email defending herself, then deleted that email and typed,

```
I was afraid of being hurt. I wanted
a child of my own. I didn't want to
share it.
```

"It" was an angry her, a her who needed help that Alicia couldn't give. How was it that when she was in the delivery room with an almost-mother screaming her lungs out, or counseling a teenager about STDs, she could be patient, understanding, compassionate—but everything her daughter said got on her nerves?

```
What's she like?
```

Alicia described Summer. She set out to be honest, to tell him that Summer was not the popular honor student and all-round athlete of what must already be his fantasies.

Yet when she read what she had written, she saw that she'd described a lonely girl who needed support. And love. In the writing, she'd realized that Summer had an inner life that she, Alicia, had never penetrated. *Summer has strengths she hasn't shown you,* the school psychologist had said.

She didn't send a picture. A picture might rope him in, but if instead he gave Alicia any sense that he was rejecting Summer based on her appearance, she would never forgive herself for setting Summer up that way, even though Summer would never know.

She didn't hear back. She went about the necessaries of the day, from showering to conducting Pap smears and dodging the laser beams of Summer's disapproval. Periodically she had heart palpitations.

The next day he replied.

```
Can I meet her?
```

Chapter 19

Read Him Like a Book

DANNIKA

Dannika was familiar with Rafe's schedule at Safeway. He worked late afternoon through closing so he could practice his drums during the day without disturbing the neighbors who were nine-to-fivers, the ones who were "wage slaves," as he called them.

She could see him more often by buying fewer items at a time, though more than once the person behind her groused, "Why don't you go through the express lane?"

Bitchiness crossed all demographics: sometimes it was an old woman, sometimes a young man. She ignored them all, and even though Rafe teased her about her one- and two-item purchases, he said that he liked seeing her. Altogether, these one-minute encounters gave her a lot of information about him: she just had to ask the right question.

Finally, one night, she was in the parking lot when he came out. Okay, so she'd been in the parking lot at the end of his shift before, but this was the night that her timing was right. He was in short sleeves, in spite of the cold, and she could see how muscular his arms were; arms that could hold a woman tightly.

"Walk with me," he said and she had the *whoop* feeling of going down an expected hill. Had he seen her waiting? Had he timed his exit?

"Shannon's out of town," he said.

Shannon was his roommate, and only a friend, but she supposed that he had a small place, and that they'd have more privacy with his roommate gone.

He didn't say, but she knew that she was walking him home. "How're the bands?"

Paying for Cocoa Puffs and cat food took long enough that over the course of their interactions she had learned that he was a drummer in two bands, Top Hats and Rabbit's Foot. One was serious, the other more for fun.

That was the right thing to ask. He talked most of the rest of the way about their various gigs and the trouble they had with this one dude, and should they kick him out or not? And the more expensive drum set, when would he save up enough for that?

His street was unlit; they could see a few stars. Rafe said the stars made him feel so small.

That's just how I feel, she thought, and shivered.

"And no matter how much music I make, how will it impact people? How can I reach people? How many musicians are going to be as well-known as Tico Torres?"

"You can make it," she said, to hide the fact that she didn't know who Tico Torres was.

He took her hand and kissed it.

She knew that Rafe was attracted to her. So it was just a matter of time before he wasn't too afraid of his feelings to express them.

They reached a dirt alley that led to another structure, this one two stories, with a wooden balcony.

Inside, she saw the set of drums first. They were bigger than she
expected, and she only recognized the cymbals.

"These are my true loves," Rafe said, caressing the head of one.

He made music. When she listened to music it stirred something deep inside her but beyond her, too. It was a little like that
feeling about God, how she was more than just a random creature
that evolved from an amoeba.

"Can you give me a lesson?" She approached the drums with the
idea of sitting at the little seat there, but he grabbed her shoulder.
"No one touches the drums but me."

"Oh! Of course not." She should have known better. Shannon
didn't support his pursuit of music, but she would.

Then Rafe threw his arm around her from behind, and kissed her
wetly. "I couldn't wait any longer."

They made love on a rag rug. Dannika hadn't had sex since Mosi
died. She'd forgotten what it was like. Wasn't it supposed to feel . . .
special? What *was* it like when she was in high school, and then right
after? She'd had boyfriends, but not like some girls, like Emma, who
was madly in love with someone new every two months.

It was over.

"Sorry about that." Rafe rolled on his back, and drew his arm
across his forehead. "It's been a while."

Been a while. That confirmed that he and Shannon were
just roommates.

Rafe produced a half-smoked joint, lit up, inhaled. He offered
it to her silently, while he held on to what he'd sucked into
his lungs.

She took a drag, held it in. Dannika had respected Mosi's antidrug stance, so much so that she declined all offers of marijuana
throughout high school. No small accomplishment, that. It was only
in her final months that Mosi had acquiesced to cannabis.

Sometime during those hideous final months (they dragged on
until Dannika wasn't sure if it was better to keep hoping for a miracle

or to get the worst over with) Dannika's desperation to check out of Hotel Reality became greater than her desire to follow Mosi's rule.

That was how Dannika had discovered weed. But she had a lifetime of Mosi's dire warnings against the evils of drugs every time she lit up, so it wasn't often.

After a couple more hits shared in silence, Dannika became enchanted with the design of the rag rug, its intricate red, white, and blue twists. She could see the variations in shade among the white pieces . . . now the red pieces . . . cardinal and garnet and ruby . . . "It's handmade," she said.

"Yeah. Shannon made it." *Sssssss*. He inhaled.

Now she envied Shannon. Dannika wanted to make things like this. Instead of throwing old clothes away you could make something beautiful with them, colors intertwining, merging, making something new . . .

. . . She thought of Catherine Earnshaw, how Edgar couldn't see what a brat she was, but Heathcliff knew her and loved her for what she was. . . . If Heathcliff had had love he would have been okay . . .

The drums looked bigger than before. She thought about the sound of drums in music, how people tapped their feet while they listened, and how the tapping matched the drummer's beat, and that was very interesting, because she'd never thought about it before.

"I gotta crash," Rafe said. "Weed makes me so sleepy."

She waited a few seconds for him to ask her to stay, and then she walked home in the dark.

————

The next morning when she heard a knock on her door, she thought it might be Rafe.

It was Howie. She did remember giving him her address, but she couldn't remember why. A good reason not to smoke weed.

She only let him in because he was carrying a box full of books that had him stooped over, just like her mother used to be over her worktable.

Five minutes later she was regretting her charity.

He was holding 50 *Successful Ivy League College Application Essays* in his lap. Raskolnikov lay in hers, his orange tabby side rising and falling with his breaths.

Howie was severely allergic to cats. That little fact had become apparent within minutes: his eyes were red, swollen, and watery. She'd brought out a box of Kleenex from which he made frequent withdrawals. "I love cats," he lied (she guessed) apologetically, "but they don't love me." Pointing at Raskolnikov, but withdrawing his finger quickly, he asked, "What's her name?"

"It's a 'he.' Rodion Romanovich Raskolnikov."

"From *Crime and Punishment?*"

She wanted to hide her surprise. "Yeah." Maybe he'd seen a PBS adaptation. "You like Dostoyevsky?"

"Yeah. I like him better than Tolstoy, even. He's more like . . . raw."

She remembered now that he'd said he was an English major. "So you read Russian novels in college, too?"

"No, on my own. I like to read." He blew his nose.

Anyone with the slightest allergy to cats would have a tough time here. Dannika liked her little Prairie-style house, with its old furniture and loose doorknobs. It smelled like her mother. But sitting with Howard, she was self-conscious about the cat hair, which was almost a second layer of upholstery. Simply stroking Razzy's back raised a new flurry.

She was tempted to apologize for it, but that would be disloyal to her mother.

And there was *Crime and Punishment* to talk about! And *The Brothers Karamazov*, which it turned out he had also read—twice!

Once they started talking about the Russian novels, they had to debate translations. Howie was a Constance Garnet purest. Dannika was firm that the new translations by Volokhonsky and Pevear were the best.

Like her, Howie disdained e-books. Like her, he went to the library and checked out books. "Cheaper that way."

Then somehow they got on to Dickens. "My favorite is *Nicholas Nickleby*," she said.

"Mine, too!" It was a girly squeal.

"Okay, favorite books by anyone." She wondered if their lists would continue to overlap.

"*Notes from Underground*."

She was embarrassed; that was a Dostoyevsky novella that she hadn't read. "Mine is *1984*." That was where she got the expression "doubleplusungood."

He shook his head. "I haven't read that one."

"Oh my God, you should! With all the government surveillance going on?"

"I'll read yours if you read mine."

He grinned as if he'd said something very clever, and for a moment she was annoyed. But that passed and she agreed. She was dying to have someone read *1984* for the first time, so she could perhaps confide in them how much she identified with Winston, for how he had to watch everything he said every second. Here she was living in the freest society in the world, in history, and she felt the same way.

Then she knew that she would never tell him. Someday maybe she'd be able to tell Rafe, because he was an artist, and he would understand. Should she go back to Safeway that night? Rafe hadn't said how long Shannon would be out of town. She could invite him back here. That was a good reason to do what she could to clean up some cat hair and maybe spray some air freshener.

Raskolnikov rose from her lap, body part by body part, doing his feline yoga thing, starting with his butt, and ending with his forelegs stretching to maximum capacity. He left a thick layer of orange hair against the black of her leggings.

"Yeah, okay." She made a futile sweep of the hair with her fingertips. "I can't work on essays today."

"No? Okay."

She had popped the balloon that had been their conversation. It drifted down between them. Yes, she wanted to discuss *1984* with someone, but she had inadvertently committed herself to more time with Howie. Maybe he was actually interesting, underneath the desperate attempts at humor. But she didn't *want* to find out that he was interesting.

"I can come back." Howie started gathering up his books. It was a slow process.

"Maybe try putting the smaller ones on top of the pile."

"Oh, sure." *Thump.* "Sure."

She rose to help him.

"I have a copy of *Notes from Underground*. I'll bring it over."

She couldn't think of a reason to tell him not to.

"And I'll get *1984* at the library."

Doubleplusungood.

Since he was carrying the stack of books, she opened the door for him.

Chapter 20

Moving Day

HUNTER

Angelica scheduled her move-in to coincide with Hunter's day off. "You can help us, right? You're not Kim Kardashian."

Maybe Kim Kardashian can help you move. But then Hunter decided that it wasn't such a bad idea: If she were at the house she could make sure that neither Angelica, nor any of her team, pocketed any of the smaller objets d'art that she'd had begun collecting. She had high hopes for some of her souvenir ashtrays, especially one from the hungry i, the fabled North Beach club.

She was spraying 409 in the bathroom when she heard the engine coming up her drive. It growled, whined, snorted, and then calmed.

Doors opened. Doors slammed.

Hunter went outside, wiping her hands on a cleaning rag. A U-Haul truck had made it most of the way up the driveway, but one of the rear wheels had fallen over the edge. Angelica stood in front of the cab, arms akimbo. A heavyset, unshaven man stood next to her.

Another heavyset, unshaven man got out of the driver's side, and immediately stumbled into the bushes.

"God has a weird sense of humor," Angelica said, loudly enough that Hunter feared the wrath of her neighbors.

"Where's Peter?"

"He's in Santa Rosa, at a meeting. Ferdinand! C'mon, man! Hunter, this is making me edgy. Take some of these boxes in."

The rear door of the U-Haul was rolled up, and several boxes were close to the edge.

"Got anything lighter than this?" Hunter asked, after she dragged one off the truck bed, but felt it slip from her hands onto the driveway.

"I thought you were in such good shape," Angelica shouted, without turning around. She was busy with her helpers: both #servingothers and #AngelicaServingOthers were trending on X.

A panicky feeling began to overtake Hunter. Was this anything like what Penelope described when she craved Valium? She'd psyched herself up as much as possible: *Be nice. Just until you can get the hell out of here.* She'd asked Preston for extra shifts, and made it clear that she was available for overtime at a moment's notice, the better to earn more money faster. There were only so many Joan of Arc Barbies in the world.

She put her shoulders back, determined to get through this day with a smile.

Fuck that.

As soon as Angelica was distracted with supervising her underlings (two men she described as "having some trouble with the seventh step, so keep a little distance") Hunter scurried around the house, and into the backyard.

Without Vicente, her former gardener, the backyard was a dangerous place, the setting for a horror movie, where the plants were not only poisonous but sentient, and able to premeditate murder. The acacias, so demure a short time ago, had already sprouted limbs like tentacles, while weeds pushed ugly, ragged leaves in the grass, and bees clustered around the bottlebrush.

She could still hear Angelica shouting.

There was a prefab toolshed in the corner of the back yard. It had been Vicente's domain, and he had crammed more inside than there was room for, including two bicycles she didn't recognize. Since she'd last been here, a few spiders had homesteaded. The cobwebs spoke of other, abandoned dwellings.

She heard voices raised from inside the house, then the clatter and thump of furniture. Her stomach clenched. Any moment, one of Angelica's henchmen would be coming in with one of those boxes from the U-Haul mounted on his bulging trapezius. He and his equally muscular partner would be making skid marks on her carefully polished floors and nicking paint off the molding.

It's not your house anymore.

Hunter had managed to close the shed door behind herself, and rest her bottom, if precariously, on the lower rung of a ladder propped against the wall, when her phone rang.

She didn't recognize the number. These days she never answered an unknown number, and not just because of robocalls. She'd had a couple of voicemails of women angry at her, "for how you betrayed Angelica's trust!" She would block those callers, even while knowing that it was an empty gesture, since it left some tens of millions still unblocked, both solicitors and enemies.

She let this one go to voicemail. Then, a minute later, she reached around the handle of a rake to listen.

"You don't know me . . . heh-heh . . . but this isn't an offer for an extended car warranty . . ."

A hesitant voice, stumbling on a couple of words. She was surprised the voicemail hadn't cut him off during one of his pauses.

"Stan Butler says he mentioned me to you. Uh . . . uh . . . can you call me?"

She did.

———

She'd forgotten about Will DeWitt, Stanley Butler's colleague who was also "all het up" about *Jesus Warned Me*. "Something about a lie that Angelica had told about one of his relatives," was what Stanley had said, and "maybe you'd like to talk to him." Once she remembered, though, she also remembered that "he was a quirky guy who lived on a houseboat."

Will asked her to meet him at a café in Sausalito. She might have demurred, except that (1) this was a good excuse to get out of the way now (she'd already parked her car at the bottom of the driveway, as per Angelica's instructions), and (2) she wanted to talk to someone who had anything negative to say about Angelica.

As an afterthought she asked, "How will I know you?"

"I'll be the only man in a suit."

———

It was an outdoor restaurant on Bridgeway. He was indeed the only man in a suit, which was all the more obvious since he was standing behind a chair at a table for two.

Her first, unkind thought was that he wasn't very attractive. He had a shaved head, and a closely trimmed beard. Bald wasn't a good look on anyone, no matter how much PR there was to the contrary, and a man with big ears and heavy eyebrows should do anything he could short of homicide to prevent it. But it wasn't a date.

When she approached, he pulled the chair back for her, then took the other seat.

"Thanks for meeting me." He dragged his own chair closer. "I chose the most public place I could think of. May I buy you lunch?"

"I guess." It was sunny, but a little windy for outdoor eating. She was dressed for running, in jogging pants and tank top, but she'd put a sweatshirt on. From her seat she had a view of the Bay, a cadet blue decorated with the white triangles of sailboats. There were shrieking seagulls, the steady rumble of conversations, and a whiff of cooking oils from the restaurant, mingling with the tang of saltwater.

All good. She'd sit at the bottom of a compost bin to get out of that house, even if she was a little worried about her ashtrays and a Bakelite letter opener.

They both ordered salads. Hunter unfolded her napkin. It blew away.

There followed a few minutes of uncomfortable small talk: He was a Marin native. Did she know that Sausalito had the largest community of houseboat dwellers in the county? He took the ferry to and from work: the San Francisco Ferry Building was just a block from his office.

Finally he explained that another lawyer at Stanley Butler's firm had pressed a hardcover copy of *Jesus Warned Me* on Will. This lawyer was now a huge fan of Angelica's ("she's so wise and funny and true!"), and she knew that Will had grown up in Lagunitas, as had Angelica. Will skimmed the book until he saw "Lagunitas," then went back to the beginning and read the whole memoir.

"Now I have to ask you a favor." Will looked around at the neighboring tables: they were all full. "You can call me paranoid, or cautious, but I want to go somewhere more private."

"What did you have in mind?"

"My houseboat."

"Oh, sure." She rolled her eyes. "I'm not getting on a boat with a strange man."

"There are things I don't want to say in a public place." He smiled wryly. "And if I tell you what they are, that defeats the purpose, doesn't it?" After casting sidelong glances at the surrounding diners, he leaned forward, tucking his tie under the edge of the table to keep it from dropping onto his plate. Then he whispered, "I need your help exposing Angelica St. Ambrose."

"I'm listening."

"So call Stan. He'll vouch for me."

She had Stanley Butler's work phone in her contacts. He promised her that she was safe with Will. "He might even be a virgin, but don't tell him I said that."

When she still hesitated, Will took a business card out from the inside pocket of his suit coat, and wrote something on the back. "This is the slip number of my boat. Call a friend and tell her where you'll be."

She called first Dannika, then Penelope, and then left a voicemail for Alicia, asking each one to check on her. This way at least one of them would.

These felt like reasonable precautions. She let Will pay the check and they walked down Bridgeway to the Sausalito Yacht Harbor.

When Hunter thought of houseboats, she thought of houses, and she was surprised that Will's floating residence gave no sign of being anything other than a boat. It looked more for an afternoon on the Bay than anything one would live on. "Yep, this is mine." There was pride in his voice. "*The 25th Mile.*"

She remembered thinking, when she was on her way to Larkspur Dock with her fliers, that she was at the twenty-fifth mile of the marathon. "That's when you don't quit," she said.

He nodded. "That's right. You get it." He leapt aboard, then held out his hand. There was hair on his knuckles. *Don't be so judgmental.* She hesitated one more moment, but then she took it, and he surprised her with his strength, as she found herself leaping over the gap.

The boat was definitely lived in. Rather dark inside, and with shabby furnishings, but she was reassured by the faint odor of cleaning supplies. The seagulls were louder, though, emitting caws like whoops of laughter.

It was also definitely worked in: on a table between two banquettes, there was a book upside down and splayed open, next to a laptop. Papers were fanned out, but secured by a model cable car that functioned as a paperweight. These days she examined every object with an eye to its value. There was nothing here to buy or sell.

"Please sit." Will indicated camel-colored cushions built into the hull so as to create a semicircular sofa. "Sorry for the mess." He rapidly gathered the papers and stacked them.

"Why do you live on a boat?"

"It simplifies life." He took his suit jacket off, and she thought, *okay, here we go*, but he hung it in a closet, opening the door just long enough for her to see a row of nearly identical suits, ranging from dark gray to charcoal to black. "I don't want to get weighed down by things. If you put too many things on a boat, it sinks." He smiled a little, "That's Science 101, courtesy of Will DeWitt. May I offer you some water?"

"What about winter?"

"What about it?"

"It rains. . . . We have storms . . ."

He shrugged.

She wanted to ask, What was the plumbing like? What was it like to take a shower? *Could* you take a shower? Whatever the answers, she would hold off using the bathroom until back on land.

Will bent over a small refrigerator. When he stood, he had a bottle of Montana Sky in his hand. "That's my new favorite brand! The water at the café was a little . . ."

"Fishy?" He handed her the bottle, then sat, as far away as the curved couch would allow.

"Yes, fishy." She uncapped the bottle. "Speaking of fishy, tell me what's so private that you can't talk about it in public."

"You've read *Jesus Warned Me.*"

"Unfortunately, yes." She was clinging to the words, "exposing Angelica St. Ambrose."

"I need to tell you things about my parents that aren't in the book. I owe it to them not to broadcast. May we stipulate that this part of the conversation is confidential?"

"You're the one taking notes." He'd grabbed a notepad from the table and was balancing it on his knee.

He sighed. "You know that Lagunitas is gentrified now, but when I was growing up it was still a working-class town."

She nodded, though she hadn't known.

Will took a deep breath, and held it for a moment. When he exhaled, he said, "Okay. My parents were alcoholics. My mother was the worse of the two. I'd have to step over her in the morning to get to the front door."

"That's what Angelica said about her own mother."

"Not true."

"But—" Hunter stopped herself. Angelica's childhood as the daughter of raging alkies was revealed scripture. Hunter had been hearing about it since they first met. "How do you know? People drink in secret."

Will rapped his pen against the notepad like a mad woodpecker. "I concede that it's possible, but I spent a lot of time at the St. Ambrose home when I was growing up." Pause. "I often went there when I needed to get away. From my own parents."

In the distance, Hunter heard a speedboat pass. Will's houseboat rocked.

Will continued. He grew up on the same street as Angelica, though she was almost ten years older. She had lifted a number of incidents from his childhood and adolescence and made them her own: It was *his* father who drank the grocery money. *His* mother who forgot to pick him and his brother up from school. It was Will himself who'd spent a night in a police station after his mother was arrested for a DUI and the cops had to wait for his father to come bail her out.

"I went to Stan to see about litigation—I was upset—and he said that you knew Angelica. Stan's wife is a big fan of hers, too. It wasn't hard to connect the dots. But more than that. . . . You're the one she does the biggest number on, in a subtle but powerful way."

Hunter looked down at her lap. She hoped that Will wouldn't cite any specifics: The times that Angelica described how Hunter flaunted the fact of her being married. Shamed Angelica about her weight. Boasted about travel: to Hawaii, to New York, to Europe. Worst of all, how Angelica hinted that Hunter was herself a high-functioning alcoholic. "Just because you call it 'wine-tasting' doesn't mean you stop at a taste," Angelica had written.

The leather cushions squeaked as Will shifted his bottom. "I can already tell . . . just after lunch . . . I mean, you're not like the way she portrays you."

"I appreciate that." Hunter was afraid her eyes would mist up. She blinked the threat away. "It's funny how everyone thinks they want to be in a book."

"Besides, how are you in a blackout, but remember so many details?" Will, seemingly embarrassed, cleared his throat. "I should be glad that she absolved my parents, but . . ." Pause. "She claims that she was molested by her Uncle Gilbert." Long pause. "That. Never. Happened."

That was the most unpleasant part of the book, and Hunter had skimmed those pages a little. Angelica said that she had repressed the memory, but reclaimed it in therapy. Her parents were oblivious, she said, thanks to their drinking.

"Are you sure?" Would Angelica invent something *that* egregious?

"I'm sure." He resumed his pen-rapping, faster now.

Another speedboat, and more rocking of *The 25th Mile*. Hunter felt slightly seasick.

"That Uncle Gilbert saved my life." There was a hairline crack in his voice. "He's the reason I'm a lawyer."

Hunter didn't ask for details. She could imagine what a steady older man would mean to an adolescent who needed one. But in these times, women had to be believed, even women who lied about other events. "How can you know for sure that . . ." She stretched out her hand, palm up.

"Uncle Gil—I call him Uncle Gil—was in a wheelchair. ALS." That was why the St. Ambroses took him in. "He's still living."

He unhooked the clasp on a door behind him, whipped out
a Kindle, then butt-hopped down the cushions until he was close
enough to hold it where she could read:

> I'll spare you the details. We've
> read them often enough. Heard them
> often enough. This is what abusers
> do. They gain your trust. Usually
> they already have your trust. T-R-
> U-ST. It what makes us human.
>   The shame of being abused held me
> back for years. It's why I became an
> alcoholic. Now all I want is for you,
> dear reader (remember when authors
> used to say "Dear Reader"?) to put
> all the shame in Jesus's inbox.

"Do you know the playwright Lillian Hellman? No? She was famous
in her lifetime. Mary McCarthy said, 'Everything she wrote was a lie,
including "and" and "the."' I'm a Catholic, you know." His left cheek was
throbbing. "The whole book is offensive. Jesus isn't your pal. He's the son
of God. She writes about him like he was her roommate last semester."

"I was r-raised Catholic," Hunter said.

"I may not go to Mass every Sunday, but I believe that Christ is
the ultimate role model. He didn't come to Earth to be exploited by
a spoiled brat. That line about Him drinking Himself to sleep? That's
blasphemous. But it actually gets worse. Gilbert St. Ambrose is a
quadriplegic now. He's living in a nursing home near Sacramento,
and when I visited him last week, some *asshole* had told him about
this. I was praying no one would."

"So he knows . . ."

"About Angelica's claims, yes." Hunter had seen the tension
rise in him, so she wasn't completely startled when he banged his

fist against the notepad. He sucked in air sharply. "Time for me to calm down."

He repeated his butt-hop in the other direction, and returned the Kindle to the cabinet.

Hunter waited a very long moment before she spoke. "Just his being in a wheelchair doesn't mean he couldn't . . ."

Will placed his hands on his knees. "During the period of which she writes, he already had very limited use of his arms and hands."

Now Hunter was embarrassed.

"Now my job is to tell him that everyone knows that she made it all up."

Hunter pounded down the rest of her Montana Sky before she spoke again. "I would like nothing better."

"I've already done as much research as I can." He wanted proof that Gilbert St. Ambrose was already a wheelchair user at the time that Angelica described. His own mother was dead and his father also in a nursing home, with Alzheimer's—not that he'd have been very cooperative in any situation. All his former neighbors were dead or had moved away, their houses dutifully remodeled and flipped. He'd found two young adults who'd been children at the time, but their memories were so contradictory that they were useless.

Medical records were confidential. He'd even tried, but failed, to get a court order unlocking them.

"I also thought of digging up the records of my mother's—" he cleared his throat again—"several DUIs, but that wouldn't prove that Angelica's parents didn't have them. Angelica's parents were very good to me." They fed him, even gave him a place to sleep. He hated seeing them libeled, but there was no cause of action when the defamed were deceased. "But Gil . . . I showed him my homework. He told me I was smart and he made me believe it."

Hunter's cell phone rang.

"Everything okay?" Dannika asked.

"Y-yes."

"You don't sound okay."

"No, I am, really." Hunter looked up over the top of her phone at Will.

"But maybe you can't say that you're okay. Like if he was holding a gun on you or something."

"I swear on the lives of your cats that I'm okay."

"Name three of them, then."

"Goodbye, Dannika." She put the phone in her purse. "If you can't prove that part about Gilbert," Hunter said, "how about proving the rest of it BS? Or I mean, some other parts that wipe out her credibility?"

"Hmm." Will nodded. "That would be a start."

"You know who could help us. Vijay Koka—her ex."

"Perfect!" Will made a fist. "I appreciate this."

"I have a stake in it, too," Hunter pointed out. "I have an old email for him. I don't know if it's still good."

Hunter's phone rang again.

"Oh my God, are you all right?" Penelope breathed.

"Yes, I'm fine. I've been fine for the last—" she looked at her watch—"ninety minutes."

"I fell asleep," Penelope admitted. "If something had happened to you—oh, my God . . ."

Hunter met Will's eyes. "I'll tell you all about it when we meet again."

"My place," Penelope reminded her. "Six o'clock. I'll have something for us to snack on."

Chapter 21

No Way to Live

DANNIKA

The pizza party had turned them into friends of a sort.

Penelope's house was a little closer to Dannika's, but it was even swankier than Hunter's, which made her feel embarrassed about her own place, with its old, cat-and-dust-covered furniture. True, the talking-stick women probably wouldn't visit her often. Or ever.

Penelope seemed flustered, but she was, as usual, perfectly put together in a gray suit that was a little short for an older woman, and patterned tights. Dannika took special note of Penelope's jewelry: the blue topaz cocktail ring and the diamond solitaire on her fingers; the gold earrings too heavy for her lobes.

Then Penelope seemed both nervous and excited to introduce them to Reyna, a cute Filipina woman. That made for a welcome change. Marin was as white as a polar bear.

When Reyna brought out the curated selection of crackers and cheeses and dried fruit to tide them over until they got home for dinner, Penelope said, "I could have done that." She clearly wasn't used to having someone who was like a servant.

The cheeses were not the kind of stuff you'd buy at Safeway. Before Reyna unwrapped them, Dannika saw "Kaltbach Cave Aged Gruyere," "6 month old Manchego" and "Grass Fed Kilaree Irish Cheddar." This was cheese for people who were never hungry.

There was no evidence of Penelope's husband. Maybe he was hiding in his room (Penelope had mentioned that they had separate bedrooms), or maybe he was Penelope's imaginary friend.

Hunter told them about the lawyer who contacted her. Dannika was not surprised to hear that there were more fabrications—no, call them lies—in Angelica's memoir. How would Hunter prove that? "I tried to email Vijay—Angelica's ex? But the email I had is no good, so I have to look elsewhere."

"'Vijay in Mumbai'?" Alicia asked. "That's a Google search that'll turn up five million hits."

"It's Vijay *Koka*." Hunter shrugged.

"Three million."

"I'm starting with people we both knew back then." Hunter reached for a dried apricot. "I bet I can find someone who kept in touch."

"Good luck with that," Penelope said. "The divorced couples I've seen draw a jagged line through the middle of their friends. Everyone takes sides."

Hunter bit the apricot in half. "I've noticed."

"Let's get back to me." Penelope leaned very far forward, and whispered, "It didn't work. I tried, but it didn't work." Her whisper became even softer. "The tapering off."

Dannika had been munching on a rye crisp, but she thought she could make a contribution. "Start keeping a journal."

"What would I write about?"

"Write about when you take them, and why you take them." Dannika remembered an exercise her mother's friends did when discussing childhood wounds. "Imagine Valium is in the room with you, and have a conversation about why it has such power over you. Maybe that will take away its power."

"I think that's silly," Penelope said, "but I'll think about it."

"It's good that you're not driving," Hunter said.

Alicia cleared her throat. "The guy I was looking for has a common American name, but he was easy to find." She looked around the small circle, waiting for a response. "Summer's dad? So I emailed him."

*Uh huh uh huh*s from the group.

"He wants to come visit us."

"'Us?'" Penelope asked.

"Me and Summer." Alicia laughed self-consciously. "Though I'm sure he'd like to meet all of you as well."

That took guts, Dannika thought. She didn't want to say anything, though.

"He's arranging to take some time off from work," Alicia said. "He's hoping to be here next week. As soon as he can, anyway." Alicia was eating water crackers as she spoke, leaving crumbs too large to be called crumbs in her lap.

Reyna returned, carrying throw pillows. "You'll need these." She tucked them behind Penelope's back.

"And Summer?" Hunter asked.

"I'll tell her once his plane leaves Logan. Just in case . . ." But then she reverted to her wry self. "I can always pass him off as a pharmaceutical rep."

"Who needs dinner after this?" Hunter put her hand on her nonexistent stomach. Reyna had come in to replenish the cheese-cracker-fruit plate during a lull ("Oh, I could have done that!" Penelope said again). "Let's make this official. I have the talking stick." She unwrapped it from its knitted blanket. "We haven't heard from you, Dannika, why don't you take a turn?"

"I don't have much to say." But she did. She wanted to tell them about Rafe; she wanted to hear them parse the clues. She had them memorized: the compliments he gave her when she was checking out (she looked sexy in that new bustier—the bustier she wore for him), the time he left his post when he didn't to have to, to help her find V-8 juice, how he let her keep him company during his break. She wouldn't mention Shannon, though. She feared their disapproval, not because there was casual sex (what was this, 1991?) but because he had a female roommate. They were too old to understand how men and women lived together now.

Maybe she'd mention how she and Howie had found some common ground in fiction. But then, they'd probably start in on how *he* was the guy for her, even with his dweeby glasses and student loan debt larger than the gross national product of Romania. She hadn't opened *Notes from Underground*.

Dannika's fingers closed around the smooth wood.

She noticed the abstract painting above the fireplace. Varying shades of the blue of lapis lazuli dominated, with some yellow spots, like fireflies. That was the last thing she saw before the room faded.

She's in seventh grade, in the after-school art class that Mosi signed her up for. She uses a pint-sized milk carton to make a replica of their house, cutting flaps where their windows are. She does a lot of mixing to re-create the forest green exterior. Over that she paints pictures of their current six cats-in-residence, in bright, non-cat colors: plums and crimsons. The teacher holds it up for everyone to see, and she says that Dannika "has the soul of an artist."

At home, she gives it to Mosi, after she gets her to look up from her work at the dining room table, which is permanently set up as her workspace. Mosi turns it over in her hand slowly, her mouth twisting into strange shapes.

"Don't you like it?" Dannika asks.

Mosi puts it down on the other end of the table.

"Is this how you want to waste your life? Do you want to ruin your eyes like me? Your back?"

"But your eyes are okay." Though suddenly Dannika isn't sure.

Mosi points to the giant magnifier she uses. "I needed reading glasses before I was forty."

"Ms. Hendricks said it was good."

Mosi squints at the little house. It looks lonely there at the end of the table. "It's okay."

"If I could make more, I was thinking of selling them on Etsy."

"Etsy!" Mosi slaps her hands on the table; the beads in her trays rattle. Suddenly she looks every day of her forty-seven years, especially those hands: bony, wrinkled. "Do you know how many people sell crap on Etsy?"

"But you always liked my stuff." When Dannika was in grade school and brought home craft projects, Mosi bubbled over with praise: "Isn't it amazing what you can do with Popsicle sticks?"

"That's when you were a little kid!"

"But this—"

"Sure, it's good. It's great. But everyone's stuff is great. I'm spending more money on your art class than you'll ever make selling this shit."

Dannika is shocked. "But Bronwyn . . ." Bronwyn is a potter.

"None of those women are making a decent living."

"But you do."

For a moment it looks like Mosi is going to sweep all her trays and tools off the table. "So, you do want to be like me?"

"Y-yeah," Dannika falters. Maybe not at this exact moment. "You're successful. You have a great life."

"Let me tell you about my great life," Mosi says. "Let's talk. I've got self-employment tax. No 'personal days.' No health insurance!"

"We have Kaiser."

Mosi didn't even hear that. She holds her fists next to her ears while she rants on. She has no opportunities to travel—unless you count driving to craft fairs in faraway places, only to sit on a stool until your butt freezes, with nothing but porta-potties, and that only if you have someone to watch your stall. Meanwhile you watch strangers paw through the pieces you spent hours—days!—on, breaking them and telling you it's your fault, because you hadn't made the wire tight enough or used the right kind of glue.

Dannika always thought that Mosi liked the fairs: the adventure. The companionship. She took Dannika with her until the year before.

Dannika certainly knows how hard Mosi works. The only table they have is the one that Mosi uses to make her jewelry, so Dannika always gets dinner for herself. Eats in her room. Mosi works under the lamp until Dannika doesn't know what time. Sometimes when she gets up, Mosi is asleep with her head resting on her outstretched arm. Sometimes Dannika hears her snuffling, like an old person, and then Dannika is scared that something will happen to her.

"I want you to have a better life," Mosi says now. Her tone shifts from the foghorn of self-pity to the screeching tires of guilt. "Go into the STEMs."

The word "STEMs" makes Dannika think of the marijuana seeds and stems that kids steal from their parents and sell cheap. But she knows what Mosi means, although she suspects that her mother doesn't know what the acronym stands for: science, technology, engineering, and math.

"It isn't 'the' STEMs," Dannika says. "It's just 'STEM.'"

"I know that," Mosi says, cranky. "Look, I want you to have some security. What about that computer stuff? That's where all the money is now."

Silicon Valley is fifty miles, and a universe, away. A lot of Dannika's classmates talk about becoming billionaires, but Dannika knows it can't be that easy. Others of her friends play the guitar, and they're going to be famous rock stars.

Actually, Dannika is really good at computers. She even helps kids with stuff like downloading drivers to connect printers. But she doesn't know how to write code, and if she was going to make the world a better place, the first thing she'd do is get rid of Instagram, because she wastes so much time on it. She doesn't have any *brilliant ideas for start-ups: her ideas are all about painted picture frames, candles designed to look like animals, plain terra-cotta pots she would decoupage, handmade purses. Even jewelry. She doesn't have the skills, but she could learn. Her skin prickles when she thinks about making new things.*

"You'll go to college," Mosi continues. "Like I didn't. And you'll study chemistry or—I guess it's biology. Whatever it is to get into med school."

That's enough. "Are you shitting me with this?" Dannika rarely talks back to her mom. "Med school? I can't be a doctor!" Anything to do with math or science, she's lucky to hang on to a C. English is her only really good class.

"So you can't go into computers, and you can't be a doctor." Mosi mimics her, using a petulant, childlike voice. "Could you at least go to law school?"

"Law school. Sure. What. Ever."

"I want a better life for you," Mosi repeats. "I could have opened my own store, but then I wouldn't have been able to work at home. I could have dated, maybe, but I was afraid any man I brought around would go after you. I had to keep you safe." Mosi looks over at the milk-carton house. "You're talented, but it'll break your heart. Give it up now."

"What?" Dannika heard Hunter ask as her eyes refocused on the painting. She saw blue clouds in it now. "You were gone there for a minute."

"Or two," Penelope said.

Dannika's head was pounding. It had all come back to her as if she were reliving it, the same way that first vivid memory had come to her two weeks before. Three pairs of eyes— brown, blue, green— under eyebrows lowered, all watched her with sympathy. More sympathy than her mother had had for her little house made of a milk carton.

"It was nothing," she said.

Chapter 22

Plenty of Blame to Go Around

PENELOPE

After Reyna caught Penelope in flagrante, surrounded by half of Reyna's wardrobe, Penelope was terrified that she would quit.

She didn't, but she did resign as keeper of the Valium. She sat Penelope down to say that this was her problem, and she was not her babysitter. "It was a mistake from the beginning. I've been to confession and said my Hail Marys, so I'm good, more or less."

This was a great relief. Time to move on quickly, to prove that Penelope was ready to take responsibility. "Dannika, you know, the punk one from the talking-stick group, said I should keep a journal."

"It's a good idea," Reyna said. "Why don't you start on Scott's computer? He wrote the password in Sharpie on the back of the monitor."

———

That wasn't like Scott, but Penelope wasn't going to complain. She needed to get used to email, and it took no more than five minutes for Reyna to set her up as PenelopeWins@gmail.com.

Penelope knew how to touch-type. She'd learned on a manual typewriter, in what they called junior high back then. There were all those new, confusing keys, but she survived her summer in Paris typing on a French keyboard, where the A and Q were reversed as well as the W and Z. Besides, she remembered the days of Wite-Out and carbon paper, so just having the "delete" and "backspace" features felt like having wings.

For her first entry, Penelope wrote about how Scott took her to see Dr. Schmulewitz.

> *I sat there like a bump on a log while Scott did all the talking. Walking into the doctor's office, he leaned on Brittany's desk and told her that blue was her color. I was so frightened right then about a lump in my breast that I was so afraid as to be certain that it was malignant.*
>
> *I have lumpy breasts. Lumpy as lumpy mashed potatoes. It's not crazy to be scared, is it? It's human nature.*

Details of that first doctor's appointment returned. The mysterious pains in her legs. Scott and Dr. Schmulewitz talking politics; she hadn't paid attention to that, but she remembered that the upshot of the conversation was that white men were being treated unfairly and that socialism in Congress was a threat. ". . .while I sat there trying to feel my boobs under my blouse without them noticing."

> *The trap of drugs is that first they do what they're supposed to do, but then they start doing the opposite of what you want them to do. That can't be the case for insulin, but my guess is that that's the problem with the hard drugs, like heroin and even cocaine. First it feels good, then it feels terrible.*
>
> *Valium did what it was supposed to do in the beginning, but now it's doing the opposite. I'm more worried than I was fifteen years ago. Maybe I would have gotten here anyway. You worry*

more as you get older. I've been accused of being a hypochondriac. But just because you're a hypochondriac doesn't mean you can't get sick. And the danger is greater, because no one believes your symptoms mean anything anymore.

Reyna leaned close to the monitor. She smelled of lavender soap. "You know, that's a good point." She straightened up. "This is good stuff, Penelope."

"No, it isn't." Penelope whipped her head back and forth.

"Well, it will be. With a little work." Reyna tapped something, and a moment later Scott's printer began to whirr. "I'm going to read it, and we're going to talk about a second draft, and we're going to post it on Medium."

"What's Medium?" Penelope asked.

"It's a website where people post their writing."

Penelope spread her hands over the keys. "Scott can't see this!"

"Huh," Reyna grunted. "I have a feeling he doesn't subscribe. But you should change names—and get a *nom d'internet*, too."

Reyna's interest and praise were like warm butterscotch syrup. "Is that like 'nom de plume'?"

"Exactly." Reyna picked up the mug that had held rose hip tea that Penelope had finished. "And we can do some kind of play on words with your name, like 'Pen Something.' I mean, if you want."

Penelope wanted. "How about 'The Mighty Pen'?"

"Love it!" Reyna leaned close again, squinting a little as she read. "This sentence . . ." She pointed. "'Frightened as to be so afraid'? Can we slim that down to 'There was a lump in my breast that I was sure was malignant?'

"Okay." But hearing Reyna read about her fears, Penelope did feel like a raging hypochondriac.

"And below that . . ." Reyna traced a few lines with her finger, "let's change 'boobs' to 'breasts.' Now—" she rested her hand on Penelope's shoulder. "How about some more tea?"

Now Penelope felt her battery truly charged. "No, not tea—coffee!" That was what writers drank. Coffee would give her the buzz necessary to write even more. And Reyna made fantastic coffee, flavored with cinnamon.

"You got it."

Reyna left and Penelope, who caught herself slumping, straightened her back. Even more than fifty years after she gave up dancing, Penelope was attentive to her posture, as every ballerina was, and sitting at a computer wasn't good for it.

She placed her fingers on a, s, d, f and j, k, l, ; again.

I don't want to play the martyr here. But I do blame Scott for getting me started. He and that damn doctor wanted to tamp down my symptoms, keep me medicated. They wanted to treat my symptoms, not my disease.

Penelope fingered her pearls. That seemed like a good observation. But then she typed,

There's plenty of blame to go around. Even if I'm not 100% responsible for swallowing that first pill, I'm responsible for each one thereafter. So however I got here, I'm the one who has to get myself out.

This was suddenly something she wanted to announce to the world. Anonymously, but still announce. She could write about how she first figured out that Scott was having affairs—after she changed the names. She could write about her first, sad marriage to Jared. Hell, she could write about growing up in Austin.

But she felt herself slump again. The pillow that Reyna had placed on Scott's desk chair wasn't helping anymore. Penelope pushed her lower back forward, but the pain persisted.

Where was Reyna with the coffee?

Penelope had taken a Valium before she sat down at Scott's computer, and it had helped her ignore the various aches that traveled around her body but never settled anywhere. That was wearing off, though. And she'd entered that danger zone in which another one wouldn't do any good, and there would be nothing to do but to ride out the pains.

She was anxious about her supply, too. It would be two weeks before she could refill the stingy prescription that her new regular doctor allowed her, so if she ran out before then she'd have to beg Tennis Club Trish to use one of her secondary contacts, who were always upping the price.

So—no!

She tried to go back to typing, but she only got as far as "this is hard why am I doing this?"

The craving was visceral. Her cheeks grew hot. And no, it wasn't a hot flash, unless you could have Valium withdrawal and a hot flash at the same time. Now her hands were shaking too much for her to type.

There was no help for it.

She returned to her room. The pills—the remaining pills—were in her nightstand drawer, and there was always a glass of water on that nightstand. It was cloudy and lukewarm but she only wanted a small swallow.

When she came back, there was a cup of coffee waiting. Reyna had left a Hershey's kiss, wrapped in foil, on a cocktail napkin next to it.

But drowsiness soon overtook her, and Penelope didn't write any more.

Chapter 23

Seems Like Old Times

ALICIA

Alicia was restless at baggage claim. She was generally restless; Summer often complained that you couldn't keep Alicia waiting.

She'd considered telling Joshua to take a cab, or an Uber, but then decided that they would get off to a better start if she made this gesture, even if it did mean canceling a few patients, and making the long drive from Marin to SFO, likely with heavy traffic. She even refused Joshua's offer to meet her outside, in the loading zone. The SFO Gestapo wouldn't let you wait any longer than the twenty seconds it took for your arriving visitor to get in the car. (She internally corrected herself: the term Gestapo applied to daily life in the United States trivialized the Holocaust.)

Would she recognize him? She hoped his profile pictures weren't as old as her own.

Finally! A tight group of weary people signaled the arrival of the passengers from Joshua's flight. The group broke up as the travelers surrounded the baggage carousel, with the biggest contingent pressing close around the delivery ramp.

Alicia swayed, looking for him. Somewhere in the huddled mass was someone who would look familiar. She didn't think she was nervous, so why was her heart beating so fast?

Now it was just stragglers: the couples with babies waiting for their car seats to come up, and one woman in a wheelchair that a skycap pushed.

Then she saw him. Khakis and a sport coat. But how had she forgotten? He was so *tall*. Six foot something, three or four. That was where Summer got her height.

He was better-looking than his picture. The photo didn't capture his gentle expression, perfect for a pediatrician. When he saw her—and he recognized her right away, too!—her hasty, last-minute visit to the hairdresser had been a good idea—he smiled, and she saw the little fan of lines from the outer corner of his eyes that look so much better on a man than a woman.

"You look gorgeous!" He put one arm around her shoulder, but didn't pull her in for a hug.

"Liar." But she was grateful. Since he'd last seen her, she was twenty pounds heavier, and already had the beginning of a sagging chin. She pulled her scarf more closely around her neck, as if that would help. "How was your flight? Uh . . . planes are so uncomfortable now."

"Not news to me." He waved his hand near his head to indicate his height.

He had blue eyes. She hadn't forgotten that as much as she hadn't stopped to think about it. That was how Summer got her hazel eyes: the ring of brown around the pupil and the outer ring of green.

The other passengers were dispersing as bags arrived. When the conveyor belt coughed up an oversized brown case, Alicia was surprised to hear Joshua say, "that's mine." Men didn't need to pack all the extras that women did: makeup, accessories, three pairs of black shoes. Although, again, she asked herself, what did she know about men and packing?

The conveyor belt took the case in the opposite direction from where they were standing. Joshua sprinted to the other end of the carousel and hauled the bag off. "There's another one coming," he said, as he dragged this first one over to her.

His second bag, only a little smaller than the first, was one of the last to travel up the conveyor belt. He hefted it from the carousel. "Ready when you are, C.B."

———

"I always wanted to drive across the Golden Gate Bridge," Joshua said.

"I bet it feels like a letdown." Alicia kept her eyes on the adjustable barrier that, at that moment, left two lanes heading north. "That's how I felt when I finally saw the Space Needle."

"No, it's not a letdown at all." Joshua was looking out the window. "That must be Alcatraz."

Alicia disciplined herself not to take her eyes off the road; she knew that Alcatraz was visible from the bridge. "Yes."

"So much color here. So much history."

"You've never been?"

Asking this acknowledged that they had lived separate lives for over fifteen years.

"No." He put his hand up on the window. "Always wanted to visit though."

They were coming up on the Robin Williams Tunnel. "You brought enough clothes for a long stay. Unless you packed an autoclave."

He laughed a little. "Hey, you never know what the weather's going to be."

She exhaled a breath she didn't know she'd been holding. She'd teased; he'd laughed. They weren't back to where they were, but there was something familiar in their exchange. It was like seeing a rerun of an old sitcom that you'd loved. When you were younger.

———

Then they were at the Embassy Suites, where Alicia had proposed that Joshua stay. *The right emotional distance.*

Alicia expected Summer to keep them waiting, but she was already in the lobby, looking at her phone while twirling a lock of hair.

She was about to stick the end of that lock of hair in her mouth—a childish habit she reverted to under stress—when Alicia spotted her. Why hadn't she thought to send Joshua a picture? Summer had dressed to impress and gotten it all wrong, in a skirt with laced flounces that she hadn't worn in years that was now too short for her, and a blouse whose buttons strained at the placket, thanks to her maturing breasts.

She stood up right away with an expression that broke Alicia's heart. It brought back everything she felt when Summer was first placed, whimpering, on her chest after the triumphant, all-natural birth. A tiny human had come out of her body. *Yes, it was still a miracle, when it happened to you.* Alicia promised herself then that her baby girl would come before everything else.

She hadn't kept that promise. Maybe it wasn't too late.

Then a wave of fear swept over her. Joshua must have imagined the ultimate California girl: Barbie thin, platinum blonde. She was afraid to look his way. How was he going to reveal his disappointment?

She was wrong. Simply wrong. After a moment they hugged each other like long-lost relatives. Which they were. Joshua had his hand on the back of Summer's neck, which was covered by her hair. Summer's head fit perfectly against his shoulder.

They stood that way for some time that Alicia didn't measure, until Joshua let her go. *Was that a tear in his eye or the reflection of the fluorescent light?* Then he clapped his hands on Summer's upper arms.

"I saw an In-N-Out Burger on the way in. You hungry?"

Chapter 24

Knock Down Walls, Build Bridges

HUNTER

Hunter was in her bedroom, laptop on her outstretched legs, the evening that Angelica launched the Fourteenth Step.

Hunter had negotiated Sundays off with Preston, so she could scour garage sales and flea markets. She'd made a few decent scores. What she lacked in experience she made up for in due diligence: When she wasn't at work or out running, she was in her room, doing research, getting an education. There, she was more or less trapped on her bed: She'd added to the acquisitions she'd moved from the Margaret Keane room, and her room was beginning to resemble the Collyer brothers' Harlem brownstone. This grated against her desire for order, but she was hardly going to pay to rent storage space. Instead, she'd cleared a path between bed and door.

She was studying the trademarks to look for on nineteenth-century figurines when she heard the front door open, followed by the cacophonous sounds of Angelica's attendees: the chatter in the key of excited but scared, the purses landing on the floor.

Angelica's Acolytes.

Hunter rose and cracked her bedroom door, but through that narrow angle she could only see Peter and Angelica themselves, and the two of them only partway. Still, it was enough to see that Peter had added sandals to his outfit. Only the socks prevented him from looking like Jesus's evil twin from one of her childhood illustrated Bibles. For tonight, Angelica had abandoned the Southwestern look for one of African royalty: a ruby headscarf subdued her red hedge-hair, but in a scarlet caftan embroidered with beads, she looked Biblical as well.

Hunter pushed her door open more widely. A crowd of people, mostly women, were drinking coffee, dispensed by an urn on a folding table. A folding table in her beautiful great room!

"I know this is going to be life-changing." "Do you follow her on Instagram?" "I've struggled so hard, maybe she can help me." "She makes you feel good about yourself because she's so fucked up."

Hunter noted that many of the women were of similar appearance: slightly overweight, with bobbed and banged gray hair and glasses.

"Jesus warned me not to buy Haagen-Dazs!" one of the woman laughed.

"She said we have to buy two copies of her memoir—"

"That's okay, I already have four!"

"—one to read and one to give to someone who needs it!"

Flee, Hunter told herself. *Flee*. When in doubt, go running. She was already in her joggers, sports bra, and tank top.

Out in the great room, one of the women recognized her. "You're the one Angelica is helping! Hunter, right? The woman who—" She cut herself off, then shook her head. "Forgiveness is truly powerful."

"Yes it is," Hunter agreed through gritted teeth.

Suddenly Peter's reedy voice, set on scream, called them to order. "Her ladyship says it's time to sit!" Then he noticed Hunter. "Hey, are you joining us?"

She shook her head.

The women, and the few men, shuffled eagerly into what had been the Margaret Keane room. Through the open door, Hunter saw rows of folding chairs, and one upholstered armchair. Angelica spotted Hunter. "If I had your body, I'd display it, too!"

Peter flinched. "You going out running, then?"

"Yeah, in a minute." She held up her water bottle, which she gripped by the neck in her left hand, then raised her right hand, so he could see her headlamp dangling from its strap.

"It's still light out," he said.

"But it won't be forever."

"Nothing is forever," he said piously. Then apologetic lines appeared on his forehead. "I guess I have to go," he mumbled, and he slid into the room, closing the door behind him.

Hunter didn't know if it was curiosity or masochism, but she tugged off her running shoes, and followed, very quietly. She leaned against the wall, then slid down against it, until her bottom made contact with the floor.

"The response was overwhelming," she heard Angelica say. "I've touched a lot of people. That's the only reason I'm doing this. I want to be a healing force and live a spiritual life."

"I didn't want Hunter to knock down those walls," Peter said. "Now I see that it was part of a plan to make room—"

"Knocking down walls is the perfect metaphor!" Angelica declared.

"Then we build—"

"Right. Bridges. Peter." Angelica's voice became firmer. "Remember, you're only as sick—"

"As your secrets!" Peter finished.

"Soooo . . . Peter is going to share some of his."

"I was a drunk and I was ruining the lives of people I love." His voice cracked.

Please don't cry, Hunter thought. *Whatever else you say, please don't cry.*

"Start at the beginning," Angelica said.

It started in high school, he said. No, he didn't drink to excess then, but now, looking back, he saw that he already had a problem. He described the various shenanigans that he and his friends got up to in order to get fake IDs until Angelica prompted him to move the story along.

Then college. Well, every frat boy drank. The more you drank, the more you were respected. So there were binges and blackouts. (Though when he said, "Girls were ready to party, and we took advantage," he didn't sound terribly remorseful.)

Then the pressures of the business world. Everyone drank at lunch. (*They didn't at Evergy-4-All,* Hunter thought.) Happy hours started earlier each week, and occurred on an increasing number of days. He left his brokerage firm to escape the culture of boozing, but it was too late. He required alcohol to get through the day. Each day he required it a little earlier.

Hunter remembered Peter saying that he was leaving his firm to go into real estate. She'd known that he'd been fired, but she'd chosen not to know it.

He bought a house to flip. Everyone was making money flipping houses. It was just a question of how much. You couldn't lose! Who ever heard of California real estate going down?

Hunter closed her eyes. She knew what was coming.

She was wrong.

"Hunter believed in me, and I let her down."

Hunter's eyes flew open. What had she just heard? Did Peter feel responsible?

"I couldn't bear the guilt. But then, poor Hunter, she had her own problems with alcohol."

I did not! She only ever drank at their parties.

"So she needed those parties, because that was her excuse to drink."

Hunter's skin burned. Did she? But she didn't drink now. There was no need to perform an autopsy on the past.

"She was disappointed in me, and I own that. But then she drank as a way of punishing me."

Hunter put her hands over her eyes, and peered out through her fingers. She remembered the parties as one long party, distinguished by random events: The time Stanley Butler brought his wife, who vomited before she could make it to the bathroom. The heat wave that had the guests taking off a few more clothes than decorum allowed.

The time the neighbor complained about the noise.

That was one time. Just one time.

She pushed her shoulders back against the wall. *This is how they get you.* They make you doubt yourself, and then they say, *only we can help you.*

"Not realizing that she was hurting herself."

He cut himself off with a sob. Hunter closed her eyes again.

She lasted a few minutes longer, long enough to hear Angelica's speech about how food was an addiction, and Jesus loved everyone no matter what they weighed. Hunter's tailbone was sore and one calf was asleep, but it was only when she heard Angelica pronounce that, "Jesus liked his carbs," that she rose with uncharacteristic clumsiness and limped to the front door. There she secured her headlamp, since she planned to be gone until well past dark.

Chapter 25

Melon Madness

HUNTER

The group wasn't supposed to meet for two more days, but Hunter felt the need of the company of women in whom she could confide.

She'd created a group text with the label "talking stick," so that with one click she could address the other three. Can we meet early? she typed. Like even this afternoon? What do you mean, early? was the response from Penelope.

After a couple of mishaps, Penelope had enlisted Reyna's support, and now her replies came back to all of them, instead of just the sender.

Hunter: How about 3:00? it's so nice out.

She suggested they meet at Larkspur Dock; even though her most recent visit had been marred by rain and rejection, it was the most central location.

Alicia: I'm taking Joshua to a car rental place at 3:00.

Penelope: I have to make sure that Reyna can drive me.

Dannika: There's a new café in Fairfax, if you don't mind the drive.

Hunter texted that Alicia could join them when she was free, reminded Penelope that Reyna was in her employ, and concluded, I think I speak for all of us when I say that yes, we do mind the drive.

After a few more rounds of texting, they settled on 4:00, at which time Hunter was at a table outside Squeeze, the juicery. School had just let out for the day, and the plaza was crowded with moms, nannies, and kids in private school uniforms. Hunter had nabbed the last empty table, and Dannika and Penelope had joined her there. They had a panoramic view of the San Francisco skyline, and the air sparkled like San Pellegrino. They each had smoothies: thick, lumpy concoctions in vibrant pastels, with more calories than vitamins, but who was keeping track?

Alicia rushed toward them, windblown and apologetic. "Joshua's using the rental car to pick Summer up from school," she panted.

"Really?" Dannika asked. "How's that going?"

"I feel like a redundant component," Alicia said. "That has to be good, right? I'm going to order. What are you having?" She pointed to Penelope's paper tumbler. "That looks good."

"It's called Take My Cherry, Please."

"That's offensive!"

"Spoken like the mother of a teenage daughter," Hunter said.

Alicia shouldered her purse. "I'll be right back!"

Hunter couldn't wait, though: She blurted it all out, including what she'd overheard from Peter. "And there were so many people at this meeting! How did she make it such a success so fast?"

"She's good at social media," Dannika said. "That's what everything is about."

Hunter had been avoiding social media, lest she see that #ofservicetoHunter was trending.

"I just wish I could get out of there!" Hunter slapped the table, hard enough that her cup of Lime Time slid over half an inch. "She doesn't even put her dishes in the dishwasher."

Alicia returned. "I got Cranberry Crazy."

"You think 'Take My Cherry' is offensive?" Dannika asked. "'Cranberry Crazy' disrespects people with mental health issues."

"I agree." Penelope was rummaging in her clutch. "So does 'Melon Madness.' "

"I wish I could offer you a place to stay." Alicia stabbed her straw through the lid of her smoothie. The lid was plastic. How did that get by the eco-police? "But you know, Joshua just got to town—"

"I'm sorry, Hunts, you'd hate my place. Cat hair."

"And I don't have an extra bedroom," Penelope said. "I can't ask Reyna to share."

"Don't worry, I don't want to move in with any of you." She pumped her own straw. "Thanks for listening to me give out yards."

"Give out yards?" Alicia echoed.

Hunter sucked up Lime Time. "My mother's expression. It means to complain."

"Oh, like 'kvetch'," Alicia said.

"Yeah, like kvetch."

Hunter sighed. What had she expected? Still, she felt a bit better. A bit.

"Any luck finding what's-his-name?"

"Vijay Koka. No." She'd now reached out to everyone in her contacts file whom she knew (or had reason to believe) had known Vijay. It was a short list; Angelica and Vijay hadn't been married that long. She powered through the names, even after the second person asked, "Are you *that* Hunter Fitzgerald?"

Time to move on. "Wassup with you guys?"

Alicia pumped her straw. "Well. Joshua."

Alicia described the reunion of daughter and dad. "I can't believe I was so nervous! And I wanted to stay and, you know, get them settled and stuff, but they wanted some time by themselves." Alicia looked at her watch.

"You have to go," Penelope said.

"No, no." Alicia covered her watch with her hand.

"Okay, well, I started a journal." Penelope turned to Dannika. "Like you said I should." It turned first into a piece about her first appointment with Dr. Schmulewitz, and then into one about her mother's own addiction to "diet pills." "Everyone in the bridge club took them."

"The Mighty Pen" was a success on Medium, according to Reyna, at least. Women responded about abusive husbands, and a few women wrote about abusive wives. Women wrote to thank her for her courage, to beg her to write more.

"I don't know if I want to write more." Penelope took a modest sip of smoothie. "But maybe."

"You should. Yeah." Hunter spotted a dab of Cranberry Crazy on the table. "I'm going to get some extra napkins."

When she returned she sensed a dampened mood.

"I hate the Salesforce Tower," Dannika was saying. "It's like a middle finger pointed at God, daring Him to give us that earthquake." Dannika was the only one of them who'd grown up in California, and she'd been raised on the promise that the Big One would come someday. *Get under a piece of furniture so you can more easily kiss your ass good-bye.*

"I didn't tell you what happened at our last meeting." Dannika paused again, and then, without ever looking up from the remains of her Take My Cherry, she told them a story about bringing home something she'd made in an art class, something she was proud of, that her mother had belittled.

"I used to love making crafts. I knew it wasn't changing the world, but I loved it. I made CDs into Christmas ornaments. I painted shoelaces. And sneakers! I melted wax and designed rainbow candles. Now whenever I get an idea for making something, there are these voices in my head that say, 'what a stupid idea,' and 'what a waste of time.'"

"Write down what they say," Alicia suggested. "Then argue with them. Like, when you hear 'this is a waste of time,' you write, 'no, it's not, I'm . . .' "

Penelope interrupted, "She's right! That's what you told me to do with the journal, and look where it led!"

"It's not just about the crafts," Dannika said. "I'm remembering all this other stuff."

How Mosi worked all day, so she couldn't drive Dannika anywhere. Public transportation in Marin wasn't much better than on the dark side of the moon, and it was hard to believe, but there was no Uber back then, so Dannika was confined to playing with kids who lived in walking distance.

She and Mosi ate standing up in the kitchen, because Mosi had co-opted the one table that was big enough for dining into her worktable. That was where Mosi toiled throughout the evening, and where Dannika was not allowed to disturb her.

"I always thought how it was like, she was working so hard to take care of us, but now I think, there was something selfish about it, too."

So maybe St. Mosi the Archangel wasn't so perfect after all. "It sounds like she was working to provide for you," Hunter said, hoping it would be productive but not sound condescending.

"Yeah, I know, lotsa kids had it way worse than me."

A seagull landed on their table. Hunter shooed it away.

"The other thing I remembered," Dannika said, "was the last craft fair."

"'The Last Craft Fair,'" Hunter repeated. "Sounds like an Australian indie film."

"Or an after-school special," Alicia said.

Dannika squeezed her cup hard enough that a tongue of smoothie reached over the lip. "I made my first earrings."

She made them out of bottle caps. She was just having fun with the caps left over from the beer that the Craftswomen's Circle drank one night, and she laid them out on the TV table that Mosi had started to bring along for her, to eat lunch and spread out the books she was always reading.

A middle-aged, ponytailed man in a denim shirt, who smelled of garlic fries, raised one of Dannika's to look at it more closely. *She's got talent.*

They're bottle caps, for God's sake. Mosi laughed.

But she's got an eye, ma'am. Watch your back.

"What did 'watch your back' mean? That I'd take business away from her? Steal her designs?"

Mosi never took her to another craft fair after that. "I told myself that it was because she thought I was getting too old to spend time with her on weekends."

"Maybe it was just a coincidence," Alicia said. "Maybe it had nothing to do with that."

"Maybe." Dannika was in obvious disagreement.

And of the man with the ponytail and the whiff of garlic, Hunter could hear Dannika thinking, *how did I forget that?*

————

The wind came up, blowing away every napkin that wasn't weighed down.

Alicia got up. "I've got to see what my daughter and—" She made a show of coughing. "I don't know what to call him, but what they're up to, anyway."

"When do we get to meet him?" Penelope asked.

"Can I bring him to our next meeting?" Alicia wiped a few smoothie drops from her cell phone before returning it to her purse.

"Boy, this stuff is like the pink goo in *The Cat in the Hat Comes Back*," she said. "Not to stay. Just if he comes by, you can meet him, and we can do potluck dinner and . . . yeah, you can meet him."

"Maybe I can cook," Penelope said.

"Maybe Reyna can cook," Dannika said.

———

Hunter couldn't find a comfortable position in bed. She hadn't slept well since Angelica and Peter had moved in—no surprise there. For the first few nights she'd worried that she'd overhear them having intercourse, especially after Angelica said that the foldout couch in the room they'd taken over (Peter's erstwhile home office) was "like sleeping on a waterbed stuffed with small root vegetables," which might mean that they'd find a more agreeable location nearer to her own room.

That night, though, the sounds that reached her were of Peter and Angelica praying.

Peter used a tone of supplication she'd never heard before as he asked for strength and guidance, while Angelica's was that of someone cheerfully reprimanding an old friend.

Hunter made a U of her pillow to cover her ears. The technique did muffle their words, but she couldn't stay in that position for long, let alone sleep.

When she gave up the attempt she heard Peter complimenting Angelica, "The Fourteenth Step is a big success."

"I don't like that it's a *step*. That model has been overbranded. Co-opted."

"I'm sure you're right."

"What do you think about rebranding as 'More Nearly Each Day'?"

"I like it."

Hunter couldn't see Peter, but she was sure that he was nodding. The Peter who loved to mansplain to Hunter about how leverage worked ("which is why you want to make a small down payment") was equally inclined to agree with Angelica. He was no longer the schemer with grandiose plans. She was starting to feel sorry for him until she remembered, *He called me a dry drunk. In so many words.*

"We need to ask for more money. We deserve it. And the publisher says they might not do another print run. It's making me edgy."

Hunter pulled the pillow up over her ears again.

It was in this state of moderate sensory deprivation that a memory returned.

> *They're a foursome. Herself with Peter, Angelica, and Vijay. It was Angelica's idea. They're hiking up the hill that leads to the main trail at Mount Tam.*
>
> *The sun is on her neck. Did she put on enough sunscreen? One shoelace is coming undone; she'll have to stop in a second.*
>
> *Peter and Vijay have gone a little ahead. Angelica seems very happy to have a man to accompany her. She's yammering about how her life had changed since she'd turned everything over to God. She's going to Overeaters Anonymous now, too. Why wouldn't Jesus take away her craving for food—was He really that busy with Afghanistan? How did Hunter stay so thin?*
>
> *Hunter is happy for Angelica, who quit drinking the month before, and who has already taken charge of her life. She has a new job, at a bank, "where they like me and there's room to grow." If Hunter also finds Angelica's self-satisfaction annoying, she has the decency to feel guilty about it.*
>
> *Hunter and Angelica are climbing the hill that will lead them to the main path. Angelica is a little short of breath, but it's not slowing down her monologue. She's reciting, without pause, a list of what she used to drink. When she drank.*
>
> *"You like the blender drinks, cuz you're a girlie girl, like brandy Alexanders and piña coladas, fuck, anything mushy*

with an umbrella, while I had what they call refined taste, but if I couldn't get the good stuff, the single malt shit, I'd drink whatever I could find, I think I could have been one of those alkies from Prohibition who drank rubbing alcohol and went blind . . ."

They reach the West Point Inn at last. Now Angelica is holding Vijay's hand. He has on new hiking boots and he's been complaining for the last twenty minutes that they're hurting his feet. He bought the same ones that Peter has, some overpriced status brand. Except that Peter's are broken in now; Vijay's aren't, and you'd think he's been asked to walk over shards of glass.

Moments later he disengages his hand from Angelica's and wipes his palm on his pants. If Angelica notices, she doesn't show it: she's smiling deliriously. They've been married two months.

Peter and Vijay start talking real estate. It's the only thing they have in common. Peter loves all the balls: base, foot, and basket, but he's as ignorant of soccer as Vijay is of American sports. "That cricket bat is so wide, it's not really fair," Peter says, and something in her snaps, at the same time that Angelica launches into another frenzied speech about how blessed she is, how she does her gratitude prayers every day and is Hunter sure she wouldn't like to try it?

They deserve each other, Hunter thinks, and right then she means all three of them.

Peter bought that house in Corte Madera that was cheap because the couple was divorcing. He borrowed against it to spend $200,000 on remodeling. She told him to wait. Yes, he got a good deal, but it's hard to sell a house in a falling market.

He lost the whole investment. Now, who's going to loan him money for the next purchase?

He needs partners, partners with unsullied reputations. And she's overheard faint buzz about another deal, an apartment complex. A deal like that requires more wallets: a syndicate, they call it. Would he be in over his head? How much more in over his head can he be? Peter likes to work alone, but so far that isn't working out real well for him.

She pulls Angelica a few steps away. "Peter's on to something big," she whispered. "He wants to keep it to himself, but maybe Vijay could get in on it, too." The hard sell.

A few minutes after this whispered suggestion, Vijay seeks Peter out. Hunter and Angelica stand a few feet away, but Hunter (and, she's sure, Angelica), eavesdrop as best they can. "Gross rents" "debt service" "return on investment" "cash flow" "depreciation write-offs."

And a name: Campbell Graves. "My property manager," Vijay says. Even an idiot is good for some things."

Peter asks if Campbell was from the soup company, and Vijay said who knew, maybe on his mother's side?

The scene blurred. She gazed at the ceiling, where moonlight from the window cast an oval of pale gray.

There remained memories of heat and anger. And regret.

She rolled onto her side. She'd been trying to help: help Peter, help Angelica, even help Vijay. Since Peter wasn't good at flipping houses, maybe he'd do better investing in multifamily housing.

But no, in the end he wasn't interested. The complex was in a declining, unincorporated section of Placer County. There were FOR RENT signs everywhere.

Vijay invested on his own.

What mattered at the moment was that unless he'd been carried off by flying monkeys, a man named Campbell Graves shouldn't be hard to find.

Angelica had been talking this whole time, but now she raised her voice to declare, "I think God wants me to build a retreat center!"

"Yes, yes, good idea."

"And I know that Jesus wants us to succeed."

Hunter tried sticking her head under the pillow, but that only worked for as long as she could hold her breath.

Chapter 26

Gone

DANNIKA

Raskolnikov was purring funny. Instead of a steady *purrrrrrrrr*, he was going *purrrr*, HICK, *purrrr* HICK. She'd noticed it, then put it out of her mind.

Noticed again, and put it out of her mind.

Then she mentioned it in group and the other women shouted, "Go to the vet!"—all three at the same time.

M. Night Shyamalan could make a horror movie called *Going to the Vet*.

Dannika took good care of her cats. That was what Mosi said made them *not*-crazy cat ladies, the ones whose homes were eventually raided by Animal Control. Cats were innocent creatures, and the Universe had entrusted them to their care.

But of all the tasks Mosi had left behind—plunging clogged toilets, leaving saucepans under leaky roofs, tending a backyard reverting to wilderness—taking the cats to the vet was the worst, with the possible exception of filing income taxes.

Mosi had kept the cat carrier in the living room, making it into an extra bed, so their pets wouldn't associate it with their trips. The cats used it frequently, since it contained a fluffy blanket, but within thirty seconds of Dannika forming the resolve to use it to take a cat on the Voyage of the Damned, all nine of them moved to other parts of the house.

She hated doing it, but she caught Razzy and closed him up overnight in the second bathroom, the one that had only a toilet. She put food, water, and a small litter box there.

The next morning she cracked open the door just enough to squeeze inside, but he escaped. Then he hid under the sofa, too far back for her to reach.

She'd learned patience from her own felines. She perched on the back of the sofa, motionless and silent, for a full ninety minutes. When she spotted a white and orange paw emerge, she waited another half-second, then dropped the large towel she'd been holding on his back.

She jumped down just in time to wrap this terrycloth shroud around him before he could wiggle away. He did not go quietly.

As she was shoving him into the carrier, many pairs of green and amber eyes watched her like she was an agent of the Thought Police. "Would any of you trade places with him, Sydney Carton–style?" she asked, as she was applying bacitracin to her arms. "Then don't look at me like that."

———

Once at the veterinary hospital, Razzy was subdued, the fight gone out of him. He lay partway on the same towel she'd used to wrestle him into the cat carrier. *Do what you must,* his limp body said.

The exam room was cold, and grim, like pictures she'd seen of hospitals in the Soviet Union, with its steel scale and wooden table. Then there was one of those abominable "hang in there" cat posters, and this one had an orange tabby kitten, which felt like a sadistic joke.

Dr. Yeung finally came in. She pressed her stethoscope against his chest. She said there was fluid in his lungs. They could drain the fluid and maybe he'd be okay. Dannika could go home; they'd be a couple of hours or more.

She opted to stay in the waiting room.

It was just as grim out there, though in a different way. There was a slatted-back bench, and the only reading material were pamphlets about fleas and heartworm, and free monthlies like *PetWorld* and *City Dog*, printed on scratchy, recycled paper, with ink that rubbed off on her fingers. She'd needed two hands for the carrier—Razzy weighed fourteen pounds—so she hadn't been able to bring a book.

This wasn't a Purse Dog kind of clinic. Instead, the women who came in were leading giant canines, most of them recognizably pure-bred: Labradors and German shepherds. They were all panting like they'd run a doggie marathon. There was a sole woman behind the counter, with a helmet hairdo from what would have been Dannika's grandmother's day, if she'd ever had a grandmother.

It was a very long wait without a book. It was times like these that Dannika indulged in a little weed, but that was the last thing she would have brought. By the time Dr. Yeung's assistant came to lead her back, Dannika's fingertips were black and she knew more than she wanted about whipworm.

"It's advanced heart disease." Dr. Yeung said.

Once again, Razzy lay still on the exam table. They'd shaved his side.

And right outside was the kennel where people boarded their dogs when they went on vacation. They were barking insanely from their row of cages. They were big cages, but they were still cages.

Why did people have pets if they couldn't take care of them?

"What can we do?" *How will I pay for it? Do we have health insurance for the cats? Why don't we have health insurance for the cats?*

Mosi had left Dannika money that was intended for college, and Dannika had been living off it for three years. Since she owned the house outright, and didn't travel or eat out, and she hadn't bought herself a single item of clothing since binge-shopping for black right after the funeral, she'd been able to go through the money slowly, but in recent months she'd realized that this was a finite amount.

"There's really nothing to do," Dr. Yeung said slowly.

"Oh." The dogs barked and barked.

Dr. Yeung stroked Razzy lightly.

"We can't do it today," Dannika said. "I have to take him home first." She needed to get used to the idea, and he needed to say good-bye to the other cats.

"That's up to you," Dr. Yeung said.

At the front desk, she didn't look at the number on the bill, just stuck her debit card in the machine's slot and hoped it wouldn't be declined.

She held the carrier handle with both hands, to keep it steady, but when it lurched, Razzy moaned. Dannika froze. Razzy was gasping for breath.

"I changed my mind," she said.

———

"It's truly humane," Dr. Yeung said, and Dannika thought how ironic it was that the word "humane" contained the word "human." "It's too bad we don't have something like this for people."

"Can I hold him?"

"I'm sorry, the angle is wrong," Dr. Yeung said. "I'm going to stick a needle in his leg and he'll go to sleep, then I'll stick a second needle in."

Dannika did not look at anything that Dr. Yeung was doing. She lay her hands on Razzy, but softly, so he would feel their presence but not their weight. There was an assistant there, too, but she was just a set of navy blue scrubs, hovering in Dannika's peripheral vision. Dannika concentrated on remaining motionless, so that Dr. Yeung wouldn't stick the needle in the wrong place, even while her tears fell fast and heavy.

"He's gone," Dr. Yeung said.

Gone was the word that would always stay with her. *Gone.* Like opening the door to a closet that had once been crammed with clothes and luggage and boxes of schoolwork that you would never throw away, and finding it was empty inside.

When the hospice worker said that Mosi had "passed," Dannika came back into the room and knew that something was different, but it wasn't like this. Mosi's body was the proof that she was there in spirit.

Whereas Razzy was gone. Mosi had gone to heaven, to be with God, like Jean Valjean joining the Bishop at the end of *Les Misérables*. But Raskolnikov looked like roadkill. She tried to cover more of him with the towel, while Dr. Yeung murmured, "He had a good life."

The woman with helmet hair at the front desk said they would cremate the body and send her the remains. In a box with a place for her to put a photograph.

Mosi had wanted to be cremated, and to have her ashes scattered on Mount Tam, but Dannika couldn't bear to think of her body reduced to what was left after you smoked a freaking cigarette.

Mosi had said that if there were ever an earthquake or fire, that she and Dannika should meet at the mailbox at the corner so that they would each know that the other was safe. So she buried her mother in the Mt. Tamalpais Cemetery, where at least there was the Mount Tam name. She still visited four times a week; she thought of it as their new "safe spot."

But she didn't know what she'd do with Raskolnikov. She was pretty sure that there were laws about burying animals, and could she dig a hole deep enough anyway?

So Dannika said to the helmet-haired woman, "Yeah, sure," and stuck her card in the slot again.

———

She drove home.

When she braked for a stop sign, the carrier in the back seat rattled, and that caused a single sob to come straight from Dannika's chest. She would have left the carrier on the street, except that she needed it for the other cats.

She would call the women when she got back. She didn't want to be alone. But she wouldn't smoke weed now because it might make her feel worse, and then she'd be trapped there, in Weed Land, where imagination could be friend or foe.

She recognized Howie's car, parked in front of her house, from two blocks away. It was a red Tercel, so old that the paint was bleached to tomato. The many dents and scratches were new, but at least he didn't pretend, like one guy she knew, whose car was so banged up it looked like a crushed soda can, that everything had happened in a parking lot while he was somewhere else. The first time Dannika saw his car, Howie had laughed off the damage. He said he needed new glasses more than he needed a new car, but it wasn't like Boss Man Ravi was giving out vision or dental.

Howie was the last person she wanted to see. She thought about driving around the block, but then decided that she wasn't going to let El Dweebo control her like that.

She swung into her own driveway, so fast that she barely missed clubbing a fresh dent into his fender, and hopped out of the car before the engine had completely died. Howie was on the other side of his car, facing her house, reading a book. *Les Misérables*.

She ran the few feet up to him, forming the words in her head: *I am not in the mood for you. Go home.*

Instead, she stopped in front of him and cried. She covered her face with her hands while her shoulders shook.

"What's wrong?" she heard him say.

She cried harder, still keeping her face covered. Then she felt his arms creep along hers until they met at her back and he was hugging her.

She collapsed into him. Anything to keep from falling down, first to the concrete, then to the abyss.

"What's wrong?" he asked again. His lips were close to her ear.

Between sobs she choked out, "Raskolnikov. He's gone."

———

He offered to make her tea, and she accepted. He went into the house, while she sat on the porch steps, even though it was getting cold. She wasn't ready to go inside, to see the cats that Raskolnikov had left behind. Howie shouted questions to her a few times, but she only picked out the words "kettle" and "spoons," so she pretended not to hear him at all.

Hunter had told her that Catholics didn't believe that animals had souls: that they acted totally on instinct, like machines. Hunter didn't believe in souls at all, but Dannika knew that Mosi had a soul. And if humans did, then cats had to, too. What kind of God bestowed immortality on one species, but denied it to another one, one that was so close on the evolutionary scale? Besides, cats had distinctive personalities as much as humans, and Razzy was more loving than most of the people she knew.

But if humans and higher mammals, like dogs and cats and horses, had souls, then where was the dividing line? Did bugs have souls?

Maybe they were all one giant soul. She and Razzy and the bugs were like drops of water in the ocean, and those drops got scooped out sometimes, but then returned to blend in with every-one else.

That wasn't very comforting. She didn't want to be a drop in the ocean of life.

Maybe there was just Nothing. That was her greatest fear. After all, in the incomprehensible vastness that was the universe, it could have happened that there was this one planet with water and oxygen, so life began there, but the rest was empty. And Godless. That was actually easier to believe than to think that a Deity had taken four billion years to get around to making sentient life and now He (or She, or They) was listening to a lonely girl trying to talk to Him.

She didn't think she could cry anymore, but the tears were coming again. She closed her eyes and let them roll down her cheeks.

Howie come up behind her and handed a mug of tea over her shoulder. When she tasted it, she discovered that it was hardly warm, and it was Earl Grey, the only tea she'd asked him not to use, since she didn't want the caffeine. Also, he forgot the sugar.

"I shouldn't have named him Raskolnikov," she said. She pressed the mug between her knees. "He was such a doomed character."

"But he's redeemed at the end." Howie took her hand. His palm was clammy.

"That's right. From prison," she said sarcastically. She freed her hand, tried one more swallow, then flung what remained into the baby acacias taking over the front of the house. "Why did this happen? He was only eleven years old. Mrs. Pardiggle is fourteen. Not that I want anything to happen to her." The terrible thought that crept in was like secondhand smoke: would she have rather it were Mrs. Pardiggle, the grumpy, overweight tuxedo cat, who wanted nothing to do with her or the others?

She waved the thought away. She loved all her cats equally.

"Thanks for letting me sit outside," Howie said.

"Huh?"

"My allergy." He tapped his glasses, and she recalled how red and swollen they were the last time he was at her house.

Might as well pretend that she was being thoughtful. "Right. Right."

"Tell me all about Raskolnikov."

"Oh my God, he was the best. I'd get in bed, and then about two minutes later, I'd hear this thump-thump—" she demonstrated by slapping the heel of her hand against her thigh— "and he'd be up on the bed and he'd crawl to me, then sniff like to make sure it was me, then I'd lift up the comforter so he could crawl underneath and purr himself to sleep."

She went on about how he'd push his chin under her hand so that she'd scratch his ears, and how funny it was to see him paw at a moth that was on the other side of a closed window. But then the image of his body, lying motionless on the vet's table, intruded, and a fresh sob escaped her. "And now he's coming home in a box."

He put his hand on the back of her neck and squeezed, in a gesture that might well have meant, "I feel your pain," but she tensed, anticipating what else it might mean.

"The box, you can decorate it with pictures of him. Maybe make a collage."

She shook her head. "Crafts are like Trix—they're for kids."

"But your stuff is good."

Even after Mosi dissed her milk carton house, Dannika had continued to make crafts; she even made an apron for Mosi out of white dish towels, and then painted a picture of herself and Mosi together. But after The Last Craft Fair, she never attempted jewelry again.

Howie removed his hand.

"Thanks for listening, anyway." And he had listened, owl eyes steady on her from behind his thick glasses.

"De nada, señorita."

She wiped her own eyes on the cuff of her sleeve.

There would be a price to pay. He'd been very patient, but he'd reach over now and, pretending to console her, would find the last trace of a tear to wipe away. Or he'd want to massage her neck. Once a dude threw himself on her bed and asked, "Do you give good back rubs?" which was almost funny. If the jerk had thought he was going to get lucky, then he might at least have offered to give *her* the back rub.

Not only did Howie not touch her, though, he tucked his hands under his armpits, so he was hugging himself. "It's all hard to figure."

Someone had left an old bike across the street. It was going to get stolen.

She hesitated. "Do you believe in anything?"

"What do you mean, like gravity?" He rocked slightly. "Yeah, 'cause that's why I don't float away."

"No, like . . ." She was embarrassed. "Like, I don't know, God or something."

"Maybe. Whatever it is has to be something we can't understand." Howie didn't look at her, but he nodded slowly. "Like a fourth primary color."

"A fourth primary color would be awesome." That was the perfect way to describe how she knew she couldn't imagine God.

"Maybe there is one, and we just can't see it." His lip turned up into a half-smile. "David Hume wrote how he couldn't believe that anything existed if he couldn't see it or touch it, or whatever, but why would we think that humans have every capability there is? I mean, we can't see X-rays."

That was just what she'd thought! "And why would humans be the most intelligent beings in the universe?"

"It's living with uncertainty that's hard," Howie said. "And no one can live with uncertainty, so they latch on to Scientology."

"Scientology," she echoed with contempt. Mosi's friends all believed in astrology, but that was fairly harmless; Dannika sometimes read Virgo, for fun.

MEEEEOOWW

It was a plaintive sound coming from inside. Raskolnikov was gone, but she still had to feed the others. Dannika sighed and picked up the empty mug. "We must cultivate our garden, amirite?" She pointed to her left eye to acknowledge his allergy. "Don't worry, you don't have to come in."

Chapter 27

Scraping the Sky

HUNTER

Campbell Graves was not hard to find. There were only two on LinkedIn, and while one was in Missouri, the other was still in Marin.

Marin Campbell Graves was a chipper guy. "I'm out of property management," he said, in response to a question she hadn't asked. "Why work for someone else? I'm in residential sales. Are you in the market?"

"Alas, no."

"Just remember that the best time to buy a house was always five years ago." He sent out a weekly newsletter, and Vijay Koka was still on his list. "Can I add your name?"

Hunter gave Campbell her name in exchange for Vijay's email. Would it still be good?

It was.

———

In his first message, Will asked in neutral terms if Mr. Koka would speak to him and an associate about the content of Angelica's book. Vijay wrote back,

```
The remembrance of that life is
fraught with so much pain to me,
with so much mental suffering and
want of hope, that I have never had
the courage even to examine how long
I was doomed to lead it.
     Charles Dickens, David Copperfield
```

Will was diplomatic but persistent.

```
You don't have to read Ms. Ambrose's
book. We would just like to ask you
a few questions.
```

Vijay declined.

Will persisted, rewording his request again. And again. And again. Until Vijay finally agreed to a Skype.

Mumbai was eight hours earlier than San Francisco—or sixteen hours later, depending on your attitude. They made an appointment for 4 p.m. Pacific Time.

———

That afternoon, Hunter remembered that she didn't like high-rises. These days she often ventured into San Francisco to scour for collectibles at secondhand stores, but those trips never took her into the Financial District.

Security at One Market Plaza was as tight as any airport, minus, at least, the pat down. A security guard programmed the elevator to take her directly to Will's floor.

When she stepped out, she saw nothing but a vast expanse of sky. She felt as if she were hovering midair. She wasn't afraid of heights—hadn't she climbed Mount Tamalpais many times? But here there was no earth beneath her feet. She kept thinking about the World Trade Center, and when a stray plane flew past, her stomach tightened.

Will had booked a conference room. It was empty except for a large monitor on the far wall. Outside, the Transamerica Pyramid, the hideous Salesforce Tower, the Bay, the water . . . and so much sky.

"Here, get comfortable." Will pulled out a chair. Yes, a man in a suit would pull out chairs for you.

A monitor hung on the wall. When the connection was made, Vijay appeared there, in close-up, scary big. It took her a moment to recognize him, even though, after a moment, she saw that he looked much the same: baby face, chipmunk cheeks. She remembered that he was younger than Angelica, but he looked barely thirty. When Will was trying to contact him, she'd thought better of trying to connect based on their previous relationship. Their interactions had been brief and impersonal. And now it seemed that he didn't even recognize her. Not flattering, but maybe just as well.

Will started with a formal greeting. "Thank you for meeting with us."

The large head spoke. "I was going to continue to ignore your emails, but I wish to conclude every interaction with my ex-wife once and for all. Please do not contact me after this call."

"We just want your help in exposing her," Hunter said.

Will picked up there. "If you can go on the record as refuting some of the claims in her memoir—"

"Hah! It's not a memoir, it's fiction, and not even good fiction. There are three honest words in that book: Angelica, 'saint,' and Ambrose. Though her eligibility for sainthood is questionable."

Will restlessly tapped a pen against the legal pad in front of him. "At the end of the book she says that you left Marin County abruptly rather than face their friends."

"Not bloody likely. I could not wait to leave California. I would have left sooner had I not had the disagreeable business of a divorce to attend to." Vijay's face was close enough to the camera that Hunter could identify the pores in his nose. "Your California is famous for being a paradise. But in fact, it is vile."

Hunter exchanged an anxious glance with Will. "W-why do you say that?" she asked.

"Look around! You have naked women on your billboards! On your television sets! I respect others' choices," he went on, "but I confess that I am made uncomfortable by the sight of two men kissing."

"Better get over it," Will said, with his head bowed over his notepad, so only Hunter could hear him.

"Parts of San Francisco look like Mumbai. If I'm going to live with the starving and the homeless, not to mention the mentally ill, I might as well live with my own starving and homeless. And we care for our mentally ill."

Angelica had written a lively description of Mumbai. "Jesus needs to get over here quick! I'm saving to send Him a plane ticket. He can fly coach."

"And by the way," Vijay scoffed, "she's never been to any part of India. She invented a trip, complete with describing her own acts of charity." His image pixelated and Hunter missed his next few words, but when his face reassembled itself, he was expanding on the same theme.

". . . and in your television programs, it's taken for granted that a woman has intercourse with a man on a first date. Understand me, she has every right to have intercourse on her own terms. And that's television. A worthy opiate for the masses. But that's what makes it so disturbing. She's a modern, independent woman, who has sex with anyone she deems worthy of a sharing a meal. Do you not realize how far you've fallen from grace?"

Hunter winced. She didn't like the idea of falling from grace, no matter how vehemently she protested her atheism.

"We've gotten rather far afield," Will said, tapping more furiously.

But Vijay had clearly waited a long time to express his frustration.

"You talk now of cultural appropriation. A white woman cannot write about a Hispanic woman. A university cannot sell sushi in its food court. Meanwhile, you in Marin County have appropriated all things Eastern. You take yoga classes and speak of karma without understanding any of the philosophical underpinnings."

Hunter was embarrassed; she took the occasional yoga class. She speculated that Will, though, was trying to think of a new, more persuasive argument with which to make their case.

"I'm not a believer," Vijay said. "If I were, I'd have dire predictions for Angelica St. Ambrose's next life. It might involve a snout."

Hunter coughed. She tried to sound serious when she said, "That's a bit harsh."

Vijay turned his face to his left for a moment, displaying a long-ish sideburn. When he faced them again, he said, "You are right. Perhaps I am the one who should be worried."

Will pressed immediately, "Because . . ."

"Because I was blunt with her. I proposed we marry so that I could obtain a green card, and eventually citizenship. I planned to be a good husband, if in name only."

"What do you mean, 'in name only'?" Hunter asked.

"I was fond of her at the start. Let's say that I found her interesting. Amusing. But I was calculating. I thought I had little to lose, if it didn't work out, that is, once we were married long enough that I could become a citizen."

It didn't work out, he went on. "In California terms, she was 'high-maintenance.'"

"You used her," Hunter said, earning an elbow poke from Will. Angelica performed entertaining monologues about her bad luck with men. Underneath the posturing was a woman who really had been hurt.

"I was quite clear that this was not a love match." Vijay moistened his lips and Hunter had an unwelcome view of his tongue. "Then, once we married, she unilaterally renegotiated the terms."

"You know that green card marriages are illegal," Will said.

Vijay tilted his giant head forward. To Hunter, it seemed ready to emerge from the screen.

"I'm sure you're aware that in my country, arranged matches were the norm for centuries. Now it exists in a modified form, and would you be surprised to learn that India has the lowest divorce rate in the world? While you Californians marry and divorce as often as you trade in cars, which you do too much of as well.

"As for the laws governing divorce, they are highly discriminatory. Half of what I bought with my own money went to your Miss—sorry, Ms. Ambrose. She's not terribly responsible when it comes to finances; perhaps you've noticed." He paused, then continued in an even more indignant tone, "The court granted her title to a large apartment complex near Sacramento, based on the flimsiest, if not falsified, evidence."

Funny, Hunter thought, how Angelica hadn't written anything about the division of property in her memoir.

"Slap the term 'community property' on a building and the offended woman can walk away with it."

Hunter was glad that Peter and Vijay had never invested in anything together after all. At least she didn't have to blame herself for that. She suspected that Vijay had heard the same you-too-can-flip-a-property and get rich stories that Peter had, stories that didn't mention that you needed to combine the ability to analyze a spreadsheet with a large serving of luck.

Will shifted in the unforgiving conference room chair. "'Our' Ms. Ambrose is also making quite a bit of money off her side of this story. We'd like to expose the untruths in her memoir, certainly those concerning you. I can record you making some of these statements."

"No," Vijay said coldly. "No good can come of any further involvement with that lady."

She would only rain further hellfire down on him, he said, starting with a lawsuit for defamation or intentional infliction of emotional distress. Americans loved no activity better than going to court. And wasn't she writing a sequel to her memoir?

Hunter allowed as how she was: She'd overheard Angelica telling Peter about it. *Let Go and Let God for God's Sake* was the working title, but she didn't share that.

"Then I'll let you imagine what further accusations she might level. Bloody hell! Wouldn't she just love to write a courtroom drama? I imagine much weeping on the witness stand in Ms. Ambrose's inimitable style."

Will made a final, calmly worded plea. Vijay could be doing good in the world by undermining Angelica, who had indeed raised the price of her workshop, thanks to its success. A success that was driving Hunter out of the house as much as she was able, so as to avoid the Acolytes. Still, she overheard, and didn't always try to avoid overhearing, requests for donations in addition to the regular meeting fee, "because of our important work."

"Hah!" Vijay snorted. "What do you care, Mr. DeWitt, how Marin County women spend their disposable income? If not on Angelica St. Ambrose, then perhaps on Botox or spa treatments? No, until she asks them to sacrifice goats, I'm at peace with her labors.

"However," he concluded. "I will give you one piece of advice, and without charge. Visit that apartment complex I mentioned. It's called Hyde Park."

The screen went black.

Chapter 28

The Father and the Daughter

PENELOPE

Penelope had her own laptop now. The problem was that she didn't yet have an actual desk, so it sat on her dresser, which meant that she could only reach the keyboard by bending over her knees.

She had planned to wait for the arrival of that desk before returning to her blog, but that morning she had a story that she wanted to write badly enough that she could tolerate a little lower back pain.

She'd been thinking about her father. She didn't think about him very often. Why would she? He'd been dead for forty years. He lived long enough to see her become the one thing more shameful than an old maid: a divorcee. Alas, not long enough to see her remarry. And he would have loved Scott.

But as the memories of her Valium years had crowded in—falling asleep in public, and searching for pills at the bottom of purses—those memories dragged memories of earlier years with them, packs of unruly dogs that barked for attention, sometimes all night.

I was an accident. My mother was 48 when she gave birth. Can you believe that? So many women think they can't conceive after 40 without medical intervention. But it happens. It happens when you least expect it.

Daddy made money in oil. Back then, that was okay. There was no global warming. Okay, there was global warming, we just didn't know about it. Okay, we did know about it, but we didn't care. Not yet. Not in time. Can I use my youth as an excuse for not knowing or caring? My high school was all about who was going to be Prom Queen.

The point is that he had a family business that he wanted to pass down, and what did dad get? Three daughters. And whoever heard of Thompson and Daughters?

Ralph Joseph Thompson. No need to change the name of a man who'd been dead forty years.

Being the youngest of four daughters, all my life I've been fascinated with how women are treated. It hurts to think about Catherine the Great, how she was such a bad mother that her son (who was probably fathered by Sergei Saltykov anyway, not the Grand Duke Peter), changed the law so that no woman could be czar again. Just think. If that hadn't happened, then the oldest Romanov princess could have inherited the throne, and maybe . . . well, I admit it. We're getting into waters too deep for me to swim in.

The howling dogs of memory brought back much of what her father had said about women over the years: Women drivers were incompetent. Women didn't belong in politics, because they were "crazy at least three days a month." And when her sisters, the two younger ones, who still lived at home, were working in the kitchen, her father, from behind the unfolded newspaper that usually covered his face, would observe, "Good practice. Cooking will get them husbands."

That was how Penelope always remembered her dad: behind the newspaper, diffusing the odor of tobacco.

She got up to stretch out her back. Damn, when was that desk going to be delivered?

She'd have to rewrite all of this. She might take out the Catherine the Great part. She might not even want to post this one. . . . But yes, she did. This one was for all the unwanted daughters of the world. Because no matter how much had changed (women doctors! women scientists! maybe someday a woman president!) too many girls were still dismissed, disregarded, and disrespected by disinterested dads.

Penelope didn't like the resentment that caused in her. She'd started this with the intention of finding forgiveness for him within herself.

She sat down again.

Daddy was a religious man. A churchgoing Methodist. When my mother told him she was pregnant—I heard this from my mother—he said, "The Lord provides!" I would be the son he'd waited for. Prayed for.

By then, he'd come to terms with my sisters. They were so much older than I that I never got to know them well, but I remember the younger two nattering on about what they would wear to the debutante ball, and how they were learning the Texas dip. I actually think he was proud of them. They were beauties when they were young. And the oldest was already married, at twenty-two, so he knew that he wasn't going to have three old maids to support.

But here comes the announcement from Marian Thompson: "I'm knocked up!" No, of course not—Mama would have said something ladylike, maybe, "we're expecting a little visitor."

Imagine Mama's surprise. She was just shy of her forty-eighth birthday. When her periods stopped, she must have thought she was going into menopause.

So here comes the son, like the Beatles said, haha. "God's timing isn't our own," the minister liked to say. God has a plan for all of us, and Marian Thompson's change-of-life baby was part of the plan. God was wagging a finger at Ralph Joseph ("R.J.") Thompson, saying, "you knew you were supposed to wait for My time!"

So now Daddy thinks, Praise the Lord! My son is going to play for the NFL, discover a cure for cancer, maybe be an astronaut, or president of these here United States, or maybe . . . okay, let's not get too far ahead of ourselves, but maybe Ralph Joseph Thompson III is the Second Coming. Mama's name was "Marian." Could that be a coincidence?

But no, it's another girl.

What did God mean, by giving him the reproductive version of clickbait?

Penelope had only learned the term "clickbait" since she'd started blogging, and it fit here perfectly, although "reproductive" struck her as wrong in that sentence.

There was no amniocentesis then and I know from my obstetrician friend that the risk of having a Down syndrome baby at Mama's age was high enough that my dad should have simply been grateful that I was healthy.

Penelope had to stop there to consider whether expressing gratitude for an infant who didn't have a developmental disability was politically incorrect. She'd have to get Reyna's, and her talking-stick women friends', opinion on that.

But no. When she felt the noose of political correctness tightening around her, she simply slackened the rope. There was free speech in America! Her daddy was the first one to say that, and he said it many, many times.

*Daddy must have thought that he would have been better off if I'd
never been born. He never said so, but then, he never said much of
anything to me about anything.*

    *Actions speak louder than words. He never went to
church again.*

    *But when he was dying, of pancreatic cancer, he made it up
to me.*

Penelope struck out the final sentence. She wasn't keeping a journal
anymore: She was writing for an audience. That meant creating a
persona, while maintaining a degree of privacy.

    She put her hands on her lower back. She was going to get up
again. But wait . . .

    The computer showed the time in the lower right-hand corner
of the screen. 3:02 p.m. She hadn't had a Valium all day.

Chapter 29

Lemon Meringue Pie

ALICIA

Alicia's usual seat was on the black leather sectional sofa across from the abstract painting that hung over the empty—perhaps never used—fireplace in Penelope's living room. It was a soft, grayish blue with some gold shapes. "What do you see when you look at that painting?" she asked.

"I see a waste of money." Penelope lay down the deli platter that would be the centerpiece of their dinner. "Scott spent I don't want to tell you how much on that. I like paintings where you can identify the subject."

Alicia saw a compass and an arrow. A sundial, maybe?

Penelope sat, tucking her pencil skirt under her thighs. "Well, I have an announcement."

She was clean. "So then I looked up and saw that I'd been writing for two hours and hadn't had a pill all day. I've been cutting down without really thinking about it. The last pill to go was the one I took in the morning. But I can write better without it.

"I know what y'all thinking. And you're right." Penelope nodded. "The price of being clean is eternal vigilance. So I got rid of the rest of my supply."

"Tennis Club Trish?" Hunter asked.

"Took her out of my address book. Ripped out the page."

They all laughed at the idea of having an address book in the first place, but Penelope didn't seem to take offense.

"Your turn, Alicia," Hunter said.

"Just a minute." Alicia had just started on a baby carrot; along with the deli platter there was a tray of crudités and dips. That tray grew more elaborate at each meeting, and now included not only a selection of raw vegetables, but three different dips, including hummus. Alicia detected Reyna's hand in this.

Penelope put the talking stick in Alicia's lap. Alicia swallowed the last of the carrot, took a sip of water, and closed her fingers around the small painted branch. She was all set to share anecdotes about Summer and Joshua.

But hardly had the nail of her left ring finger prodded the tip of her thumb, when the room began to spin.

> She's in her mother's kitchen. Debbie closes the shutters over the sink to block out the sun, as it dips below the level of the frame. Everything in her mother's kitchen is yellow: the walls, the appliances, the window treatments, the linoleum. It's like living in the center of a lemon meringue pie.
>
> It's Passover, when Debbie cooks for extended family: three aunts, two uncles, six cousins. Alicia likes some of them.
>
> Debbie returns to apple-chopping. "Do you have any idea how lucky you are?" Her knife hits the counter with angry whacks. She's making charoset.
>
> Alicia isn't feeling lucky. The smell of gefilte fish, arranged on plates with daubs of red horseradish, is making her queasy, even though the plates are at the far end of the counter. She's hated the

smell of gefilte fish all her life (the taste is even worse), so maybe
that doesn't count. She breaks off half a slice of matzo from the
box; sometimes eating makes her feel better.

The notion that the indisposition of pregnancy is confined to
morning is another myth created by the patriarchy, but it was
thanks to a wave of nausea Alicia suffered when she entered a
Boston Market that she looked at a calendar. Yes, she'd missed a
period. Maybe even two.

"I threw up daily for months!" Whack-whack-whack, goes
the knife against the cutting board.

Alicia is sure that this is an exaggeration.

Whack-whack. The pieces of apple get smaller and smaller.
Isn't there a Cuisinart or something that will do that for her?

"I'm going to have an abortion."

That was cruel. She should have said "I'm going to terminate
the pregnancy."

"No, you're not!"

And why did she tell Debbie anyway? Because she has to tell
someone, and when you have to tell someone, you tell your mother.

"Ma, I can't have a baby now, I—"

"Having a baby takes one day. I had you in two hours."

Debbie's experience with childbirth varies in the telling. Sometimes she had a painless, precipitant labor. Other times she was in
agony for seventy-two hours.

"You do know who the father is, right?"

Alicia straightens her back. "He's a guy in my year. Joshua—" She stops. Okay, yes, she had to tell her mother, but she
can't run the risk of Joshua finding out. It's her body, her decision.

"Joshua who?"

"It doesn't matter."

"Yes, it does!" Debbie slams down the bowl of chopped apples.
Then she recollects herself, and squeezes lemon juice on them to keep
them from going brown. "Can't he take some responsibility?"

"He dumped me when I said I was pregnant." She adds, for
effect, "He said it was my problem."

It's time to take the matzo meal out of the refrigerator. Debbie likes to give it the full two hours. "I'll take care of it."

What does Debbie mean? She'll arrange for an abortion?

"I said, I'll take care of the baby. This might be my one chance to be a grandmother."

Debbie must think that Alicia will never marry. Alicia knows that Debbie doesn't think much of Alicia's appearance. It's also true that Alicia hasn't dated much. But what medical student does?

Debbie holds her hands under the faucet. She needs damp hands to roll matzo balls.

Watching Debbie cook for the relatives over the years, Alicia has vowed that she will never cook any more than is absolutely necessary.

"Your brother—" *Debbie stops.*

Alicia's older brother has been troubled since childhood. As a teen he got into drugs; later he dropped out of college, and now, though clean and sober, works as a lowly (by her mother's stand- ards) drug-and-alcohol counselor.

"When's your due date? Okay, so not perfect. But you can miss two weeks of school—you're so smart—and then we'll take over. Your father and I will take the baby until . . . until whenever you want."

Alicia tries to get her mind around this offer. What if her mother reneges? But somehow Alicia knows she won't. Debbie can be a nag, a noodge. She's also queen of the kind of contradictory messages that the psychiatric community used to think caused schizophrenia in children. "Are the girls wearing their hair that long?" *one week and then, after the haircut,* "Are the girls wearing their hair that short?"

But she's also a nurturer: The abundance of food surrounding them is only one manifestation, the way that the segment of matzo in Alicia's hand is only a chunk of the slice, for Debbie is always standing by the front door with an extra layer of clothing, and she even sews! Replaces loose buttons, hems dresses and skirts; made costumes for that most un-Jewish of holidays: Halloween.

Grandparents are so much easier to bond with than parents.
"I'll think about it."

But she can't think about it. In another week she'll tip into her
second trimester, when the procedure isn't drive-thru anymore. And
although Alicia could be a PSA for reproductive rights, for her the
second trimester has some moral ambiguity.

Debbie has dropped the matzo balls into the boiling water. She
takes a brush to scrub the matzo meal that has stuck to her hands.

Debbie is a woman meant to be a mother.

———

Alicia's first sonogram revealed that the baby was a girl. Alicia
was glad: she could raise a feminist! She went to Lamaze and had
a natural birth. The sonogram also revealed that she was further
along than she'd realized. The baby came in late August, and
Alicia didn't have to miss school after all.

She named her Summer. She liked the name, but she was
sticking it to Debbie, too, who wanted to name her Nora, for her
deceased father Norman. "And the woman in A Doll's House."

Alicia breastfed for two weeks at her parents' house,
then departed.

"Hoo boy." Alicia put her hands on her face, pressed her eyelids with
her fingertips.

The other women looked everywhere but at her. Finally, "you
remembered something," Hunter said.

"M'm." Was this what some drugs were like? What about the hal-
lucinations that women had under the influence of "twilight sleep,"
the sinister drug that the medical profession had at one time forced
on women in labor? And that only after they shaved their pubic
hair and gave them enemas. "It's obviously a kind of mass hypnosis."
Alicia couldn't be hypnotized. People trained in hypnosis had tried.

"If you say so." Dannika folded her arms across her chest.

"It doesn't really matter, does it?" Hunter had raised this before.

Penelope *heh-heh*'d. "I hope I don't remember that I killed someone in a past life." She paused. "I don't believe in past lives. Just to be clear."

"In my mind, all these years . . ." Alicia didn't finish.

In her mind, Debbie and Mark had "helped out a little." Taken Summer during exam week. Given Alicia a break. But that wasn't how it happened. Alicia had parked Summer with the Liebermans, and didn't see Summer for weeks at a time, for the first two years of her daughter's life.

"I guess . . ." Alicia started to reach for another baby carrot, then stopped. "I guess I owe Summer an apology."

And when, a little later, Penelope brought out a virgin box of Godiva chocolates, Alicia didn't have any.

———

When she got home, Alicia found Summer in the kitchen with Joshua, where he was showing her how to separate an egg. "You two do not need to eat takeout every night. If you were my patients . . ."

The sight of the rich yellow of the yolk put Alicia back in her mother's lemon meringue kitchen for a moment. Maybe this was what PTSD was like.

Joshua dropped the yolk into one bowl, then poured the white into another.

"Let me try, Dad," Summer said.

Summer had started calling him "Dad" a while before, but the sound still startled Alicia.

"All right, sweetie." Joshua tossed the eggshell into Summer's recent addition: the compost bin.

"What are you guys making?"

"An egg-white omelet," Summer said. "It's healthier."

"How was your group?" Joshua asked.

"Uh . . . fine, fine. Can I talk to Summer for a minute?"

"Huh." Summer was less than enthusiastic, but Joshua said that he should check in with the office.

When they were alone: "Wh-what do you want to talk about?"

Summer leaned against the refrigerator, and again, for a split second, Alicia was back in her own mother's kitchen. But then she focused on Summer, almost as tall as Joshua, with those hazel eyes. Something was different, though. Alicia squinted. Summer was wearing her standard jeans-and-T-shirt, but instead of the oversized pieces that rendered her shapeless, she was in skinny jeans and a black T-shirt, half-tucked. And was that an ear cuff? It was difficult to see under Summer's hair.

"I want to apologize to you."

"Whoodee-doo."

Alicia had done some rehearsing in the car, and when she spoke, it came out in a rush, awkward and insincere. "I'm-sorry-I-left-you-with-Grandma-and-Granddad-when-you-were-a-baby."

"Huh." Again. "That's what you want to apologize to me for?"

"Uh . . . yes?"

Summer shook her head. "I love Grandma and Granddad."

"I know you do, but—" Alicia was about to say that these were formative years, that her own absence was the root cause of the tension between them now. Did she have some fantasy that Summer would fall into her arms and say, thank you for not having an abortion? But she couldn't, because she'd first have to tell Summer that she'd wanted an abortion, and there was no coming back from that.

"You should have left me there." Summer pushed herself off the refrigerator.

"What?"

"Grandma Debbie and Granddad Mark loved me the way I was."

"I love you the way you are."

"Grandma and Granddad had time for me. Especially Grandma."

Alicia bit her lip to keep from shouting. *What did you want me to do, quit my residency, work as a waitress? Yeah, that would have been a life for us!*

Not long before, she would have said all that, and worse.

But now, she stood still, a firm canvas sail against Summer's windstorm list of Alicia's failings as a mother. She didn't decorate her brown paper lunch bags like Tiffany's mother, or leave Post-it "I love you" notes in them like KC's mom. She didn't cook dinner. (Here Summer gestured to the cork board of takeout menus that still fluttered there.) She wasn't even home for dinner half the time! She never chaperoned field trips. She was never a room parent, like Hannah's mom and the other Hannah's mom. And now that Summer was in tenth grade, and chaperoning field trips or being a room parent was no longer of value, the only way Alicia contributed was by throwing money at the school, and anyone could do that.

And still Alicia battened down the hatches, while thinking, *next she'll hate on me for not kissing her favorite doll goodnight.*

"But worse!" Summer said. "You made me take clarinet."

All the fifth graders had to take an instrument.

"And ballet!"

"But you wanted—" Summer had begged to take ballet. Hadn't she? But even if Summer had wanted ballet there were things Alicia knew that she hadn't wanted. Private Spanish lessons at age six. Science camp at eight. Oprah's latest book club selection left on Summer's bed.

"I wanted control." Alicia interrupted, but spoke hardly above a whisper. "I thought I'd get tabula rasa and I could make you whatever I wanted."

"What's tabula rasa?"

"Blank slate." Alicia was staring at the wall calendar that advertised Clomid, given to her by a pharmaceutical rep. Each month had a different picture of a happy infant. "I wanted you all to myself." Alicia found the courage to look her daughter in the face again.

"That's why I lied to you about Joshua. I wanted to make sure that no one else would have any input about you. But . . ." Alicia reached for something that didn't exist: an excuse. "I lied to myself, too."

Summer locked eyes with her.

"So you let me grow up thinking Dad didn't want me."

The boat tipped over. Alicia went down, deep, swallowing so much salt water that she was unable to speak.

This was the terrible, irrevocable, unforgivable act. A mother-daughter war crime. Alicia broke eye contact, looking everywhere, at everything, the takeout menus and the calendar, and the table where there was a half-empty carton of yogurt.

Alicia was sick of hearing about the infamous twelve steps, as if, instead of a mere Ten Commandments, Moses had brought them down on two tablets from Mount Sinai. But at the moment, she thought of the one about making amends, and discovered that it was bullshit.

When she could finally get the words out, she said, "I'm so sorry."

"Well, I lied to you, too." Summer looked very proud of herself. "There wasn't any Prophet John."

"You told me."

"Yeah, I told you that part. I didn't tell you that I ran away to find Dad." Grandma Debbie, after years of silence, had told Summer what she knew: that Summer's father was another medical student and that his first name was Joshua.

"There was a medical convention in Las Vegas and I was going to try to find him there. How stupid was that?" Summer said, which was a relief, as it obviated the need for Alicia to point out that there were likely more than one "Joshua" at a typical medical convention.

"You didn't even know that he was a pediatrician," Alicia said before she could stop herself.

This was a memory that would never fade: the vision of Summer in the trunk of a car, mouth duct-taped . . . then her corpse . . . she shuddered the images away; Summer was here, safe and healthy.

"I was naive, I admit it," Summer said haughtily. "I've matured since then."

"It was four months ago!"

"Well, it turns out that he was there. I just didn't have the hotel name right." She turned abruptly, with a grace that Alicia had not seen before. "Anyway, Dad is in my life now."

Chapter 30

Rock the Boat

HUNTER

The following Sunday, Hunter and Will made the long drive north to Placer County, northeast of Sacramento, and Hyde Park Apartments.

Hunter suspected—as did Will—that Vijay wanted them to find fire code violations and other signs of neglect egregious enough that they could sic the authorities on Angelica.

They explored the complex in nearly unbearable heat. "WTF?" Hunter asked when she stripped down to her tank top. "It's only spring."

"Global warming." Will used a handkerchief to pat down his scalp, then replaced the UC Berkeley cap he'd been wearing.

The place was run down: the pool had been drained (FOR MAIN-TENANCE, a sign declared ambiguously) and only one of the washing machines in the laundry room was functioning. As for the landscaping, everything that was supposed to be green had turned brown, but Will approved of that: "There's no water to waste on lawns."

"We could get a reporter out here, maybe?" Hunter asked.

Will thought such a move would backfire. "If we were to investigate any of the buildings around here, I bet we'd see this and worse." Indeed, in this part of Placer County, Hyde Park was upscale. "So we get a story about how apartment life in Placer County is subpar. Nothing to do with Angelica."

When they entered the community room, at least, the air-conditioning made Hunter feel as though she could breathe again.

It was a large space, with a pool table on one end, where several twentysomethings gathered. Billiard balls clacked, and a few cans of Coors Lite rested on the rails.

The rest of the room was set up for a meeting, with chairs in neat rows, facing a long table and a blank monitor. But the most striking features were the posters, affixed at intervals on the walls, which showed large, hagiographic photos of Angelica, her giant red curls its own halo, over the announcement, ANGELICA ST. AMBROSE, MORE NEARLY EACH DAY.

YOU DON'T NEED 12 STEPS TO OVERCOME ADDICTION!!! MY WORKSHOP WILL EMPOWER YOU WITH GOD'S LOVE IMMEDIATELY.

"You're hurting," Hunter said under her breath, "and only I can fix it."

One of the pool players, a young woman, approached them. "Oh, she's phenomenal! You have to come hear her speak! She will change your life!"

The woman was dressed for the weather, in flip-flops, lavender short-shorts, and what appeared to be a sports bra. More of her skin was covered by tattoos than by clothing: dragons in red and blue predominated. "She does these incredible inspirational talks. They're all about forgiving yourself and moving on."

"She owns the building!" Hunter blurted.

"She knows everybody's name," Tattoo said rapturously. "She makes a connection with everyone individually."

"She owns—"

"No," Tattoo snapped. "She used to. She got it from her ex-husband, who was a real jerk, so she sold her share to a giant corporation, at a big loss! Did you know that she was an alcoholic, and her partner, too? So they started doing support groups for people with addiction problems, but it just grew and grew out of that."

The sound of the billiard balls stopped. "Tyler!" someone called.

Tattoo—or Tyler, as she must be—seemed not to hear.

"There's no price here." Will lightly touched the bottom of the poster. "What do these workshops cost?"

"She only charges what you can afford!" Tattoo pushed Will's hand off the poster. "And she's a survivor of sexual abuse, so she gets that, too."

"Are a lot of people coming?" Will asked.

"Oh, yes! And if you can't afford what she thinks is fair, she has a payment plan."

Will's left cheek was throbbing.

"Tyler!" someone else called. "Are you going to forfeit or what?"

———

The drive back seemed longer than the drive up. The words "payment plan" hung in the air. Will especially seemed preoccupied.

She thought to distract him when she did as much of a victory dance as her seat belt would allow. "If I sell that Catalin radio for a fair price, I'll have enough for my security deposit. Then I'll be moving out."

"Catalin?"

"It's latter-day Bakelite, but it comes in better colors. We call everything Bakelite. It's like Q-tips. Or Kleenex."

Will kept his eyes on the road. "I'm glad you were able quit Starbucks."

A protein shake rolled out from under the passenger seat. Hunter reached for it, but her seat belt locked, so she let it roll back.

———

"Do you want anything?"

That was Will's first question when Hunter came aboard, having jumped the slice of green water lapping between dock and boat without needing help.

The cabin felt less cramped, now that she'd made a few visits. Hunter plunked down on the semicircular sofa that was built into the hull. She was grateful for the calmer waters that would probably prevent a recurrence of queasiness. "How are you fixed for H_2O? I drank all the water of my own that I brought."

"Here's one with your name on it." He handed her a bottle of Montana Sky.

Hunter tried stretching out but, thanks to the curve of the sofa, could only manage to recline with her knees bent, while resting her head on her folded arm. She happily inhaled disinfectant on top of the plastic cushions.

Will liked to clean, though not in the obsessive way that she did. He was busy picking up the few dishes that must have been left from the morning.

Hunter reached down for her purse. They'd stopped for gas, and Hunter, possessed by evil spirits, had grabbed a bag of Lays' Chile Limon potato chips from the convenience store. Dannika swore by them.

This would be the point of no return. She hesitated . . . but then, *riiiiiip.*

The bag was open. Will wrinkled his nose but didn't say anything.

Hunter plucked out the biggest, saltiest, and crispiest one she saw at the top. "OMG, these are good. I won't offer you any." Still, she extended the bag.

Will only shook his head before he cracked open his own bottle of water. He hated single-use bottles, but he didn't entirely trust the water that came into his sink. He drank a long time while she munched, wiping her fingertips on a Kleenex from her purse.

"Oh my God, take these." She crumpled up the top.

"I'll throw them in the Bay, is what I'll do," he grumbled, but he emptied the chips into compost.

Then he sat at the end of the banquette, with hands folded between his knees, leaning forward. He didn't speak for an uncomfortably long time. Finally, though, he sighed. "My Uncle Gil is declining."

Through the porthole behind him, she could see hull of the boat in the slip next to his.

"Well . . ." What could she possibly say? *We expected that? That sucks. I'm sorry.*

"I feel some pressure."

To expose Angelica.

She was ashamed. She'd been talking about her business, and even eating potato chips.

"I want him to know, before . . . you know."

She forced herself to ask. "What's changed?"

"He's having trouble swallowing. That means tracheotomy, and . . . well."

He got up and she watched as, in slow motion, he put a glass in a cupboard.

"But he can still understand," she said. "That's what matters."

"You never talk about your own parents." *The alkies.* He hadn't mentioned them since their first meeting.

He smiled grimly. "What, so I can write a memoir about them?"

"No, I . . ." *Wasn't talking supposed to make you feel better?*

"I despise the culture of victimhood," he said. "I suppose I should be grateful that she didn't write about them. She picked up all those stories from me, you know, when I was hanging out with Uncle Gilbert. I don't think she liked that I was . . . well, kind of a surrogate son."

It was growing darker inside, though there were several hours of daylight left. She wanted to cheer him up. And she was rusty, but unless there had been a dramatic paradigm shift that she'd missed during the decade, she knew one reliable way to cheer a man up.

"Will?"

"Yes?"

"This sofa is very uncomfortable. I'm getting a cramp in my calf."

"I'm sorry."

"There's a real bed belowdecks, right?"

He started. "Um . . . yeah."

"Let's check it out, Running Man."

———

It was semi-dark belowdecks, which helped her feel less self-conscious. And down here, the swaying of the boat was soothing. Will had a full-size bed covered with a thin duvet, navy, the material wearing thin at the seams.

He seemed unable to believe his luck: he touched her as if she might vanish. She took the lead, pulling off her tank top, then pulling his polo shirt off. She was feigning all signs of confidence. It had been a very long time since she'd had sex, and she couldn't remember when she'd last had sex with someone for the first time.

Will was thin, muscular, and agile, but shy in lovemaking. Hunter's feigned confidence evidently sparked confidence in him, though. He finished undressing himself and then they were in bed.

It was awkward, as first times usually are, but it was awkward in the way of people who don't think it will be the only time.

At least that was how it felt to her, when, later, he rose to use the head, and quickly covered his hairy chest with his polo shirt. "I know I'm too thin."

"I think you look great," she said. How had she thought him unattractive? She liked even the hair on his knuckles; it was masculine.

In a few minutes he came back to bed, sans polo shirt.

She snuggled closer to him. She wanted to maximize skin-on-skin contact. From this vantage point, she saw, peering out from behind the edges of a curtain, the shoulder of one of his suits.

She pointed. "Those must be hard to keep. On a boat."

"Yeah, it's a bitch."

"Take 'em to the dry cleaners?" She curled strands of his chest hair around her finger.

"Mm."

"And your regular laundry?"

"Gotta take that out, too."

She rested her head on his pecs. "You told me you live on a boat because it simplifies life. None of that sounds very simple to me."

He put his arm around her shoulder, pulled her even closer. "Let's not talk laundry."

This next time around he wasn't shy.

Chapter 31

Four Very Good Years

PENELOPE

Penelope had become comfortable enough with her computer that she used a website to email digital invitations to the other three women. "It's a special meeting of the talking-stick group! Early dinner! Be there or be square!" They'd probably never heard that old expression, the young whippersnappers.

The dinner that she and Reyna planned was a large undertaking. First, Penelope had to dig out the Wedgwood china and sterling silverware that dated back to when she and Scott had had dinner parties. That was years before. Before chest pains, muscle spasms, mysterious moles. Before Scott's unexplained absences, and longer hours at the office. Before Dr. Schmulewitz, and little blue pills. Before Tennis Club Trish.

A different life. A different woman. She'd been miserable.

Penelope had managed to keep two husbands fed, because anyone could broil a steak and cut up lettuce for a salad. When she and Scott had had those dinner parties, she'd hired someone to cook, a woman who did wear a uniform, and whose name she'd forgotten. This would be something different.

"We make the sauce first," Reyna said. "No, wrong, first you need an apron." Reyna found one that Penelope had forgotten she had: red linen from Williams Sonoma on which her name was embroidered. Reyna put the neck strap over Penelope's head, then stood behind her to loosen it. "Your hair is growing out!" Penelope felt Reyna's fingers on the back of her neck.

"Yeah, I need to see Cassandra." Her hairdresser.

"No, I like it. It's so thick! Let it grow." Reyna lifted some strands, let them fall. "I like long hair. It's so womanly."

That night, Penelope discovered the sensual pleasures of cooking: kneading the ground meat, tasting the white wine before a cup went into the sauce. Steam from the pots that condensed on her face.

While the sauce was simmering, the scent of meat and tomato filling the kitchen almost made Penelope euphoric. She did let Reyna chop the onions, since those always made her eyes sting. Perhaps cooking was a hobby they could share.

———

Hunter was the first to arrive. "What are we celebrating? There was so much digital confetti on those invitations that I was going to get out a whisk broom."

"Only you would want to clean up an email," Penelope said.

"What do I smell?" Hunter inhaled. "Garlic? Cheese?"

"It's lasagna." Reyna was putting rings around the napkins. "But there's a vegetarian and a meat one. Beef and pork."

"Whoa. Two pans? That was a lot of work."

"We didn't want to leave Dannika out," Penelope said. "Also, Reyna and I like things really spicy, so we made the meat lasagna that way. Anyone who doesn't like spicy can have the vegetarian one. And there's a Tex-Mex salad. Total culture clash!"

Hunter collapsed dramatically in one of the dining chairs. "Well, I have news, too. I wanted to wait, but if our friends are going to be late—"

"You were early," Penelope corrected her.

"Let's just say I can't wait. Will and I went up to Hyde Park . . ."

Penelope didn't pay close attention to Hunter's description of visiting the apartment complex. She was busy perfecting the table. Then she heard Hunter tell Reyna, "So you could say we 'took it to the next level.'"

"Is that what they call it now?" Penelope moved the candlesticks farther apart, then stepped back to see the effect.

"He called today, but he didn't leave a message."

"He called?" Reyna echoed. "That's major. No one *calls* anymore."

"Do I call him back?" Hunter asked. "If he didn't leave a message?"

"Text an emoji," Reyna suggested. "Not an eggplant or a heart. Maybe a smiley face or a wink."

"Don't ask me, anyway," Penelope said, "I'm out of the romance game. Officially. Scott rented an apartment in the city."

"Oh!" Hunter waited a moment before asking, "Am I happy or sad for you?"

"Happy." Penelope repositioned the candlesticks again. Could they turn off the light, or would that make it too dark?

"I think you're fine." Reyna hugged Hunter. "If he called today with nothing urgent, I mean, just to check in, you're all set."

"We're supposed to be more evolved than this." Hunter grimaced. "And not care about men."

"But everyone cares about romance!" Reyna hugged Hunter again, held on a little longer this time. "When you stop caring, you're dead."

———

Dannika was often late, a bad habit which the others had tried to correct, but tonight it was Alicia who came rushing in after the appointed hour because of an emergency C-section. She waved her hand over the table. "An embarrassment of riches!"

The place settings complete, Penelope had added a massive floral arrangement in the center. Then there were the two baking dishes of lasagna, each resting on a trivet, and the Tex-Mex salad in a bowl that also qualified as leviathan. Two bottles of red wine, and two bottles of water: sparkling and flat. A large loaf of French bread, with a few slices precut on the bias.

The table could seat twelve, but the five of them gathered at one end. This meant that someone who wanted food or drink from the other end either had to get up or ask multiple people to pass dishes.

But watching them cut into the lasagna and dish up salad, Penelope felt something unfamiliar in her chest. She decided to call it happiness.

"You're killing me here." Alicia tore off a slice of French bread. "Now pass the butter. Please."

"Have some wine, Hunter! Don't let Angelica St. Ambrose define you."

"Speaking of Angelica—"

"Let's not."

"Okay, but let's drink!" Hunter raised her glass for Dannika to fill. "I'd forgotten that wine is really cool."

———

Talking, drinking, and a lot of moving around. Leaves of romaine and stray black beans on the tablecloth.

Wine made Alicia voluble. She talked about Summer, how she had a lot to make up to her, but she would make it up, oh yes she would.

Then she spilled some wine on Penelope's white linen tablecloth.

"Don't worry about it." Penelope was holding on to her news. She could only share it for the first time once. It was like losing your virginity, but this would be a lot more fun.

Hunter had found an apartment in San Rafael, and she was pretty sure she'd be moving soon—did anyone have any empty boxes?

The candlesticks prompted Dannika to mention that she was rereading *Les Misérables*.

Reyna stopped the chatter when she tapped her knife against her wineglass—gently, since it was Waterford crystal. So gently that she had to repeat the process a few times.

But finally, "Penelope has an announcement."

"I've been asked to write for a website," Penelope said. She was suddenly embarrassed, and she looked down at the napkin in her lap. "It's called OurVoicesBoom.com."

Three times she heard, "Really!"

"Boom as in baby boomer," Reyna said. "It's an underserved demographic. I mean, on the internet. And they're going to pay her."

"Not very much," Penelope said.

"You don't need the money anyway." Dannika was between bites; she was devouring the vegetarian lasagna. "You should donate it to charity."

"Make sure it's a good charity." Alicia poured herself more wine, dribbling some over the edge of the glass. "Not one of these corrupt behemoths. Even the Red Cross—"

"The point of the money isn't the money," Reyna said. "It means that they value her."

"And I'm still writing under the name the Mighty Pen, so I can say whatever I want without worrying about Scott or his minions reading it." She was going to change Scott's, and even Dr. Schmulewitz's, names, not that they deserved anonymity.

"We're proud of you." Alicia was cutting herself another piece of the meat-filled lasagna.

"Let's say that we're 'impressed' instead," Hunter suggested. "'Proud' is kind of condescending."

"Y'all can be proud and impressed and just plain happy for lil ol' me." Penelope reached for a slice of bread that she didn't want. Now that she'd made the announcement, she did feel let down. In spite of their enthusiasm, she suddenly saw it as small accomplishment, something that not only anyone could do, but that anyone could do in their twenties. And she wasn't in her twenties.

Maybe that was what spurred her to make the next announcement, though it wasn't anything to brag about either. Not really. "I'm still, um, Valium-free."

"Good for you." "Not surprised." "Mazel tov."

Penelope shot a glance at Reyna, on her right. "That woman from the tennis club—Trish—called me yesterday."

"Dealers have a sixth sense." Dannika nodded.

"I got her to take my number out of *her* contacts."

Penelope reached over to Reyna, who was sitting next to her, and squeezed her hand. She still felt ashamed for having tried to make Reyna responsible for her addiction.

Reyna seemed to understand the gesture. "It's past! I'm going to get the Godiva."

"It's another *fresh* box," Penelope added.

———

They all helped clear the table, though Penelope thought it would have been easier to let Reyna and her do it, rather than to have so much traffic coming and going between kitchen and dining room.

"Godiva chocolate is my trigger," Alicia said. "Put it away."

"Someone else might want one." Hunter slit open the seal with her fingernail.

"Then when you pass it around, skip me."

"Good luck, you guys," Reyna laughed. "I'm going to a yoga class."

They moved to the great room.

The moment she sat down, Penelope pounded her fists on her thighs, though she knew it looked childish. "I want to go first!" Obviously, she had no more secrets to keep, and she was eager to continue talking, maybe even bragging, a little, about the grateful emails her writing engendered, how many comments she had, and how many new followers. With talking stick in hand, she might not be able to resist boasting a little.

And she would tell them about the pieces she was planning to write for OurVoicesBoom.com. She'd describe how going down from ten milligrams to five milligrams wasn't very hard, but going from five to zero was terrifying.

Alicia leaned over the Godiva box. "One piece. Just one piece."

The most important thing, Penelope thought, was telling her readers that just because she had taken a path of tapering off slowly, did not mean that they had to do the same. That rehab, twelve-step programs, and absolutely, religion—Buddhism and Hinduism as well as Christianity—all of that was a good way to get help. And yes, admitting you needed help was a first step. She had mixed feelings about interventions, because of that old joke, about how the light bulb has to want to change.

When finally the wooden stick emerged, Penelope reached for it with both hands. "Come to Mama." She thought of the Sistine Chapel, with God reaching over to Adam.

Her fingers grasped the wood.

The room went dark.

———

At summer camp there were two counselors for her cabin: Chrissy and Patti. Patti was fat. Chrissy was beautiful. When they were all outdoors, Chrissy's hair became sunlight.

At meals Chrissy wanted Penelope to sit next to her. The girl who sat on her other side had braces with that hideous headgear; her name was Martha and the other girls called her Metal Mouth Martha. Chrissy must have felt sorry for her.

Penelope couldn't dive, because she was afraid of going head-first into the water. The closest she could get was bending over and jumping off the side, so that when she dropped into the water her feet still went in first.

One afternoon Chrissy whispered, "Pretend you're a swan, and there's food underneath," and then Penelope closed her eyes, and stretched her hands out, and let them lead the way. Her head broke the surface, while her legs rose up behind her. She landed deep in the water and became a mermaid.

They weren't supposed to wear two-piece swimsuits, but Chrissy did sometimes, so you could see how flat her tummy was. All the girls wanted to be tan, but Chrissy's skin was white like vanilla ice cream, and Penelope wanted to stay white like her.

Then the second week Chrissy had a one-piece. Penelope asked why, and Chrissy said in a gravelly voice, "Ask the Man." Then she laughed. "If they can't handle a woman's body, it's their loss."

Penelope missed the two-piece.

The session ended and most of the other girls went home but Penelope was staying for the whole summer. Her sisters were all married by then and her parents wanted to travel.

Chrissy and Patti were still the counselors, but the new crop of girls seemed younger than the last. Penelope had more in common with Chrissy. During naptime, while the new girls slept, Penelope stayed with Chrissy, and sometimes they took walks, and sometimes, on the steeper trails, Chrissy held her hand.

Metal Mouth Martha was staying for the whole summer, too, and she still sat on Chrissy's other side at meals. But two weeks later, another session began, and one of the new girls had very bad acne. The first time Penelope saw her she felt bad for her, thinking what name the girls would have for her, and how Penelope would have to call her that, too.

But the worst was that night, when Penelope brought her tray, with the iceberg lettuce salad and the spaghetti and the Jell-O fruit mold, to her cabin's table, and there was Chrissy, with Metal Mouth Martha on one side and the new girl with acne on the other.

Penelope told herself that Chrissy felt sorry for Pizza Face (for that was the name that had already stuck to her), but the rest of the summer wasn't the same.

Penelope heard someone speaking.

"Whoa, Penelope, where did you go?"

"That must have been a real BFD."

This was like waking up from a colonoscopy. One second the doctor was saying, "You'll feel something cold," and the next second she was opening her eyes in the little curtained-off area.

"You don't have to tell us," Hunter said.

"No, I want to tell you." Penelope looked across the room at the blue abstract painting, by the artist whom Scott thought would be famous after he died. Every one saw something different there: Penelope saw blue clouds, with the sun trying to peek through.

"Just maybe not tonight."

———

Over the next few days, the memories came back like champagne bubbles floating to the top of the flute. Penelope remembered more Chrissys. There was Miss Montgomery (the title "Ms." didn't exist then, or, if it did, no one in Texas had heard), and Mademoiselle LeGrand, the French teacher. By high school, her crushes were on girls her own age. Her mother thought it was lovely that Penelope had close girlfriends, and that she and her friends didn't fight over boys.

The young women of the twenty-first century, even middle-aged women, had no idea what it was like back then. You could get married, or you could be (1) a teacher, (2) a nurse, or (3) a secretary. If, later, you did get married, you quit your job.

Since Penelope wasn't married when she graduated from high school, she got to go to college. Her mother had attended a small, private all-girls school in the Northeast, which made Penelope a legacy, so even with her mediocre grades and unimpressive list of extracurriculars ("Yankees don't care that you were a cheerleader"), they accepted her.

At least some of the girls were having lesbian relations, or even full-on affairs. Maybe a lot of them. It was hard to know, because that was another thing that was different: girls were discreet. Not like today, when women were on television talking about sex the same way they talked about recipes, and half of Gen Z was so "woke" that they didn't know if they were male or female, let alone homo- or heterosexual.

Penelope never went beyond kissing. Kissing and some touching. And sometimes, more intimate touching. She was very popular. She was tall, athletic, blonde, green-eyed, with beautiful, long-fingered hands.

There were a few girls in particular, several named Elizabeth and at least two Margarets, who spent the night in her dorm room while her regular roommate, Mary, was spending the night with one of her friends.

It was the best four years of Penelope's life.

Penelope's dad would call an unmarried woman an old maid after her twenty-fourth birthday, so Penelope married Jared when she was twenty-three. That lasted seven desolate years.

She didn't like sex. She agreed with Sylvia Plath's description of male genitalia: "turkey neck and turkey gizzards." But she was still in junior high when her mother told her that most women disliked sex: It was just something you had to do for your husband. "Close your eyes and think of Texas," her mother said, though it was only later that Penelope got the joke. It turned out that Jared didn't like sex the way her friends' husbands seemed to, which helped.

Penelope read the alumnae magazine for the first ten years after graduation. One by one (and in very short order) her friends got married. One of the Elizabeths became a lawyer, but her name never showed up in the "Best Wishes" column. (The alumnae of Penelope's college knew that you only congratulated the groom.)

Penelope wondered how many of those marriages had ended in divorce—and why. What difference, though? By now, a lot of her classmates would have passed away. Maybe even the Margarets.

Penelope saw her life through a new filter: The aerobics classes she loved until her health—really, her Valium addiction—interfered. All the times she paged through swimwear catalogues when she had no intention of going swimming.

A week later, she told the other women about these memories, and they made her realize that she was still the same person she had always been, only more so, because she wasn't hiding this from herself, and, for God's sake, there was nothing to be ashamed of. No wonder she'd hated being married.

Hunter said, "It seems that a lot of us have a large capacity to not know what we don't want to know. It's better to know."

"And you can write about it," Dannika said, "oh, Mighty Pen!"

Penelope did not share, though, even then, the thoughts she'd had during the past week concerning Reyna. How often she wanted to touch her. Penelope wasn't merely a lesbian: She was a lesbian in love.

Chapter 32

Off the Beaten Path

HUNTER

The next time Will called, he did leave her a voicemail. The message rambled but he ended with a question: "Go running together tomorrow?"

They met at Depot Square. He was wearing black running pants and a T-shirt with the slogan, "THERE IS NO PLANET **B**." A baseball cap covered his shaved head. He did look a little too thin, but the muscles on his arms were ripped.

"I'm going to show you my secret trail," he said as they drove toward Muir Woods. "Once people find out about this one, it'll be ruined for everyone. It's the tragedy of the commons." He swigged from his water bottle. "I'm selfish about running spots."

After many turns down small side roads that she'd never noticed in the past, they ended up at one end of a narrow path bordered by pine and eucalyptus. There was no off-road parking: he wedged his car between two trees, adding a few tiny scratches to both sides of his car.

"How did you find this?"

"Luck." Will bent over to retie his shoelaces. "Better check yours."

She could see why the trail hadn't been widely discovered. Within the border wall of tall cypress, pines, and eucalyptus, it was narrow, with just enough room for the two of them to run side by side, and sometimes not even that.

They saw only the occasional runner coming toward them (Will would jump off the trail, long enough for the interloper to get through) and no one overtook them.

They exchanged a few words at the beginning, mostly having to do with him warning her about upcoming curves and knobby roots. Hunter had regained most of her endurance, and it was good to feel the tiny bubbles of perspiration form on her neck and shoulders. Will was perspiring, too: the back of his T-shirt had a map of South America. On men, sweat maps were a sign of accomplishment.

After a while she attempted speech through her panting, "When was the last time you ran a marathon?"

"It's been a while." *Pump-pump-pump-pump*. "The training takes a lot of time. Away from—" *Pound-pound-pound-pound*. "Other things."

"We're – so – lucky – to – have – this – land," Hunter puffed.

"We have it for now."

"It's protected." Sixty percent of the land in Marin County was protected by Federal agencies. No one could come along and deface it with luxury condos or theme parks.

"Protected by the government?" Will pumped harder. "Or by God Himself?"

Hunter's lungs contracted. She took two more strides, then stopped to rest her hand against the bark of a pine tree. "Just a sec."

Will leaned against the tree trunk next to her. "The Russian aristocracy thought their land was protected by the government *and* by God. You think your money in the bank is safe, when it's just a number on a piece of paper that anyone can tear up."

This made Hunter think of how much time she spent raking through what the dead relatives of potential clients had left behind.

"Actually, it's just a number on a screen," he said. "Nothing belongs to us."

She'd wasted enough of her own life that she didn't want to dwell on the fragility of the time that remained. She inhaled the leafy, earthy air. But what was that other smell—a dead skunk somewhere, or perhaps some manure? Welcome to nature.

Something more than the Russian Revolution was bothering Will, and that scared her. "I'm rested. Let's go."

———

The last part of the trail was uphill. Hunter could feel each rock as her shoe made contact with it. *Are we there yet?* She was too proud to ask.

Then, finally, the trail ended at a thick cluster of eucalyptus, cypress, and bay laurels that allowed in only strips of blue between.

Will turned sideways; Hunter followed, and they squeezed between the last two trees on the edge of forever. It was a sharp drop, and Will took her arm. "Careful. But it's a beautiful view, isn't it?"

"Yes." Of the East Bay hills and a hazy San Francisco skyline in the distance. Up closer was the Richmond-San Rafael Bridge, the one that looked like it had been put together from an Erector Set. The sky was clear except for a few high clouds.

Hunter didn't need a Fitbit to know they'd gone about two and a half miles, though on the rough terrain it felt like more. Most of her hair stayed pinned atop her head, but a fringe of shorter strands had come loose and formed a tickly veil on her neck. "Just when you think you've seen every spectacular view Marin has to offer. . . . But you were born here. Maybe you have seen 'em all."

"Oakland." Pause. "But then we moved to Lagunitas."

Silence.

She guessed. "Your Uncle Gilbert died."

"I wanted to tell you somewhere private."

Her brief impulse was to say, "He's in a better place," but that was so clichéd—and quite possibly untrue. *We knew it was going to happen?* No.

"I'm so sorry."

"It would be a relief, if only . . ."

But maybe she and Will could be in a better place. "Your Uncle Gil was a very special man." She hated to use the word "special," but she didn't have time to dwell on more original synonyms. "But we can't help him now."

Although *Jesus Warned Me* was still holding on to the lower slots of the *New York Times* list, Hunter was feeling the ramifications of Angelica's traducement less. The latest print run of her memoir was only maintaining traction with readers of spiritual self-help, while Hunter, in daily life, was dealing with buyers and sellers, the most unspiritual of cohorts. These people didn't know or care who she was, weren't interested in religion of any kind (at least not when she was with them), and, for the most part, they didn't even read.

"Does this trail have a name?" she asked. Many trails did.

"Not that I know of."

"Let's christen it the Gilbert St. Ambrose Memorial trail. We can put a sign up—or a bench." The Marin outdoors was full of benches with plaques "in loving memory."

"That's not enough," Will said. He gazed in the direction of the East Bay. "Let's put it this way: we're at the twenty-fifth mile."

Chapter 33

Only Human

DANNIKA

Dannika was out biking in the afternoon, so she decided that she would just keep going and cycle all the way to Penelope's for their meeting. The forces of good were triumphing over the forces of both the internal combustion and electric engines: Every month there were bike lanes on more roads, making the world safer for two-wheeled vehicles.

It was a long ride, though, from San Anselmo to Tunstead Avenue, and then on Sir Francis Drake, where there wasn't a bike lane, so she had to be careful.

She was glad of the time to think. She was still grieving Razzy. She'd told the other women about how he died, and they were sympathetic, though since none of them were pet people, they couldn't truly understand. At least none of them said something like, "But it's not like losing your mother, is it?" and she was grateful for that. Loss was loss was loss, and saying "This is how bad you should feel, no more," was pretty pathetic.

These days she was having nicer memories of her mother that balanced the not-so-nice ones: When Dannika was sick, Mosi would wait on her, read to her, keep her company. Okay, if she had a looming deadline for a big commission she had to take care of that, too, but that was money for both of them.

Mosi was always worried about money, and for a while Dannika could only recall the occasions when her mother had denied her: a new bike when the old one was falling apart; a black leather jacket like the one her friend Sophie had. But now she also remembered the times when Mosi had denied herself, say, when the Craftswomen's Circle went on a retreat and Mosi stayed behind, unwilling both to spend the money and to accept help from the others, since all of them lived by cobbling together income from private lessons and the occasional sale.

Razzy was only a cat, and Mosi was only human. Loving, and limited.

———

As usual, Dannika was the last to arrive. "Sorry—I biked here."

"Isn't that dangerous?" Penelope asked.

"Not the way I do it."

She sat. Dannika liked Penelope's black leather sectional sofa, because they could be reasonably close, but still have enough elbow room, and whoever got the end seat could stretch out. Now there was a new, larger, glass table in the crook of the L. "The better to eat off." They'd continued to experiment with the menu, but they stuck to dishes that could be consumed with minimal utensils.

Alicia had brought sushi and Hunter spring rolls. Damn! Dannika had Italian sodas to contribute, but she hadn't gone back to get them once she'd started cycling.

"I'm all moved in!" Hunter announced as she plopped down while simultaneously unwrapping the talking stick. "Woo hoo! No more Twin Terrors."

Then she told them about Will's uncle's death. Dannika thought it was a blessing, but she kept that to herself. Had she thought it a blessing when Mosi finally passed away after weeks of hospice care? She had—in part. And that was understandable.

At the end of her story, Hunter said, "I feel like I let him down."

"Will? Let him down?" Alicia echoed. "No, you didn't. How can you say that? You did everything you could."

"Catholic guilt," Penelope said.

"Whatever." Hunter held out the talking stick. "Someone else take a turn."

Dannika wanted to tell them about her attitude adjustment toward her mom, so she stuck out her hand. She felt the forked end stabbing her palm. She hadn't eaten anything yet, so maybe that was why she felt woozy. Then she was swaying—or was it the room swaying?

> It's like watching YouTube, but with no sound. She sees herself in the art studio, in middle school, with Jim Kelly, and she's making him laugh with a story about her mother's friends, and his girl-friend Jeanie Jordan is laughing, too. . . .
>
> There's Perry, from drama class. They're supposed to be rehearsing a scene together in an empty classroom, but they're making out instead. . . .
>
> Then the English teacher, Mr. Schmidt, with the prosthetic arm, who writes poetry, and sometimes he drives Dannika home from school because it's on his way, but he says, no, it isn't right for him to take advantage of her, there's a power imbalance. . . .
>
> Mosi's first oncologist, Dr. Mastriano, is always hugging her to make her feel better, though he won't say what she wants, which is that everything will be all right.
>
> Jana's dad has moved in with her because he split with Jana's mom, and he's a lot older, but he's still really handsome. . . .

Dannika felt the talking stick land on her thighs. The leather of the sofa was stiff against her back.

"Dannika?"

Hands on her shoulders.

Alicia pressed her fingers against Dannika's wrist. "Someone get her some water."

The first thing Dannika saw clearly were the blue swirls of the painting above the fireplace across from her. "It's nothing," she said. "I'm fine."

Alicia and Hunter exchanged glances; Penelope appeared with a glass of water in unsteady hands.

"You remembered something," Hunter said.

"Well, yeah." Dannika heard the tremor in her own voice. "But it was just some, like images from things. Not things I'd forgotten."

She convinced them, or at least tried, that she had probably dozed off for a few moments. "You know how you start dreaming sometimes when you're not fully asleep yet?"

"Yeah," Hunter said. "We know."

———

By the time she got back to the west side of 101, she felt as though she'd been pedaling since childhood. Every muscle ached. Her helmet covered her hair, but the wind was making her cheeks sting. She needed a new helmet, one with a windscreen.

She needed even more to stop thinking about that montage of men. But no matter how much she tried to do the mindfulness thing, and focus just on her pumping legs, and her fingers around the handlebars, their images kept coming back, like swiping down an Instagram feed that had the same pictures over and over.

Rafe was different from them. Wasn't he? He was a musician. An artist.

It had been three weeks since Dannika and Rafe had last been alone together. They'd catch each other at Safeway and go back to his place, if Shannon wasn't there.

It was time to find out where she stood. Rafe had said that the only reason he had Shannon as a roommate was because he couldn't afford to live alone. Well, let him move in with her! He wasn't allergic to cats. (Though she wasn't sure they'd ever talked about cats.) He'd be a little bit farther away from work, but she wouldn't charge him rent, so how could he resist?

She was passing Safeway anyway, so she might as well go in. This was his regular night. He wouldn't get off until 11:00, but she could see if he was available for later.

The store was fairly empty, but as usual, the lines were long; management only opened two lanes during off-hours. Word on the street was that self-check was coming, but it hadn't happened yet. Rafe joked that he would be replaced by a machine once they invented one that could play drum solos.

She recognized the cashier at one of the registers, so she grabbed a package of Oreos, and waited her turn. "Hey, I haven't seen Rafe here for a while"—intending it to sound totally caj, but coming out like, "Is the cross-burning still on for tonight?"

"He left," the cashier said. "Papa was a rolling stone."

"Oh." She dropped all pretense of casual. "Did he finally get that touring gig?"

"More like wanting to avoid a gig at San Quentin." The cashier laughed. Then he closed one nostril with an index finger, the international symbol for cocaine use. "Wow, you must really love your cookie fix."

Maybe Rafe had been fired after one of his coworkers—even this self-righteous dude in front of her—had started a rumor about him using cocaine. They were jealous of him for being in a band, and for how the manager, a middle-aged divorcee, had a crush on him.

"Oreos are vegan, you know," she mumbled.

Outside, she remounted her bike. Up ahead she saw the white glow of the movie theater marquee that meant that she was, finally, close to home. But it felt like what her seventh grade algebra said was Zeno's paradox, that she'd keep getting closer, but never arrive.

Now the YouTube–like montage of men made sense. Jim, Perry, Mr. Schmidt, Dr. Mastriano, Jana's dad. They didn't look alike; they weren't the same age; they didn't have the same jobs. The ones from high school weren't married. Actually, the only one who was married was Dr. Mastriano, and she didn't know about Mr. Schmidt.

The point was that they were all unavailable, sometimes because of another woman, but sometimes just because. She'd been in love with each one, pursued each one, pined for each one. Then finally accepted that Nothing Would Happen.

Rafe had been lying to Shannon all this time about fucking other women.

A large capacity to not know what you don't want to know.

The house was dark when she got home. She turned on lights and began the—okay, it was damn tedious—process of cleaning cat boxes and making sure there was the right food and water, and she had to give Pumblechook his eye drops. She was smart enough to keep all the cats indoors, except for the occasional monitored excursion to the backyard, which was completely dead thanks to the once-a-millennial drought. Cats that were let outside got run over; even the smarter ones got lost.

Finally she was able to sit on the couch. She was about to get up to make tea, but Grushenka crawled on her lap, and after the poor kitty had made that much effort, with her arthritis, Dannika wasn't going to dislodge her. Grushenka was also overweight. Dannika tried different ways of getting her to eat less, but then she thought, *what's the long game here?* She was twenty years old. Let her enjoy herself.

Purrrrrrrrr.

Dannika stroked her back, and Grushenka revved up the purr. She wouldn't live much longer. Would she and Raskolnikov be together in some way? Dannika had to think so. She had to.

The memories of the men now led to the memories of how she'd embarrassed herself while pursuing them: Googling names. Driving past houses. Once she slipped a note through the vents in Perry's locker, asking him to call her. He didn't, but he did tell his friends. She was only a sophomore then. But he was a senior, and thank God, the tale didn't survive his graduation.

A few of Grushenka's hairs came off between her fingers. Cats had body language—flattened ears, flicking tails—but no facial expression. So it was easy to imagine, when Grushenka was staring at her, irises slitted, that she was jealous that Dannika had spent more time petting Dunya Romanovna, the white-and-gray tabby , than her. Or that she was relishing her victory over a bug. But would Grushenka really have hurt feelings if Dannika raised her from her lap? Or was she, even with angry black slits or flattened ears, only ever thinking *eat . . . sleep . . . poop?*

To say that the men Dannika had loved were thinking *eat-sleep-poop* wasn't entirely fair, but they weren't contemplating the possibility that humans had immortal souls. They were thinking, *stock market . . . Super Bowl . . . sex.*

When Dannika was a senior, there was a boy who transferred to her high school from southern California. Michael. She had a huge crush on him. He looked like the total LA boy: golden hair, golden skin. A broad chest. Every girl, and about half the guys, were infatuated with him.

A month later, he asked Dannika out. Unbelievable! And he took her to a club where they didn't card, but he didn't get drunk or obnoxious. The music was too loud for them to talk, and they drove to Stinson Beach and made out. But she lost interest in him after that night.

And now she knew why. He wasn't God, either. He couldn't heal her.

Chapter 34

Round and Round She Goes

ALICIA

In all her years in Marin, Alicia had never been aware that there was an indoor ice rink in Santa Rosa. But Joshua, here on his first visit to Northern California, had found it on Yelp, packed her and Summer into the Pathfinder, and schlepped them up Highway 101 to the Redwood Empire Ice Arena, more commonly known as Snoopy's Home Ice.

Now, in the Warm Puppy Café, surrounded by life-size statues of Charlie Brown, Snoopy, and Woodstock, Joshua was watching Summer glide around the ice rink. Alicia recognized love on his face: an expression that reminded her of her own father, who, unlike her mother, approved of her no matter what she did. It was her father's belief in her that had made her a doctor. Now Summer had *two* parents who believed in her.

Summer herself was a nearly anonymous figure, bundled in purple Gore-Tex, with a red-and-white, Christmassy knit hat pulled down over her hair and ears, but Alicia could pick her out from all the others, and follow her wide arcs, even when she was on the far side of the rink.

Joshua had ordered a hamburger and fries. Alicia had a salad, which gave off a whiff of vinegar, while the smell of grilled beef and oil from Joshua's plate made her half-crazy with desire.

"Is this the first time she's been ice-skating?" Joshua asked. He dipped a fry in a generous pool of ketchup without taking his eyes off Summer.

Alicia's first impulse was to take this as a reproach: *Did you never think to take her?* But then she said, "Bay Area winters aren't cold enough for outdoor skating." There was an artificially created outdoor rink in downtown San Francisco, but it was only open two months a year.

"She's a natural," he said.

Summer, completely self-absorbed, arms extended, swooped like a condor in effortless circles. Alicia had expected her to cling to the wall, but no, she could even skate backward. She wasn't exactly ready for the Olympics, but . . . *but that's my problem*, Alicia realized. Summer didn't have to win a gold medal to enjoy a sport. Alicia had always pushed herself so hard, and achieved so much, that she'd set unreasonable—no, *insane*—standards for her daughter. Instead of living up to what Alicia demanded, she'd sunk to what Alicia feared.

And what exactly were Alicia's own great achievements? Yes, she was a board-certified physician. Yes, she was listed in *Marin Magazine* as one of the top fifty obstetricians in the county; yes, she'd been honored by more than one nonprofit for fundraising efforts. And yes, she'd raised a child without a partner.

But she couldn't speak a second language, or play a musical instrument. She couldn't cook anything more complicated than pasta with canned sauce, and the last time she was on a dance floor, the women she was with had laughed at her so hard that she never danced again, not even when alone.

Joshua was refilling his ketchup pool. He was a big eater. She remembered that, and so many other details now. After the first, awkward week, a decade and a half had crumbled away. They'd picked up where they left off, bantering, and balancing each other, she serious, him playful.

Alicia didn't believe in soulmates, but maybe this was how it was meant to be: the two of them growing into early middle age on their own. Establishing their careers without quarreling over the division of parenting duties. Now they could come together for the easier-harder part. Harder, because they had to shepherd Summer into womanhood, but easier because there were no more diapers, or parent-teacher conferences, or snack weeks.

Joshua was lucky to have missed all that, and she'd experienced a brief period of resentment that he'd been able to dive in and reap the benefits, an employee cashing in his stock options. Her talking-stick friends had reminded her that the situation was entirely her own doing, because she had never told him; since then, she allowed herself simply to enjoy his company, and to watch Summer thrive.

They had many years ahead, and it would be easy for Joshua to establish a practice here. In this land of helicopter moms (and dads!), Marin was screaming for more good pediatricians.

"I FaceTimed with Lawrence today," Joshua said.

Lawrence was his therapist back home. Alicia was still skeptical of the efficacy of psychotherapy, but Joshua claimed that the process had helped him. "Yes?"

"Well . . ." He hesitated. "Can we talk?"

That never means anything good. "Yeah, sure."

"I'm working on letting go of the anger."

Alicia's fork slipped out of her hand. "What anger?"

"You really don't know?" His eyes widened; his blue eyes were shaped like Summer's: round and shallow-set. "Because I missed out on all these years."

"Missed out?" she echoed.

"Missed out on her first steps. Her first words. You know I see what that's like for parents. Every day."

Alicia almost blurted out her own version of what he'd missed, but was stopped by a memory: Summer at Alicia's parents' house, letting go of the sofa where she'd been cruising, looking straight at Alicia as if to say, "I saved this for you, Mommy!"

Her first step. Saved it for when Alicia had taken time to visit.

Other memories formed a multicar pileup. Those Mother's Day cards from grammar school. The part of George's mother in *Our Town*. Alicia didn't remember the character's name, but Joshua would have loved all that.

"I wish you'd told me. I became a pediatrician because I love kids."

"You're right." Alicia pulled in her lower lip, wishing away the memory of Summer's eighth birthday party. Alicia hired a magician, and the whole class came.

There were happy years before the puberty tide came in. Stressful, but often happy. For a long time, Alicia had been remembering only the stressful part.

"Lawrence reminded me that you were only Dannika's age when you got pregnant."

Joshua had joined the group at Larkspur Dock one afternoon. He wanted to meet them, since Alicia spoke of them so often. He and Summer only stayed a few minutes, but during that brief visit Joshua had up close and personal conversations with each woman. They all seemed to like him.

"So, I'm processing how young you were—how young we both were—and beginning to understand. And forgive. For the sake of *shalom bayit.*"

You could revise memories, Alicia thought, *or repress them outright.* But once recaptured, once you knew they were true, you couldn't change them—you could only change how you felt about them.

She wanted to say all this to Joshua. She was poking at limp lettuce leaves, trying to find the words, without telling him about the talking stick, which she had promised not to do, when Summer came into the café, letting in a blast of cold air as well as a guitar-heavy

song from the speakers about how true love lasted forever. Snoopy's
Home Ice was playing KOIT, Summer's easy-listening station, one
that no cool kid would ever listen to.

Summer stomped on her skates over to their table. "Those fries
smell good!" She helped herself to a plump one.

"Easy, girlfriend," Joshua teased. "I'll get you your own order."

Summer yanked off her knit hat. "It's warm in here." Her hair
was in French braids. Now that she was spending so much more time
outside, her dishwater blonde hair had lightened to honey, to match
Joshua's, while her skin no longer looked pasty, but ivory.

"Have you told her yet?" Summer went for another fry, sliding
this one across the pool of ketchup, dividing it like the Red Sea.

"Not yet." Joshua pointed back to the rink with his thumb. "Hey,
isn't this your favorite song?"

"Told me what?" Alicia asked quickly. Had he been reading her
mind? Had his tale of his "breakthrough" with Lawrence been a
lead-up to saying that he wanted to move out west?

"One for the road." Summer picked up a fry, and stomped out
again, sending in another blast of cold air and a few lyrics from Katy
Perry, or Taylor Swift, or perhaps the new, even younger singer who
would replace them.

"So, I was thinking . . ." Joshua pushed his plate to one side, and
folded his arms on the table.

Alicia's heart pounded.

"I want Summer to come back East with me when school lets
out," he said.

Her heart didn't stop. She only wanted it to.

"Don't take this the wrong way, but I don't like Marin. It has
nothing to do with you."

Who wanted to live in the Northeast when they could live in
California? "I can't move back East," she said. "I have a big practice here." She was embarrassed to add how attached she was to the
talking-stick group.

Joshua stared, his mouth open slightly. "I was assuming you'd stay here."

"But what about us?" It slipped out.

"Us?" He freed a new napkin from the dispenser. "I . . . should have said earlier, I guess, but I'm seeing someone."

"Oh?" Of course he was. Just because she had stopped dating years ago, why would he? "Tell me about her."

Joshua kept his eyes on the table while he folded the napkin. "I figured you knew. . . . It's a 'he.'"

Alicia felt the café floor tipping. Why didn't the talking stick magically fill her in on this part?

Joshua fidgeted. "His name is Taddy. Isn't that such a cliché?"

Medical students made love hastily, urgently, with a sense of triumphing over the system. Besides, they had roommates, and early-morning classes. So why would she think there was anything strange about their rare lovemaking? Or notice that she was always the one who initiated it?

"Thaddeus Louis Bartholomew IV." Joshua spoke in a rush. "I tease him about the fourth, because, you know, it's 'IV,' like intravenous?" He raised his left hand from the napkin and held his first two fingers up in a peace sign.

"Right," Alicia said absently. *Joshua was the one who taught Summer to French-braid her hair.*

"Don't worry, if they don't hit it off, Taddy is history." Joshua snapped his fingers. "Besides, he's not Jewish."

Alicia was too preoccupied with trying to get the floor to stop rolling from side to side to process why that might matter.

"I'm sure you got that from the name." Joshua laughed a little. "It didn't matter before, but now that I have a family—I belong to a synagogue, Am Tikva, that's mostly gay families. She can have a bat mitzvah."

The excitement in his voice was palpable. But he misinterpreted her expression, for he said, "I'm not criticizing you for not getting

her involved in the Jewish community. It would be good for her
now, though."

Alicia felt profoundly criticized. Her mother had pushed her to
try Jdate when Summer was a preschooler, and later, to join a synagogue herself, "where they had groups for single women."

Alicia hadn't seen the point.

"Oh my God, has she ever even been to a seder?" Josh asked.
Presumably rhetorically.

Time to push back. "You don't know what's involved." Alicia
sucked up the last of her Diet Pepsi. "Raising a teenager. You've had
her for—what? A month? At her best." She used her straw to stab at
the remaining ice cubes.

He looked surprised. "Are you kidding? It's like a Hanukkah miracle in May. I guess we can call it a Shavuot miracle."

Alicia had forgotten what holiday Shavuot was. She did remember that it was one of the important ones, but even the important
ones were easy to forget if they weren't close to Christmas or Easter.

"I always wanted to be a dad." He concentrated on the napkin,
and after a moment he held it up. It was shaped as a crane. "Last
year's hobby. Origami. So you see there's space in my life for a kid.
And especially a daughter."

"Why?"

"Nothing depraved, if that's where you're going. I just like—
women. And girls. She's delightful. She's creative. She's funny."

Alicia narrowed her eyes. Summer? Funny?

Joshua liberated another napkin. "I thought about adopting, but
I didn't have a partner, and I could see how hard it was for the single
parents, never mind the divorced parents—I mean, I don't want you
to think I was a loser. I dated." He raised an index finger. "But I wasn't
going to get myself in a situation where I was doing some uncon-
scious uncoupling or whatever it is now."

He put one last fold into this new napkin, then held it up. It was
in the shape of a heart.

Summer came back then, panting a little, exhaling steam. "That was way fun." She started unlacing her skates.

"Summer, hon." Joshua pointed to a sign with a picture of Snoopy that said, "Don't change skates in the café."

"Whatever." Summer shrugged, but she cheered up quickly. "He told you. I can tell." She spoke fast, tugging on the end of one lace. "He already has a second bedroom—"

"For when my parents visited. I'm going to let Summer do a little redecorating."

They went on making plans. Summer couldn't wait to see snow falling, and to pick out new linens. Could he *believe* that she still had Mulan sheets? "Mom got them for me when I was five! You'll let me pick out my own."

All you had to do was to ask me for new sheets, Alicia thought.

Summer said that wherever she went to school, she wanted to get on the newspaper, and maybe the student council.

Alicia forced a rogue cherry tomato off the plate. She hated salads.

Joshua finally included Alicia. "There'll be no sodas in the house. I'm giving them up totally." He tilted his glass of Pepsi, half-empty and now flat. "Also, I have season tickets to the symphony, but that's where Summer draws the line."

This was when Alicia would normally make a smart-ass crack about Summer's irremediable taste in music. And a crack was a fissure that could expand invisibly, until the entire structure collapsed. She forced a smile. "Yeah, no. Summer hates classical music."

"Whew!" Summer showed all her teeth, now straightened by two expensive rounds of braces. She abruptly dropped the smile, and looked unexpectedly timid, when she asked, "Will you come to my bat mitzvah?"

Alicia couldn't speak for the ache in her chest. After a moment, she squeezed out the words, "Of course." For once, at least, Summer wanted something that Alicia could give.

Chapter 35

A Large Capacity

HUNTER

The text message that Hunter received from Alicia had Penelope and Dannika on the thread as well.

> Emergency pls meet me at Marin
> Rick's.

Hunter and the others responded quickly, promising to come to Alicia's aid, but the thread lengthened with questions (you're not sick, are you?) and excuses (Reyna not here I have to take Uber) before the meeting was set.

Marin Rick's was an old-fashioned steakhouse. Alicia was already seated in the lounge section, at a table for four, and already drinking. As Hunter approached, Alicia was slapping her hand down on a cocktail napkin and barking at the waiter, "My friends will be here any minute!"

Mid-evening Saturday, and it was packed. Dim light and soft recorded music. What was she hearing? It sounded familiar. After a moment she recognized a slow-tempo instrumental cover of "Don't Stop Believin'."

Hunter slipped into the empty seat across from Alicia. "What're you having?"

"It *was* a gin and tonic." Alicia slurred a little. "This is my second. Where've you been?"

"I was unpacking boxes." In her new apartment. "I got here as fast as I could." That was a lie, because she was constitutionally incapable of walking out on a half-full, *or* a half-empty box. But it was only another fifteen minutes of putting plates on the contact paper she'd already installed.

"I need help." It was Penelope. Yes, in high heels. "Can you show me how to add a tip? The driver was so nice."

Dannika rolled in almost immediately after. "There's always so much traffic on 101!"

Alicia tossed back the last of her drink. "You're probably wondering why I asked you here," she growled with mock importance. "I couldn't wait to tell you a funny story." Then she announced, far too loudly, "Joshua is gay!"

Hunter and the others immediately shushed her, while looking over their shoulders to see who might have overheard. No one wanted to sound homophobic. But everyone Hunter saw was looking at their phones, even the elderly couple at the table next to them.

"This is what couldn't wait?" Dannika picked up the bar menu. "Not that I minded pausing *Bridgerton*."

"I was watching *Grace and Frankie*," Penelope said. "But a lot of these new shows run out of steam after two seasons."

Alicia was waving to get the waiter's attention, as desperately as if she needed to warn him about the iceberg ahead. "Isn't that just hilarious?"

Penelope and Dannika must not have picked up on the same note of hysteria that Hunter did, for they both laughed.

"I thought you knew!" Penelope said. She looked at Hunter. "Didn't *you* know?"

Hunter knew, but she didn't want to add to Alicia's pain by saying so.

"He took her to that musical theater revue," Dannika confirmed.

"Why—" Hunter wanted to ask, *why do you care?*

But then she understood.

"How did you not know?" Dannika laughed again. "He liked taking her to the mall, too."

"Because," Hunter answered on behalf of Alicia, "people have a large capacity to not know what they don't want to know."

Now they were all silent.

The waiter, a young man with a boxed beard, finally arrived, and, after apologizing for the delay, he remarked that Alicia was now free to stop waving.

"Well, excuuuse me. This round on me, ladies."

Penelope and Dannika each ordered a glass of the house red. Hunter studied the wine list. *Don't let Angelica define you.* Still, since nothing on the list appealed to her, she ordered mineral water. If she were going to drink, she was going to have something worth drinking.

"Another G & T for me, *sir*," Alicia said. She raised her glass of melting ice. "Here's to the three gay men in California who haven't come out yet!"

She tilted her head back to pour the last of the ice down her throat. The straw nearly poked her in the eye.

Hunter didn't think that Alicia's love for Joshua was either wide, or deep, or even real, but rejection was rejection (didn't Hunter know?) and Alicia was hurting.

"I thought we were going to be a big—well, a little happy family, and I was going to make it all up to her." Alicia let her face fall into her hands.

"You're being too hard on yourself," Penelope said. "She's a teenager. All daughters hate their mothers at some point. Then they get over it and move on."

"I didn't say she hated me!" Alicia glared at Penelope over her fingertips. "What do you know, anyway?"

"I had a mother once," Penelope said calmly.

"I might even miss her." Alicia spoke into her palms.

A different waiter, this one a few years older and sporting a circle beard, arrived with four glasses on a tray that he balanced on one splayed hand. "I know, I know, men are evil," he said as he swapped out Alicia's empty glass for a fresh gin and tonic, then delivered the others their drinks.

Alicia downed a sizeable swallow of hers, while the others took polite sips. "Two hours ago I was ready to marry him. Is that crazy or what?" A few gulps, then, "He wants to take her back East with him."

"He can't if you don't want him to," Hunter said. "Can he?"

"Is his name on her birth certificate?" Dannika asked. "I don't know if that matters. I don't know anything about this stuff."

"I could probably stop him, but . . . oh, what's the point? Summer wants to go, and God knows she's not happy here."

The plan was that Summer would finish out the school year in Marin. There was only a month remaining. Then she and Joshua would have the summer to get settled in. "It's the Summer of Summer!" Alicia raised her hand and waved at nothing. "Hey, can I get more lime in this?"

Hunter reached across the table, entwined her fingers with Alicia's, and gently lowered their joined hands.

Penelope sipped wine. "I'm trying to imagine an openly gay pediatrician back in Austin when I was growing up." She stifled a ladylike burp. "An openly gay *anything*."

Alicia put her hands over her eyes again. "He says it's a plus, can ya believe that?" She slurred, "He says that he's the go-to guy for gay parents, okay? And if Mr. and Mrs. Suburb think that little Johnny might be gay, well, then isn't Dr. Josh the one to let Johnny talk to!"

Dannika cleared her throat. "If you ask me, it's a happy ending."

"Huh?" Alicia's eyelids were drooping.

"Wellll . . ." Dannika took her time. "It's the elephant in the room, isn't it? My mom did the same thing to me. I never knew who my dad even was. *She* never knew who my dad was. It's okay." Dannika made eye contact with each of them, one at a time. "And she decided to have me, and she got herself to a safe place where I could have a nice middle-class life." She shrugged. "It's affected my relationships with men. But obviously she had trouble with that, too." Dannika shared a sad, wry smile. "So, Summer's had her time with you, now she'll have her time with him."

Alicia put her head down on her folded arms. Dannika patted her back.

"She's a cheap date," Penelope said, indicating Alicia. "That's an old expression for someone who can't hold her liquor."

Alicia's voice, audible but barely intelligible, rose from her folded arms. "She needs the ladies' room," Dannika interpreted. "I'll help her."

Alicia rose unsteadily. Dannika held onto her arm. After a couple of swerves, and one bump into another table, followed by Dannika's apology, the two of them headed toward the back.

"I've heard from Peter," Hunter told Penelope. She hadn't meant to bring this up; it was Alicia's night. "He wants me to find his high school yearbooks."

"Really?" Penelope asked. "Why? Don't tell me. He was the star quarterback."

"I don't know. And there's no way I'm going back to the house to look for them."

"Why can't he look for them?"

"He's not staying there right now. He's 'on retreat.'" She made air quotes. "Whatever that means in his world." Hunter found this amusing, or at least as amusing as a future ex-wife could. They weren't legally divorced yet, though with the process underway, at least he couldn't get her into any more debt. "He sent me a DM on Twi—X."

"Tweety Petey. Why can't Angelica take him his yearbooks?"

"He says he doesn't want to disturb her, 'cause she's busy with something new."

"Trouble in paradise?"

"Maybe." Hunter smiled. "Would you think less of me if I said that I hoped so?"

Penelope shook her head.

"But mostly, really, I'm ready to move on," Hunter said, and it felt true.

———

A few minutes later, Dannika returned with an abashed Alicia. "I feel better now."

"Then let's eat something." Hunter held up the bar menu.

They ordered quesadillas, and stuffed clams, and fried artichoke hearts, and sliders, all to share. Hunter was deferential to the new waiter when she asked for extra plates. As they played four-card monte with the dishes, their chatter was about new streaming services and the food itself.

"This is enough for dinner." Alicia sucked grease off her thumb.

"Well, I'm glad." Hunter signaled for the check; she was planning to make sure that the waiter got a large tip. "Where's your car? You can't drive home."

Chapter 36

Back to the Boat

HUNTER

Hunter had been on her way to see Will when she got Alicia's "emergency" message, but she'd texted him to postpone. Now she postponed again so that she could drive Alicia home, with the promise of bringing her back to her car the following morning.

But finally, she headed south.

Passing the Civic Center—the famous public building designed by Frank Lloyd Wright—she wondered again if Will's determination to force a retraction from Angelica had lessened. When he gave her the news at the precipice at Muir Woods, it had only been a few days after Gilbert's death.

But she guessed that Will needed a cause the way Peter had needed a get-rich-quick scheme.

———

"You shaved your beard!" was the first thing she said, after Will handed her aboard. "It looks good. You look . . ." *Younger.* "Good."

Will bowed his head, embarrassed.

Facial hair was for men with something to hide. That has been Peter's maxim. Will had nothing to hide, and she was becoming ever fonder of his hot fudge–brown eyes under expressive brows. Even his shaved scalp had acquired a certain insouciant charm.

"Water?" He extended a bottle of Montana Sky.

And life was for the living, even if one is a gallant crusader.

So, after a revitalizing swig of water, they proceeded belowdecks.

There was no more awkwardness. Nor shyness. Will had even become adventurous.

In the final year with Peter there'd been very little sex, and when there was, they uncoupled and re-dressed themselves immediately. But that evening with Will, Hunter found herself naked under his duvet, arms and legs intertwined, skin on skin. Had she and Peter been this way, those many years ago? She couldn't remember. She didn't try very hard. "Pretty soon, you're coming to my apartment."

"Still a no go?"

"Don't take it personally." Will had his quirks, and he respected hers. She couldn't spend the night on a houseboat, not with bilge pumps anywhere in the vicinity. "I need more furniture."

"How much furniture do we need?" He smiled.

She did have a mattress and box springs on the floor of her bedroom. But that wasn't good enough for an overnight guest, even when the alternative was a bed that lurched and the briny smell that came through the portholes.

"And I want to do some more decorating." She was looking for an étagère on which she could display collectibles, both those for sale and those she planned to hang on to until the right time.

"The dude who bought the radio bought all my Bakelite jewelry." It was enough to clear another chunk of Peter's credit card debt.

"Proud of my girl." He tucked a lock of her hair behind her ear.

"Say 'impressed.'" She'd explain later.

"But how does a plastic necklace turn such a profit?" He hesitated. "Asking for a friend."

She traced the freckles on his arm. "Tell your friend that it's like anything else in this vale of tears—it depends on how rare it is, and how much someone wants it. And one someone is all you need." It wasn't even a large necklace, she said, but the beads were of the most desirable colors. "The thing about my business is that God is in the details. Two coins look to be worth the same, until you see that one has an S stamped on it, for the San Francisco mint."

"And to think, I've never looked for an S on any of my money."

"It reminds me of saints' relics." Hunter shifted in his embrace, and he moved to realign them. Skin on skin. "Putting a price on inanimate objects, as if they have magic."

"You're not telling people that a Hummel figurine can cure them of leprosy, I trust."

"No." Her left arm had grown numb; she reluctantly pulled it out from under his torso.

"There's a reason they call it 'memory'-abilia," Will said. "People save things to remember people by. To keep them alive in our hearts."

"At least you can wear jewelry." It served a practical purpose. But then there were the items that acquired value from the magical touch of another. If she found a vinyl album cover signed by one of the Beatles, she could turn it into a small fortune. Being famous made you a deity.

"Some days are hard," Will said. "If going through a photo album, or even holding onto a celebrity autograph helps, let it help."

Relics had been big business back in the Middle Ages, but the Catholic church had outlawed their sale. "My mother would have loved to own some awesome relic." She ran her finger along his newly naked jaw. It was a firm jaw that didn't need to hide.

"Like the Shroud of Turin."

"Or one of those cloths that has the Pope's blood on it—" But she stopped.

"Too soon," Will agreed.

The Shroud of Turin was two thousand years old, but the Pope's blood was from the twenty-first century.

She shivered. He held her more tightly.

After her first communion, Hunter's mother warned her that she must never take communion unless she was in a state of grace. It didn't happen all in one day, but that was the beginning of Hunter turning her back on the church. Bernadette's church, anyway. If Will didn't like the culture of victimhood, Hunter didn't like the culture of fear.

She had told Will about some of this. He was looking for a down-to-earth, welcoming church where he might resume attending Mass. He might have doubts about some of the details ("Let's say the Assumption of the Virgin Mary is a metaphor"), but "if they get you early, they've got you for life."

———

They moved to the upper deck, where Will said he would make dinner. Hunter wasn't sure how he would manage that, or, if he did, how he would serve it, since an earlier inspection of the galley revealed only two mismatched glasses.

He did make eggs that were marginally edible on a stove that attained marginal heat. They sat at the built-in table, after he moved away the notepads and books stacked there, and used mismatched forks.

"I'm just going to come out with some news," he said.

She braced herself.

"There's a new film option on *Jesus Warned Me.* 'The struggles of a recovering alcoholic bringing her spirituality to others.' The key word is 'spirituality,' because it's for Daylight."

"I beg your pardon?"

"I hadn't heard of it, either. It's a new cable channel."

Bankrolled by Lindsey Van Gelder, he went on. Van Gelder was a gay, not-quite billionaire tech, looking to fill the programming gap left by conservative Christians. "He wants shows for LGBT Christians. And a lot about recovery, of course. So it's recovery meets Marianne Williamson meets . . ."

"Angelica St. Ambrose. A film of her life story."

"That's what the option is for."

"Won't they have to talk to real-life people to confirm the facts?"

"It'll be 'inspired by,' not 'based on.'"

She took a moment to digest this, since it had become difficult to do so with the actual food. "Why didn't you tell me before?"

He grinned apologetically. "I didn't want to spoil the mood."

Suddenly Hunter wasn't as eager to move on from the Angelica Project as she had been. If there were a miniseries out of Angelica's journey from mid-forties alkie to pious leader of the recovery movement and a new, liberal Christianity, every lie she told—not just about Hunter, but about so much else—would be enshrined forever. "Wait—how do you know about this?"

He waved this off. "Oh, I read the trades."

"The trades?"

"There'll be a press release any day now, but actually, I heard about it from one of Angelica's fans at the law firm. The same lady who introduced me to the memoir in the first place."

"A dark day."

"Not entirely, at least." Will put his hand over hers.

Hunter acknowledged this with a nod.

"It gets worse. This same colleague is such a die-hard fan that she set up More Nearly Each Day as a 501(c)3 corporation for free."

Which meant that any donations to MNED were tax deductible.

"She'll be rich." Though no matter how rich, Angelica would spend it.

"Personally, I think the tax exemption for religious organizations is wrong," Will said. "L. Ron Hubbard said he wanted to start a new religion because that was where the money was."

"What sexy talk. You're getting me in the mood again." She stabbed at her remaining eggs. They represented a valiant effort.

Will pushed his plate aside. "I don't claim to see into anyone's heart. If she's using the money she raises to promote the liberal Christian values she espouses, then it's none of our business if people want to give it to her. If she's using the money to enrich herself, that's a very un-Jesus thing to do."

He grimaced. She grimaced back, then returned to redeploying egg away from the chips on the plate's circumference. "Maybe I can get up close and personal and see just how she is using this money." She looked up. "Talk to Peter."

"Good idea."

Had she hoped to see a flicker of jealousy? "He's on retreat. And he wants something from me." She told Will about the yearbooks. "I don't have them, but I have something else." The baseball cards that she plucked out of his collection for safekeeping.

"Where is this retreat?" Will asked.

"I don't know." She picked up her phone. Yes, it was always close by, even when she and Will were making love, though she *had* set it to "Do Not Disturb." "But I know how I can find out."

After all, he was *Tweety Petey*.

Chapter 37

Calling All Creators

DANNIKA

Dannika wanted to take Howie's advice and make Raskolnikov's ash-box into a shrine worthy of him, but she'd been blocked. She didn't have photos of him, or any of the cats. She thought about cutting pictures out of magazines, but she didn't have any magazines, either, since she only read on her computer.

Finally she decided to look for ideas in the basement. The basement was both an archaeological site and obstacle course: Mosi saved everything except bread-bag clips, and Dannika wasn't sure about the bread-bag clips. Cast-off clothing, electronics with dead batteries, and any item with the faintest whiff of sentimental value, from birthday cards and party invitations to Dannika's fourth grade spelling tests—it was all down there. "I'm one dented can away from my own reality show," Mosi had joked. There were a few dented cans, too.

Dannika rattled around until she unearthed some surplus wrapping paper patterned with kittens. Then, on the way up, she banged her shin against the Box.

On the afternoon when Bronwyn awoke Dannika from the nap-that-wasn't-a-nap, Mosi's supplies—tools, beads, clasps—were still strewn on the repurposed dining room table. But before she left, Bronwyn packed everything up. "Your cats could hurt themselves on these pliers," Bronwyn had said, but that was silly, unless her pets managed to bypass a hundred thousand years of evolution and grow the thumbs they needed to handle them. Bronwyn's real message was, *move on.* "We all loved her," she reminded Dannika.

Bronwyn wanted Dannika to donate the tools and supplies to a battered woman's shelter, and Dannika put on an adequately convincing act, solemnly promising that she would, but when Bronwyn left, she took the box to the basement. There it had remained, just as her mother's clothes had remained in her closet, though they were becoming musty now.

With her shin still throbbing, Dannika decided to bring the Box upstairs. There would be beads inside, and she could glue those onto Raskolnikov's ash-box as well. Mosi wouldn't mind sharing.

Unlike Mosi's boxes, which had been randomly scavenged from grocery stores, and which left their contents exposed to the world, Bronwyn's Box was taped up like a dead pharaoh. Dannika had to use a knife to slice it open, and unfold the flaps. There was a bead board on top, but underneath were the tools: They looked sinister, like something you'd use for surgery. Or an autopsy. There were about six different kinds of pliers, but the names all came back to her: snub nose, round nose, flat nose, chain nose, bail. There were wire cutters. Crimp covers.

When Dannika was little, Mosi said she could watch her work if she were quiet. Dannika would sit with hands folded, not making a sound; what sounds there were came from Mosi, after Mosi forgot she was there. Her mother would groan, and grunt, and curse, as she flung down one tool and picked up another. Sometimes she'd throw her shoulders against the chair, tilt her head back, and cry *aaargh* at the ceiling.

These memories of Mosi working were a series of pictures that Dannika saw the way she might flip through a photo album. There was no photo album IRL; Mosi had taken few pictures of Dannika, and she certainly had never gathered any into an album, even while Dannika's friends' parents were sending snapshots off to Shutterfly to turn into mousepads, calendars, and coffee mugs.

During Dannika's Resentment Month, she'd added the absence of photos to the list of Mosi's failings. Today, at least, her internal album generated feelings of pride and respect. She saw Mosi wrapping Scotch tape around a finger to pick up crimp beads. Mosi adjusting her magnifier. Even Mosi cursing the ceiling was the act of a woman who pursued her craft with integrity.

Dannika removed the tools one by one. Underneath, there were plastic containers with the detritus of Mosi's work: the beads, the wires, the bead stoppers and S chains and spacers. Dannika let her gaze hover over it all, trying to get in the zone, where inspiration for the Raskolnikov project would come.

Then she noticed, in the corner, a lacquered box, shaped like a miniature pirate's chest. She lifted it out.

When she opened it, she gasped. It was full of reds: beads and stones in crimson, scarlet, maroon, candy apple. Dannika passionately loved the reds, and these dark, vibrant shades collected together gave her the dopamine hit other people associated with accumulating likes on a Facebook post.

Mosi must have been collecting these for a long time. Maybe they were for a commission that she'd been unable to complete. But who loved this spoke of the color wheel as much as Dannika? So she must have been planning to make something for her.

Except that Dannika wasn't her target customer. Mosi made jewelry for older women who were trying to look young and hip. "Statement" pieces, she called them, like necklaces with pendants that pointed to cleavage, and earrings heavy enough to make earlobes droop. Mosi knew what those women wanted. She never wore her own creations, though. "I'm not a jewelry person." *So why did you start making it, Mosi? There was a woman in New Mexico who taught me.*

It was a rare time when Mosi spoke of those years.

She left this for me to do. Dannika couldn't reconcile that with Mosi's melodramatic insistence that Dannika not pursue either arts or crafts. Had her mother had new thoughts near the end?

The man at the Last Crafts Fair said, *watch your back.* After that Dannika thought that Mosi feared Dannika surpassing her, and maybe that was the case, but what Dannika knew for sure now was that Dannika herself feared being better than Mosi.

There were several chunks of red coral. Dannika picked up the largest one, held it in the air, turned it ninety degrees and then back again. Red coral was valuable. It was probably endangered now, but throwing it in the ocean would be an empty gesture.

Then she saw it in her mind, as if it were another page in the photo album. A finished piece. She just had to make it. It would be a necklace of red coral and turquoise. There was turquoise here, wasn't there?

She dug through the plastic containers, plucking out each turquoise piece she found. Some were pierced for stringing, and she set those aside.

Then she laid the beads out: red coral alternating with smaller turquoise stones. She didn't want just red/turquoise, red/turquoise, though, and the beads were different sizes and shapes, so she rearranged them. Wanting to create a powerful, if not perfect composition. Rearranged them again. She added and subtracted until she had the effect she wanted. She didn't use the bead board on principle.

Throughout, her hands remembered Mosi's hands in motion: the pliers and the wires, the tools and the spools.

She cut off a length of a twenty-four-gauge wire; that was what Mosi used most often for necklaces. It was only after she used the wire cutter that she realized that she needed a heavier wire, to support the bigger stones. She hated to waste, but c'est la guerre. She searched for, and found, a spool of twelve-gauge.

The bead reamer to smooth out the holes. The crimping beads for the ends.

. . . Then she was holding a necklace by its two ends: the lobster claw and the tiny jump ring on the other. *I made something where nothing was.*

Pride was sweet, but it soured quickly. This was an entry-level project. Any high-schooler could do it. She wasn't even sure she'd done it right. She peered at the lobster claw. Was it really the best clasp for this? And why hadn't she used spacer beads? The necklace screamed for gold spacer beads.

All she could think of was of what she didn't know. She wanted to be able not just to smooth the hole that would turn a stone into a bead, but to pierce that first hole herself. She wanted to learn how to solder. She wanted to know what metals were good for what kind of jewelry.

A text came in on her cell.

```
Yo it's me just in the neighborhood
can I drop by?
```

Howie.

Even though she wasn't proud of it anymore, she did want to show Howie her work. He wasn't the judgmental type. She tapped out yes.

———

"That's really good! Are you going to sell it?"

Howie was at the other end of the table, munching an apple.

"No." She was packing up the box again. She'd have to reorganize all the tools and beads and supplies from scratch, and she dreaded it, since she had a *tiny* touch of the hoarder in her, too. "I'm going to keep it as a kind of souvenir."

What she wanted was to be able to look back on it someday and see how much better she could do.

Howie came for a closer look. "I mean, the colors are really pretty."

Dannika appreciated his praise, but what did he know about jewelry? Literature, sure. San Francisco State swag, okay. Jewelry, no.

"You could sell it on . . . what's that site?"

"Etsy."

"Yeah."

Etsy was the best she could do, without actual training.

Dannika now knew the meaning of the word *ambition*. She wanted to make things and have the world see. She wanted other people to wear what she made.

Mosi had made a success of her business, teaching herself what she didn't learn in New Mexico, flying without instruments. She never created art. No, that wasn't fair. Who knew what art was? But that wasn't the point.

Dannika wanted to be better than her mother.

Crunch. Howie took a final bite. "Any more apples?"

"Yeah, in the fridge. Help yourself."

Dannika closed her eyes. She had visions of other necklaces, and earrings, and bracelets, or she knew that's what they were, but she couldn't get them to come into focus. She saw shapes and colors but they kept moving, like blobs of wax in a lava lamp.

"Where's the compost bin? For the apple core?"

"Next to the fridge."

"Oh, I see it." *Womp.* "Ooops. Missed."

She *was* going to be better than Mosi. She hoped that Mosi would be proud. But she wasn't going to worry about that anymore.

Chapter 38

Let's Get Cookin'

PENELOPE

"Look," Penelope said to Reyna, "she didn't have a home health aide the last time we saw her."

It was rude to point, so Penelope bent over the grocery cart and spoke in a low voice. Reyna would know to whom Penelope referred: an elderly woman in a navy dress, hunched over a walker, entering the automatic doors at Whole Foods. A much younger Asian American woman held onto her arm. The younger woman wore a cotton print wraparound top in an appalling baby blue floral print, with navy blue cotton pants. It left room for some ambiguity: was she a servant, or a friend with hopelessly bad taste?

"That's going to be me in a few years."

"Stop that," Reyna said.

"How much older than I do you think she is?"

"At least a hundred years."

"Then let me push the cart."

Reyna bumped her hip against Penelope's. "You are more than welcome to do so, Madame."

Before the night of the lasagna dinner party, when the talking stick had stirred up so many memories, Penelope had touched Reyna unselfconsciously. Now each time their bodies made contact, Penelope felt a tingling mix of excitement, fear, and recognition.

"Are you sure I'm ready for this?" Penelope asked, as she grasped the cart's handle.

That morning, Reyna had asked, "What do you say to learning to make my justifiably famous mushroom risotto?"

Penelope was thrilled. She'd been trying to get up the nerve to suggest another cooking project.

"I forget," Reyna said now, "does Dannika eat seafood?"

"Officially, no," Penelope said, "but unofficially . . ." Everyone found a way to bend their own rules when necessary. Her father had watched sports on the sabbath, even after Pastor Bob said they shouldn't.

"I was thinking about cacciucco," Reyna mused. "But no, let's stick to risotto. But then we should make it just for us. It's only really good when you first make it."

"Are there onions?"

"There are shallots. But you're going to have to get over the onion phobia, Penelope."

Penelope didn't like that, so she changed the subject. "Where did you learn all this Italian cooking, anyway?"

Reyna shrugged. "I bought a cookbook. Then I watched YouTube videos."

"Everything is on YouTube now, isn't?" But Penelope was now more interested in the world outside. She had returned to the tennis club, not to see Trish, but to swim, for the first time in many years. She asked Reyna to drive her there, and then to pick her up, because she didn't want Reyna to see her in a bathing suit. She was in good shape for seventy-three—but she was seventy-three.

Chauffeuring (though she preferred to think of it as "driving") was just about all Penelope needed Reyna for anymore. The hours

she'd used to spend googling symptoms of pancreatic cancer she
now spent writing, and answering emails from—dare she call them
fans? Readers, anyway. Her piece about growing up as an unwanted
fourth daughter, who was still forced into the role of debutante,
continued to generate responses. My parents divorced
because I wasn't a boy. I'll carry that shame
for life. . . . Thank you for standing up for
all the ignored girls of the world. . . . some
countries they don't even educate the women.
However, she had not written about her recovered memory of her
college years, *nom d'internet* or no.

"Let's start with the broth." Reyna was holding a list, though
Penelope doubted she needed one.

They headed down the canned food aisle. Penelope slowed, so
that she could walk behind Reyna—and admire Reyna's behind. It
was good, Penelope thought, to have gotten Reyna out of that stupid
white uniform early on, but Reyna had a kind of uniform of her own:
a small selection of jeans in different washes, but all showing off slim
thighs and her plump but firm derriere. She rotated through an assort-
ment of T-shirts and sweaters, depending on the weather. When that
weather permitted—as it had since April—she wore sandals, displaying an immaculate pedicure and one toe ring. Today she was in a hot
pink tank top, snug over her breasts. God, she was beautiful!

"So, are you down to make lasagna for your friends again?" Reyna
asked. "There's a lot of demand." She picked up a can of Progresso,
squinted at the ingredients, then put it back. "If I do say so myself."

"Sure." *I just want Reyna near me.* Penelope would have to get used
to longing for more. Hadn't she lived without sex for most of her
life, unless you counted those years with Jared, when she stared at
the ceiling and occasionally inserted a grunt of counterfeit pleasure?

Yes, except now the locks on the overstuffed suitcase of sexual desire that she'd been sitting on for decades had popped open,

letting spill memories of plump breasts with swollen nipples and parted thighs.

Reyna stopped to put a box of Lundberg arborio rice, which was labeled as "sustainably farmed" and "gluten free" as well as kosher, in the cart. "Make a woman mushroom risotto and you feed her for a day," Reyna said. "Teach a woman to make mushroom risotto, and you feed her for a lifetime."

In the pasta aisle, Reyna gave a TED Talk about the most common mistakes cooks made with regard to risotto. Trying to speed up the process was the first and worst, she explained.

Penelope nodded. A long process meant more time in the kitchen together. An image of herself with Reyna next to the stove appeared. Then Reyna appeared, in the same place, but naked.

Penelope squeezed her eyes shut.

"Mushrooms!" Reyna announced. "We need two different kinds."

———

In the car, Reyna seemed to take longer than necessary to flip through the ring of keys. When she finally started backing up, she said, "I need to take classes in group dynamics and mental illness."

"What? Why?"

"Well, I'm interested, for starters," Reyna said. "But also, I need to take classes to keep my license active."

"D-do you have to do that soon?" Penelope had a sudden attack of dry mouth.

"Mmmm," was Reyna's vague response. She came to a stop at the parking lot exit. "This is a busy street," she observed, as if to herself, but then, "You might think about getting your driver's license back from Scott, you know."

———

At home, while they were putting the groceries away, Penelope was nervous, which was why she started a long, directionless story about her eight-week summer sojourn in Paris, sponsored by the college, in between her junior and senior year.

"And the women at the corner boulangerie were so nice! Parisians are supposedly hostile to Americans, but I didn't find . . ."

Reyna was usually inexplicably patient with these tales, but she interrupted, "Let's have some tea in my room."

She's still calling it "my" room, Penelope thought, grabbing at this moonbeam of hope.

Once there, though, the first thing Reyna said was, "You know that it's time for me to move on. You don't need a nurse. Let alone a babysitter."

They were semi-reclining on the bed, mirroring each other, propped on elbows with cups of tea between them.

"What's her name?" Penelope asked.

"Excuse me?"

"You know what I'm asking."

Because there it was, as obvious now as it should have been to Alicia about Dr. Josh. Reyna was a gorgeous thirty-five-year-old who had never been married, had never mentioned a boyfriend, and had never spoken of dating.

Well, maybe not quite as obvious as Dr. Josh, but Penelope knew it now. That she and Reyna might have this common ground, that Reyna wouldn't judge her for her past, was something to be grateful for—so why did she have to learn it on the same day that Reyna said she wanted to leave? It was like that joke from Penelope's childhood, about how ambivalence was watching your mother-in-law drive off a cliff in your new Cadillac, although it would have to be a Ferrari now.

"There's no special her." Reyna pressed her finger against the handle of her teacup, then pushed the cup into circles. "There are a few casual 'hers.'"

Penelope was appalled to find herself picturing the "hers" as broad-shouldered women with butch haircuts in UPS uniforms.

"It's just like I said, I want to go back to school—"

"But there's no reason you have to move out!" Penelope thumped the duvet, sending a few drops of tea over the edge of her cup. "I have an idea—why don't we fix this place up a little? New furniture? What if we paint? I've never liked these colors." The walls were taupe, and the molding was white: a scheme left over from its days as Scott's home gym. "Or, or . . . you could even have your own study here! Now that Scott has his apartment." Except for the barbells in the closet, almost all that remained of Scott in the house was his subscription to *White Collar Crime Monthly.*

"I want to go back to school to become an RN," Reyna said. "I was in an LVN-to-RN program. But back when I needed a job really badly, I made a novena to Saint Teresa, and then Scott found me online on the SF State job board. He made me an offer I couldn't refuse. So. Much. Money!" She waved at an invisible bank account. "I don't feel right about taking it anymore."

Penelope didn't want to hear about Scott's money. Or Scott.

"So you see," Reyna continued, "this was meant to be. The time that you and I have had together, I mean."

This should have made Penelope feel all warm and fuzzy, but she thought of all the young, stylish women who would be in that same RN program. She feared a return of her old heart attack symptoms, this time caused by jealousy.

"You know I love you, Penelope, but in Marin I'm a person of color, and in San Francisco, I'm just a person. Didn't you notice, when we were out today, that every single aide, or nanny, or cleaning person we saw was a POC, and every customer Caucasian?"

Penelope registered something about Reyna being a person of color, but her heart caught on the word "love."

As was so often the case, Reyna knew what Penelope was thinking.

"I do love you, Penelope."

"But not that way."

"What way is 'that' way? Do you mean . . ." She sat up, and cupped both sides of her mouth to imitate a bullhorn, but she spoke softly when she spelled out, "S-E-X?"

Penelope wondered if she were blushing. She might have feigned some level of ignorance, before her talking-stick memory, and the more fragmented memories that followed, but her feigning days were over.

Reyna put her hand on Penelope's outstretched thigh. "I know I have to make allowances for your generation."

Now with the word "sex" spelled out, Reyna's hand on her leg was an electric current. She sat up, too. "Do you know what San Francisco rents are like?" Penelope heard a bit of a shriek in her voice. She herself had no idea what San Francisco rents were like, but they had to be prohibitively high. They had to be.

"I'll work something out." Reyna swallowed the last of her tea.

Yes, with some similarly inclined roommate. "And finding a roommate on . . . whatever those websites are, is dangerous. I've heard—"

"—about women being murdered by roommates they found on Craigslist?" Reyna smiled. "Now you're just being silly."

Penelope had only one last card to play, but it was a platinum American Express.

"You know . . ." She traced the stitching on the duvet, "how disappointed Daddy was that I was a girl."

Reyna sucked air through her teeth in a way that told Penelope that Reyna had heard the story more times than necessary—along with those stories about Penelope's time in Paris, and about preparing to be a debutante.

"Okay, okay, but this is new. He made it up to me in the end."

When he was dying of pancreatic cancer, Penelope said, her father changed his will so that Penelope got his shares of his oil—sorry, *energy* business. She sold them to his partners, put the money in Treasury Bills, and never touched it except to reinvest when the bills matured. The rate of return was low, but compound interest was a powerful force.

"Mama was already dead, but there were some pissed off grand-kids. Stepgrandkids, too. That generation is so entitled!"

"So Scott—"

"This was a little before I married him, and when I did, he knew I had a little mad money, but he had no idea how much. I'll give him credit where credit is due, he's never been stingy with me." Scott liked things the way they were: he had a wife—and an ailing wife at that—to use as an excuse if a Jennifer or a Tiffany got insistent. "I can use that money now to put you through school, and—and you can stay here."

"Penelope, no. But I appreciate the gesture."

Reyna leaned forward and kissed Penelope on the cheek. It was a thank-you kiss. A friendship kiss.

Then Penelope couldn't help herself. She'd wanted this for so long, for so much longer than she knew she wanted it, that the wanting took over her body. She scooted on her knees to close the gap between them, knocking over both cups, and kissed Reyna on the mouth.

Then she pulled away, hating herself, waiting for the slap across the face. "Oh, God, look." She'd spilled the remains of her own tea on the duvet.

Reyna laughed then, the laugh that had charmed Penelope on that first day. "I wondered if you were ever going to get up the nerve to do that."

There had been no slap, but Penelope's cheeks stung as if there had.

"I've been meaning to wash this anyway," Reyna said.

Penelope conscientiously keep her eyes down as she gathered the cups and saucers and slid backward off the bed. Now she only had to erase this memory, forever: attempt the talking-stick phe-nomenon in reverse. Maybe it was a good thing after all that Reyna was leaving. "I'm so . . . I'm so . . ." Saucers and cups clinked against each other.

Reyna laughed again. "C'mere, sweetie." She patted the space next to herself.

"What?"

"C'mere." Reyna patted the duvet again. "I wasn't going to make the first move, you can understand that, right?"

Penelope wondered if this could really be happening.

But when Reyna slid her arms under Penelope's waist, she knew it was real, and she knew where it was going, and she was happier than she'd been in a very, very long time. Frightened, as well.

"We'll take our time," Reyna said. "And we'll stop whenever you say 'stop.'"

Penelope nodded.

They kissed for a while and Penelope let herself love it.

Then Reyna slid one hand between Penelope's legs.

"Riddle me this," Reyna said. "How do you stand pantyhose? I find them so uncomfortable."

"It's funny," Penelope squeaked. "A lot of women say that, but I've never had a problem." Her heart galloped. She closed her eyes. When she opened them, Reyna was looking at her.

"Are you sure you want this?"

"Yes . . . it's just that . . ." In college, she had a flat tummy. Now it was a pouty lip. Now her standup-and-salute breasts pointed downward. And her arms . . . swimming was starting to help, but she would never be thirty again. "I'm not a young woman." If she hadn't wanted Reyna to see her in a bathing suit, well, now she wanted to hide under a burka.

"Really? Let's see your driver's license. No, wait, Scott took that away." Reyna put her free hand on Penelope's breast, still encased in a white Oxford shirt. "We're lesbians, not gay men. We see past surfaces."

The knot of tension Penelope's stomach loosened. "Can we just draw the curtain?"

There was more clinking china when Reyna put the teacups on the floor. Then there were the sounds of clothing being stripped away. Later Penelope's nervous giggles and later still, her faint moans.

No one had touched her intimately for a very long time, besides the doctors and technicians who performed Pap smears and mammograms. Her clitoris had become like her appendix: existing not only without a purpose, but its exact whereabouts unknown.

All that changed that afternoon. Reyna knew exactly where it was and what it was for. And all one needed was a tongue.

"Oh . . . my . . . God." Penelope arched her back. "Oh my God."

"Not bad, huh?"

Penelope had to wait for her heart to slow down. "Does this mean it's my turn?" she asked finally.

Reyna lay down next to her. "Next time."

Next time. What beautiful words.

"Of course, next time could be in ten minutes." Reyna looked at her watch.

"I'll need . . . um . . . help?"

Reyna chuckled. "It's not a test." Pause. "I'll give you all the feedback you need."

Reyna took her hand, and they lay there for a little while, next to each other, looking at the ceiling, where there was a frosted glass light fixture from the previous century that needed dusting. "This is better than Valium," Penelope said.

———

Hunter was telling them all about her plans to drive up to a town called Moskowite Corner to talk to Peter. Penelope was pretending to listen. She didn't care about Peter Fitzgerald or Angelica St. Ambrose at the moment.

Will thought this and Will said that. Penelope was happy for Hunter's burgeoning romance, but heterosexual relationships were so bourgeois.

While Penelope felt like the first woman who had ever fallen in love. And Reyna was at her yoga class, so she could share the story without embarrassing her.

"Here ya go, Pen."

Hunter handed her the talking stick. Finally!

She told them how Reyna was leaving to pursue a nursing degree. "And . . . and . . ."

"You made out," Dannika said.

Hunter shushed her. "She's holding the talking stick."

"Well, yeah." Penelope tugged the hem of her skirt down over her knees. "Let's leave it at that."

Nervous laughter.

Then Hunter said, "We never talk about you behind your back—I mean, that's my story and I'm sticking to it—but I think I speak for all of us when I say, I'm not surprised."

Penelope described Reyna's plans to move to the city, trying to sound casual about this next step. "But! She's going to be my social media manager."

"So you'll be in constant touch." Dannika reached for a broccoli floret.

"That's the plan." Penelope sighed. "The age difference, though . . ."

"No one would think anything of it if you were a man!" Dannika said.

"Almost no one," Alicia qualified.

Penelope held up a carrot stick. It was a baby carrot, which seemed appropriate. "I've realized something. Women don't have penis envy—men do! They worship the Almighty Dick!" Her mother would have fainted.

"Let's not write off male genitalia entirely yet," Hunter said.

Penelope basked in their attention a little longer, sounding ever more like a teenager to herself, as she extolled Reyna's beauty, intelligence, and wit. So this was what it was like when you were in love, but didn't know what was going to happen—whether you had a future with your beloved, or if they—*she*—was going to leave you the next day?

"And now you can write about all this," Dannika said. "Coming out . . ."

". . .a little later in life," Hunter finished.

Alicia smiled. "You're an inspiration."

Chapter 39

A House Is Not a Home

HUNTER

Peter's first DM to Hunter had requested his high school yearbooks without further detail.

When she was on Will's boat she responded that she did have his yearbooks. It was a lie that would get her two hundred years in purgatory, especially as she elaborated that she wanted to return them, so where exactly was he?

She heard from him the next day. Moskowite Corner, he replied.

Then, in a separate message: Can you leave them at the Moskowite Corner post office?

I'd like to give them to you personally.

I'm on retreat and need to be alone.

But she was tired of using her thumbs and nostalgic for an old-fashioned conversation.

Peter had the same cell phone number that he'd had since before they married. She'd tried, but failed, to forget it. She got voicemail several times, but finally he answered. "Hunter!"

In spite of his earlier rebuffs, he sounded happy to hear from her. "It has been lonely," he admitted. "All this introspection."

She wrinkled her nose, squeezed her eyes shut, and repeated the lie about his yearbooks. "You sound funny," he said.

She coughed. "Sorry. Tell me where you are and I'll bring them to you."

"I told you, Silly Jilly. Moskowite Corner."

She tapped her phone. On Google Earth she saw mostly mobile home parks. Also a church, an actual volunteer fire department, and a food pantry.

"I'm a few miles out of town," Peter said. "I'll email you directions. It's not far from Silverado."

The mention of Silverado, the posh wine country resort, caused a pang. They'd spent a few weekends there. "Why do you want these yearbooks, anyway?"

There was too much static for her to hear his answer.

Then the call dropped.

———

Moskowite Corner was more depressing on the ground than on her phone. There was a restaurant/bar that appeared to have been closed for some time, though a few trucks were parked in front. A grocery store had a Sputnik-era sign and a pay phone.

She took the one paved road out of town.

A few miles up she spotted the red mailbox that Peter had told her was her cue to turn right. She drove onto a wide swath of gravel that disappeared into a mix of weeds and dirt. There was a slight grade, though, which meant that the house ahead came into view in stages: first, there was a wide, front-facing gable that sported four disproportionately large dormers. A moment later, there was the floor below, with four bay windows, and then, two gravel crunches later, the first floor: thirty feet high, at least, with two ornate Palladian windows on each side of the front door, which was framed with a portico.

It made her think of an Irish convent—if one had been designed by a first-year architectural student who figured on points for every window design from the last five hundred years.

There was a bulldozer on the western side of the house, with its blade bowing low. An excavator was on the eastern side, its long arm bent in supplication. Several young men were running around, shouting in Spanish.

She stopped the car some yards away from the door, when her tires begged for a rest. She stepped out, and smelled freshly turned earth and newly sawed wood.

"I heard you coming." It was Peter, standing under the portico. He was wearing a belted forest green garment that reached the ground. "I'm sorry there's no driveway yet. This is a work-in-progress. But then, we're all works in progress, amirite?"

"You seem cheerful." She sounded cheerful, too, which surprised her. She'd left Marin with a carload of hurt and anger, but much of it had taken an exit off Highway 80. Both emotions might reconnect via an internal back road, but at this moment, she was actually happy to see him. Although that long, dark green gown was kind of creepy. And he'd grown a beard! When had he forgotten his own mantra regarding facial hair? "You—you're not thinking of joining . . . becoming an oblate, maybe?"

"I don't know what that is."

"It's a person who dedicates himself to a life of Christian service, but without taking vows." Her mother had often spoken of becoming one, but she liked alcohol and costume jewelry too much. "Like

even, a vow of chastity." She was teasing now. "I asked because . . ."
\She drew a circle in front of his chest, indicating his pious and
somber attire.

"This?" He laughed. "This is a bathrobe."

He undid the belt, giving her a moment's panic, but it revealed
only his University of Michigan T-shirt and pajama pants. There
was a surprise, though: He'd gained weight, perhaps twenty pounds.
It was mostly in his belly, but all his muscles had slackened.

"What is this?" She tilted her head toward the huge house.

"The retreat center! Ain't she something?" He placed his hands
in the namaste position and bowed slightly. "Come in."

He stood aside, and Hunter entered to find herself in a room
that was two stories high, with a ginormous crystal chandelier hanging from the vaulted ceiling. There was another vast space off to
her right, ringed by pilasters. She smelled mass quantities of san-
dalwood incense burning, but it wasn't enough to mask the odor of
fresh paint.

"Hey, what about my yearbooks? I'm working the steps, and
there are a lot of people I need to make amends to. Trouble is, I can't
put together all the names, faces, and misdeeds. I think the pictures
will help."

How's Angelica doing with that ninth step? That was the one about
making amends to people one has harmed. "The yearbooks!" She
covered her face with her hands, and rocked, bending at the waist.
"Oh my God, Peter, I couldn't find them after all. I'm so sorry!" She
kept rocking, hoping she might work herself into tears. "I should
have told you before I came, but I wanted to see you."

When she finally dared peek through her fingers, she saw him
look so disappointed, that she truly regretted not just the lie, but
hurting him.

"I do have something for you." She unshouldered the trim suede
backpack she'd started carrying as a purse.

"I see you're dressed to run." He still sounded disappointed.

"Always." She unzipped the backpack and brought out the base-ball cards she'd rescued from his collection. They were in protective sleeves and bound with a ribbon.

"Oh, awesome." He tugged the ribbon open, then fanned the cards out. "I am glad to have these."

"Too bad Jesus never played baseball."

Peter raised one finger. "That we *know* of." He squatted, and placed the cards one by one on the floor, which was of an expensive-looking hardwood.

He'd bought these cards hoping to make money on them, but watching him, Hunter saw the little boy who simply liked baseball cards, in spite of the flecks of gray in his honey-blond whiskers. She promised herself that she would actually search for the yearbooks, even if it meant returning to Chardonnay Heights.

"This was sweet, Hunter." He rose from his squat.

"So . . . on retreat, hmm?" She pulled the straps of her backpack up on her shoulders. "No human interaction?"

"That's right. Except Twitter, I mean 'X'. Huh! I keep forgetting." He tilted his head. "And Facebook."

"And Instagram?"

"No! I'm off Instagram!" He shifted from foot to foot in a dance that said, *and I miss it.* "The whole point is to shut out the noise."

"What about all those workmen?"

"They don't count." His foot-shifting accelerated, and he made a restless, almost fluttery circle around her. "Hey! I've got to put these somewhere safe in my room."

Perfect. "How about a tour?"

———

A staircase disappeared into the second floor. "How do you spend your time?" she asked, as they climbed. "I mean, without human interaction."

"I read a lot. The Big Book and the Bible."

"No contact with Angelica?"

"She's giving me the gift of this space."

On the landing Hunter heard pounding. "They're still working on the third floor," he explained. "We don't want to go up there. There's lots of nails and stuff."

"How many bedrooms?"

Peter shrugged. "It depends on what you want to call a 'bedroom.' There's a master suite, but someplace will be Angelica's home office . . . Maybe eight altogether?"

"Where's the money coming for all of this?"

"Didn't you read about it? The Vershwender Grant."

The Vershwender Grant was like the MacArthur Fellowship: half a million dollars with no strings.

"Uh huh." She kept nodding, trying to keep her expression neutral. "This is going to be quite the retreat center."

"Or we might want to make it our weekend home. Angelica needs a place to decompress."

"How did Angelica swing a Vershwender? Did she know anyone on the committee?"

"I stay out of that." He puckered and looked at her very seriously. "But she's helped a lot of people, and they're grateful. Hey, let me show you her room."

It was at the end of the hall: a large room with a canopy bed at its center. "Angelica says that her childhood dream was to have a canopy bed." He smiled. "I'm happy she has that now."

It was a king-size bed (possibly a California king, but tomato-tomahto), covered with a pink duvet dotted with fluffy pink balls that resembled cotton candy. The frame was festooned with matching trim, and four king-sized pillows were tucked neatly into matching shams. Wait—was that a teddy bear on the pillows? It did seem like a little girl's fantasy. Even the wannabe Margaret Keane painting, with the big-eyed girl holding the big-eyed cat, that hung on the wall seemed to fit.

Hunter dearly wished to ask Peter if they shared not just this room, but this bed, but how could she?

Peter volunteered the answer. "Angelica and I are moving into a more spiritual phase of our relationship."

"Ah."

They retraced their steps, and Peter showed her other rooms, some furnished (including a small, creepily bare one that Peter was apparently using: twin bed, and a handmade poster advising SMILE, BREATHE, AND GO SLOWLY) and others, as he'd said, works-in-progress. Overall, Hunter hadn't seen such an accumulation of outrageously bad taste since she and Peter had stopped at the Madonna Inn, the hotel in San Luis Obispo famous for imitating nineteenth-century bordellos.

"Angelica grew up poor," Peter explained, when they looked at a room wallpapered with a pattern of palm trees. "She's aware that she's compensating."

They returned to the first floor, where Peter described how the cavernous rooms had multiple potential uses: seminars, a pop-up Pilates studio, performances by the Napa-based Indigenous People's Dance Troupe, a gallery where local artists could display their work. Yet another large space was going to be a home theater. "A jumbotron is coming," Peter said, "and seating for forty. She's paid her dues," he insisted. "Growing up with two alcoholic parents and surviving that? Wow."

"How much is the Vershwender Grant for, again?" Disingenuity at its finest.

He laughed. "Google it." Then he elbowed her gently. "I'm sorry, I couldn't resist. It was half a mil." Most of it was gone, he added casually.

All into the house? she wanted to know.

"Some of it, yeah. But she also invested in a renewable energy start-up with a guy who turned out to be a con artist. She's so trusting. Actually, there were a couple of start-ups. Silicon Valley!" He genuflected in a comic attitude of worship. "I'm glad I'm out of all that! Plus, she's got a new banker who's a solid Christian, and who's going to up her line of credit."

"A lot of figs on this tree."

Peter laughed again, and she felt happy that she had made him laugh.

He walked her to her Prius, but then lingered at the driver's side. She rolled down the window. "I've been thinking . . ." he began.

"Yes?"

"I love Jesus and Jesus loves me. We have a good thing going on. But there have to be other ways to God, don't you think?"

She started the engine. "You're asking the wrong person. You know I'm an atheist."

"Don't tell Angelica I said that," Peter insisted. "Promise."

"When would I ever see Angelica?" *But that's not what he asked.* "I promise."

"And the yearbooks! Please find my yearbooks. And anything else that can help me work the ninth step."

———

Hunter was a little late to that night's meeting.

"That house," Dannika said. "Wow. Wish I could see it."

"Me, too," Penelope agreed. "Just out of curiosity."

"I was able to take a few pictures." Hunter rummaged in her backpack, then brought out her phone. "When he went to the bathroom and stuff. Then I got more from a distance." She passed around the phone and let the other women scroll through. Alicia pronounced it hideous; Penelope shook her head grimly; Dannika laughed.

"I couldn't take too many, because I didn't want Peter to ask why."

"Now you've got her." Alicia leaned back with a kosher pickle spear; they were having a deli night, at her suggestion. "It's like Tammy Faye time. Post those online."

"Yeah!" Dannika pounded her fists on her knees. "And we'll spread the word all over social media."

Hunter used her thumb to scroll through the photos again. The last one she'd taken was from farthest away: it still showed the tops of the Palladian windows, but the construction equipment was outside the frame. Why did iPhones never have decent wide-angle lenses? Probably the new ones did.

"This looks like revenge porn." On the drive back to Marin, Hunter had savored the prospect of documenting the evidence of Angelica's excess, and the hypocrisy it revealed. But now she worried about how she would be perceived by doing so.

Penelope snapped her fingers close to Hunter's nose. "Wake up, lady. If you don't care that she accused that poor disabled man of molesting her, we do. If you don't care that she's raising money to spend on herself, we do. You need to confront her in front of the people she's ripping off before they start stockpiling weapons."

"You're right. Thank you." Hunter put her phone away.

Alicia sighed. "If you hand me the talking stick, I'll tell you about Summer's preparations to head back East. Although she's made it clear that she wants as little help from me as possible."

Chapter 40

Until We Meet Again

ALICIA

Alicia had been to the San Francisco International Airport many times, but never when it wasn't under construction. The parking structure, on seven levels, had an equally Sisyphean feel, with its twin circular driveways.

"It's in-*terminable*," she said.

No response from Summer, who was sitting in the passenger seat of the Pathfinder.

Secretly, Alicia was in no hurry to find a space. They were ridiculously early, thanks to Joshua drumming into Summer's head that they had to allow for extra time. (*Lots* of extra time. "You never know about traffic! And long lines at security!")

Alicia envisioned herself and her daughter sitting in excruciating silence for an hour that felt like a year before she could in good conscience let Summer go through security to wait alone. Alicia's greatest fear was that they would have one last, never-put-that-toothpaste-back-in-the-tube fight, and that that would be the

memory of their parting, like passing by a freeway sign: YOU ARE NOW
LEAVING THE POSSIBILITY OF RECONCILIATION, POPULATION 2.

Joshua had returned to Brookline shortly after their ice-skating
venture. Now that Summer's school year had ended, she was joining
him, so they'd have time to tour new schools, to decorate her room
to her liking, and . . .

"Dad is going to take me shopping!"

Alicia had lost count of how many times Summer had said this,
or some variation.

Joshua had further influenced Summer's look: She'd adopted a
palette of jewel tones: dark, vibrant colors like sapphire and emerald.
"No orange," Joshua said firmly. "Never wear orange unless you're
dressing up as a pumpkin for Halloween. P.S.: Never dress up as a
pumpkin." The new colors made her ivory skin glow, and her hazel
eyes a shade more green.

"Well, he's also going to keep a close eye on what you wear, so
don't get any ideas about tattoos."

"That's against Jewish law anyway." Summer raised her chin.
"You're not supposed to mutilate your body."

Summer reminded Alicia of those gentiles who converted to
Judaism and became more observant than their fellow "members of
the tribe." This functioned as yet a new boxing ring in which they
could spar: just how Jewish was she going to become, and at what
point would Alicia push back?

"I'm going back down," Alicia said. She meant another level of
the parking lot.

"There was nothing there before!"

"Maybe someone has vacated a space. No one parks here very
long. It's too expensive."

"Did I tell you Dad's having a housewarming party for me?"

Alicia refrained from pointing out that it would be more correct
to say that it was a welcome party. And yes, she'd heard about this,

too, more than a few times, both from Summer, and, via email and phone calls, from Joshua.

"He's inviting everyone from his office, and don't worry, they're not all gay—"

"Summer! You know I don't have a prob—"

"—or Jewish! His office is really diverse."

What does that mean, they have an African American receptionist?

But Alicia had placed an imaginary binder clip on her mouth. Though the tension was rising today, the past few weeks had passed pleasantly. What started as a truce became a sojourn on Mother-Daughter Island. Mother-Daughter Island was a place where confidences were shared, where counsel but not lectures was given, and where hugs were exchanged. From the older woman, there were cures for PMS and stories of her life pre-motherhood. From the younger woman there was a dictionary of current slang.

Summer studied hard for finals, and Alicia helped her when she wanted help, but didn't nag when she didn't. They went to the movies and dinner. They went back to the ice rink, bringing two girls from school whom Summer had befriended.

Later, they laughed at the pretensions of those two girls, who had delusions of Princeton as their safety school. Another time, they even made fun of Summer's beloved Grandma Debbie, who was on and off Weight Watchers like a former child star in and out of rehab.

Oh, they'd had their disputes, like over how much Summer needed to have with her when she arrived at Logan. She wouldn't need winter clothes, Alicia reminded her, not until October at least. And books—so much cheaper to mail them, fourth class, later! She should take only what she'd need for a few weeks, and let Alicia pack up the rest. Why enrich the airlines?

Summer acceded: "If you want to do all that packing and shipping, it's fine with me."

They left San Rafael in good humor.

But in the parking lot there was a new reality: it was a Friday afternoon at one of the nation's busiest airports, the weekend after the school year ended for a few hundred thousand Bay Area students. There was the smell of exhaust, the screech of tires, and the occasional shout, "I saw that first!" *Motherfucker*.

Finally Alicia saw a spot where the drivers on either side had parked on the white borders, rendering the space accessible by vehicle, but not allowing any room to open the car doors. Alicia let Summer out before squeezing in, and climbed out through the hatchback. Let the assholes who took more space than they deserved deal with it.

———

Alicia had loved airports when she was a child, especially the departures area, where everyone was anticipating a trip to a place better than where they were. Then, as a med student, she imagined the time she'd have a career as a famous doctor-researcher, and she'd be flying to conferences, which were always in glamorous places, like in the Caribbean or Switzerland, or, at worst, New Orleans.

"What happened to baggage check?" she wondered aloud. The computer terminals at the counter had no one manning them, and no one was waiting in line. She spotted one broad-shouldered man moving behind the counter, whose body language repelled interaction.

Summer gasped in frustration, "We have to do it ourselves now."

Alicia only now noticed that there were little rows of kiosks with the United logo. They resembled R2-D2. "KC told me about this," Summer said, more patiently.

Here were the lines, four deep at each kiosk. Alicia hated lines the way she hated health insurance companies. "I was so *farmisht*," Alicia said, half to herself. "I don't know how I let your father get you on a flight on a Friday afternoon."

"You made the reservations, Mom," Summer said coolly.

That kept Alicia quiet until it was their turn. She already had Summer's boarding pass, and she typed in the locator number quickly, feeling a little smug, after watching the couple in front of them struggle with the onscreen instructions.

The machine spat out a long strip of paper with Summer's flight, the Logan Airport code, BOS, and instructions on how to attach the tag. It reminded Alicia of a mobius strip. *I'm an MD!* she thought. *And a goddam Phi Beta Kappa! I can certainly attach a luggage tag!*

She was still staring at it when Summer ripped off the backing, looped the strip around the handle, and hefted the case onto the scale, leaving Alicia feeling old and stupid.

And defeated. She gave over to the feeling, letting Summer haul the suitcase to the baggage handler, then head straight in the direction of security.

There she discovered that she'd had no reason to worry about having too much time before the flight. The line folded back and forth on itself, defined by nylon ropes.

No, nobody *liked* lines, but Alicia wondered if there might not be something in the physician's desk reference about an actual allergy to them. Standing in line made her skin itch, and she couldn't stop shifting her weight from one foot to another. Why had she never enrolled Summer in TSA PreCheck? Those passengers were practically galloping by.

Summer was chattering about snacks she'd brought, reassuring Alicia that she hadn't purchased any at the airport, "I know you hate that, 'cause they're overpriced," and what movies did Alicia think they'd be showing on the plane, and how she was thinking about giving classical music one more chance; she was still debating about what new linens she wanted in the room that was to be hers (Joshua had sent her pictures); and then, suddenly, "You'll keep my room here the way it is?"

Alicia's throat tightened. "Of course," she choked out, but then, "unless I decide to start a garage band and we need a place to practice."

"Dad and I talked a lot about you, you know. He said you were always hypercritical so I shouldn't take it personally."

Alicia had to squeeze her fists tightly, lest the binder clip on her mouth come loose.

"Then he said that you were even harder on yourself than you are on anyone else, and he wished that you could appreciate how wonderful you are."

Alicia's fists opened.

"He said you're more beautiful now than you were in med school." Summer shook her head slightly, perhaps wondering how anyone Alicia's age could be considered attractive. Then she bent over to reorganize her carry-ons yet again, moving potato chips from her purse to her backpack, then returning them. Alicia smelled bananas that were ripening too fast.

The line had suddenly sped up. They were only moments away from having to part.

"Summer, *now?*"

"I don't want to have to get up to get the backpack down!"

Of all the evil those nineteen men had done, years before, this must be least of it, yet at that moment it burned: Alicia couldn't accompany Summer to the gate.

A uniformed Asian American woman behind the lectern waved her gloved hand at them.

This was it.

Then she nearly toppled over as Summer grabbed her around the waist. Or really, the rib cage, since Summer was so much taller. "I love you, Mom!"

Just for a moment, Alicia felt she deserved it.

———

Alicia had to pass baggage claim on the way back to her car. A second escalator would return her to the parking structure, but she stopped, in the sudden grip of desire for a Coke.

Could one feel nostalgic for a quarrel? Every time Summer returned from visiting her grandparents in the East, she wanted a soda from the vending machine in baggage claim. Every time they argued over it. Alicia could give in and feel like a terrible mother who was rotting her daughter's teeth, or she could refuse, and endure a very long ride back to San Rafael with a teenager who blasted more frosty air than an open window on a Boston winter night.

But now Alicia was alone, and *she* could drink as much damn Coca-Cola as she wanted.

The carousel closest to Alicia had only a few lonely bags making their eternal, circular journey to nowhere.

A flight had recently landed: the first deplaning passengers were hustling toward the closest carousel. True, baggage claim was less crowded now that airlines were charging for checked bags, and passengers were squeezing "carry-ons" the size of Model Ts into the overhead bins.

But if the upper departures level was full of excitement, the lower level was full of despair, or at least that's how Alicia saw it while she drank her Coke. People returning reluctantly from vacation, exhausted from hours crammed into narrow fuselages (themselves shaped like toothpaste tubes), being elbowed by strangers who reeked of whatever chemically preserved abomination they'd been eating on the plane.

A pregnant woman—at least thirty-two weeks, by Alicia's count—was waiting alone. Alicia hoped someone was coming to meet her; she shouldn't be lifting anything heavy.

But someday soon she'd be here with Summer, picking up her bags, when she came home to visit. And if Summer wanted a Coca-Cola from the vending machine, Alicia wouldn't say no.

Chapter 41

Looking for Love in All the Wrong Places

HUNTER

"More shenanigans!" was how Hunter described the results of the further research that she and Will done into More Nearly Each Day. Angelica was getting paid large fees for suspiciously short speeches, speeches she sometimes didn't even give. She had a salary in the mid-six-figures. And this in addition to the half-mil Vershwender money.

"How do you even *spend* all that?" Dannika asked.

"Oh, you can spend it," Alicia said. "I could spend it if I had to."

"And I can tell you more," Hunter began.

But Alicia, who had just finished her story of taking Summer to SFO, handed her the talking stick. "This makes it official."

Hunter's fingers closed around its wood. She heard herself ask, "Is it warm in here?"

Then she was gone.

———

Twelve Years Earlier

*A hotel ballroom in downtown San Francisco. A view of the
Ferry Building.*

Sororities weren't like the "mean girls" of the old days: they
were philanthropic organizations, and once a year Hunter's Beta
Gamma Delta alumnae group had an event on behalf of Sisters
Fighting Hunger. Hunter had attended each one since she'd moved
to Northern California.

Something had changed since last year, though: She'd "cele-
brated" her twenty-ninth birthday.

Twenty-nine. "It's just a number," another woman (two years
her junior) on the planning committee said.

Yes, Hunter thought, it's the number right before thirty.

Over the past few years, her former sorority sisters had been
getting married: contestants winning a game show and going on to
the championship round.

Hunter had been a bridesmaid three times. The first time it was
fun, with all the joking about the unstylish dresses in a purple so
ugly it rubbed off on your brain, with the fabric pumps dyed to
match. Everyone in the wedding party was in their mid-twenties
then, and one of the bridesmaids had said of the couple, "I give
them a year"—or was it Hunter herself who had said that? She
could joke back then. In one's twenties, one was a free spirit—too
independent, too adventurous for marriage! After thirty, suspicions
arose. Is she too choosy? Is she gay? Does she have low self-esteem?

Hunter was someone who cared about suspicions. And optics.
Besides, after thirty, the pool was shrinking, and many of the
available men came with potential stepchildren, most of whom were
already medicated with Adderall, Ritalin, Prozac, or all three.

Then there was the possibility of children of her own. She
didn't want children as much as she wanted the option, and having
children was not something she would do on her own.

Coincidentally, she was wearing purple that night—lilac,
really, that set off her freshly highlighted blonde hair. White was

her favorite color in most clothes, and Californians were indifferent to the Labor Day rule, but that evening, a white dress would send off the wrong subliminal message.

Hunter also knew how to use her small breasts to advantage. She didn't need a bra for this retro satin dress, with its deep V-shaped neckline, and many men preferred that silhouette to the bovine one that a larger bosom created.

Brad would marry her. He'd already asked her once. They were semi-living together, which by her definition meant that he was spending at least three, but fewer than six nights at her apartment in Mill Valley. Hunter hated spending too many nights alone, but she was bored.

There was always a man, and she was always bored.

He was with her tonight, and her first job was to unload him. Ideally she would park him with an acquaintance, but anyone who could discuss the Forty-Niners roster would do.

When she recognized a sorority sister's boyfriend who was as devoted a pro football fan as he, she moved quickly. "I'll let you fellas catch up." She gave Brad's arm a caress, in the manner of a good girlfriend, ready to sacrifice time with her beloved so that he could get his testosterone fix, then headed for the bar.

Once she had a plastic cup of second-rate chardonnay to hold, she stepped out of the way of others in line to do early reconnaissance. The hotel ballroom was enlivened with helium balloons in the Beta Gamma Delta colors, purple and white, and a banner with the BGD slogan: Greeks Not Geeks. The food would be good, because Hunter always took charge of the menu. This was limited to hors d'oeuvres, cheap wine, and mineral water, but serving even a modest dinner to those buying tickets to end hunger seemed grossly unclear on the concept.

Bingo! A tall man with thick, honey-blond hair, an athletic build, and dark blue eyes she could see halfway across the room. He was talking to two other men. Those two (much shorter) men were doing the listening, laughing at his story, which he accompanied with lively, but precise hand gestures.

She took long strides toward them, lest any other woman get there first. She wasn't worried about competition; she just didn't want to take the time necessary to get rid of it.

She paused in front of the trio until he looked her way. He was in a three-piece suit from an earlier year, but still outclassed his friends, who were in jeans and loafers. "You must have come straight from the office," was how she introduced herself.

The other two men took one glance at her and made their excuses, recognizing that she was above their pay grade.

Her prey tilted his head back with something like a laugh. "Now, how did you know?"

"Nice tie, too." Brad owned one suit, and it needed a trip to the dry cleaners.

"Oh, this old thing." He tugged at the full Windsor knot. "I just threw it on."

He was joking, but he was also being modest. This was a tie of the highest quality navy silk, with lighter blue stripes gathered in groups of five. So he had money, and nascent good taste. He only needed a good woman to refine it.

"Hunter Talbot." I don't need a large ring. Better to put the money toward a down payment on a house.

"Patrick Fitzgerald. Irish enough for you?"

"My mother is Irish!" she exclaimed. "And not Irish American. Irish-Irish." She affected the accent. "County Wexford. 'Barn' and bred."

"That's very good."

"It had better be." She took a delicate sip of her wine. Patrick was drinking mineral water. *"I grew up listening to it."*

A female server passed by with a tray of garlic prawns. Hunter declined, because she was worried about the effects on her breath, while Patrick said, "No, thank you," making eye contact with the woman, but breaking it immediately. He was no player; only polite. And she'd never seen such a finely sculpted, aristocratic jawline. Had social niceties not dictated otherwise, she would have conducted a thorough husband interview, including, "Where do you see yourself in five years?"

Since she couldn't be that blunt, she danced around the permissible. But whatever Patrick was, he was not eager to talk about himself. She learned that he worked for a real estate company. And he was going to law school at night, at Golden Gate University! So in five years . . . But he kept turning the conversation back to her: where did she live, what did she do, where was she born. Did she like growing up in Stamford? Did she like working at a gym?

When another plate of hors d'oeuvres—smoked salmon mousse canapes—came around, he took one, and she took one herself, and made it into three bites, each one eaten more slowly and sensuously than the preceding. Salty and tangy, the salmon spread around the inside of her mouth, and yes, she arranged for a tiny dab to remain on her lip, so that her tongue darted out to catch it.

But suddenly, Patrick's attention was diverted to another man. "There you are! I swear, dude, if you were ever on time for anything . . ."

Hunter blinked. Was she seeing double? A second blink and all came clear: This was obviously Patrick's brother. He was the dating app photo version of Patrick: He had the same distinctive, well-defined jaw, and the same dark blue eyes, but his hair was a shade lighter, and noticeably thicker. Maybe that was an effect created by the fact that it was a little longer, and tousled in a boyish manner that might or might not have been accidental. His face was missing the laugh lines and faint creases that only moments before had given Patrick's character.

"This is Peter, my baby bro." Patrick had an affectionate smile for Peter as he took his elbow. "Peter, this is Hunter Talbot."

Peter sported the very latest fashion: He was in a pinstripe suit that still smelled of the department store, but in lieu of a briefcase, a high-end backpack dangled from his right shoulder.

"Traffic, man," Peter said. "The bridge was like Wu-Tang Clan was doing a reunion concert." He let the backpack slide to the floor and extended his hand. "Hunter? Hi. Nice to meet you."

Finally, she got what she was used to: the acknowledgment, in the form of raised brows, that she was an attractive woman in a very low-cut dress.

"But, dude, you are always late," Patrick said. "And always with some lame excuse. Like, how many police actions can happen on one man's route?"

"I'm unlucky." Peter flashed dazzlingly white, even teeth. "And I attract trouble."

"You work downtown?" Hunter asked. She raised her plastic wineglass. It trembled slightly in the air.

"Yep, yep, but I made a detour to a gym South of Market."

Which might be the real reason you're late, she thought, but Patrick either didn't notice or didn't care. Instead, he said, "Hunter told me she works at Energy-4-All. You know, the gym?"

"Yeah. I gotta get something to drink."

"Have some of mine." Hunter impulsively thrust her cup at him.

Peter took it, gulped, and frowned. "For the two-hundred-dollar ticket, I'd expect something not from 7-11."

"I paid for your ticket!" Patrick laughed.

While Hunter feigned offense. "This is from Trader Joe's."

Peter snorted. "Game changer. You know how I get mine . . ." He had a contact somewhere who knew someone who got him deep discounts on exclusive wines.

She enjoyed wine-tasting herself, and weren't they in exactly the right place for it, here in Northern California?

It wasn't hard to get Peter to talk about any number of subjects. He was a foodie, like Patrick. Like Hunter.

Then she got her full husband-interview after all, though from this younger brother, when he talked about his job, and his job prospects. The promotion he expected in six months. "Which I sort of don't deserve, but sort of do."

He talked about travel. He'd go to all seven continents, but maybe he'd give himself a pass on the Arctic Circle. He talked about golf. About skiing. About taking up mountain-climbing someday.

Patrick remained with them, inserting the occasional remark. "Hunter wants to open her own gym down the line."

Mostly she wanted to start a business, and here she was, learning a lot about marketing and fitness equipment, so—

"You work out a lot, I can see," Peter said. "I'd invest in you."

She had a moment to bask before he continued, "You know, running a business is a full-time plus job. You willing to put in those kind of hours?"

"Yes." She pushed her shoulders back.

"What you need is something high concept. Like 24-Hour Fitness has."

"They're having trouble," Patrick said. "No one goes to the gym at 3:00 a.m. Or not enough people, anyway. Now, if they'd targeted—"

Peter interrupted, "Like I said, you need a gimmick. Something beyond the first-month-for-five dollars routine. Something like free Wi-Fi pumped into your brain."

"Or . . . or . . ." Hunter wanted badly to throw out her own, never-before-heard-of idea that would impress both brothers. She had nothing.

"I've been to so many meetings I can recite marketing plans like the Pledge of Allegiance." Peter had finished her wine; he turned the glass upside down. "Let me buy you a better drink sometime, so we can talk about it more," he said. "I can give you a lot of ideas."

She was back in Penelope's living room, slumped against the sofa cushions. She was clutching the talking stick as if it were the crucifix with which she was going to be buried.

The faces of the other three women hovered over her.

"What was it?" The frown line was deep between Alicia's brows.

"I wanted his brother," Hunter heard herself say. "I thought he'd be like his brother."

"Whose brother?" "What brother?"

Alicia put her hand on Hunter's forehead. "I bet you keep a thermometer around here, Penelope."

Hunter held out the talking stick. The wood felt dry in her hands. "Ew, get this thing away from me."

Dannika took it from her. "What's the deal about a brother?"

"I met Peter's brother first," was all she could say for a moment.

Then she told them about the fundraiser, her lilac dress, the hors d'oeuvres, and Patrick: handsome Patrick, interested-in-people-besides-himself Patrick, and how she let Peter's silver-plated surface outshine Patrick's silver, silver that only needed polishing.

"I went to that event wanting so much to meet someone. . . . No excuse, I know." She looked at the others, her gaze resting a moment longer on Dannika. "Peter was late the first time we went out, too. He'll be late to his own funeral." She sighed. "And he had a Porsche. I was so naive, I thought if you had a Porsche, you could afford a Porsche."

Alicia gave a short laugh.

On that first date, Peter soliloquized about some of the ideas he had for new businesses, "good karma businesses," like training coal miners for other careers. She liked how he used the word "career," instead of "job." A friend, he said, had designed a new, more efficient windmill. And solar! He described how scientists were at work on improving it, using terms she didn't understand. She realized only later that he didn't understand them, either.

Patrick steered wealthy, savvy clients his way, and he was learning from them even as he gave them advice. Did she know that there was no five-year period of history during which the stock market didn't go up? You had to have the courage to stick with something, not get scared off when there was a dip.

Yes, Peter was fun, and funny, and some of his many ideas might even have been good ideas, too, but he couldn't follow through on any of them, and it wasn't because his drinking-to-loosen-up developed into drinking-to-relax, and then into problem drinking. This was long before that.

Hunter eventually learned that Patrick was the one who'd gotten Peter his brokerage job, the one he was fired from a few years after he and Hunter married.

"Patrick was the better man," Hunter said now, "but I went for the even better-looking one with plans to be rich." She sighed. "Why was I so desperate to get married anyway? To either of them?"

"You shouldn't be so hard on yourself," Alicia said. She'd been feeling Hunter's pulse. But she turned away now and walked over to the window.

Over Alicia's shoulder, Hunter could see the great expanse of Penelope's lawn. It reminded her of what Will had said once, how people who migrated from other parts of the country created landscapes that were ultimately unsustainable in California's mostly desert climate. "There's a story I remember from Hebrew school."

"Will this one be on the test?" Dannika asked.

Hunter shushed her.

Alicia's shoulders tensed. "Pharaoh puts a bowl of gold and jewels in front of Moses, and a bowl of hot coals next to it. If Moses reaches for the gold, it means that he wants to usurp Pharaoh, but if he puts his hand in the coals, it means he's no threat."

Hunter had never heard this particular tale, which hadn't made it into the Catholic school curriculum.

"Moses reaches for the gold and jewels, but an angel pushes his hand away. He puts his hand in the coals instead, then puts his fingers in his mouth, and that's why he has a speech impediment."

"I didn't know he has—had a speech impediment," Penelope said.

"I think the moral of this story is clear," Alicia said. "You didn't have an angel to push your hand away."

Chapter 42

Thank You for Your Inquiry

DANNIKA

Dannika's search to further her education did not have a promising start.

Dannika found it easiest to use her laptop when she was lying on her couch, with pillows propped up behind her. The computer was on her knees, and Miss Havisham the tortoiseshell cat was on her thighs. That made it difficult to reach the keyboard, but she was bound by the inviolable Arenescu household rule that one did not disturb a sleeping cat.

```
Dear Ms. Arenescu:
Thank you for your inquiry.
Admissions are closed for the upcom-
ing academic year. The next applica-
tion deadline . . .
```

Wait *another* year?

Dannika had written to UCLA and given them her story about her mom, about her paralyzing grief, and about her awakened ambition. Why had she bothered? Because she'd had a fantasy: that the old (and in some cases now probably dead) white men who ran UCLA would *understand*.

Maybe her mistake was in the salutation itself. If only she knew someone in the admissions committee, rather than writing "To Whom It May Concern."

But the Good Ship UCLA had sailed.

In a way, it was a relief. She didn't want to wait four years to start learning her craft. "So go to college and work on jewelry in your spare time," Alicia had said.

Spare time? She'd need every minute to get her head back around doing *homework*. And she'd have to take at least one real science class, like chemistry or biology—or physics! Not. Gonna. Happen.

So—to hell with the four-year college route! She was twenty-four. She'd go straight to a design school.

Back to the internet. She typed in DESIGN SCHOOLS NEAR ME.

The first hit was the Academy of Art University in San Francisco. The website excited her. They had programs in architecture, photography, art history—*and* jewelry and metalwork. She could commute. Or even telecommute, since they offered courses online.

Hmmm . . .

Hunter and Alicia both told Dannika horror stories of a Time Before Google. "We called it AO-Hell." "It was America On Hold."

Penelope said, "Don't get me involved in this. When I was your age we used to send smoke signals." She looked up from her cuticles. "What? Is a joke about smoke signals cultural appropriation?"

Dannika had designed an entry-level WordPress site for Penelope (TheMightyPen.com), so she could blog there, and not be tied to OurVoicesBoom.com. When the site went live, Penelope was as awe-struck as if Dannika had built the world's first perpetual motion machine.

But how do you make jewelry online? You had to be able to put your hands on a piece of metal, feel its weight and texture. You had to see colors with your own eyes, not through the fickle lens of an integrated camera.

And AAU had open admissions. That meant they'd take anyone, even high school dropouts.

A few Yelp reviews and a Wikipedia entry later, she self-righteously put AAU on her "no go" list. Dannika Arenescu had become a snob.

There were other possibilities in the Bay Area, but the snobbishness—call it *discernment*—didn't leave her. When she found a school with a more selective admissions policy, it didn't offer any programs centered around metallurgy, let alone jewelry design, so she dismissed that one, as well.

There was another problem, too: There were gaps in her education. Yawning chasms, more like it. Yes, she knew a subset of nineteenth-century literature, and a lot of trivia about the old movies that Mosi liked, but when it came to history and geography, she was an embarrassment. Hunter and Alicia especially looked surprised and concerned when they stumbled into these gaps, like when she couldn't find Germany on a map. "That's definitely a place you need to know how to find," they insisted.

Miss Havisham stretched, placing her front legs on Dannika's right thigh, and her back legs on her left. Then she arched her back, seeming to announce, "Nice nap. Five minutes till the next one." Dannika felt the pain in her stomach that appeared when she thought of Raskolnikov.

What she needed was a program that would fill some of the gaps in her education, but also get her into the World. A place where she'd find a mentor, the way Mosi had found one for herself in New Mexico.

Miss Havisham jumped off, and Dannika took the opportunity to head to the kitchen in search of juice. But when she opened the refrigerator door, she found herself gazing at a life in stasis. Lettuce gone bad, eggs from three months ago. Even the light bulb was burned out.

She stared at it, pulling on her lower lip. There were other options. She could take some classes at College of Marin, as Howie had suggested the first time they met. If she became what she wanted to become (and she hardly dared admit to herself what she was imagining: the display case at an upscale department store, the museum exhibit—she was still young! It was still possible!) it wouldn't matter where her degree was from.

But she had to get out of here. She had to leave this house, with all of Mosi's boxes and "pieces of string too short to save."

The cats! OMG, the cats! No, she wouldn't leave them, but . . .

She returned to the couch, empty-handed, but more focused. No, she didn't just want to learn how to solder, she wanted to learn economics. *Let's not get carried away.* She was never going to be a scientist. *Sorry, Mosi.* If she found a cure for cancer it would be too late for her mother anyway.

Finally she found a few places that looked promising—or rather, their programs looked promising. Was Howie's offer of help with an application essay still good? No, she had to do this on her own. (Also, she didn't want to ask him.)

She sucked her upper lip between her teeth and bit down hard. These were all private schools, some for profit, some nonprofit, but all expensive, too expensive even if she had never touched the money that Mosi had scraped together to leave her.

She had to hope to get a scholarship. Pray to get a scholarship. Dannika grimaced. She did believe in God. She believed in God because she had to. But she detested the evangelicals who believed in the power of prayer. There was a study that claimed that sick people recovered more quickly if people were praying for them. Really? Was God like the Quinnipiac University Poll?

No, God might be Dannika's imaginary friend, but He-She-It-They was all she had right now, so she closed her eyes and prayed.

Chapter 43

We Love You, Penelope

Penelope

You've saved me. I talked to my husband. I'm leaving.

Kudos to you for coming out as an
older woman. I send your blogs to
the women I know who think it's too
late for them.

You're a sick bitch and you've
ruined my marriage. Fuck you.

Why did the outliers—the nasty ones—have so much power over
her? "That's the way it is," Reyna said. "Try growing up gay in
Stockton." She put her hand on Penelope's shoulder, then kissed
her cheek.

Penelope still felt like the first lesbian in the world. And she wanted to shout it from the rooftops, or, barring that, tweet all day long. #lesbiansrock #lesbianlove #lesbiansrule

Penelope had waited until Dannika had designed her website before she came out. The administrators of OurVoicesBoom.com were supportive of the revelation, but anxious about the specifics. "We have a lot of conservative subscribers."

With her own website, Penelope could write whatever the hell she wanted. Eventually, she'd have guest bloggers, too. Reyna would both solicit and review submissions, since she had agreed to accept a modest salary for taking on the job of Penelope's social media manager.

Writing that first coming out essay had taken some time, some additional prodding, and several drafts. Finally Penelope had written, in part:

```
When I think of the joy I've been
missing for decades, it breaks my
heart. It's hard not to look back
and think of the partnership I might
have had.
    But I can't get that time back,
and regretting the past only post-
pones my future.
```

Besides, in that parallel universe she would have missed Reyna, wouldn't she? When Reyna was born in the Stockton community hospital, Penelope was married to Jared, and living (if you could call it that) in Austin. Now she thought that she had more years left than she'd imagined just a few months earlier. She was going to make the most of whatever time that was, and Reyna could have her pick of the cologne that survived her.

Reyna, who had started packing that afternoon. She was going to become an RN through a program at the University of San Francisco. "Three moves is as good as a fire. I'm getting rid of a lot of stuff."

Penelope was sitting halfway on Reyna's bed: one knee on the duvet, the other foot on the floor. "Am I a coward for not using my real name? On my website, I mean?"

Reyna did hesitate, but then she said, "No, this way you create a persona that's not you. Besides—I mean I hate to say it—but the way things are these days . . . you know, threats from toxic men."

"Was that an actual threat?" Penelope started sliding off the bed. The words, "sick bitch" felt like a tattoo.

"No, no, no. I'm just saying that Scott may not be a saint, but he's still entitled to his privacy."

Reyna was folding up her thong panties. They were all pastels, with lace trim. How did she wear those? Pantyhose would feel like a second skin by comparison to a thong, which Penelope imagined would be like having a permanent wedgie.

"I'm going to miss you." Penelope suddenly felt very sorry for herself.

"And I'm going to be your social media manager, remember?"

Yes, that would give Penelope an excuse—better, would *require* Penelope not only to email, text, talk and FaceTime with Reyna, but to be in the same room with her occasionally. Let the young'uns have their smartphones. It wasn't called being "in touch" for nothing.

At least thongs didn't take up much space in a suitcase. Watching Reyna tuck them between twin piles of sweaters, Penelope relived the shame of searching Reyna's room. She was so lucky that Reyna had forgiven her for that.

It also prompted her to speak. "I did some research. Turns out that you can take a few classes and then just take the test to become an RN!"

"Penelope, I don't want to cheat my way in. I love you, but . . ."

"There's always a but, dammit."

"But I've never even set up an IV for you."

Of course Reyna didn't want to cheat her way in. Penelope scrunched her brows together, then released the muscles, knowing how many more wrinkles were visible on a scrunched brow. "I'd feel better if you had a male roommate. A gay male roommate."

Reyna was not a one-woman woman. She had said as much. She wanted her own place; she did not explicitly say that she wanted her own place so as to have sex with other women, but why would young, beautiful Reyna want to be with an old hag like her?

As had been the case from the beginning, Reyna read her mind. "You are a very attractive woman, Penelope." The zipper of her suitcase screeched as she ran it around the border of her suitcase. Halfway around, it stalled, the top straining. "Help me close this, please?"

Penelope put both hands on the suitcase top and pushed down so as to make the clothes inside more compact. She didn't want to think of Reyna's lingerie inside, but she did. She saw the veins in her hands swell with the effort, and she closed her eyes. She'd been trying to squeeze a lot of things into a too-small space for too long a time.

Chapter 44

The Truth Hurts

HUNTER

"Ta-da!" Hunter turned her front door key, then pushed the door open. "After you, monsieur!"

"Well, finally." Will stepped over the threshold.

The tour was brief: kitchen, living room, bedroom, bath. The only thing worth hovering over was the chrome-and-glass shelf, visible from the entryway, where Hunter had arranged, as planned, her most valuable collectibles.

Will respectfully lifted an ashtray, holding it by its edges. It was from the Carnelian Room, once an expensive restaurant at the top floor of the Bank of America Center, in downtown San Francisco. It was from a time long, long ago, when restaurants had ashtrays.

"I know a man who is collecting ashtrays who will pay big bucks for this." She put her index finger across her lips. "Believe it or not."

"I *am* skeptical." He raised one eyebrow.

"And there's no need to insure something like this." Not that it made financial sense to insure any but the most valuable collectibles.

"If someone breaks in, they'll go for my computer, not an innocuous ashtray." Which ashtray she took back from Will, to replace on the shelf. "Look! It's decor and merch at the same time! By the way . . ."

Will was running his thumb and forefinger down a lock of her hair. "Yes?"

"I want to talk to Angelica alone." She adjusted the position of the ashtray.

Years ago, Angelica had come to her, looking for a job. Hunter didn't hire her, because she wasn't qualified. But that was the beginning of Angelica wanting what Hunter had, and she started with Peter.

"Hey, I've got a stake in this, too." He playfully tugged on the lock of hair as a reminder.

"I know, I know." She decided to be direct. "Uncle Gilbert is gone—requiescat in pace—and I want to take care of this part myself." She smiled. "It's personal."

"Okay." Will's return smile was hard to read. "And here I wore my good luck tie."

———

That morning, Hunter had called the landline at Chardonnay Heights. She got a recorded message (a male voice, with a slight East European accent) touting the achievements of More Nearly Each Day ("our new retreat center will open soon—come feel the love") and referring the caller to "our newly designed website, MoreNearlyEachDay.org." She was encouraged to leave a message.

She spoke slowly: "I need to talk to Angelica. St. Ambrose," she added, lest Angelica's swelling ranks included anyone with the same first name as hers.

The return call was from what sounded like a young man enduring puberty. His voice alternately cracked and squeaked when he asked, what was the purpose of the interview? Who referred her?

Hunter reflexively agreed to ground rules that included no recording devices and Angelica's preapproval of any articles before they were posted.

They were set for that afternoon at 2:00.

———

Hunter had not set foot in Chardonnay Heights in months, and when she saw the line of cars parked along the narrow roadway she wondered how the neighbors felt about it. Back in the days of their parties, Hunter had taken care to keep the noise level manageable, and she'd also invited every neighbor, including the octogenarian up the hill who had binoculars as well as a handgun. Hunter could turn on some charm when necessary, in addition to leaving gifts on porches.

She parked behind a Ford Fiesta. There was no sidewalk, so she walked back to where the hedge that bordered the street ended, and turned into her driveway. There she saw that Peter's and her project from years before had finally been carried out: the driveway was now wide enough for two cars to pass at the same time.

This didn't make it any less steep, and Hunter climbed awkwardly. She'd dressed in a white linen pantsuit, and her white high-heeled sandals, while also appropriate for early summer, were a challenge. But she wanted to make an impression, in the way that Will's dark suit had impressed her when they first met. (At least, it seemed *now* that she'd been impressed by it.)

Under her arm, she carried an accordion file, thick with documents she would show Angelica.

Finally, the top: Someone had enlarged the patio in front of the house, uprooting two beautiful black pine trees. And the house had a new door: wider than the old one, and institutional-looking. Gold letters across the center spelled out: MORE NEARLY EACH DAY. It was unlocked, and when she opened it, she found her view blocked by newly constructed drywall only a few feet in front of her. It was painted bubblegum pink—that was, what was visible of it, for it was almost entirely covered with photos of Angelica, many with celebrities. The narrow space, which reminded her of a new age doctor's waiting room, was filled with displays of Angelica's books, including her recently self-published *Jesus Warned Me* workbook, and the new audio adaptation, read by the author.

She heard people from the other side of the wall. "It's starting." "Be quiet!"

"Yes, yes, yes, I have news I want to share!" Angelica's voice. "Lindsey Van Gelder is on board with having me write the screenplay. He's read my book and loves—"

The long line of cars on the road . . . Angelica was holding a meeting. And it was starting—yes, Hunter looked at her watch— right at the time that Hunter had said she'd arrive for their one-on-one "interview." *Well*, she thought, *game on*.

Another snatch of Angelica's speech penetrated the thin partition. ". . . attached to direct, but I'm not allowed to name names!"

Hunter followed the wall, heading in the direction of what should be the bedrooms, and fearing that in this parallel universe she might step off a newly constructed cliff built especially for her. Instead, another wall blocked off the part of the house where the bedrooms had been. What Hunter needed was a flask marked "drink me," with a potion that that would make her able to pass through solid objects.

". . . *Let Go and Let God for God's Sake* is the sequel . . ."

At last she identified a swinging door that flew open at a gentle touch.

The light blinded her for a moment. The floor-to-ceiling windows that faced west made the room look like heaven's gate, with the afternoon sun against white walls. (*Freshly painted*, Hunter noticed.) The breakfast bar was still there, now sporting a coffee service, but the rest of the kitchen was blocked off by a sliding rice paper screen. Her great room was half its former size.

While still in the doorframe, she heard Angelica, "The reality show component would have parts for everyone, especially the most committed."

Then Angelica spotted her. "Look who's here, folks! Hunter Fitzgerald, my old—well, not *old*—friend. Old as in longtime." She stretched her hand out from a kimono sleeve: silver rings glinted. "Long, long, *long*time."

Anyone listening would have thought Hunter was a welcome guest—and they had all been listening. They were also watching her closely: thirty people at least, sitting in a double row of folding chairs, arranged in a semicircle.

That was the calculation behind Angelica making the great room smaller: it made the place looked packed. In spite of the dense seating, though, the front row stopped at a distance from Angelica, creating a space equivalent to the sanctuary. Angelica herself was enthroned in a deeply padded club chair, slightly raised from the floor on cinder blocks, in the place where the altar would be. And while it had been many years since Hunter had been inside a church of any kind, she shivered at how this reminded her of the small church of her childhood, with the selection of Jesus statuary displayed where the kitchen counter had been—and right next to the coffee creamer.

"I'll wait outside until you're finished," Hunter said.

Angelica shook her head. "There's nothing you can say that you can't say in front of my peeps."

"But—" Hunter involuntarily rattled the accordion file under her arm.

"Nothing." Angelica surveyed the assembly from her perch. "We need a chair for Hunter!"

A woman in the back raised a chair. "Last one!" She stumbled toward her, with the chair raised above everyone's head. She tripped on a few feet, provoking "oww!"s and "careful!"s. When she got close enough, Hunter saw that she had a large silver cross around her neck.

She also had hair just like Angelica's: tight, dark red curls. She set the chair down with a forceful plunk and an equally forceful glare.

Uncomfortable as Hunter was, she had become interested in the proceedings. She squeezed the chair in between a man who smelled of cigarettes and a woman who stuck her elbow in Hunter's rib cage.

"Saturday is another Love Building Day," Angelica announced. "Seven a.m., bring your own tools—the kind made of metal, not the name you used to call your partners."

Laughter.

"We'll finish up with a barbecue in the backyard."

The group clapped, loudly and at furious speed.

Love Building Day. This must be the source of both the landscaping and the hatchet-job-cum-remodel inside Chardonnay Heights: "volunteers" from her followers, the people Hunter thought of as the Acolytes.

When the noise finally receded, Angelica addressed Hunter again: "We were just about to start the 'coming clean.' Owning our addictions." She held Hunter's gaze a moment. "Feel free to participate."

A young woman raised her hand. "Hi, I'm Lynne, and I'm addicted to negative thoughts."

As everyone turned to look at Lynne, Hunter scrutinized the rest of the audience-congregation. The group included many more redheads, most with the perfect, tight curls of a permanent wave. She gradually picked out the Southwestern accessories: the turquoise jewelry; the bandannas; the cowboy boots alternating with sandals. String ties on plaid shirts on the few men. On one woman, a long skirt printed with cacti. Enough crosses for a revival meeting.

One step more and they'd be in uniform.

Lynne described how she kept thinking that her boyfriend was cheating. She didn't read his text messages, there was a password on his phone anyway, but there was a picture of him on Instagram with a blonde woman, who was skinnier than her, so what should she think?

Angelica told Lynne she had to love her body exactly the way it was and then encouraged her to put her problem in Jesus's inbox. "Nuns have it so easy. Jesus is their boyfriend, and it's okay for Him to hang with other women. Or men, of course. I wrote an essay, 'Jesus Is No Homophobe.' It's on my website for free."

Hunter was numb to hearing Angelica speak of Jesus so cavalierly, but she was surprised to find that she didn't like hearing her laugh at nuns. She'd wanted to be one herself—granted, about thirty-five years earlier.

There were more stories, all leading with the obligatory introduction: I'm Emily, Ashley, another Emily. I'm addicted to loneliness. I'm addicted to FreeCell. Starbucks coffee. Reruns of *Hogan's Heroes*. And the usual suspects: cocaine, alcohol, sex, online gambling.

"Hi, I'm Nevin, and I'm addicted to candy bars."

This from a man noticeably older than the others: perhaps seventy-five. Perhaps even older. His bowed head showed a bright pink scalp, with a few stripes of white hair.

Hi, Nevin.

"But I can't afford them anymore, so I take them." His shoulders trembled. "Hershey bars or Nestle's Crunch."

It was all too easy to forget that there was actual poverty in Marin County. Not just the handful of welfare recipients tucked away between Sausalito and Marin City, safely out of sight, but the Nevins: people on Social Security, people who'd lived here for decades, now forced out by rising costs and the condescension of neighbors.

Angelica was taking money from Nevin. And when Hunter pictured Nevin shuffling toward home with the purloined chocolate in the pocket of ill-fitting trousers, all contempt she felt toward Angelica's followers fell away: every leaf from a tree in a sudden storm, leaving only thin, dead branches.

Again, murmurs of encouragement. Jesus would provide candy for the soul.

Hunter raised her hand. "I'd like to come clean."

Angelica acknowledged her with a regal nod.

Hunter stood, the better to command attention.

"My name is Hunter, and I'm : . . ." She hesitated. "I'm addicted to the truth."

The others were only halfway through an uncertain *Hi Hunter*, before she rushed on.

"Your Angelica St. Ambrose has used More Nearly Each Day, which is supposed to be a *charity*, to enrich herself."

This earned her a few seconds of silent surprise before the rumbles of protest began.

"She used her Vershwender Grant money to build a mansion in the wine country, telling you that it would become a retreat center, but it never will—"

"That money was hers!" a man shouted.

"She's building that for us."

"Yeah, where do you get off?"

Now it was Hunter's turn to be surprised. But she collected herself quickly. She just had to explain better.

"The original grant money is long gone, and now she's using *your* money to finish remodeling—"

"For us! She's building it for us!" The woman who called this out was sniffling in a way that promised a full-blown crying jag.

That was the last accusation Hunter could clearly identify from an onslaught that followed. ("Who the hell are you?" "What do you know?")

But fine, then! Hunter reached into her accordion file, grabbing whatever papers her fist would hold. She yelled to make herself heard. "Angelica is paying herself a huge salary, using money that you've donated—"

"All those nonprofit CEOs get huge salaries." It was another redhead, her face almost hidden by an Angeli-fro.

"There's that group that takes high school kids on field trips to the Sierras . . . what's it called . . ."

"Yeah, the nonprofits that work with kids pay the most—there's that Read to a Kindergartener—"

And Nevin himself declared, "Kaminsky gets three hundred thousand for running his Fingerpaint Museum."

How was it that so many of them knew highly paid executives from the nonprofit world?

Someone in the back whom she couldn't see called out, "The Society for the Promotion of Czech Filmmaking pays its president more than that!"

Angelica, as serene as Lake Tahoe, said, "The president of the board of ProPublica—that's where you got your information, is it?—is paid half a million dollars a year. To provide information like this to people like you, who are contributing nothing to the spiritual growth of anyone."

Everyone stopped talking. Hunter flailed for her next argument. It was like searching for your cell phone in your purse when you know you've left it behind. She wanted to say to the people in this room, *if you love Jesus, go to church! Pray at home! You don't need Angelica St. Ambrose to tell you fanciful stories about her past in order to reach Him!*

Angelica went on, "I devote all my time to helping people recover from addiction and discover God through Jesus." Her gaze swept the circle; her amber eyes were wet and red-rimmed. "Everyone here should be recognized, and rewarded, for what they do."

Ah! But she didn't know what more Hunter knew, thanks to the work she and Will had done!

"Angelica also charges enormous speaking fees—"they'd say she deserved that, too, but she was ready!—"for speeches she doesn't give!"

"What? What speaking fees? Where?"—came the questions from different parts of the room.

"I'll tell you!" Hunter waved the papers in her hand. "Angelica was scheduled to appear at the Marin Civic Center Speakers Series last month. She was paid ten thousand dollars. But she canceled due to a so-called illness, the speech is marked postponed, and—"

"And rescheduled for September, when the series resumes." Angelica finally spoke, still serene.

"I've heard her speak." A young woman with a nose ring made herself heard. "It's life-changing!"

"She's so wise and funny and true," another Acolyte said.

Somehow, the empty space that Hunter had thought of as a sanctuary had shrunk. People were closing in on her in a mass of red hair, crosses, turquoise jewelry, and sweat that combined with Angelica's heavy gardenia cologne to make Hunter woozy.

She acted out of instinct or desperation when she said, "Her memoir is full of lies, her parents didn't even drink—"

She was cut off by laughter. The loudest and jolliest came from Angelica.

Then the attacks resumed. "Of course you'd say that, after what you did!" "There's an empty seat here, if you'd like to join our meeting!"

"Vijay Koka will back me up!" she cried.

Angelica laughed again. "Oh, good old Can't-Stay-Vijay. He took off for Daddy and Mummy in 'Mummy-bai.' And do you know, I still haven't been to India? And I'd really like to go."

The laughter devolved into jeers.

"Angelica's a threat to everyone who's using," someone said.

"You have your own agenda."

"What are you doing to help anyone?"

"We know about your history with Angelica, Hunter Fitzgerald."

"Stop!" Angelica raised her voice for the first time.

The silence was a border wall. Hunter could hear the squeak of the chair legs on her once-beautiful hardwood floor. She heard a cough. She heard her own shallow breaths.

"We all know what happened. But why are we here anyway? God always has a plan, doesn't He? This way, I can do this publicly." She caught Hunter in the high beams of her amber eyes. "I. Forgive. You. Hunter."

———

Hunter hadn't cried since the second meeting of the talking-stick group.

She cried that night in Will's arms.

He stroked the back of her hair. "It's over now. Let's not follow our enemies into Hell."

Chapter 45

Search but You Will Not Find

HUNTER

"Have you ever been in a nightmare," Hunter asked the other women, "and you know it's a nightmare, but you can't wake yourself up?"

"You can't save them from themselves," Alicia said.

"Angelica is using them to do the construction on the house." This was how a cult evolved: asking not just for money, but for participation. For loyalty.

"I don't care what they think of me," Hunter lied. "I wanted to help."

The women continued murmurs of sympathy and encouragement. But underneath their words she heard their disappointment. She heard them wondering if there hadn't been more that she could have done. She heard them wondering why she'd bothered in the first place, and if perhaps revenge hadn't truly been her motive all along.

Then she knew she was hearing all these things only from herself.

Don't give up, she thought. *There has to be a way.*

Penelope said, "Let's break out the talking stick," and Hunter returned to her body with a snap.

"Yeah. 'Kay." Hunter reached for the piece of Zelda's knitting at her side. When she lifted it, she noticed that it felt light, but that didn't fully register until a few moments later, when she unwound the cloth. "It's gone."

"What?" "No." "Huh?"

Hunter shook out the material, as if it might have gotten caught up in its folds. "The talking stick is gone."

The other three women closed in, leaning over her shoulders. When did she last see it? Was it ever out of her hands? Could she have left it in her car/in her apartment/in a restaurant/CVS? Did she take it to Moskowite Corner?

She couldn't remember. She felt the ground shift under her: 6.9 on the Anxiety Scale.

"I thought you were going to get some sort of lockbox for it."

They were panicking. Even Alicia, once she'd seen Zelda's knitting laid out empty, began pacing. "It's just weird, that's all," she said.

When they started meeting at Penelope's, Hunter had given the talking stick to her to keep, feeling it was safer with her than under the same roof as Angelica. But the day she signed the lease on her own apartment, she'd taken it there. She'd kept it at the back of her closet, snug in its colorful wrap.

Could Hunter have been the victim of a car break-in? Might Will have taken it, even by accident?

Hunter sat with her head in her hands, thinking how easy it was for conspiracy theories and unfounded accusations to foment.

Dannika put an end to this when she stamped her foot. "All right, stop, you guys. We need to work together."

Reyna was the one human outside their group who knew about the mysterious ways of their wooden accessory, but Penelope didn't want to ask her about it. "That's racist! She'll think I'm accusing her of stealing it!"

"No, she won't," Hunter reassured her. "Just call her and ask if she saw it around the house. You'll know how to put it." Hunter imagined an ad on eBay: SPECIAL MAGIC OAK STICK THAT HELPS YOU RETRIEVE REPRESSED &/OR REVISED MEMORIES.

Penelope left the room, but returned a few minutes later. "She said, 'I don't know nothin' 'bout no talking stick.'" Penelope frowned. "I really hope I didn't offend her."

"C'mon, guys." Alicia addressed them, arms akimbo. "It's very weird that it's gone. We can keep looking, but in the meantime, this is our chance to see what life is like without the talking stick."

Penelope cleared her throat. "That's what people used to tell me about Valium. Just try life without it."

"What people?" Hunter asked.

"Oh, you know, like doctors, when I was begging them to give me more."

"And now, you are living without it!" Alicia said.

Dannika pressed, "How do you explain what happened to us? I mean, I had like real visions of things."

Alicia shook her head. "Freud started out with hypnotizing people, and he only stopped because he discovered that he couldn't hypnotize everyone. But hypnosis is a real thing. Some people truly believe they're regressing to past lives, for God's sake."

"I don't want to be born again." Dannika shuddered. "By the time I come back, the oceans will be boiling over."

"But you believe in astrology."

"Prove to me that it's not real!"

"You can't prove a negative," Alicia said. "Like, a giraffe isn't going to walk in this door. You all know I'm right, but you can still say, well, it could happen."

"C'mon everyone," Hunter mumbled. "We agreed that we'd respect—"

"Hunter." Alicia turned to her. "You must know the story about the shepherd children who had a vision of the Virgin Mary and how she made the sun twirl in the sky."

"The Miracle of the Sun." Hunter squirmed. "Fatima."

"Thousands of people were there that day and swore it happened. Do you think it happened?"

"It's hard to believe," Hunter said.

"So, it was a case of mass hypnosis. People are suggestible. The children say this is going to happen, and people wanted to believe it badly enough that they think it happened."

When Angelica's followers were berating Hunter en masse, there was room in her heart for nothing but rage. Through the telescope of a single day, though, she felt their desperation. They wanted someone to care for them. Someone to link them to that Higher Power, which in Hunter's great room they called Jesus, and standing in the center of their semicircle, she was also standing in their way.

"And what about the people who swear they've encountered aliens?" Alicia asked. "I'm not talking about one crazy person. I'm talking about a lot of crazy people, who claim they were there at the same time and all confirm each other's stories."

Penelope spread her hands apart. "There's something to be said for being willing not to have the answer."

"Here's another theory." Hunter arranged the empty knitting over her lap. "What if the talking stick has done what it came here to do, and now it's gone?"

"Where?" Alicia asked. "To talking-stick heaven? Or to that woman's RV?"

"That is beneath you, Dr. Lieberman," Penelope said.

"I'm sorry." Alicia took the talking-stick cover from Hunter's lap and held it up to the light from the nearest window. "I guess I'm upset, too."

"We can stick with facts," Hunter said. "We got together and we each had a couple of memories. No one thinks the memories aren't real, do they?"

All three women shook their heads.

"You know," Dannika said after a moment, "maybe all those people really *have* encountered aliens."

Chapter 46

Return to Treasure Island

HUNTER

When the group met again, Dannika brought what she called, "Son of Talking Stick." Then she changed her mind. "No, let's call it Daughter of Talking Stick."

"Talking Stick 2.0.," Alicia suggested.

Dannika had broken off a small branch from a tree in her backyard, sanded it, and wrapped bands of different-colored yarn around it at intervals. She used twine to attach several feathers and small, polished stones.

They all agreed that it was beautiful. Why did it feel so wrong?

Penelope was a longtime consumer of soap operas and she explained that this was how she felt when a favorite character was replaced by a new actor. "And they expect you to shift all the feelings you had for the character on the new person!" She pinched the feather at the end of the new stick. "Actually, you do, it just takes a while."

———

But Hunter wasn't ready to let go of the talking stick. Alicia called it idolatry. Hunter, though, thinking again about holy relics, wanted to hold the talking stick one last time, *knowing* that it would be the last time. What she really wanted was an explanation, but she would settle for closure.

Closure meant Treasure Island.

Did she think that Zelda would replace it? Maybe.

"Let's not tell the others," Hunter said to Dannika on the phone. The "others" would be Penelope and Alicia.

"Why not?"

"They'll think I'm crazy."

"So why are you telling me?"

Dannika had, from the beginning, been the one most receptive to the mysteries of the talking stick, so Hunter wanted her for company.

"And you already think I'm crazy."

"I don't like keeping secrets."

"We can tell them when we get back." *Or not.*

"You want to find the talking-stick lady."

"Bingo." She added, "I need to find the talking stick to know *why* I need the talking stick."

"That's like Howie." Dannika *ha'*d. "He needs his glasses to find his glasses, poor dude. Oooh, field trip. Let's do it."

———

Dannika was generally a fidgety person, and now her fingers were dancing on the dashboard of Hunter's Prius. "Can you hear that? It's 'Don't Stop Believin'.'"

"No, it just sounds like *tap, tap, tap.*" Hunter checked her blind spot, then moved to the far left lane for the Treasure Island exit.

"I think once we all fix up my new talking stick it'll be just as good."

"Danni, there's nothing wrong with your new talking stick."

"Oh, God, no." Dannika pointed.

Hunter disciplined herself to keep her eyes on the road. "What?"

"See that sign? They're building these high-end condos on Yerba Buena. They can't do that!"

Hunter sighed.

"It's so rocky, I thought it was safe from being developed," Dannika said. "Why crowd more people into the Bay Area and spoil it for everyone?"

Hunter took one hand off the wheel long enough to rub thumb and index finger together in the universal gesture that denoted *money*.

"Well, it sucks."

T.J.Maxx, a chain of discount clothing stores where Hunter had shopped as a teenager, had once had a slogan, "It's never the same place twice." Treasure Island was like that: constantly evolving, as old buildings from its time as a Navy base were torn down, and new housing built. Meanwhile, DANGER—RADIATION signs remained.

Dannika regarded the new construction with dismay. "Someday this whole island will be a resort and casino."

For now, at least, parking wasn't a problem. Hunter left her car in a large empty lot, refreshingly devoid of "permit parking only" signs. Then they started down Avenue of the Palms, the road where the palm trees framed the eastern half of the city.

"Do you know where we're going?" Dannika asked.

"No," Hunter admitted. "There's something about Treasure Island that makes me get lost immediately."

It wasn't immediate, but before they'd walked far, Hunter was disoriented. "If it's June, the sun is in the northern part of the sky, right?" she asked. "I could have sworn the apartments were this way."

The sun was quickly becoming a moot point, as the fog began to roll in, first as an invading mist, then as a thickening veil.

They walked another hour, past chain link fences covered with sheeting, past telephone poles, past spontaneous sculptures made of wood and stones. They passed an upscale bar and grill that was closed.

Then Hunter noticed a lamppost. It was an ordinary lamppost, yet somehow she knew that they had finally wandered into the same warren of apartment buildings she'd visited before.

"It's like the Casbah." Or what she imagined the Casbah to be: a maze of narrow passages, perhaps with no exit.

Puffs of fog followed them, drifting in between the buildings, almost as if from behind the walls or through the open windows, turning afternoon into twilight. The buildings looked even shabbier than Hunter remembered.

"My feet are tired," Dannika said, though as an observation rather than a complaint. She was in leather over-the-knee boots and her black hair was in a ponytail. The hair on the shaved side of her head had mostly grown in.

"The last time I was here you could hardly see a No Trespassing sign in front of your face," Hunter said.

"Are there dogs around?" Dannika asked nervously.

"Only cats, don't worry. Um . . . you believe me that there was an alley here, right?"

"Sure," Dannika said. "They're always closing up alleys."

"I think we've already been down this street," Hunter said.

"Okay, time for a break." Dannika sat on the narrow concrete that passed for a sidewalk. "Did you ever read *The Lion, the Witch, and the Wardrobe?*"

"Of course," Hunter said, though feeling a little defensive. She only vaguely remembered it.

"So you know how, when Lucy tries to take the other kids back to Narnia the first time, it doesn't work."

"Yeah." Hunter scanned the concrete sky. "Sure."

Dannika looked up at Hunter. "No, do you really? Okay, so it's a portal to Narnia, where for some reason everyone speaks English, but sometimes it closes up."

"Yeah, it's funny how the whole galaxy speaks English," Hunter said absently. She wasn't ready to give up: she stared down the row of apartment blocks to the vanishing point, where there were more apartment blocks. As before, these streets were oddly quiet. Maybe because it was a weekday.

"The lamppost made me think of Narnia, too."

Hunter didn't get the connection, but decided not to reveal her ignorance.

"It's funny that you always call her 'the Talking-Stick Lady,'" Dannika said. "Didn't she have a name?"

"Yes," Hunter said. "It's Zelda."

Dannika didn't say anything for a moment. The moment stretched on, while Hunter continued to alternate examining street and sky, growing impatient to start moving again.

Finally she looked down. Dannika, still on the sidewalk, was hugging herself. "What?"

"Zelda was the name of my mom's BFF in New Mexico."

"What BFF?"

"You know, the one I mentioned, who taught her how to make jewelry."

Hunter shivered. It was getting cold. She did not remember Dannika describing Mosi's mentor, but she didn't need to admit that, either.

"Then she took the name Zelda in honor of her. She even went to court and made it legal."

Hunter looked back down the street, as if two of the buildings they had passed would slide apart, and create the alley.

"Her real name, on her birth certificate, was Patty or Cathy." Dannika pulled on her lower lip. "I can't even remember. She only told me once. She hated it because it was so bourgeois. She used to say 'bourgey.'"

"That sounds like her," Hunter said, then added quickly, "I mean, from what you've told me."

A two-toned Oldsmobile passed by. It was the first car they'd seen in a long time. Spanish music played from the open window, but Hunter couldn't see the driver.

"The name—is it a coincidence? It feels like something more." Dannika opened her hands, and stared at the palms. "I want it to be something more."

Hunter gave in to gravity and sat next to Dannika. "I guess we'll never know."

Chapter 47

The Final Bridge

DANNIKA

Once they got back on the bridge, Hunter put on a podcast, "from the Justuff League." It was an episode about comic books, and that gave Dannika permission to pay no attention. Perhaps Hunter was playing it for the purpose of making discussion unnecessary.

Which was good, because she wanted to daydream. She daydreamed that Hunter's Zelda was the same Zelda that Mosi had learned from, and that Zelda was—she didn't want to think an *angel*, because it was just too corny, but okay, some sort of spiritual messenger. That her mother had asked Zelda to bring the talking stick to them.

Harry Houdini had exposed a lot of mediums, and he said that if there were any way to come back, he would.

He hadn't.

Maybe he had better things to do, wherever he was. Or the *one rule* of the next world was that you couldn't go back to comfort your family. After all, it went against everything Dannika wanted to believe, that there were certain people who had a gift for contacting dead relatives, leaving everyone else out, unless they had money to pay those people.

She did wish she knew someone who had had a near-death experience, someone who would describe it so passionately that Dannika would believe them and feel reassured, but the closest she got was someone saying that they knew someone who knew someone who had one.

So she always returned to the same hope: that whatever it was was beyond what she could imagine, and it had to be true, it had to be real, because of the feeling she had, the longing for God that transcended even her love for her mother.

She loved her mother in a new way now. Not the way she'd fancied herself in love with Rafe, or Mosi's oncologist, when she thought those limited (actually, sometimes pathetic) men could do something that only God could do, but as one human to another. One human daughter to one human mother. Before Mosi was a mother, she was a single woman living in an artist's colony, and she could have had an abortion, easy. Instead she gave up all her friends, and came farther out west, the way seekers always do, to the Seeker Capital of the World.

From the radio: *Don't ever take an action figure out of its box.*

Dannika felt the need to tell Hunter one last story. "After my mom died, when I was throwing out her things—"

"I thought you didn't throw out her things."

"Well, there was one thing I did throw out."

They were on the Golden Gate, the final bridge of their trip home. The fog was so thick that the north tower was completely obscured. But Dannika had Marin County faith that when they got close enough to need it, it would become visible.

"It was the notice that she was due for a mammogram. I'm pretty sure that she just didn't go."

"Oh. I'm sorry." Hunter didn't look at her, but Dannika saw the frowny eyes, and her hands tighter on the wheel.

Dannika looked back out over the Bay, though even Alcatraz was enshrouded. "I think I'm ready to forgive her for that."

Chapter 48

Believe It or Not

HUNTER

In the week that followed, Hunter and Will attempted to interest various media outlets, online and off, into looking into Angelica's nonprofit. *Another evil church story? No thanks.*

It didn't help that their sources—the people who had given them their data—had evaporated. Phone calls, emails, and texts went unanswered.

"We'll think of something," Will said.

"We have to," Hunter agreed.

Meanwhile, she did her best to avoid social media. But it was like avoiding oxygen. And her news feed was possessed of demonic powers: Whether she tapped on a story about flooding in Tennessee, or a HuffPo piece on "The Best Way to Groom Your Bikini Area," she somehow ended up with news about Angelica: the Daylight Channel had greenlit *Bread upon the Water,* the reality show "featuring Angelica St. Ambrose and her loving and fun-loving 'medevac team,' bringing her message of inclusivity to her friends and followers!"

More Nearly Each Day was soaring through the layers of the atmosphere, on the verge of going into orbit.

Then she heard from Peter. Would Hunter meet him at the old place? Yes, Chardonnay Heights.

"I'd rather not risk running into Angelica."

Angelica wouldn't be there. She was setting up shop at a house in Tiburon. "Three stories. Hundred-and-eighty-degree views. Anyway, I have something to tell you, and it's better in person."

————

Hunter leaned forward, pumping her arms hard, to take the last fifty feet up the now-widened driveway.

Peter was at the top, holding a large black compost bag. He looked up as she approached. "Wow, you're still in great shape."

"'Still,' huh?" Hunter panted. She bent over, resting her hands above her knees, to catch her breath, then pulled on the collar of her tank top to create a draft under her neck.

"You're early! I was trying to clean up a bit."

Hunter wasn't early, but since Peter ran chronically late, he might have fixed an even later hour for their meeting in his mind. While she had covered the distance as fast as she could, trying to outrun her sense of impending doom regarding what he wanted to talk about. His demeanor now reassured her a little: in a T-shirt and cargo shorts, he strutted across the newly constructed front patio, yanking out weeds that had sprouted in the seams of the concrete.

Let's get this over with. "What's up?" *And no, I will not be a bridesmaid.*

"Well . . . Angelica and I split."

"Oh!" She reached under her tank top to adjust the strap of her sports bra, the better to look away. "What happened?"

"Angelica is pretty intense. And, um . . . very insecure." He leaned back to look up at the sky. "But I don't want to say anything bad about her."

Hunter had a visceral memory of being surrounded by hostile acolytes, and being accused of at least five of the seven deadly sins. "Oh, c'mon, for old time's sake."

Now Peter directed his gaze into the bottom of the compost bag. "Well . . ." She saw a smile start on one corner of his mouth before he curbed it. "She's pretty concerned about her weight."

That was her opening. Who could blame her for wanting to know? "I have to ask . . ."

He didn't make her finish. He looked at her, his aristocratic chin jutting forward, his eyes clear. For a moment he was as stunning as the night they met. Then she was forced to acknowledge the signs of age: the weight gain in his middle, the gray in his blond hair.

"She seduced me with her spirituality. If a Buddhist or Muslim had come along then, I'd be a Buddhist or a Muslim, but Angelica was there, and she made me feel like I wasn't a failure after all, so Jesus got me." He held her gaze. "And she got me to stop drinking, so I'll always be grateful to her."

"You needed Jesus for that," she said.

"Atheism is a belief, too, Hunts."

He'd heard her rant for years against her mother's Catholicism. Lately Hunter did wonder if she'd thrown the baptized baby out with the holy water. Just because some people used religion for their own selfish or cruel ends didn't mean there was nothing in it for anyone.

"Arrgh, it's disgusting when people litter!" Peter removed a candy bar wrapper from under what remained of the Japanese box-wood. "Anyway, the reason I needed to see you right away is that I'm headed to Santa Cruz tomorrow. Dharma Gate? No? It's a Tibetan Buddhist temple." He looked up expectantly. "They host a lot of retreats and learning sessions. I'm going to be a volunteer, like, cook-ing and gardening, so I can stay and learn for free."

"It's not free if you're volunteering. Don't sell yourself short." In the past she would have mocked him. In the present, she wasn't sure about his gardening—at least, not as she watched him struggle with a buckhorn plantain, but he'd learn. He'd learn.

"Ouch!" He'd pricked himself with a foxtail. He stuck his thumb in his mouth. "Moving on to more important things." He reached into one front pocket, looked puzzled, reached into the other. On his third try, from a back pocket, he withdrew an envelope. Even at this distance she recognized the logo of the bank. He shook the envelope; the contents rattled. Then he held it out to her.

She held up her hands. "No, no, I'm sweaty."

"You are way too phobic about stuff like that." He narrowed one eye. "I've seen you naked, remember?"

He held out the envelope again. It was already open, so she pulled out a wad of pages. The top sheet was a statement from the infamous credit card, and she read, THE AMOUNT YOU OWE: $0.00. "Oh, my God."

He tilted his head, in a show of comic modesty. "I sold the Margaret Keane."

"But—" She'd last seen it in Moskowite Corner, in Angelica's bedroom.

"Angelica said that she should keep it, because Keane was a Christian, but I said that it should go to you, because you were the one who found it."

A dealer bought it. Both Peter and the dealer knew it was fake, but it was such a *good* fake.

Still. "Isn't that 'bad karma'?"

He raised one shoulder. "We were both totally honest about our beliefs."

"Thank you, Peter." *Darling? Dear?* She'd never used such endearments; this wasn't the time to start. She stared at the bill. Who could imagine that a zero, let alone one in a font almost too small to read, could be such a powerful and beautiful symbol?

Probably a lot of people.

"Besides, it *might* be real," Peter said. "The universe is full of surprises."

Peter would have had to carry it out, maybe get one of the workmen to drive it back to Marin in the bed of his pickup.

"It gets better, or it would, if you'd take the time to unfold *all* the papers there."

The page underneath the credit card bill looked legal. "It's a quitclaim deed," Peter said.

Yes, across the top of the paper were printed the words QUITCLAIM DEED. "What does it mean?"

"It means I'm giving you the house, Silly Jilly."

He took a few steps to his left and gestured to the front door like a game show host's assistant pointing to a prize. The house wasn't exactly the prize it had been a few months before: All signs of More Nearly Each Day were gone, and there were uneven splashes of whitewash over what she suspected was graffiti. This looked like a job for GetOffMyLawn.com, a.k.a. Nextdoor.

"There's more paperwork to do. Here." He scrounged through several pockets again, and finally withdrew a small square. "Call this dude and he'll fix you up."

It was the business card of an attorney. "But where would have been the drama in meeting you at a law office? And I'm not a JD like my bro."

Hunter winced. "I don't know what to say." She held the quitclaim deed in one hand and the attorney's card in the other, staring at them so she wouldn't have to look at Peter for a few moments. Her mouth was dry when she said, "Thank you isn't enough."

"Give thanks to *your* karma." He formed namaste, and bowed.

She had no pocket or purse to put the deed in, so she folded the pages and tucked them in her sports bra as best she could. The top half protruded.

"You can fix the house up and move back." Peter pointed his thumb over his shoulder.

"Mmm." She couldn't live here again, even if she knocked down every remaining wall, but . . . *but I could still put it to good use.*

"Hey! I found the yearbooks! Now, where are those damn keys?"

She pointed to one of his front pockets. "There's a bulge there. Or are you just happy to see me?" She held her new lanyard away from her chest, from which her own keys dangled. Dannika had made lanyards for each of them: Alicia could use hers for her hospital ID, but Penelope said that she'd give hers to Reyna. "Where did you find them—the yearbooks?"

"In the house. I forget where. Damn, this thing is hard to open." He was struggling to remove the house key from the ring.

"I'm glad." She leaned a little to one side, to see the front door.

"There's still some junk, but you can just throw away anything you find."

"Did you happen to see a piece of wood—like a small branch—with beads and feathers on it?"

He looked puzzled. "You're kidding, right?"

"Actually, I'm not."

"I'm sorry, Hunts." He shrugged. "I had some of Angelica's buddies helping me. I told them to toss anything that was obviously worthless. Is it really important?"

"No," she lied.

"Here!" With a final yank, he extracted the house key, and handed it to her. "The burglar alarm code is the same. Hey, um . . . You seeing anyone?"

"Well, sort of." She focused all her attention on prying the house key onto her own ring.

"I hope he's worthy of you."

I hope I'm worthy of him. But there was no need to talk about Will, no need to give Peter details about another successful man he could compare himself to.

Now she had to get inside the house to search under every plank of the hardwood floors for the talking stick. Though it was true that the group had been chugging along without their original. And they were getting used to the new one. They personalized it: Penelope twisted a short gold chain around the midsection. Alicia attached a speculum, using wire, but the others objected, and she replaced it with a Band-Aid. Hunter was waiting for inspiration.

Dannika also continued to experiment with alternatives. The latest was a kind of necklace made of socks for which she could no longer find mates. The ultimate found object. But although she swore each sock had come straight from her clothesline, no one would drape it around herself.

Like the weeds that surrounded Chardonnay Heights, secrets would emerge on their own.

"I'm truly happy for you." He'd spent most of his life trying to be Patrick. Now he could learn to be Peter.

He opened his arms. "C'mon, a hug."

"I need a shower!"

But she obliged. He did release her pretty quickly, but perhaps it was his eagerness to turn her attention to the house again. "You don't need to do much inside. I wish I could pay someone to do it for you—"

"Don't worry about Chardonnay, Peter." She put her hand on his cheek. "I'm very grateful for the gift."

Chapter 49

Food for Thought

ALICIA

"Peter gave you the house? Talk about letting go of material things!"

Alicia was sitting across from Hunter at her new office on 4th Street, a tiny room she'd rented above a small dental practice. A large white paper bag with a grease spot stood on Hunter's desk, between them. ("I told you I didn't want lunch," Hunter said when Alicia set it down. "But I do," Alicia replied.) "You can move back in after you fix it up a little."

"A little? It needs fixing up like that house in Sausalito that was crushed in that mudslide."

"Oh, yeah. Back when it used to rain." Alicia unfolded the top of the bag. "So . . . that was why you wanted to see me alone?" They would be meeting as a group the following night.

Hunter spun a black ashtray, imprinted with the words CONCORD PAVILION. "I need to talk to you about something."

Alicia could only think of one explanation for Hunter's urgency: she was pregnant, and she needed to make a decision quickly. Of course she'd come to Alicia, who could most discreetly arrange for a "procedure." This would be when Hunter's Catholic upbringing would come back to haunt her.

Alicia knew how it went: the women who, the previous month, were longing for a baby, but who now, pregnant, suddenly weren't so sure that they wanted to interrupt their climb up the corporate ladder at Crate & Barrel, or wherever they might eventually get stock options.

Alicia hadn't wanted to interrupt her education. She was one of the lucky ones: she had a family who could, and did, help. Had it not been for her own mother's offer, Alicia would have had the fastest abortion the state of Massachusetts had ever seen.

She was so grateful that she hadn't.

"Here, I have Montana Sky." Hunter brought out two bottles from a minifridge. "It's Will's favorite, too."

"I knew I liked him." Alicia said. She learned that she could be jealous of Hunter, and happy for her at the same time. And Will DeWitt wanted children, or so Hunter had said.

"But what the hell were you thinking, with this?" Hunter used her own bottle to point to the white bag.

It was two orders of burgers and fries. "It's from Phyllis' Giant Burgers," Alicia said, "not McDonalds." Alicia pulled out her own burger. The smell of well-done beef made her stomach contract with longing. The only thing better than the first bite was the anticipation of the first bite.

"Just the smell is making me nauseous," Hunter said.

Not surprising.

If Alicia had had that abortion, she wouldn't have Summer now. They spoke almost nightly; the time change worked in Alicia's early-to-bed-early-to-rise schedule. Alicia had become the mother she wanted to be by letting Summer go. In two years, Summer would be ready for college, and then, instead of fleeing across the country as she would have in the time before Joshua, she might reverse-flee, back to the Bay Area.

During those phone calls, Alicia learned that Summer, too, remembered the good times. She remembered the swings at the park. Homework help. Disney on Ice.

What had happened when Summer turned thirteen? Oh, right. Puberty. No wonder thirteen was considered such an unlucky number.

Hunter slipped a paper plate under Alicia's burger. "You know how they say that cops have the best weed? I guess doctors have the highest cholesterol?"

Alicia' s cholesterol *was* a little high. But she was proud of herself for remembering paper plates and extra napkins, knowing what a neat freak Hunter was. She squeezed the contents of a ketchup packet onto one of those plates, and made the unwelcome comparison to a pool of blood.

She didn't envy Hunter's decision; she'd be forty-two in a few weeks. This might be her last chance for a baby. Well, she'd support Hunter in whichever decision she made.

"So here's my idea." Hunter slid her elbows forward on her desk. "A mammovan."

"You're not pregnant?"

"Me? No!"

"Oh." Alicia was a little disappointed. "But what's this about a mammogram? I hope you had one when you turned forty!"

"Yes, but you know that Mosi didn't."

"What's Mosi got to do with it?" She took another bite, tasting mustard, onion, and pickle at the same time. What was better than a hamburger?

"And I didn't say mammogram. I said mammovan. A van, or a bus, that parks, like, in malls in underserved neighborhoods, and gives free mammograms to women without insurance." She paused. "Or without good insurance."

The word "insurance" triggered anxiety in Alicia. America's healthcare system was a mudslide all its own, and it crushed more than houses.

"Dannika told me something the other day." Hunter spun the Concord Pavilion ashtray again. "Her mother didn't have mammograms. We're not sure why, but Dannika thinks maybe she couldn't afford the copay. The copay. I want to do this for the Mosis and Dannikas of the future. Maybe Dannika herself in fifteen years." She slammed her hand down on the twirling ashtray. "So what do you say? Are you in?"

She'd done some research. Yes, mobile mammography was already a thing ("I knew that," Alicia grumbled), but those big buses weren't parking in underserved neighborhoods. Oh, no. They were lumbering into office parks to screen women who were too busy with board meetings to take time off from work.

"Yeah, yeah, I like it." Alicia nodded.

"I'll use the money from selling Chardonnay Heights to get us launched, but I need someone to help me, a doctor—not any doctor. A gynecologist. A breast surgeon would be even better, but I don't know any. I mean, and . . . we're friends."

Alicia liked it a lot.

She and Hunter talked a long time, interrupting each other and then returning to finish broken-off sentences. Hunter knew business, and Alicia knew medicine, but there was much more to learn.

Alicia had more time for learning now.

Alicia's hamburger had vanished, as had the fries, though she didn't remember eating them. When it became clear that Hunter really wasn't going to eat her lunch, Alicia bagged it all up, promising to compost it at home, though really planning to have it for dinner.

Alicia had to rush back to the office. The waiting room was filling.

Yes, she was happy that Hunter had Will. But now—might it possibly be Alicia's turn? Since reclaiming Summer full-time from her parents, Alicia had had no more than the occasional blind date that ended in a hotel room with the curtains and her eyes closed.

Alicia had been afraid to bring a man home, because that could go one of two ways: Summer got attached or Summer got abused. Alicia had been downright paranoid about that. It wasn't inevitable: Alicia had patients who were parenting stepchildren, and although those patients often complained that the stepchild "was just like his/her mother," there wasn't any abuse going on. There was usually plenty of tsuris, though.

Alicia was a few months away from forty and twenty pounds away from skinny. Thirty pounds by the eating-disorder-inducing standards of Marin County. But she wasn't going to let that stop her anymore.

Meanwhile, she couldn't wait to tell Summer and Joshua about Hunter's idea. They'd not only love it, they'd be impressed. Bringing a mammogram to a woman who otherwise wouldn't have one was healing the world: *tikkun olam*. Joshua and Summer were very big on *tikkun olam*.

Chapter 50

Time and Tide

DANNIKA

"Their big mistake was letting Airbnb come in," Dannika said.

She and Howie were in Bolinas, sitting on a wooden bench outside a hotel that was done up to look like a Hollywood director's version of an Old West saloon. The whole of the tiny town looked much like that. Most streets didn't have sidewalks.

Lack of sidewalks didn't mean lack of automobiles, though. Howie said that he'd never heard so many broken mufflers rattle by. But in between the VW bugs from the previous century came cruising Porsches that had rolled out of the dealer's lot only that week.

Bolinas was an insular community, surrounded on three sides by the Pacific Ocean. The locals had wanted it to stay that way, badly enough that they had removed the signs from Highway 1 that would have led visitors to their hamlet of artists' communes, possibly not unlike the one in New Mexico where Dannika was conceived.

But then came the internet, with pictures of the views, and Siri, to tell tourists how to get there. Now millionaires and billionaires fresh from Silicon Valley outbid each other for houses newly vacated by aging residents or their heirs.

Mosi's old friend Bronwyn had been one of those very same locals who had trooped out, armed with flashlights and shovels, to wrest those freeway signs from the earth. Bronwyn had lived here for forty years, in a roomy wooden house in need of paint, mounted atop a cliff. But she was selling the house now: "I can get ten times what I paid for it."

Everyone has a price, Dannika thought. But she didn't blame Bronwyn for wanting to get out before a frozen yogurt place opened. Or a Burger King.

Bronwyn had invited Dannika to her farewell party, and no, she didn't mind if Howie came along. Then Howie had the idea of arriving early, so that Dannika could check out the Bolinas Museum. She appreciated his support of her interest in art.

"People only come here to Instagram," Dannika said. She'd seen so many pictures of Bronwyn's house that going to it IRL felt anticlimactic.

"Is Instagram a verb now?" Howie grinned.

"Isn't everything?" It was too bad that people with dreams of becoming influencers had to flock to Bolinas, like the swallows to San Juan Capistrano, except every darn day instead of once a year. The Marin she'd grown up in was sinking under the weight of outlet malls and Starbucks.

Even with the help of Siri, Howie had ended up parking his battered Tercel much farther away from their destination than he had intended. After walking this far, both of his shoelaces had come untied, so Dannika had directed them to this bench where Howie could safely bend over and tend to them.

Two middle-aged women, each carrying a straw tote bag larger than her head, strolled past. Their free arms were linked.

"Hey, did you ever read *1984*? I read *Notes from Underground*."

He hung his head. "I haven't finished it yet," he mumbled.

"I can't say that *Notes from Underground* is my favorite, but—"

"It's the torture," Howie said. "I can't read about O'Brien torturing Winston."

She'd forgotten how difficult that part was.

Howie was so much smarter than Dannika had given him credit for. He'd read all of Proust, and he'd read *The Stranger* in French! But he lacked ambition, and by ambition she didn't mean fame or money, just achieving something more than drawing designs in the steamed milk on top of cappuccinos.

She had no right to judge him, since she'd had no ambition of her own for so long. But now she did. Now she had visions of earrings and necklaces and belt buckles dancing in her head.

Howie put his hand on her arm. "You told me to stop you when you do that."

She'd been picking at her black nail polish. "I changed my mind." She didn't look up when she went on, "I'm sorry. You're right." She blew a black fleck off her finger. "Well, I've got some news. I found a school."

Howie rested his arm on the back of the bench.

"There's a college in upstate New York." Dannika returned to picking; she couldn't help it. "They combine general ed with training in different arts, like jewelry design." She rushed through the next part. "It's super expensive, but Bronwyn knows people there and she thinks I can get in. I mean, I got into UCLA, before . . . you know."

He took his arm away. "Where in New York?"

"Rochester." The New York Institute for Education and the Applied Arts. "I'll have a BFA. That and six bucks won't even get me a latte now, but I'll get caught up with where some of my high school friends are academically, and I'll learn the—some of the stuff that my mom never learned." *Not to worry, Mosi,* she thought. *I'll have that miserable artist's life you didn't want for me, and I'll love it just like you did.* "Do you still want to help me with that application essay?"

One of his Howie's shoelaces had mysteriously come undone again. He bent over and spoke from that position. "How will you pay for it? Can you get a scholarship?"

"I doubt it. Student loans."

When he straightened up, he looked relieved. "Permission to speak freely? That's *not* a good idea. You'll end up like me."

That prospect did not appeal. At the moment Howie looked like an absent-minded professor: clean but rumpled clothes, glasses with frames from an earlier decade, and black curls getting shaggy. She could picture him in thirty years, still working at the Café Ravi, maybe tutoring high school kids in English.

She didn't know how she'd pay tuition, and she would be embarrassed to share her fantasy with Howie, that her mother, wherever she was, would now use her own high-level contacts to make it work. While having these thoughts, she automatically looked up at the sky, even though she didn't think that Mosi's soul occupied the same space as United Airlines.

Now she slapped her hands on her thighs, and announced, "We'd better get to that museum, if we're going!" She got out her phone. Yep, it was on Google Maps. So much for keeping tourists out. "It's that way."

———

They started walking, circling around the Porsches and VWs. Bicycles were the real threat, as their riders observed no traffic laws.

It was Howie who noticed the little wooden box sticking out from the side of a wall. There was a slot in the box, and, printed on the side in black: GIVE ONLY WHAT YOU CAN. The door next to it had a small, barred window near the top. Below that, the sign read, CONCEPTUAL ART: WHEN YOU DON'T THINK IT BELONGS IN A MUSEUM.

There was a bell, which Dannika rang. When there was no response, she rang again, this time pressing and holding the button until they heard a buzzing sound, and she was able to push the door open.

She climbed a very steep and narrow staircase, Howie behind her, making wisecracks about how many bones he'd break if he fell.

"I'm just closing up."

It was a woman with wavy hair in that color that could be platinum blonde or gray. It reached the waistband of a skirt in a dark floral print that caressed the floor, leaving just enough room for Dannika to see Birkenstocks. When Dannika was at the bottom of the stairs, and saw her from a distance, she would have said that the woman was about thirty, but when she reached the top she saw that she was even older than Penelope.

"We're busy," the woman said. "We're packing up our last exhibit and putting out a new one."

"We are weary travelers." Howie thumped his chest lightly. "We seek succor." He pretended to gasp. "Water!"

"Can we see what was on display?" Dannika's interest was piqued by the woman's desire to keep it hidden.

The woman sniffed. "Five minutes. And don't touch anything."

The space looked like someone's attic: a slanting roof with skylights, and exposed brick on the opposite wall. The smell of sawdust; low shelves, empty except for a few brackets and screws. A row of empty liquor bottles. A bicycle tire. A floor that needed sweeping.

Howie sloughed off his jacket, and made a move to hang it on the coatrack next to the stairs, but another woman called out, "No! That's part of the new exhibit!" This woman held a microfiber cloth in one hand and a spray bottle without a label in the other. Her auburn hair and floral-print skirt were as long as her colleague's, and she, too, had the lined and leathery face of a woman who has seen eighty in the rear-view mirror.

"I told you we should put it somewhere else, Alexandra," the white-haired woman complained.

"I didn't know," Howie apologized, then asked, "how is it an 'exhibit'?"

"You either get it or you don't," Alexandra said. "Waimea, if you want it somewhere else, move it."

"I'll help you," Howie offered.

Waimea agreed and Alexandra said, "Suit yourself."

Howie embraced the coatrack's neck; Waimea wrapped her hands below his. But they started lifting at different moments, and the items already draped over its hooks—one looking suspiciously like a straitjacket, and another a fox fur scarf with the fox's head attached—dropped to the floor.

"I said on the count of three!" Waimea snapped.

"No, you didn't," Howie objected.

"What's the new exhibit?" Dannika asked.

"Tools of Women's Oppression." Alexandra pointed to a corner of the space, where there huddled a vacuum cleaner, a dustpan, and a mop. "Trans *and* cisgender."

"Just let me do it!" Waimea and Howie were still disputing the fate of the coatrack.

Dannika was about to intervene, when she spotted an unsealed shipping crate next to the vacuum cleaner. The tip of a feather poked out over the top.

Dannika pointed. "That's it! That's our talking stick! It's the same feather. White, with a black tip." She bounced on her heels, then stepped toward the box.

Alexandra flung her arm out, hitting Dannika just below her bosom. "We asked you not to touch our pieces!"

Waimea wrested the coatrack away from Howie one final time, then dragged it across the floor. The screeching sound should have cracked the glass in the windows.

Dannika bent over Alexandra's arm. Now she could see at the top of the box a woven basket and what looked like a dream catcher. "Are these Native American artifacts?"

"They're not Native American," Alexandra said coldly. She dropped her arm, but held her hand up like a traffic cop. "They're *Navajo*."

"Well, *sorry*." It was hard to stay ahead of the PC curve.

"This box was delivered to us by mistake." Alexandra folded her arms over her chest.

"And we're returning them to their rightful owners in New Mexico." Waimea was defiant. "It's not our fault they ended up here."

Dannika glanced sideways at the goose feather. She could grab it and run. But the stairs would slow her down.

"I know what you're thinking," Howie whispered. "Don't."

Alexandra heard him. "Your friend is right. It would be a mistake."

Dannika felt sure that the feather was attached to their talking stick. But no, it wasn't theirs anymore. It was just passing through, like Blanche DuBois, on her way to the sanitarium in *A Streetcar Named Desire*. Like all of them. Dannika was glad that it wasn't going to stay with Alexandra and Waimea.

Alexandra broke her out of her trance. "We have work to do. Waimea, hand me those rubber gloves, will you? No, the ones *with* latex."

Howie tugged at Dannika's elbow. She got the message.

The stairs were so steep that Dannika held onto the banister on the way down, though she declined Howie's offer of additional assistance. As they passed the donation box, she put in a dollar. "They weren't very nice," she said, "but this feels like the right thing to do." *And a contribution to the shipping costs.* She wanted the Navajo artifacts to get back on the road. Zelda, or Mosi, or God, would see that it ended up with its rightful owner.

Broke as he was, Howie put in a dollar of his own.

Chapter 51

The Bottom of One Mountain
Is the Top of the One Below

HUNTER

Hunter turned her face to the sun while she stretched, hands on the small of her back.

She and Will were back on Mount Tamalpais. They had run together up the hill from the tiny area where one could park off-road, and then the three miles along the flat, though rocky, path to the West Point Inn.

"You really are quite the runner," Will said.

"It's the uphill part that's hard."

"You could join a running club." Will pulled one ankle toward his butt, stretching his quadricep. "We could join one together."

"Hah!" *That's a very married thing to do.* Did she still have some qualms about marrying Will? How could she not? Hunter reached back to unpin her hair, which she then shook loose over her shoulders. "Look, we're alone here." *We can kiss.*

Will didn't like physical demonstrations of affection in public, beyond holding hands. *Showing off*, he called it.

They weren't completely alone. Only the inaccessibility of the spot by automobile prevented it from being packed with locals and tourists. As it was, the yuppie brigade was out in full force: twenty-something hikers in nylon pants, carrying daypacks, shielding their faces with baseball caps or straw hats. A few sturdy older folks.

But they had enough of a zone of privacy, beneath the picnic tables and below the line of rocks that separated the official path from the hill, that Will couldn't resist, as she'd expected, and she felt his hand on the back of her neck, under her hair. He whispered, "Only God, my dear."

He liked to recite the Yeats poem.

"Could love me for myself alone," she finished.

"And not your yellow hair."

"You'll have to give it your best shot."

It was a sunny September day. Recent, if inadequate, showers had polished the air to a mirrorlike shine. Thanks to the warm weather, many visitors had their extra layers tied around their waists. There were a few babies and toddlers who'd been transported by strollers. Hunter tried to picture herself making the same journey that way.

Suddenly there was doubt. "Are you sure about this?"

His hand still on her neck, caressing now. "Yes."

Will had "proposed" the night before. It was not the stuff of rom-coms. He hadn't made eye contact, had in fact been half-mumbling when he said, *We could get married, you know.*

"We're not living on your boat."

"No."

"And you know I'm forty-one."

"So am I."

They'd left the possibility of children unresolved. A good Catholic girl would leave it up to God, right? But she was back on the pill. *Trust in God, and tie your camel.* Alicia insisted that she *could* get pregnant.

Will dropped his hand suddenly, so she knew that they were no longer alone. It was Alicia, strolling, as much as one could "stroll" after a four-mile hike, toward them. "I got almost an hour's head start! I'm sooo out of shape."

She had brought them bottles of Montana Sky and small towels, so they got busy drinking and patting down sweat.

"I am so proud of what you ladies—I mean, *women,* are doing," Will said. "I mean, I'm impressed."

He meant the Ma'am-o-Van, now officially a 501(c)(3) organization. Will had agreed to be on their board of directors, and though Hunter might be biased, he was a formidable addition, as a respected attorney. She and Alicia wanted a diverse board of community members, people who, like Will, were reliable, honest, smart, and yes, had some contacts in the world of business.

"We have a very long way to go," Hunter said. So far, the Ma'am-O-Van project had all been paperwork. Lots of paperwork. Mind-numbing, soul-draining paperwork. Both she and Alicia had considered giving up the idea on more than one occasion, but reaching this first milestone gave them a boost. Hunter sustained herself on images of the RV-sized mammogram-on-wheels with their logo, which had yet to be designed: how to stand out while being tasteful? And they didn't want to use pink—probably *couldn't* use pink, as it was strongly enough associated with the Susan G. Komen foundation to be a de facto trademark.

"There's a Jewish proverb," Alicia said, "that 'saving one life is like saving the whole world.' And we'll save our share of Mosi Arenescus before we're through."

"Thank God there's a breeze!" It was Dannika and Howie. Dannika sported a hiking-friendly look—baseball cap, loose nylon pants, and T-shirt—but there was something else different about her that Hunter couldn't pinpoint.

"Did you leave Penelope and Reyna behind?" Hunter asked.

Dannika looked sheepish. "They insisted we keep going."

Howie held up his glasses to the light, then cleaned them on his T-shirt. "So we'll wait. The mountain isn't going anywhere."

"Just tell me that Penelope is wearing appropriate footwear," Hunter said.

Will pointed west. "Like the woman said, 'Just when you think you've seen every drop-dead view . . .'"

He didn't need to finish the sentence. They were facing a wide vista of hills, and beyond that, the slate blue of the world's largest ocean. Hunter could smell the pine trees behind them.

"And you were born here," Hunter said.

"I was born here, too!" Dannika put indignant hands on her hips. "Almost, anyway."

Finally they spotted Penelope and Reyna: the one tall and big-boned, the other short and curvy. Penelope had on a red tracksuit, and, as they got a little closer, Hunter was relieved to see that she was wearing a pair of black Nikes. They were holding hands.

"I have got to sit down!" Penelope announced. "I'm not so young anymore."

There were picnic tables a short distance from the Inn's porch which were open to the public. There was only one with enough room for all seven of them to sit, squished together. The two couples at the other end of the table were deeply involved in a conversation about the best time of year to plant coriander.

Reyna unshouldered her daypack, and brought out trays from the new vegan Japanese restaurant in Mill Valley. There were avocado and cucumber rolls, spicy watermelon rolls, nigiri topped with eggplant, shiitake mushrooms, and vegan "tuna," as well as a container of edamame.

"Dannika has an announcement to make," Penelope said as she was passing out chopsticks.

"Penelope! You said we were going to wait."

"I changed my mind. I'm too excited!" Penelope prolonged the moment by drinking from her water bottle. "Dannika's going to college, after winter break."

Dannika covered her face with her hands.

Howie's eyes already looked disproportionately big behind his thick glasses, but they grew wider now, telling Hunter that this was an unpleasant surprise. "I thought you decided not to go."

Because that's what you wanted to hear, Hunter thought.

"Upstate New York!" Penelope exclaimed.

"That's why I wanted to wait." Dannika removed her hands, and Hunter saw that her nose ring was gone.

"Didn't you—" Penelope began. "I'm sorry." But she moved on quickly. "It's a program tailor-made for her," Penelope said. "She can earn a bachelor of arts in jewelry design, and then an MFA at the same school."

"Winters are terrible there," Howie said.

"That's why they take all of January off," Penelope said.

"So not till February," Howie reassured himself.

Dannika folded her arms on the picnic table. "My mom learned everything she knew from the artisans in the commune. She was good, but . . ." Dannika stumbled through a description of what she wanted to achieve by combining the upcycling that was popular in craft-making with advanced metalwork. She concluded with a hesitant, "I think I can build on what she did."

Alicia positioned her hands like a conductor. "All together now."

Mazel tov, they chorused—except Howie. "What about the cats? You can't take eight cats back to New York."

"I can take a couple, the ones who need the most care. I'll find good homes for the rest." Dannika looked at Hunter. "I'm hoping that one or two of the women here this very afternoon will take one, and my mom's old friends will take whichever ones are left." She slapped the table. "No one's asked me how I'm going to pay for all this!"

"Because we're too polite," Reyna said.

"Dannika—" Penelope warned.

"You can't have it both ways," Dannika said. "You can't tell everyone I'm going and then not tell everyone that you're paying my tuition."

"What?" "Wow!" "That's very generous."

Penelope put her elbows on the table, and rested her chin in her hands. "I can afford to make a donation to your mobile mammography, too, down the line. I want to take care of Dannika first. By the way! Reyna and I joined an LGBTQ+ book group. We're reading *Rubyfruit Jungle.*"

"Penelope's never read it." Reyna dabbed wasabi on her "tuna" nigiri. "We've got to patch that pothole in her education." She tasted the nigiri, then puckered thoughtfully. "Doesn't really taste like tuna."

"No, because it's made from roasted tomatoes," Dannika said. "It's good, though. If you were a mother tuna, you'd appreciate it."

"By the way . . ." Reyna added more wasabi. "Did you read about More Nearly Each Day?"

"No," Alicia said. "What about it?"

"The IRS is investigating." Reyna made eye contact with each of them, one at a time. "I read that they're looking into their finances."

"Really," Hunter observed neutrally. "Are there more napkins?"

"Yes," Reyna said. "There's a form they're supposed to file—"

"A 990," Will said.

Reyna bit off the first half. "This article said that they listed officers who weren't real people and paid them big salaries."

"No." Dannika splashed soy sauce on her avocado roll. "They wouldn't do that, would they?"

"Tsk, tsk." Hunter tucked a napkin into her waistband, since there was enough wind to blow it away.

"Someone complained." Reyna quoted, "'Speaking on condition of anonymity to discuss a sensitive topic.'"

"I wonder who." Will was plating edamame.

"It sounds like there are a number of fishy transactions." Reyna pointed to her nigiri. "Nothing fishy here, obviously."

"Really." Hunter didn't look up. "You know, it was the Center for Medicare and Medicaid that brought down that big shot Silicon Valley woman."

Dannika pointed to her plate of avocado roll. "I'd like to go vegan, but I really like cheese. Can there be cruelty-free cheese?"

Hunter spread her hands in an I-don't-know gesture. Within the borders of her peripheral vision she captured Will raising his own hands to mirror hers. He was already thinking, she was sure, about his next quest against those who would exploit the gullible.

"Want to trade for tuna?" Penelope asked.

"Sure." Reyna held up her tray. "The same article said that the Daylight Channel had broken off discussions with her on both their projects due to creative differences."

Will stood up. "I want a picture."

No one wanted to move, but Will persisted until he posed them in front of the West Point Inn sign. "This is like herding cats!" he joked. "Speaking of cats." He was enough excited by the prospect of this photo that he importuned a pudgy man with a moustache at the next picnic table.

"Sure thing!" the man said. He stood up to reveal a gray T-shirt that read, MY LIFE IS BASED ON A TRUE STORY.

Will realigned them in front of the row of stones that bordered the Inn, with Hunter on one end and himself on the other. Dannika said, "Arms around each other!"

"I'll take a few," the man said.

Hunter turned around to admire the view. She remembered Angelica asking, "How can you not believe in God when you look at all this?" and her own defiant atheism. If a religious person can have doubts, an atheist can have doubts, too, right? Perhaps it was the more congenial company that let the wind blow some doubts about the nonexistence of God into her ear. *Atheism is a belief, too.* Being here with real friends, friends who wouldn't desert her if there was a scandal, was even better evidence.

And a man. No shame in loving a man, even one who saw a crusade in every cigarette not put in the proper receptacle. Especially one like that.

The stranger in the gray T-shirt was not only friendly, but fastidious. He took picture after picture, until there was one with everyone smiling and eyes open. It might be one for Instagram.

Acknowledgments

I once worked with a prospective author who kept insisting that once he got the opening pages down, "the book will write itself." He was actually surprised when that didn't happen.

I had no such delusions with regard to this novel. I was, however, fortunate enough to find help from the best. First, the gifted and beloved women of my writing group: Sheri Cooper, Phyllis Florin, Terry Gamble, Suzanne Lewis, Mary Beth McClure, Alison Sackett, and Linda Schlossberg. This book would not exist without them.

Author Donna Gillespie brought her usual perspicacity to a late draft. Steve and Carol Acunto were encouraging throughout the process.

Some of the most valuable help comes from people who are simply willing to listen to a writer complain—I mean, work through a problem aloud. The good, patient people who listened to me include Doug Gordy, Jacob Levin, Christine McDonagh, and Steven Drachman. My apologies to those who I'm sure I've omitted. As we see in *The Talking Stick*, memory can't always be trusted.

I owe special gratitude to the team at Skyhorse: Tony Lyons, Louis Conte, and the extraordinary editor Michael Campbell.

And once again, to Michael Bernick.

About the Author

Donna Levin is the author of four acclaimed novels: *Extraordinary Means, California Street, There's More than One Way Home,* and *He Could Be Another Bill Gates.* Her novels are part of the California Fiction collection in the California State Library, and her papers are part of Boston University's Howard Gotlieb Archival Research Center.